A one-time legal secreta͟[...] charitable foundation, Su͟[...] bliss when she became a r͟[...] Mills & Boon. She's visited͟[...] factories for 'research', and ͟[...]͟mas. But the real joy of her job is ͟[...]͟ories about women for women. With over ͟eighty published novels, she's tackled issues like infertility, losing a child and becoming widowed, and worked through them with her characters.

Karin Baine lives in Northern Ireland with her husband, two sons and her out-of-control notebook collection. Her mother and her grandmother's vast collection of books inspired her love of reading and her dream of becoming a Mills & Boon author. Now she can tell people she has a *proper* job! You can follow Karin on X, @karinbaine1, or visit her website for the latest news—karinbaine.com.

ONE-NIGHT BABY WITH THE BEST MAN

SUSAN MEIER

CINDERELLA'S FESTIVE FAKE DATE

KARIN BAINE

MILLS & BOON

First published in Great Britain 2024
by Mills & Boon, an imprint of HarperCollins*Publishers* Ltd,
1 London Bridge Street, London, SE1 9GF

www.harpercollins.co.uk

HarperCollins*Publishers*, Macken House, 39/40 Mayor Street Upper, Dublin 1, D01 C9W8, Ireland

One-Night Baby with the Best Man © 2024 Linda Susan Meier

Cinderella's Festive Fake Date © 2024 Karin Baine

ISBN: 978-0-263-32143-2

11/24

MIX
Paper | Supporting responsible forestry
FSC™ C007454

This book contains FSC™ certified paper and other controlled sources to ensure responsible forest management.

For more information visit www.harpercollins.co.uk/green.

Printed and Bound in the UK using 100% Renewable Electricity at CPI Group (UK) Ltd, Croydon, CR0 4YY

ONE-NIGHT BABY WITH THE BEST MAN

SUSAN MEIER

MILLS & BOON

I dedicate this book to all my Facebook friends,
who listen to my silly stories
and put up with my offbeat sense of humor.
You make my days brighter.

CHAPTER ONE

RICO MENDOZA DROVE his Bentley along the Tuscan road leading to the expansive vineyard owned by his unofficial family, the Salvaggios. Abandoned as an infant, Rico had been raised in various foster homes and group homes. At twenty-eight, he'd met Antonio Salvaggio at a meeting where they were discussing a potential business venture. When it was over, Antonio had insisted he come to the Salvaggio villa for dinner. He'd met Carlos and GiGi, Antonio's grandparents, and Lorenzo, Antonio's dad. Ten years later, he gambled with Lorenzo in Monte Carlo, popped in to spend afternoons with GiGi every time he was in Florence and was like a brother to Antonio.

He'd flown in from London two days early for Antonio's engagement party on Saturday night because he knew there'd be wine and laughter. He hadn't even been told Antonio was dating someone, but apparently, the whole romance had happened quickly. Antonio had met the woman he now described as his one true love, romanced her a few months, got engaged and was not wasting a minute getting married.

The man was smitten.

Rico snorted when he thought of Antonio calling a woman his one true love. Rico wasn't a big believer in love. But Antonio was. Though his first marriage hadn't worked out and he'd been a happy playboy for years, there had always been something wistful about him. He hadn't been lost—Rico knew exactly what lost looked like—it was more that Antonio seemed to want something different from his future.

The vineyard lane appeared on Rico's left, and he turned the Bentley onto the long strip of pavement. He'd barely noticed the fields as he'd driven along the road, but heading toward the Salvaggios' massive vineyard, he saw row upon row of resting grapevines, the huge wine-making facility and the beautiful yellow stucco villa.

He eased his car along the curving driveway and stopped in front of the enormous garage. Though he knew there were plenty of people arriving for the engagement party weekend, there were no other cars parked in the driveway.

Not wanting to leave his Bentley in the way when other vehicles might need to drive up to the portico, he pulled out his phone and texted Lorenzo, asking where he should park his car.

A few minutes later, Antonio's dad stepped out of the villa. Tall with dark hair and serious brown eyes, he approached the Bentley.

Rico eased out of his car into the crisp December air. Given that Lorenzo wore jeans and a cashmere sweater, Rico was appropriately dressed in a T-shirt and jeans with a black leather jacket. He caught Lorenzo in a big hug.

"Good to see you, old man," he said, slapping Lorenzo's back.

Lorenzo snorted. "I'm far from an old man."

"I know. Rumor has it you have a new lady in town."

Lorenzo gaped at him. "What?"

"I know. I know. It's a secret. The way all your relationships are."

"Not all my relationships are a secret!" He stopped his little rant, shaking his head as he grinned at Rico's teasing. "Just leave your car and one of the maintenance guys will park it inside. We can text them to get it for you when you're ready to leave."

Rico tossed his car starter in the air with a laugh, then set it on the front seat. "Don't think I didn't notice you're evading the question about your mystery woman."

They walked to the front door, which Lorenzo opened, offering Rico entry first. But Rico laughed. "Age before beauty."

"You know, you're so cocky, but you're going to get old too."

"I hope so. The alternative isn't appealing."

Lorenzo snorted and entered the foyer. Rico followed him. He paused to take in the gorgeous space with its crystal chandelier and curving staircase, then Lorenzo motioned for him to go into the sitting room to the right.

Antonio and a gorgeous brunette sat on a chair catty-corner to the sofa. As Rico and Lorenzo entered, Antonio rose and caught the hand of the brunette, saying, "Riley, that troublemaker with my father is my best man, Rico."

Riley laughed as they walked over to him. "He doesn't look like a troublemaker."

Antonio sniffed. "Give him time." Stopping in front of Rico, he added, "Rico, this is my fiancée, Riley Morgan."

Rico hugged Riley. "It's a pleasure to meet you." It really was. Rico himself might not believe in love and might not want to get married, but Antonio did. It gave him great joy to see his friend happy.

Antonio pointed to the sofa. "And of course you know GiGi."

He walked over and took her hands. She'd lost Carlos at the beginning of the year and Antonio and Riley's wedding seemed to be bringing her back to her usual, happy self.

He kissed the back of her hands. "The only sweet one in this family."

GiGi laughed. "Oh, you love my boys too. Otherwise, you wouldn't tease so much."

"Next to her," Antonio continued, "is Riley's mom, Juliette Morgan."

He faced the stunning blonde with the most expressive green eyes Rico had ever seen. "How do you do."

"It's nice to meet you," Juliette said.

"And next to her is Riley's maid of honor, Marietta Fontain."

Rico eased down another step to be in front of her and said, "It's nice to meet you."

She looked up at him. Her soft blue eyes caught his gaze and his heart jerked. Strawberry blond hair to the middle of her back framed a face with high cheekbones and a pert little nose. She looked like a sprite or a pixie. Someone from Celtic folklore.

She smiled and his heart thudded.

"It's nice to meet you."

He stared at her. Her voice had the cutest accent, a sort of twang. She was obviously from the American South. "Your voice is beautiful."

She laughed. "I grew up in Texas."

She said that as if it explained everything, but unexpected curiosity about her filled him with a million questions. The kind of questions he normally didn't ask, if only because he didn't want anyone asking him about who he was. He didn't know anything about who he was, except that his mom had left him in a train station in Spain and he had the coloring and stature of a Spaniard.

Stifling his curiosity about Marietta Fontain, he sat in the thick chair across from Antonio and Riley. Lorenzo walked behind the bar and got everyone wine.

Through drinks and dinner, Rico joined in the fun, laughing with everyone as they discussed the upcoming engagement ball. Then Antonio and Riley suggested that Marietta and Rico join them in the wine-tasting facility for dancing that night.

As they entered the building, Rico smiled. Most wine-tasting rooms weren't tricked out the way the Salvaggio Vineyards' room was. Most had tables and chairs and happy employees pouring samples. But Lorenzo had seen wine-tasting rooms in the United States that had fancy bars, with backlit rows of wine, tables for conversations and a dance floor, and had decided to copy the idea. Tourists didn't merely sample the Salvaggio wines; they enjoyed the atmosphere and the ambiance of mingling with other tourists and dancing and returned home talking about the experience. As a result, a visit to the Salvaggio Vineyards was on everyone's not-to-be-missed list.

The band began to play. Antonio smiled at Riley, took her hand and led her to the dance floor.

Anticipation filled Rico. This was his chance to get to know Marietta, away from GiGi's curiosity and Lorenzo's teasing. He turned to face her, and she smiled at him.

His chest tightened. He didn't know what it was about her that made his heart stutter and his brain turn to mush. But he was not letting this opportunity get away. "Would you like to dance?"

She laughed. "Yes and no. Yes, because I love music. But honestly, I'm exhausted."

The urge to talk her into a dance, just one dance, nudged at him, but the gentleman in him won. He directed her to one of the empty tables. As they walked over, he said, "That's right. You flew in from the States today."

"And took a train and drove the last few miles with Juliette in her maiden drive in Tuscany. If she offers you a ride anywhere, politely decline. At least until she knows her way around better."

He laughed. Not only was it pure joy to hear her Southern drawl, but she seemed to be a good sport about things. "After she held her own with Lorenzo at dinner tonight, I'm not sure Riley's mom takes no for an answer."

Marietta snorted. "She doesn't. She and Riley shared office space and me. I was the receptionist and office manager for both. When she sets her mind to something, she doesn't back off."

Even in the dim light of the room, her skin glowed. But it was her eyes that seemed to charm him the most. Pale blue, like the sky on a perfect day.

His lips lifted into a smile. But as he walked to the bar to get glasses of wine for himself and Marietta, he wondered if he was beginning to feel a little bit of what Antonio seemed to feel for Riley.

Smitten.

Good Lord. He could not be smitten. Smitten was for guys like Antonio who wanted to be devoted, to have children, to be selfless and self-indulgent with the same person. Not for people like Rico who liked nightlife, who lived and breathed freedom. What he felt for Marietta was simple attraction. Nothing more.

Still, there was nothing wrong with that. Especially if she was feeling the same thing. If the attraction was mutual, they had a whole weekend to explore it.

The song ended. Antonio and Riley walked over to their table holding hands. Riley looked from Marietta to Rico. "What are you guys talking about?"

Marietta chuckled. "Your mother."

"Oh! How she and my dad have a thing?" Antonio asked.

Rico set down his wineglass. "*Juliette* is the woman your dad has in town?"

Riley batted her hands, indicating he should keep his voice down. "We're not sure yet. We've been trying to trap them into admitting it. But my mom is like a vault when she wants to be…"

"And my dad is the king of never giving a straight answer."

Rico laughed and took a sip of his wine. "That could make this weekend a lot of fun."

Antonio gasped. "Don't say anything, Rico. Riley and I have been treading lightly in the way we're edging them into admitting the truth. We don't want to do anything that might cause a problem at the engagement party."

Marietta hid a snicker by taking a drink of her wine. It would be a cold, frosty day in hell before Juliette broke down when challenged. Looking around the room dripping with finery, she took in the tall walnut tables that matched the shiny bar in front of the backlit rows of fancy bottles of Salvaggio wines. They'd made the room bigger than other wine-tasting rooms she'd seen in Texas, but she'd been to plenty of vineyards that had music and dancing to attract customers.

The Salvaggios certainly took the wine-tasting room to the next level, though. Which was probably why their vineyard was a standout in their industry. Of course, Salvaggio Wines was only one of many businesses they owned. The Salvaggios were billionaires. Juliette owned a home nursing agency. Even Riley owned a company.

Of course, she didn't know Rico's status—

Except that he was gorgeous. And yummy. Thick, curly dark hair was complemented by a sexy black leather jacket that he wore like a man so accustomed to luxury he could dress casually and still reek elegance. He was probably wealthy too.

No matter how tempting she found him though, she knew she should keep her distance. Stay in her own lane. She was a Texas girl, making a life in Manhattan, who'd barely dated since her divorce. Rico Mendoza was way out of her league.

Even if he did make all her nerve endings shimmy and her chest tighten with longing.

The band began to play again. This time a slow song. Antonio immediately led Riley back onto the dance floor.

Marietta pretended great interest in her wineglass. She'd already told him she was too tired to dance.

"Do you want to get out of here?"

Marietta's gaze leaped to his. "Out of here?"

"Antonio mentioned that we're staying in the same hotel. You're tired. I have a car. We'll wait for Antonio and Riley to get back from this dance, then say we're going to our hotel because I understand tomorrow's a big day."

She could have gazed into his beautiful dark eyes forever. "A big day for what?"

"I don't know. Whatever it is people do to get ready for an engagement party."

"We're choosing my maid of honor dress tomorrow. Maybe something along the lines of choosing a wedding tux for you?"

"I own a tux."

Of course he did. No matter how appealing, he was way beyond her. Not somebody she should even consider flirting with.

She changed the subject. "If it was summer, I'd be hoping we were spending tomorrow afternoon at the pool. Did you see that outdoor space? GiGi said she just redid it."

"I've seen it. You're right. It's perfect."

"But not in the winter."

"No. Not in the winter."

Silence fell over their small table. She worked to think of something to say. Her instinct was to flirt. But she'd already discounted that. They weren't merely from two different worlds. They were from two different continents. Best to simply try to make friends and keep it that way.

Except she was really attracted to him. Tall, dark and handsome…and just *yum* with that mop of curly hair.

But she wasn't in the market for a guy.

She'd had a bad marriage and didn't want another—

Maybe that was the answer? She really didn't want to marry again. But that didn't mean she couldn't flirt…or have some fun.

Did it?

Antonio and Riley returned to the tall table, cuddling and happy. Marietta smiled at them, as Rico shoved away from the table. "Marietta is tired from traveling and I need to get back to the hotel to make some calls to the States."

Riley said, "Oh."

Antonio said, "Okay. We'll see you tomorrow."

"Any special time you need for us to be at the vineyard?"

"No," Riley said. She squeezed Marietta's hand. "Sleep in. Have a leisurely breakfast."

She slid into her jacket. "That sounds like heaven."

"Especially since you have your own room."

They headed for the door and walked out into the starry night, taking the cobblestone path that led to the pool area that GiGi had just redone. Instead of turning left toward the pool, Rico went right, through a garden that had a few shrubs but no flowers, given that it was December. Then suddenly they were at the far side of the house.

"I'll text Lorenzo and see how I get my car out of the garage."

She stood in the cold night, fighting a shiver.

A garage door suddenly rose.

Rico laughed. "That Lorenzo. Everything's connected to his phone."

They walked inside. He eased over to a Bentley and opened the door for her. She slid inside. While he rounded the hood, she glanced around.

Holy cats.

The villa had clued her in that the Salvaggios had more money than everybody she knew put together. But suddenly the sheer volume of wealth around her overwhelmed her. New York City, Manhattan in particular, was filled with beautiful things.

But this was *luxury*.

She didn't belong here. And she most certainly did not belong with Rico. Not even to flirt a bit.

Ridiculous disappointment filled her. She knew all about life not turning out the way she thought it should. Not getting what she wanted. She'd learned to temper her wishes and goals into something that fit her life.

But telling herself no tonight felt wrong.

CHAPTER TWO

RICO STARTED THE car and drove them to the country road that would take them to Florence. He hadn't missed the way Riley had said that Marietta should sleep in because she had her own room. Meaning, she usually slept with someone and was probably married! If that was true, it would put an end to all his unusual longings around her—and his plan to turn this into a fun, romantic weekend with the maid of honor.

Not being able to come right out and ask, he hedged a bit. "So…you get a room to yourself?"

She laughed. "Riley always teases me about the fact that I have three roommates in a two-bedroom apartment. There are two of us in each bedroom."

He glanced over at her. "You aren't married? You have roommates?"

"It's not unheard of in New York. Rent is through the roof. And I wanted to be there, in the thick of things to find myself, to make my mark." She shrugged. "I wasn't afraid to sacrifice."

He knew all about sacrifices too. Or maybe more like life necessities. "My first apartment was two rooms above a garage. Cold in the winter. And smelled like mold."

She burst out laughing.

He peered over at her. She didn't feel sorry for him? She didn't dismiss his past as something that was over so he should forget it? She saw the humor?

"The stairway to the entry was outside. Cats would congregate by my door every morning. I think the tenant before me probably fed them and they expected me to keep up the tradition."

She laughed again. "And did you?"

He took a breath. "I'm a sucker for anybody or anything who needs a little help."

"It's connection. I had a crappy end to my marriage, and two of my three roommates are women who also left bad relationships." She shrugged. "I knew exactly what they were going through. I happily accepted them when they applied. What's your connection to the cats?"

The question should have gotten his shackles up. But she wasn't asking out of curiosity. They were simply talking honestly. And it wasn't like he hid his past. In this day of technology, no one could hide their past. All she had to do was research him. Everything was there.

"I was an orphan." Which was a cleaner way of explaining his life than admitting someone had left him in a train station. Everyone assumed it was his mom since there had been a lipstick print on his cheek from where she'd kissed him goodbye. "Raised in foster homes until I eventually ran away to be on my own."

She glanced around the Bentley. "Looks like you did okay."

"I did. I jumped around, worked mostly as a waiter until I was twenty-one. I couldn't seem to get anything together in Spain, so I went to London. When I got there, I found a job as a limo driver because those guys get really great tips. A couple weeks in, I picked up this man at the airport and rather than sit in the back he sat in front with me."

"That's odd."

"He told me his daughter was considering starting a ride-share company. He wanted to talk her into getting limos instead of using the cars of people who worked for her. He asked a million questions and when he found out how much money I made, he looked at the worn jeans beneath the company jacket and asked me what I was doing with all those good tips." He smiled at the memory. "I said paying rent and he rolled into this long speech about how lucky I was to be young and if I would start saving and investing now, I could be a billionaire someday." He chuckled. "He was right."

She frowned. "Maybe I should run into him."

"I could arrange it. Not only does he live in Manhattan, but we're still friends because every time he came to London, he requested me as his driver. We'd have these great talks. He told me things I had no clue about. Like living off my hourly wage and saving every cent of my tips so I'd have money to invest. Four years later, I'd scraped together enough to start a limo company that competed with the one I had worked for. Two years after that, I was going to his business meetings with him. That's how I met Antonio. We bought a company together and became friends. Ten years and a few really good opportunities later, I'm the billionaire Ethan O'Banyon had said I would be."

"That's amazing."

He released a breath, suddenly so comfortable with her that his over-the-top attraction to her made sense. They both knew life wasn't easy. "It's really a matter of two things. Living below your means and getting lucky with investments."

"Sounds like it didn't hurt that you found a mentor."

He laughed. "No. It did not. I always considered my meeting Ethan to be life's way of making it up to me that I was abandoned."

"That's a healthy way of looking at it."

"It is. There is absolutely no point in dwelling on the past. Making a future is a much better use of your brain."

"That was how I looked at it when my husband dumped me."

He winced. "Ugh. Sorry."

"Don't be sorry. Our marriage had been deteriorating. I just never got the gumption to leave myself." Even discussing something unhappy, her pretty accent gave him goose bumps. "Wish I had. But I didn't dwell on that. I asked myself what I wanted, and I decided what I really, really wanted was my freedom."

"Your husband must have been extremely difficult to live with if your big goal was freedom."

She took a breath. "He was. We didn't start out that way. We dated all four years at university." She laughed. "Even had the same business management classes. We were like two peas in a pod. But after being perfect together for so long, about a year or so into our marriage, his temper began to make ugly appearances when we'd argue. He blamed things on me. Yelled a lot. Then I realized he used his temper to make everything look like my fault." She paused, then shrugged. "Anyway, I was relieved when he told me he wanted to end our marriage."

Just from the little she'd said, he knew there was more to her bad marriage than she was letting on, but nobody told the entire story of their life in the first private conversation they had with someone. From the way she fiddled with her jacket and purse, he knew she was embarrassed to have even said what she had.

But she shouldn't be. He didn't condemn her for a bad marriage or even for letting details slide into a getting-to-know-you conversation. He understood having a difficult past.

To ease her discomfort, he said, "I felt the same way when I'd be moved away from foster parents who were abusive."

She winced. "Your foster parents were abusive?"

"Not all of them. But there were many who believed in using a belt or the back of their hand to get a confused kid to fall in line."

"That's awful."

"It's also the past. I guess what I'm trying to say is that it sounds like we're both survivors."

She smiled. "It does."

This time her smile didn't throw him for a loop. This time, he actually felt the softness of it. Along with a click of connection. And why not? They *were* both survivors. And not survivors who wore their hearts on their sleeves. Survivors who knew life was sometimes about moving on.

"Tell me more about your life now."

"I'm having a blast being myself."

He laughed. "Really?"

"In Texas, towns are small and everybody knows everybody. In Manhattan, I can do what I want without worrying what anybody else thinks because most people aren't paying attention."

He chuckled. "That is true. I never thought of it that way."

It was another area in which they were similar. He liked being able to do what he wanted too. Though for a different reason. She liked the freedom of choices, but he liked that he answered to no one.

It was no wonder they had a click of connection. They might come at things from different angles or with different motivations, but their bottom lines were the same.

They arrived at their hotel. Both had already checked in, so they simply walked by the noisy glass-walled bar to the elevator. She reached to hit the button for her floor. He reached to hit the button for his. They hit the button for three simultaneously, their hands bumping against each other.

At the feeling of her soft skin beneath his fingertips, he froze, then swallowed hard. Touching her—even so innocently—was wonderful. And here they were, both in the same hotel—not staying at the villa—giving them privacy and opportunity to do whatever they wanted.

She laughed nervously. Their accidental brush seemed to

have had the same effect on her as it had had on him. The stars seemed to be aligning for them.

"I see we're both on three."

She said, "That's convenient," then her very pale skin turned pink.

She'd blushed?

Because she'd said that's convenient?

Oh, yeah. He understood. If they were sleeping together, it would be very convenient to be on the same floor. She might not have intended her comment that way. But once the words had slipped out of her mouth, she'd realized they could have that meaning.

The doors swished closed.

He smiled at her. She smiled at him. Attraction washed through him again. Not the simple urge when a person meets someone physically attractive. But a strong intuition that they could have something wonderful this weekend—and the week before the wedding when everyone was supposed to gather to prepare for the big day.

Living on different continents, they'd never have a relationship. But this was exactly the kind of situation that one-night stands were made for. An incredible attraction. No chance of anything permanent. Just a moment stolen out of time.

Still—

They were in the same wedding and neither one of them wanted to do anything that might somehow affect Antonio and Riley's big day. He'd have to think all this through before he acted on what appeared to be a very happy impulse.

The elevator bell rang. The doors slid open. He motioned for her to exit before him. They both turned right.

She dug out her key as they walked down the hall. He ambled past his room, continuing on with her. The hall was empty, but a person never knew if there was someone around a corner, waiting for an unsuspecting tourist. A gentleman, he decided to walk her to her door.

They reached her room and Marietta's breath shimmied. All her confusing thoughts about Rico had been banished. He might be extremely wealthy now, but he knew what it was to struggle. They were more alike than she ever would have guessed, and it was going to be a lot of fun to hang out together at the engagement ball and during the week before the wedding.

If they started something romantic, that might actually make the engagement party and wedding week even more fun.

She stopped at her door and displayed her keycard. "This is me."

"Then I'll say good-night."

"Good night."

He didn't move.

She stood in front of her door awkwardly waiting for him to leave, then realized he might be considering kissing her good-night.

And would that be so bad?

No. It would actually be perfect. She was blissfully attracted to him. That didn't happen to her every day. Heck, it had never happened. Plus, he wasn't merely good-looking. He was a nice guy. They had enough in common to be great partners for the wedding. But she was also attracted enough to him that she'd consider a fling—

But it was up to him.

Kiss her?

Not kiss her?

All up to him.

"It's customary that you open the door so I can make sure you get inside safely."

"Oh!" Her chest swelled with the foolishness of her thought

process. Dear God. It probably hadn't even crossed his mind to kiss her. It had simply been so long since she'd even thought about kissing someone—and even having a fling—that she'd gotten all the signals wrong. Or gotten so wrapped up in her own hopes that she'd—

Well, she might have made a fool of herself.

She slid the card across the doorknob. The lock clicked. She opened the door and stepped inside. Before she closed it, she said, "Good night."

He paused. She refused to think that he might be reconsidering kissing her. Good grief. They'd just met. And she'd already made herself look foolish once. That was enough.

He said, "Good night."

She closed the door and leaned against it. The problem was, the man was simply too yummy. And she hadn't even flirted with anyone in years. Worse, she was looking at this weekend and the week before the wedding as a vacation of a sort. He would be the perfect candidate for a vacation fling. But not if he didn't think of her the same way she thought of him. They might have enough in common to be friends, but that was it.

Still, they had enough in common that she could see them having a great time at the engagement party and wedding.

From here on out, she'd behave, treat him like a friend, stop all the wonderful tingles of attraction she felt around him and enjoy herself.

For Pete's sake! She was in Italy, with her best friend, celebrating a wedding. She didn't need any more fun than that.

The next morning, Rico woke and ran his hands down his face. He'd thought the whole thing through when he returned to his hotel room that night and decided it was a lucky break for him and Marietta to have found each other and they should take full advantage. He wanted nothing more than an entire day to woo her, but he was best man in Antonio's wedding and like it or not, that was where his priorities lay. He had no idea what Antonio had planned for them that day, but he was ready to be a dutiful best man.

Unfortunately, Antonio didn't seem to have anything that needed to be handled. After breakfast, Rico, Antonio and Lorenzo spent most of the day hiding in Antonio's quarters at the villa, staying out of the way of the bride, her mom, her maid of honor and Antonio's grandmother while they plowed through their planning and organizing duties.

But he wasn't concerned. He had a car and he and Marietta were staying at the same hotel. When they left the villa that night, they could get a nightcap at the bar and things could progress from there.

Immediately after dinner, that plan went to hell in a hand-basket when Juliette announced she was driving Marietta back to Florence because they had some business to discuss. Something about her new duties now that Riley would be living in Italy.

Disappointed, Rico watched a movie with Antonio and Riley, who made popcorn and cuddled, making him feel like a third wheel, even though they assured him he wasn't.

The next day, the entire villa buzzed with activity for the ball that night. If Marietta had been around, he hadn't seen her. When he returned to the hotel to dress for the ball, Lorenzo sent him a text saying he would be sending a limo for him around six. He wanted Rico to enjoy the party, not be worried about having to drive home.

Alone and feeling very much like the third wheel again, he arrived for the ball. The butler, Gerard, opened the door for him.

"Good evening, sir. I've been instructed to tell you that Antonio and Riley will be down shortly, and you should go back through the hall to the anteroom for the ballroom where the wedding party will gather before being introduced."

"Thank you, Gerard."

"My pleasure, sir."

Head down, hands in his trouser pockets, he eased his way to the side entry to the ballroom.

When he looked up, he saw Marietta standing alone in the little room that was more like a corridor. A vision in a shiny emerald green gown, she smiled at him.

"Hey."

All his thoughts of boredom and being an unnecessary part of the festivities disappeared. He walked over to her. "You are ravishing."

She snickered. In her down-home way, she said, "I bought this gown for a Christmas party last year. Riley said it was perfect for her engagement ball. So here I am, wearing it again. It's not like I'm going to see anybody who went to a charity ball in Manhattan last year."

Her Southern drawl was like music to his ears. But just seeing her took his mood from pensive to unbelievably happy.

"Well, you look wonderful."

She brushed her hand along the lapel of his jacket. "You're pretty spiffy yourself."

"This old thing?" he teased, motioning to his tux.

She laughed.

"So what have you and Riley been doing for the last two days?"

She laughed. "What haven't we been doing? First, Riley had a million little things she wanted my opinion on." She rolled her eyes. "Especially the vows. Then she wanted lunch out yesterday and today. After which we shopped. The girl wants all new clothes for her honeymoon." She paused and caught his gaze. "Do you know where they're going?"

"I think it's a secret."

She huffed out a sigh. "These people and their secrets."

Lorenzo and Juliette appeared at the end of the corridor.

Rico leaned into Marietta and whispered, "Speaking of secrets."

He expected her to laugh. Instead, their gazes caught and held. Attraction rippled through him. His heart chugged to a stop. She was about the most beautiful woman he had ever met. And she wasn't just pretty. She was normal around him, as if they'd been friends forever.

Something clicked in his heart. He ignored it. He wanted this night. She lived too far away for him to worry that the engaging of his heart meant they were starting something he couldn't stop. After the wedding, they might not ever see each other again.

He simply wanted this night.

CHAPTER THREE

ANTONIO AND RILEY arrived all smiles. Though they obviously tried not to, Juliette and Lorenzo gave off romantic vibes. Marietta could barely believe she was there, in this lap of luxury, in the private hall, waiting to be introduced.

She peeked into the ballroom. Light from the chandeliers glittered off gold flatware, crystal stemware and diamond necklaces on the slim throats of wealthy matriarchs. She swore at least four of the guests were royals.

The master of ceremonies introduced her and Rico. They walked into the ballroom to applause and proceeded over to the main table. There was a short set of steps to the platform that was raised just high enough that everyone could see the bride and groom and their wedding party.

Marietta couldn't help it. She was charmed. The Salvaggios might be wealthy, but they were wonderful people. Her friend was happy. The ball itself was exquisite. Rico thought she looked ravishing. And the champagne flowed like water.

The master of ceremonies introduced everyone again for the bridal party song that started the dancing for the evening. Rico pulled her into his arms, and they glided across the floor. The touch of his hand on the bare skin of her back sent tingles through her. The way he smiled at her filled her heart with joy. If anyone had ever felt like they were in a fairy tale, it was her. Right now. In this minute.

After a second dance, Rico plucked two glasses of champagne for them off the tray of a passing waiter. They slid through the tables, easing away from the noise of the band. When they were far enough, she tugged on his jacket sleeve to stop him.

"I know you know a lot of people here, so don't feel that you have to stay with me to entertain me. Go talk to your friends."

"I am." The way he held her gaze shot electricity through her. The man could charm the angels if he wanted. "I'm just taking you with me. I'll introduce you to everyone."

Like a couple.

She did not let her brain go there. They were partners in a wedding. He knew people that she didn't. He was being polite. But she couldn't stop the acknowledgment of how attracted they were. And how that meant something. And how she was due, really due, for an inconsequential fling with a gorgeous guy. If that's what this was leading up to, she was ready.

She smiled at him. "That'd be great."

Walking through the crowd, he introduced her to two race car drivers who were friends of Antonio's.

She shook hands politely. "How do you do."

They glanced from her to Rico and back to her again. The tall blond who'd just won a major race smiled at her. "You're Riley's friend?"

"Maid of honor. Rico's the best man."

The blond guy acknowledged that with an, "Oh."

The shorter, dark-haired man set his champagne glass on a table, saying, "Would you like to dance?"

Rico slid his hand around her waist. "Next dance is mine." He led her onto the dance floor.

The proprietary gesture should have made her wince, except she'd made the mistake of making herself and Rico sound like wedding partners when they were beginning to feel like so much more. As if they were leading up to something… And she wanted it.

She wanted this night.

After the dance, Lorenzo came over. "I'm stealing Marietta for a dance."

Marietta sort of froze, but Rico politely handed her off to Lorenzo. He led her to the dance floor, where Antonio was dancing with Juliette, and she hid a smile.

But even as she and Lorenzo chitchatted through their dance, her gaze searched the crowd for Rico. Their eyes met across the crowded room, and warmth poured through her. At the end of the dance, Lorenzo walked her back to where Rico stood and, in that minute, she knew she wouldn't be dancing with anyone else that evening.

It wasn't wrong to want a romantic interlude with him, something as special as he was. And something that could last for the few weeks they would be in each other's company for the wedding. And when the wedding was over, they would be over…and that would be fine because she had a new job to get to.

It would also be wonderful.

At the end of the night, the crowd began to thin out. Riley and Antonio came over and said good-night. More people left. In the almost empty ballroom, the few remaining conversations echoed around them.

A dutiful best man, Rico said, "Let's go find Lorenzo, see if there's anything he needs us to do."

Taking her hand, as he had been doing all evening, he led her across the dance floor, where Lorenzo stood alone by the bar.

Rico said, "Is there anything we can help you with?"

"No. Gerard and I will close the room. I'll text the driver that you're both ready to go back to the hotel."

They laughed about the party on the drive through the dark countryside. But her insides tingled with the idea that they were about to make love.

She didn't have to say it. He didn't have to ask. They'd been building to this all night.

When they reached the hotel, the driver pulled up to the portico and Rico got out. He turned to take her hand to help her out of the limo and kept it as they walked to the elevator, where he pushed the button for the third floor. He kept holding her hand as they walked down the hall to her room. When they reached the door, he didn't hesitate to pull her into his arms and kiss her good-night.

His soft lips met hers. Delicious warmth poured through her. She leaned in. He deepened the kiss, opening her mouth to let their tongues twine. Her arms tightened around his shoulders. His tightened around her waist.

Everything was perfect, but a strange fear gripped her. She didn't want to misinterpret things the way she had her wish for a good-night kiss at her door that first night.

She stopped the kiss and took a slight step back so she could look in his beautiful dark eyes. The urgent need not to miss this chance overwhelmed her.

"Don't go." She motioned to her door. "Come inside."

He held her gaze. "Are you sure?"

She inched over to him and straightened his bow tie intimately. "Absolutely."

Not giving either one of them a chance to think, she turned and used her keycard to open her door. He followed her into her room. As the door closed, he caught her wrist and spun her to face him, kissing her deeply.

Her entire body breathed a sigh of relief. It could have been embarrassing if she'd misinterpreted that kiss. But she hadn't and he was here in her room. He was hers for the night and she wasn't wasting a minute. She broke the kiss and undid the bow tie she'd straightened only minutes before. He reached behind her for the zipper of her dress. It slithered to the floor, leaving her standing before him in her pale peach bra and panties and high heels.

She began unbuttoning his shirt. He slid his hands from her shoulders to her wrists. "You have the softest skin."

"It's my mom's Irish heritage. Pretty sure that's where I get the red hair, too."

He laughed and she smiled at him. It felt so wonderful to simply be herself. To laugh with him and enjoy everything. And that might be the greatest gift of the night because this night certainly was a gift.

He lost patience with her undressing him and took off his trousers as she removed his shirt. He shrugged out of his undershirt and briefs and she reached for the clasp of her bra but he stopped her.

"Leave it." He chuckled. "And the sexy high heels."

With a quick nudge, he dropped her to the bed. She laughed, edging away from him as he climbed on the soft comforter with her. But he was quick, like a panther, and before she really knew what was happening, she was beneath him as he enjoyed the satiny fabric of her bra and panties.

Pleasure spiraled through her. She breathed in, enjoying every sensation before she began touching and tasting. She wanted to go slowly, to take in every moment of tingling delight, but their movements quickened as each became greedy. Her bra and panties disappeared as if by magic, then he kissed her like a man drowning in need and joined them.

For ten seconds it felt as if the world had stopped. She knew for sure her breathing had. She basked in the delight of being with him before they moved again. Not wanting to miss a thing, she ran her fingers through his thick, curly hair, then her hands smoothed down his back, memorizing the texture of him as their desire built to a stunning climax that stole her breath.

They lay together as each came down from the pleasure high, then he rolled to the pillow beside hers, taking her with him, snuggled against his side.

"I knew you'd be delicious."

She levered herself up on her elbow with a wince. "You might be confusing *delicious* with *desperate*."

"Desperate?"

"It's been a while."

"Really? I wouldn't have guessed."

She laughed. "I moved to New York right after my divorce, and honestly I've simply been too busy establishing myself to date."

"Well, I'm glad you're free now. From the second I saw you, I knew you were something special and I was right."

"I'd think you were a sweet talker or funnin' me, except I think you're pretty special too."

He slid his hand up to her neck and bought her to him for a kiss that heated within seconds. They made love again and fell asleep nestled together.

Rico had never been happier, never been with a woman who was simultaneously sweet and sexy—and something about her Texas accent made her voice even sexier. But by the time he woke the next morning, she had already gone. A note leaning against the lamp on the bedside table said she had an early flight.

Which was fine. Technically, they'd had a one-night stand—

With the promise of romance the entire week before the wedding.

They might not be in each other's world but GiGi had

insisted the entire wedding party be in Florence the week before the wedding. So they had seven days to be together.

He wondered if they should be open about their relationship or keep it a secret. Secret relationships were such fun. But it was also great to be openly affectionate.

Didn't matter. What they had was fabulous and it came with a natural expiration date. When the wedding was over, she'd return to Manhattan for good and he'd go back to London.

It was perfect.

Arriving in Manhattan, Marietta felt a lot like Cinderella returning to her normal life after a night with a handsome prince...but that was fine. She wasn't going back to sweeping cinders. After years of working with Riley as office manager and her right-hand person planning the marriage proposals that were the bread and butter of her company, she was the new general manager of Riley's proposal business. She couldn't wait to be with Rico again at the wedding, but she reminded herself that it was good that they had a three-week span without seeing each other because for as much fun as they had together, they didn't belong together.

Number one, she was at the beginning of a new job, the start of a new life. Number two, he was a billionaire. She was a worker bee. A smart woman would accept that, enjoy what they had, and then after the wedding put her nose to the grindstone.

Besides, once-in-a-lifetime romances were supposed to end. Right now, she had wonderful engagement ball memories and strong confidence about the rest of her life.

Things had never been better.

Monday morning, she went to the office, wearing something one step above the T-shirts and jeans she'd typically worn as the office manager. Sissy, the new receptionist, told her that Juliette had already arrived. She'd gone directly to her office, closing the door, and she didn't want to be disturbed.

Respecting that, and also knowing her duties, she went back to work. There were proposals to be planned. But she couldn't stop thinking of Rico. Wondering how he would propose if he ever found a woman he'd want to marry. She tossed that thought right out of her head because she knew the woman would not be her. Not wanting to dwell on that, she threw herself into her work.

They still had the week before the wedding to enjoy each other.

Then that would be the end of them.

CHAPTER FOUR

THE NEXT WEEK passed in a blur of hosting Christmas Eve and Christmas Day marriage proposals for her clients, as she put the finishing touches on the planning of New Year's Eve and New Year's Day proposals.

Juliette spent the holiday in Italy with Riley and the Salvaggios, leaving Marietta to manage Riley's company and the office itself.

The pace of the business didn't surprise her because she'd worked for Riley for years. She'd simply gone from being the one who helped plan the proposals to the one who did all the planning...and she loved it. It seemed like every day she was going to a party.

On January 2, with the excitement of all the holiday proposals out of the way, she realized she hadn't gotten her period. Confused, she looked at her calendar. She should have gotten it the end of the week before. Another three days went by. Still nothing. Passing a drugstore on the way to her apartment, she almost stepped inside. But that was ridiculous. Foolish. She was a week late. Lots of women had odd periods.

Except, she didn't. And for the first time in a long time, she'd actually had sex—

No. There was no point worrying about this. She'd tried to get pregnant for years in her marriage. She genuinely believed she couldn't have kids—

But what if it was her husband who couldn't have kids?

Oh, Lord. Her husband had always blamed her for their lack of children. But nobody had ever had anything checked out.

What if Keith had been the problem?

She didn't pass the pharmacy on her way home that night. She ducked in and bought a pregnancy test. The next morning, it was positive.

After all these years of never conceiving? It seemed improbable. So, she bought another pregnancy test. Actually, she bought three and used one every morning until they were gone. Because the goofy things always came back positive. After four tests, she now believed them.

She was pregnant.

The week before the wedding, Rico's private plane arrived at the airport in Florence earlier than he had planned. The Salvaggios weren't expecting him this early, so he'd tried to delay himself by having lunch before he'd left London. But eating alone didn't waste much time. Plus, he'd missed Marietta so much that he'd barely been able to focus. Was it really a surprise that he arrived at the airport early?

The Bentley he kept in his private hangar awaited him, but knowing he was early, he drove to the hotel and unpacked, wasting time again, but eventually he gave up. He simply could not wait to see her.

In the villa driveway, he texted Lorenzo, who texted a garage employee who came out to get the Bentley. With his car squared away, he strode to the front door. He rang the bell before he entered so no one would be surprised when he walked into the foyer.

Gerard greeted him with a smile. "Mr. Mendoza. A pleasure to see you." He took Rico's jacket.

"It's good to see you too, Gerard." He could hear noise in the room on the left, so he pointed. "Is everyone in there?"

Gerard winced. "GiGi's holding court."

Rico laughed. "When isn't she?"

As Gerard walked away with his coat, Rico turned to enter what he called the Salvaggios' social room. His gaze made a quick swipe of the area. He instantly saw Marietta in jeans and a peach-colored sweater that accented her pretty red hair. But just as quickly, he also realized the room was filled with women only. GiGi, Juliette, Riley and Marietta.

"Looks like I'm in the wrong room."

GiGi waved him inside. "No! No! Sit! Tell us what's going on in your life."

He winced. "Don't you have things you're supposed to be doing?"

Lorenzo's mom batted her hand. "They can wait."

His gaze slowly shifted to Marietta, who unlike Riley, Juliette and GiGi, was not smiling at him. In fact, when their gazes caught, she jerked hers away.

He thought it odd, but this was clearly girls' time. Plus, she might not want anyone to know they'd slept together after the engagement ball. He could respect that.

"I'd rather go look for the guys," he said with a chuckle, making light of the whole situation.

"They're in Lorenzo's quarters," Riley said. "Undoubtedly someone on TV is kicking a ball, or hitting a ball, or tossing a ball."

GiGi laughed. *"Si."*

"And Lorenzo's quarters are…where?" He'd watched soccer matches with Antonio, but had never gone to Lorenzo's quarters.

"Third floor," Juliette said. "Last door on the right."

"Okay."

No one seemed to think it odd that Juliette knew where Lorenzo's room was, but he said nothing. Just nodded and returned to the foyer. He took the elevator and walked down a hall that smelled of perfume. It wasn't unpleasant. Just different. The hall to Lorenzo's quarters smelled like a woman. Apparently, he and his mystery woman were still an item—

Antonio and Riley thought *Juliette* was his mystery woman. And wouldn't that explain why she had known which room was Lorenzo's?

No. He wasn't going to touch that with a ten-foot pole.

As he had done with the front door, he knocked then didn't wait to be invited in. He opened the door and strode into a foyer that took him to a huge main room with oversize leather sofas and a huge TV mounted on the wall above the fireplace.

Lorenzo saw him first. "Hey! Rico! Grab a beer and take a seat. We found a Bruce Willis movie."

"Everybody gets beaten up?"

Antonio laughed. "Yes. And the bad guys are sorry they tried anything."

A quick glance around showed Rico there was a refrigerator in the open floor plan kitchen. He walked over, grabbed a beer and plopped down on the sofa beside Antonio.

"Don't you guys have things you should be doing?"

"I have three contracts I should be reading," Antonio said with a sigh of disgust.

"No. I mean wedding things?"

"Like what?" Lorenzo asked. "If I even make a small suggestion GiGi goes bananas. You'd swear it was her getting married."

Rico snorted and took a long drink of his beer.

"She made us both take a week off work just so she can tell us not to touch anything."

"So you're watching movies?"

"And Knicks basketball," Antonio said. "Riley's taken me to Madison Square Garden to watch them play."

"Sounds fun?" Rico said with a wince.

"It is. We'll show you later."

He glanced around. This was not at all how he pictured this week going. First, for some reason, he imagined himself and Marietta meeting in the foyer and sharing a passionate kiss. Then, he'd thought there would be tons of prep work for the bridal party. Though now that he thought about it, he wasn't sure what he'd believed they needed to do. Employees would set up the ballroom for the celebration and the vineyard where Antonio and Riley would exchange vows. And they'd probably hired a chef to prepare the food, and undoubtedly that chef came with staff.

Wine could be gotten from the vineyard supply.

Good God he was going to be bored—

Unless he and Marietta could sneak away. Now, that would be fun. Making up a reason they couldn't come to the vineyard, figuring out somewhere to go where no one would see them, or just staying in one of their hotel rooms and making their own fun.

"Rico?"

His gaze jumped to Lorenzo.

"I asked if you wanted some snacks."

The sense of severe boredom nearly overwhelmed him. But he declined with a smile and began plotting how he and Marietta could spend the next few days together.

By the time the gentlemen came downstairs after the movie, Marietta, Riley and Juliette had taken GiGi to town for a break. According to Gerard, it had been Marietta's idea.

Rico frowned. If he were a suspicious man, he might think she was avoiding him. But he wasn't suspicious, and he also knew Marietta had a good heart. The past year since Carlos's death had been hard on GiGi. Marietta was simply injecting some fun into her life.

Lorenzo suggested they go to the wine-tasting room. After getting coats, the three men walked past the new pool area to the big building that fronted the vineyards. Lorenzo got behind the bar and entertained himself and customers by pouring the samples.

Antonio began taking calls. From his replies, they were business calls.

Had there been more than a smattering of customers, Rico might have joined Lorenzo behind the bar, but there were just enough people to entertain Lorenzo.

Rico sat on one of the tall stools by the shiny walnut bar.

When the sun finally set on the boring day, he announced that he was going back to the hotel to change for dinner.

Lorenzo shook his head. "GiGi wants everything casual this week. She'll be happy you didn't change out of your jeans and sweater."

He did his best to smile. But, seriously, boredom was killing him and damn it, he wanted to see Marietta.

Finally, finally, they went to the dining room. He took his seat beside Marietta, who gave him a weak smile. Just when he would have given her a questioning look, Lorenzo walked behind Juliette's chair, leaned down and kissed her.

Rico blinked. That was the first interesting thing that had happened all day.

Antonio must have noticed his odd expression because he said, "My dad and Juliette decided to admit they were in a relationship."

"On Christmas," GiGi said. "Such a wonderful surprise."

Rico cleared his throat. "I'm glad for you," he said to Lorenzo and Juliette. "And you too, GiGi."

She laughed. "I just love love. It makes me happy when people are happy."

Rico smiled. "Yeah. It makes me happy too." He lied because this felt like his opening. "And speaking of relationships—"

Marietta kicked him under the table.

He jerked his gaze to hers.

She pointedly said, "If you're wondering when Lorenzo's going to ask me to set up a proposal for him, don't. They're taking things slowly."

She drew out the word *slowly* so much that he knew she was sending him a message. Apparently, his second guess for why she seemed so distant was correct. Marietta didn't want to announce that they were an item.

Which was fine. He couldn't believe he'd almost let the cat out of the bag just because he'd been bored and restless all day...and hadn't seen her.

He was simply antsy. That's all. He could keep a secret with the best of them.

Dinner was served. The conversation was lively. Especially from Lorenzo, who behaved like a man who'd finally found happiness. The guardian of the family had apparently passed on his duties to Antonio, who was thrilled to be running the Salvaggio empire—which explained why he'd made business calls while his father entertained guests in the wine-tasting room.

They took dessert into the social room. After the chocolate cake was gone, Rico finally had his real opportunity. He rose from his chair. "Well, it's been a long day, so I'm going to the hotel." He flicked his gaze to Marietta. "I'd be happy to give you a ride."

She looked at him ruefully, but eventually forced a smile and said, "Yes. That would be great."

Because it was late, Lorenzo walked out to the garage with them. He used his phone to unlock the door, waited while they entered the Bentley and waved goodbye as Rico drove out of the lane.

At the road, he turned to the right, went a half mile, pulled off to the side, shoved the car into Park, undid his seat belt and reached for Marietta. He heard the click of her seat belt unlocking.

She turned into his arms, and he pulled her to him for a desperate, happy, passionate kiss. For a second, he was tempted to pull her onto his lap, but she shifted away.

"We need to talk."

"Hey, no worries. If you don't want anyone to know we're being romantic, I can keep a secret."

She winced. "I'm afraid the secret's a little bigger than that."

He frowned, absolutely confused about what she was talking about.

She sucked in a breath. "I'm pregnant."

All the blood drained from his body. He swore it puddled at his feet, rendering him frozen and speechless. He tried to blink to bring himself back to life and even his eyelids refused to cooperate.

"Here's the deal," she said in her cute little Texas way that reminded him of exactly how attracted he was to her—

Except she wasn't just a gorgeous woman anymore. She was pregnant.

Pregnant.

"After spending years unable to conceive in my marriage, it never occurred to me to worry about getting pregnant. Actually, I never thought I'd be a mom."

She spoke in a rush. In his befuddled state, he couldn't tell if she was trying to get all this out or genuinely excited. But it did explain a few things about her broken marriage. She'd said her husband blamed things on her. She'd said she was happy to get away.

"I have a great job. A secure job. The only thing I need is an apartment of my own and now I can afford that. With all the hubbub about the wedding, Riley and I never actually discussed how big my raise is going to be, but Juliette did say it will be substantial. So." She faced him. "Seriously, I'm thrilled."

He heard everything she said, but simply couldn't process it because the reality had finally sunk in. He was going to be a dad? Hell, he'd never *had* a dad. At least not one that he knew. He had no clue how to be a dad. He also knew how difficult life could be for a child who grew up believing he was unwanted.

He pushed all that out of his head to think about later so he could deal with the situation at hand. "You're happy?"

"Honestly, Rico, I'm so thrilled I could dance."

"But this was why you weren't glad to see me?"

She inched a little closer. "I was glad to see you. I simply was concerned about your reaction."

"Oh, I was surprised. Still am."

She laughed. "Imagine my shock. For the past eight years I've believed I'd never be a mom. Now, here I am, pregnant." She took a happy breath. "And at such a good point. You know... I can do this by myself. Don't need anybody's money. Don't need anybody's help."

What she was saying sank in a bit more. That bad marriage she'd told him about had left her incredibly independent. Which he already knew. But did that leave room for him? What would it be like to parent with a woman who didn't need him—hell, as independent as she was, she probably wouldn't *want* him around.

"By the time the baby's born I will be settled in both the job and whatever apartment I choose."

Another man might have been okay with that. Rico had conflicting feelings. As a guy who'd spent his life free and unfettered, her words told him she wouldn't mess with his life, wouldn't change his life. As an abandoned child, the thought of ignoring his own son or daughter sent hot arrows through him. He'd lived a life of not being wanted. He would not do that to a child.

He peeked at her. Before he said anything that might sound

wrong, he needed to understand her position fully and accurately. "You're saying you don't want anything from me?"

"I don't *need* anything from you."

He felt totally and completely edged out. Even as he knew how bad that would be for his child, he wasn't sure what to say. Or even if this was the right time to discuss it. There were so many things to consider before he could even decide the right thing to do.

"I see."

"Oh, no!" Her happy eyes filled with horror. "I'm not saying you don't have rights. You do! If you want them. I'm trying to assure you that I've made my choices now you can make yours."

"You mean I can decide how involved I want to be?"

"Yes!"

"And how will this work? I live in London. You live in Manhattan."

She playfully punched his arm. "You have a plane, remember? You can come visit."

"That's it?"

She studied his face for a few seconds. "You know what? I've had days to get accustomed to this. It's also something joyful for me. I've always wanted to be a mom and suddenly that dream is coming true. I've thought things through. I'm happy. I'm healthy. I'm financially stable. And I really, really want to be a mom. Now, you need to take a few days to consider what you want."

Marietta watched as Rico leaned forward, started the Bentley again, then wrapped his fingers around the steering wheel. At first, he'd clearly been shocked. Now, the expression on his face confused her. She'd run every possible reaction from him through her brain and somehow this one hadn't made the list. Oh, sure. She'd considered that he'd be shocked. But this new expression flummoxed her.

Rico seemed like a great guy, but technically, she didn't know him. She had to be very careful how she navigated the waters of his place in her life. After all, her last connection to a man had been horrible.

The drive to the hotel was silent. The walk to her hotel room was equally silent. When they reached her door, she faced him with a smile. "I guess we can talk tomorrow?"

He ran his hand along the back of his neck. "Honestly, I still haven't wrapped my head around all of it yet. There are things I have to consider that you don't."

For the first time since she'd realized she was pregnant, she remembered that he was a billionaire. She'd laid out that she was fully capable of supporting their child herself. Surely, he wasn't thinking she wanted money from him, and he needed to protect himself and his fortune—

Righteous indignation roared through her. Of all the chauvinistic—

She squelched that thought. He was allowed a knee-jerk reaction or two. He could have all the time he wanted to "think things through." She'd made her plans. She was fine. Better than fine. She was about to become a mom. Something she genuinely believed would never happen for her. She did not want his money, and she would not let him ruin her happiness.

CHAPTER FIVE

THE NEXT MORNING, Marietta woke feeling a little dizzy. She waited until her head cleared before she got out of bed. She'd read about morning sickness and if this was the worst it got, she would be lucky. She was totally prepared to not only get through the pregnancy but to enjoy it.

She slid into the shower thinking about Rico. She wasn't angry with him for needing time. She'd even stopped worrying that he seriously believed he had to protect his fortune. Those were his choices. If he wanted to be angry or bitter or suspicious, that was on him.

But she also realized that his needing time to consider all the ramifications wasn't out of line either.

She also hadn't forgotten that if she'd had a child with her ex, he would have demanded rights far beyond what she would have wanted. He probably also would have sued for custody. In a way, that was Rico's world. He had money. He had power. He was accustomed to being in control. He could sue for custody.

Her chest tightened and she stopped her thoughts. She would take this one step at a time. Which meant she wouldn't worry about things that hadn't happened. Though, she did intend to be prepared to fight if she had to.

No one would walk all over her the way her ex had.

It took an hour to dress and check her emails. When her phone hadn't pinged with a text or a call from Rico, she assumed he either wasn't awake, or was still thinking things through. She went downstairs and got breakfast at the hotel restaurant. She sat in front of the wall of glass, so he could easily see her if he came downstairs.

He didn't.

So, she called a rideshare and arrived at the villa without him. He needed space. She didn't like awkward situations. She also didn't want them to discuss things they weren't ready to talk about. His staying away from her might just be a good idea. It wasn't like they were a couple. They'd had a one-night stand and created a child. A child she wanted very much. He could have as much or as little involvement as he wanted. And if he pushed too hard or too far, she'd hire a lawyer.

When she reached the doorway of the room where everyone always gathered, Juliette and Riley sat on the sofa, drinking coffee. GiGi was giving them instructions to relay to the staff who would be setting up the area between the pool and the vineyard for the vows.

She stepped into the room just as Juliette said, "So we're doing a dry run with them?"

"*Si*. I don't want them setting up the chairs or the trellis until Saturday morning. But we'll all be busy on Saturday morning. So, if we run through everything today, they'll know what they're doing when the time comes to actually set up everything." GiGi glanced up and saw Marietta. "Good morning."

She sat beside Riley on the sofa. "Good morning, GiGi."

"Did you sleep well?"

She smiled. "Very well." Unlike Rico, she'd already adjusted to her pregnancy and she was happy—

An unexpected thought struck her. She'd never considered telling Riley and Juliette that she was pregnant. She'd instinctively known that was something for later, after the wedding, after her job was official, when she was far enough along that it would be exciting to tell them. The news wouldn't get jumbled up in Antonio and Riley's celebration or the chaos of learning a new job.

But what if Rico wanted to tell the Salvaggios? He seemed very close to them. He might want advice.

She was going to have to chat with him about that and the sooner the better.

"We're actually getting lucky with the weather, if the forecast is to be believed," Riley said. "It's supposed to be sunny with highs in the fifties."

Marietta said, "That is lucky," as the front door opened. She couldn't see who'd entered from where she sat but she did hear Gerard's muffled voice and laughter a few seconds before Rico stepped into the room.

GiGi said, "Rico! Good morning!" Then she glanced at Marietta. "I thought you two were riding together?"

"I got up early," Marietta said. But the truth was she was happy not to have another awkward car ride with him. She wanted his decisions to be his decisions and she did not want him asking her too many questions. She wanted him figuring out what he wanted on his own. So that if they did go to court, she wouldn't have said things that he could misinterpret.

Rico caught her gaze. "Could I see you in the foyer for a second?"

She held back a wince. Apparently, he did not agree that he should make his decisions on his own. "Sure."

When Juliette, Riley and GiGi gave them a confused look, Rico smiled. "We're going in together on a wedding gift."

GiGi said, "Ooh, I know what's happening here. She probably has better ideas than yours."

Rico laughed. "Exactly."

Riley rubbed her hands together in anticipation. "Wonder what it is."

Marietta chuckled, grateful he'd used discretion but also enjoying the moment and this wonderful family, as she rose from the sofa and followed him into the foyer. He caught her hand and eased them down the hall to the elevator, far enough away from the social room that they probably couldn't be heard.

She caught his gaze. "Do you really want to go in together on a gift?"

He snorted. "I already paid for a trip to Tahiti."

"I thought Antonio had a honeymoon planned."

"Tickets are open-ended. They can go on my trip whenever they want."

"Better put my name on the card or GiGi will know you lied."

He rolled his eyes. "She still has a mind like a steel trap."

She laughed. He eased her a little farther down the hall. "What was this morning about?"

"About?"

"Why'd you come here on your own... How *did* you get here?"

"Rideshare. And I didn't bother you this morning because it seemed like you wanted some time alone to think about things. Speaking of which, I don't want to tell anyone I'm pregnant until the wedding is over. I don't want to overshadow Riley and Antonio's special day."

Not sure if he was relieved that she was safe or relieved that they were holding off on telling people, Rico drew a long, life-sustaining breath. "Okay. Good."

"I mean, I know you're friends with Antonio and Lorenzo, so I sort of feel bad asking you to keep the secret for a while—"

"It's fine." He took another breath as all kinds of odd thoughts bombarded him about her taking a rideshare. Not that he was against them, but she was in a strange country.

And pregnant with his child.

For the first time since he'd arrived, he really looked at her. Her long hair fell around her in beautiful, curly chaos. A soft white sweater and jeans outlined her sexy little body. Her beatific smile reached all his screaming nerve endings and calmed them.

He actually, physically felt himself relax. He smiled, took a breath and said, "Good morning."

She laughed. "Ah. You're finally awake."

He shook his head. "I've been awake. Just not coherent." His smile grew. "You know, I've never asked how you're feeling."

"I've had a week to adjust to this news. You heard yesterday. I think it's normal for you to be off your game. And I also think some things should be off-limits for us to discuss. Actually, we both might want to get a lawyer."

He rubbed his hand along the back of his neck. "I guess."

"And I'm feeling fine. Woke a little dizzy this morning, but if that's the worst my morning sickness gets, I'm okay with it."

He studied her. He knew nothing about babies and pregnancy. The only kids he'd been around were those with him in whatever foster care house he'd been assigned. Now that he was an adult, children simply never entered his world. He worked in boardrooms and offices. His coffee company had a corporate office and staff. But he had a CEO running it. His primary function was managing his money as an independent investor. The closest he came to a child was a picture on someone's desk.

His nerve endings popped again.

"Look, I need to get back in the sitting room, and you should probably find Antonio and Lorenzo, unless you want to hear the back-and-forth about who should sit where during the wedding reception."

That sounded like fingernails on a chalkboard.

She was right. He needed to calm down, forget about the pregnancy and do wedding things. "I'll be going, thank you."

She snickered. "That's right. Save yourself while you can."

She turned away, but the oddest sense rolled through him. As if he should hug her or kiss her the way partners kissed when they parted. Luckily, he caught himself before he could do something so—

Intimate?

Connected?

Committed?

He knew all these weird feelings were the result of the pregnancy but that was the problem. He'd never been "attached" to anyone by anything other than friendship or sex. He had absolutely no idea how to handle the waves of unfamiliar emotions bombarding him. Or even how to process them. They sat on his skin like prickly sensations.

And then there was the matter of both of them getting a lawyer. That should have been the first thing he'd thought of. So why hadn't he?

He turned and almost bumped into Gerard. "You wouldn't happen to know where Lorenzo and Antonio are?"

"Hiding."

Rico laughed. "I would like to hide with them if possible." He pointed toward the foyer stairs. "Second floor. Last door on the left, right?"

Gerard nodded.

"Thank you."

He walked away grateful that he would spend the next couple of hours watching a movie or a sporting event—

Or sneaking out with his two best friends to do something foolish like find a shooting range—or play paintball.

If he needed to get his mind off the pregnancy until they each saw a lawyer, entertaining himself was exactly what he should do. Anyway, the wedding had happened so fast they hadn't arranged a bachelor party for Antonio. Maybe he could get a private minute to talk to Lorenzo and set up a paintball outing and lunch.

Having something to do for the wedding took his mind off everything and as they watched a movie, he was grateful. When Antonio left the room, he mentioned the paintball outing to Lorenzo and he laughed.

"That's a fabulous idea. I'll get a few names and we'll give him an outing he won't forget."

They kept silent when Antonio returned. Eventually, Lorenzo left, saying he had some work to do, and when he returned an hour later, he slipped a list of names to Rico.

The note also said his assistant had already secured a facility for Thursday morning and had contacted the people on the list.

Rico relaxed. It was good to have something wedding related to do, not just to get his mind off the pregnancy but also to put his focus on the wedding so no one got suspicious.

The three men ambled downstairs at noon for lunch.

As always, the conversation was spirited, but rather than split up into two groups when they were done eating, they all converged on the social room where Lorenzo poured wine. Twenty minutes of looking at GiGi's seating charts ensued because GiGi wanted everyone's okay on who would sit with whom.

No one but Rico seemed to notice that Marietta wasn't drinking her wine.

Holding her glass delicately, GiGi said, "That's the final chart! No more second-guessing. Saturday is going to be amazing."

"Not to mention Thursday," Rico said.

Everybody looked at him.

"We've arranged something of a bachelor party for Antonio."

GiGi said, "Ah."

Riley glanced at Lorenzo and Rico expectantly.

Marietta didn't even react.

Rico's heart stuttered. She looked worn down. She'd eaten lunch but now suddenly she appeared to be exhausted, and she'd barely spoken. She could be tired. Or sick. Or worse.

"A bachelor party?" Antonio said, surprised.

"Not so much a party as an outing," Lorenzo said. "And the only thing you get to know is don't wear good clothes."

Everybody laughed.

Rico looked at Marietta. Her face had gone pale.

He rose from his seat. "You know, if there's nothing else for us to do, maybe Marietta and I should head back to the hotel."

She finally smiled. She was definitely sick. Or something. Probably tired. He would not panic.

GiGi looked from Rico to Marietta. "You're going to the hotel?"

Marietta rose. "Yes. I think jet lag is setting in. I wouldn't mind a nap."

Glancing around the room, GiGi frowned. "Why aren't you staying here?"

Rico casually said, "For the engagement party, we were in the hotel. We got rooms there again."

"I had you staying there for *your* privacy," GiGi qualified. "But this is the wedding week. We need everybody here."

"Here?" Rico said, not liking that idea at all. Driving Marietta back to the hotel or being at the hotel was their private time, when they could discuss things like their one-night stand and her pregnancy.

"*Si.* You will stay here," GiGi said with finality. "Go back to the hotel and get your things."

CHAPTER SIX

MARIETTA ALMOST SIGHED with relief. Though they'd barely talked today, she could tell Rico still hadn't adjusted to the reality of her pregnancy. She'd also noticed the way he kept looking at her through lunch and when Lorenzo handed her a glass of wine. He needed to forget about the pregnancy, and the best way to do that would be for them to spend no time together. None. Let him take Antonio to whatever bachelor party event he had planned. Let him focus on the wedding.

Both of them staying at the villa would actually accomplish that. Not to mention cut down on uncomfortable drives to and from the hotel. Now all she had to endure was one ride to the hotel and the return trip here and then she could focus on Riley. Like a good maid of honor.

Gerard brought their coats to the foyer, and they exited through the front door to find Rico's Bentley waiting for them.

He opened the door for her, and she smiled her thanks. Now that she had a plan for keeping them apart until after the wedding, she intended to lead him in the direction of forgetting about the baby until he'd had a chance to come to terms with it. On his own turf. In his own world. Where he'd get the sense of what having a child really would mean to his life.

He slid behind the wheel talking. "I know you're probably mad at me for calling attention to you…but you looked sick."

"I'm not sick."

"Tired, then?"

"A little. But pregnancy is different for everyone. So far, with the exception of wanting a nap today, I'm fine. Maybe even better than fine."

He snorted.

"I'm serious. I'm starting a new job, running Riley's company. I can't have you calling attention to every yawn. Riley is my friend, and she loves me, but I will not put her in a position of thinking I can't do the job she promoted me into."

He drew a breath, as if considering that.

"Please. Just ignore me for the next couple of days. Not only is this Riley and Antonio's wedding week, but you're getting yourself more confused trying to make decisions before you can. You need to think this through in London, in your condo, doing your normal work where you'll have a perspective of your life so you can decide how much involvement you can logically handle. And I meant what I said about talking to your lawyer. I have no idea what he's going to say. I have no idea what *my* lawyer is going to say. But I think before we make any decisions or have any great discussions, we should both talk to lawyers."

"You're right."

"And stop watching me. I swear I'm taking good care of myself. There is no need to watch me like I'm a ticking bomb."

"I don't watch you."

"You do."

He sighed. "Okay. Maybe a little. I'm concerned."

"And I'm telling you that you don't need to be. I can take care of myself. I *will* take care of myself."

He said, "Fine."

He didn't say another word in the car and she hoped he was pondering her take on things—especially the part about the lawyer.

As they walked through the hotel lobby in the direction of the elevator, Rico said, "I'll get my things and come back for yours."

"Or I could get a bellman to help me."

He stopped but she kept going to the elevator doors. She pressed the buttons for their floors because this time he was on two and she was on three.

He entered the elevator two seconds before the door would have closed and stood stonily silent beside her until the door opened on his floor.

He hesitated, looking like a guy who was going to take charge again, when he didn't need to. She was very good at managing her own life—even when something unexpected happened. He didn't behave the way her ex-husband did, but having someone hovering over her did remind her of those days, sending a cold shiver of warning down her spine.

Still, he wasn't Keith. While she would be careful about keeping their dealings fair, she wouldn't punish Rico for things he hadn't done.

"Go. I'm not mad at you. You and I are fine. I'm also done telling you what to do. But really. Think about waiting until you're in London to try to acclimate yourself to becoming a dad. The baby won't be here for eight months. We have plenty of time."

"We do," he agreed, though he didn't seem enthused about it.

"We do!" she said, trying to help him relax in that knowledge. "And I'm fine. In fact, I want to make a few calls before I pack. So drive back to the villa yourself."

He gaped at her. "And you'll call a rideshare?"

"Or if it will make you happier, I'll call Lorenzo and ask him to send a car for me."

His mouth twisted with the effort not to smile. "Just not with Juliette driving."

She laughed. Of all the reactions she'd suspected he might have, overvigilance was the one she hadn't considered. Still, she could handle this. "God forbid."

He sniffed, then smiled, then laughed. "All right. Your points are taken."

He walked out of the elevator. When the doors closed, she blew her breath out on a sigh. Rico was a man accustomed to getting his own way and she was a woman who'd learned a hard lesson about letting anyone take over even a small part of her life.

No matter how happy they'd been at the engagement ball, they were people who barely knew each other, who were about to have a baby together. She would be more than careful. She would hang on to her life, her independence, with both hands.

Rico headed to his room to pack, knowing exactly why he was getting everything wrong. He was accustomed to taking control, but he wasn't sure how to do that in this situation. First, Marietta wanted control. Which was fine. But that left him feeling as if he was standing in the middle of an open field with no sense of where he was or why.

He hadn't had this feeling since he was a kid, being sent to another foster home, somewhere he would probably be ignored, or, worse, beaten or bullied by older kids. And there wasn't a damned thing he could do about it.

He reached his room, opened the door and walked inside. He hated those memories of being out of control. And this situation brought them all back. He knew Marietta was right about him waiting until he got to London, in his normal surroundings, to figure out his place with his child. But that didn't feel right. It sounded right. But it didn't *feel* right.

Nothing felt right.

With a sigh, he pulled his phone from his pocket and did

the other thing she suggested, the thing a person does when their whole world seemed to have been flipped upside down. He hit the speed dial number for his lawyer.

"Pete?"

"Calling my direct line, Rico? This must be serious."

"It is. One of my female friends told me she's pregnant."

Rico swore he heard the sound of his lawyer coming to attention. "She told you because the baby is yours?"

"Yes."

"So she says."

Rico frowned. "This woman has no reason to lie."

"You know her well enough to be sure of that?"

He winced as foolishness rose from his gut and engulfed him. He was a wealthy man and no matter how sweet and nice Marietta appeared, he didn't really know her. She didn't seem like the type to pull a con, but he couldn't say that for sure.

"No. I don't."

"Oh, Rico. Are you falling for the oldest trick in the book?"

"Honestly, Pete. I don't think so." He didn't believe Marietta was conning him. He also didn't believe she was lying. Actually, he got the impression she'd be perfectly fine if he said goodbye after the wedding and she never saw him again.

But the logical reaction of his legal counsel did corral some of his emotions and infuse them with common sense. "She's a friend of a friend. Someone I'd never met until last month, but for her to be as close to Antonio's fiancée as she is… Well, let's just say Riley's not the kind of person to trust someone without reason."

"Your first move is still to have a DNA test to be sure."

"When the baby's born?"

"Two months into the pregnancy it can be done."

He leaned back. "You're saying I shouldn't do anything until we can get a DNA test?"

"Yes. Don't make promises. Don't agree to anything. Do

your best to stay away from her for a while." He paused. "How far along is she?"

"About a month."

He sniffed. "Okay. You have some time before we know for sure this is your child. That gives you a chance to consider everything and decide on the right outcomes for you. Best thing to do is keep your distance until you can get the test."

"Okay." After another few minutes of conversation, they disconnected the call. He felt better. It would not be difficult to keep his distance from a woman who wanted him to stay away from her.

They barely saw each other for the rest of the week. She seemed to be happily busy with the wedding, while Rico kept Antonio entertained.

Friday night's rehearsal dinner was small, intimate. Just Riley and her mom, the three Salvaggios, and Marietta and Rico in the regular dining room, along with Antonio's godfather, Marco. Antonio had told him they had decided to keep it private because there were concerns about his mother. Lorenzo and Annabelle's divorce hadn't been amicable. Which made him think of Marietta's divorce and her attitude that he could be as involved with their child as he wanted. For as much as he didn't understand family and connections, Marietta had had them, and her marriage had hurt her.

It was no wonder she didn't want anything to do with him. No wonder she wanted him to keep his distance. The last man she'd trusted had hurt her.

The wedding party said their good-nights early. Everybody wanted to be rested for the afternoon wedding. But Rico couldn't sleep. Thoughts of Antonio's mom juxtaposed his own mom, the woman he'd never known, and somehow Marietta's pregnancy got drawn into the confusion, along with her ex-husband.

At three, he gave up trying to sleep and went to the restaurant-style kitchen to make a sandwich. He took it to the huge center island and sat on one of the stools.

He'd be the first to admit he didn't understand family. But tonight, with fears about how he would handle being a dad rolling around in his brain, he couldn't stop wondering about his mother. She'd left him in a train station. If the lipstick stain on his cheek was any indicator, she'd kissed him goodbye. She'd kissed him goodbye but walked away—leaving a baby alone in a world that could sometimes be brutal.

How could you kiss someone, a baby, and then leave them to fend for themselves?

The kitchen door opened and Marietta walked in, reaching for the switch to turn on the light. She saw him sitting beside the island in the already lit room, and her hand fell to her side.

He expected her to turn and run. Instead, she ambled to the island. "So? Sandwich?"

"I was more restless than hungry, but I'm hoping a full stomach will put me to sleep."

She bit her lower lip. "I'm glad you're here. I was having trouble sleeping too."

"If that's a hint that you want half my sandwich, I'm not sharing. But I will make you one."

She walked over to the industrial-sized refrigerator. "No. I'm fine. I can do it myself."

"I know. You've told me that more than once."

She winced. "Actually, that's why I'm glad you're here. I want to apologize for being so bossy the other day and insisting you do what I say." She brought bread and deli meat to the counter. "It's just that I worked for years to get an opportunity like the one I'm getting with Riley's company. I don't want to risk losing it."

"You think Riley would fire you for being pregnant?"

"No." She pulled in a breath. "But she'll be a newlywed,

on her honeymoon, this time tomorrow. I don't want her to worry. I don't want her to rush home because she's wondering if I can handle things."

He shook his head. "Women. You worry about everything."

"Hey, Mr. Pot-Calling-the-Kettle-Black. Until our chat, you kept watching me as if you thought I'd explode."

"Not explode."

"Then what?"

"I don't know… Honestly, I've been around pregnant women, but never for long and not one in which I had a vested interest."

She chuckled. "Are you telling me you're curious?"

"Yes. And maybe a little confused. *My* mother left me in a train station."

Her hand stopped midway to the bread. "Oh. That's awful."

"I didn't even know her name." He snorted. "Hell, I don't even know my own name. Rico was embroidered on my T-shirt. So they assumed that was my first name. Turns out it could have also been the name of a company that made baby clothes at the time. So, really. I have no idea who I am."

She abandoned her sandwich making and sat on the stool beside his. "I'm so sorry."

"I think…" He paused. "No. I *know* that your being pregnant is making me remember my situation and that's part of why I'm acting so protectively. I don't want to hover over you. I don't want to interfere where you don't want me. I'm not going to ask you to marry me tomorrow because I grew up without a family. Honestly, Marietta, I don't know what I feel."

"I get that." She squeezed her eyes shut, then popped them open. "I think my past is affecting how I'm reacting too. Except maybe while you're going a little wacky, I'm being a too guarded."

"Really?"

"My husband fell for me the day we met. He doted on me while we were at university. His marriage proposal was legendary. He didn't change over the years, but he did stop being over-the-top nice. And when we couldn't get pregnant, he started yelling at me and blaming me and making me feel so worthless it was hard for me to even go out of the house. I should have seen the handwriting on the wall and left him. But it was almost as if trying to please him became so important I lost myself. I will never trust anyone the way I trusted him again."

He could only imagine her confusion, her pain. "He sounds like a real piece of work."

She nodded. "He was. But I don't want you to think I'm assuming you're like him, and as a result I'm going overboard with rules. The truth is, I learned a very hard lesson in that marriage, and had to fight to be who I am now. I won't ever put myself in that kind of position again."

"Which was why you wanted me to talk to my lawyer."

"Sometimes things are better negotiated through a third party."

"It's a basic business principle. Always have an agreement drawn up by a lawyer."

"And if both of us have a lawyer, we'll take the emotion out of our decisions and do what's best for our child."

He nodded and eased off the stool. She'd told her story coolly, analytically, helping him to understand her side of things. But her marriage had not been easy. And while her pregnancy reminded him of his unhappy beginnings, it probably reminded her of her first marriage and not being able to get pregnant. No matter how happy she was to become a mom, those memories lingered and touched a part of her that might be healed but still had a scar.

"Let me make that sandwich for you."

She shook her head. "No. I think I can sleep now."

He smiled. "Now that things are back to normal between us?"

"Oh, honey, if things were back to normal, we'd be ripping each other's clothes off."

He laughed.

She smiled. "You know I didn't plan this. I don't want your money. I do want this baby."

"I know." She hadn't merely told him, but also he believed her. Still, the very fact that she was so honest with him made him feel guilty that he hadn't admitted he'd already called his lawyer.

He sighed. "I called my attorney the other day."

"That's good. What did he say?"

"That we should get a DNA test before we agree to anything."

"I don't have a problem with that. Neither one of us expected to be creating a child that night. So we should be sure. But I'm perfectly capable of raising a child myself. I'm not going to demand anything from you. For what it's worth, if you want to be part of our baby's life, I'm happy to have you. You're smart. You're successful. You're a nice guy. I'm sure you could teach our baby a hundred things I don't even know about."

Watching her happy face as she spoke, he wondered about that. It almost seemed she didn't realize just how smart and strong she was. Plus, he might be successful, but he knew nothing about raising a child or being in a family. He was a former foster kid who would not be where he was now were it not for his mentor. If anything, he'd be smart to let her raise their child without his input. He *wanted* his child having her spunk, her drive, her happiness, her enthusiasm.

A lonely ache gnawed at the pit of his stomach. At first, he thought it was sadness about missing out on raising his child. Then he realized the lonely feeling was actually about her. He'd missed her the weeks they were apart. He missed being the object of her attention, her affection. Right now, he'd like nothing better than to sweep her off her feet, hear her laugh, have her touch him…be able to touch her.

But that was wrong. They had a child to consider. A potential lawsuit happening between them.

He cleared the crumbs from his sandwich. "As you've said before, there's plenty of time for us to think about my involvement."

After the DNA test.

Until then, his lawyer had advised that he stay away.

Disappointment swamped him.

He wasn't accustomed to being told what to do. But it was more than that. They'd created a child. It seemed wrong to always discuss it so clinically. Through lawyers. Just to be sure they got it right.

She paused at the kitchen door. "Wanna share the elevator?"

He joined her at the door. "I can walk to the second floor." He gave her a stern look. "But you take the elevator to the third."

"So bossy."

He shook his head. She loved to tease and so did he. The empty feeling he had inside was also about the way they weren't being themselves with each other.

But she gave him that beatific smile and he decided he could not have picked a better mother for his child. She was wonderful.

After the childhood he'd had, he knew a baby needed a good mother far more than a child's father needed to get his own way.

The next day the sun glowed down on Antonio and Riley's wedding. Riley was stunning in a white velvet cloak over a beaded gown, standing in front of handsome Antonio. For a second, Marietta almost cried with joy. She knew that perfect weddings didn't always mean perfect happiness, but she had a good feeling about Antonio and Riley.

They were going to make it.

They said their vows smiling at each other, while Juliette wiped tears from her eyes and held Lorenzo's hand.

A lot of good had come from that fake proposal Antonio had hired Riley to plan for him as a way to convince his grandmother to get her chemotherapy treatments because she had a lot to live for.

Filled with happiness for the entire Salvaggio family, Marietta glanced past Antonio and Riley to Rico. So handsome in his tux.

A slight breeze ruffled his black curls and he smiled at her.

She was glad they'd had their conversation the night before. She knew everything would be okay once he adjusted to becoming a dad. She also knew he would carefully consider how much involvement he would have. Though he seemed carefree, he lived his life deliberately. There would be no judgment if he decided to ride off into the sunset.

As horrible as the last few years of her marriage had been, they had made her strong. Incredibly strong. She could handle raising a child alone.

Actually, it would probably be easier to raise their child alone.

The ceremony ended. Riley and Antonio walked down the aisle between the two rows of white chairs that were filled with their family and friends.

Marietta and Rico came together from their different sides of the aisle, and she slid her hand into the crook of his elbow. He smiled down at her and her heart melted.

He was so damned handsome. And really he was a nice

guy. He'd also lived a terrible childhood. It seemed wrong to be so suspicious of him.

They survived an hour of posing for pictures and arrived at the villa ballroom for the reception. Rico helped her up the three steps onto the platform for the bridal table. Dinner was filled with toasts, making it almost impossible to eat because they raised their glasses so often. The whole room swelled with love and happiness.

When Rico took her into his arms to dance the bridal party dance, a million sensations hit her. She loved the feel of him. She loved how she felt in his arms. He was so sexy, she couldn't look at him without getting a sprinkle of goose-flesh. She was pregnant with this man's child because she was attracted to him. Ridiculously. Somehow in all the hub-bub over the wedding and her pregnancy she'd forgotten that.

She drew in a quick breath to steady herself. But all that did was bring the sexy scent of his aftershave to her.

"Everything okay?"

"Yes." She actually croaked.

He laughed. "Are you sure?"

Memories cascaded through her brain. How he made her laugh. How she could be herself with him. How he'd seemed to like her just as she was—

Of course, those were all easy things to do in a one-night stand. It was simple to impress someone when you knew you weren't starting a relationship, simply enjoying each other's company.

He spun her around the dance floor, making her laugh, and the wide skirt of her burgundy-colored ball gown fan out around her.

"Just giving the crowd a little thrill."

She laughed again.

Holding on to her one hand, he released her other hand

and nudged her back so he could twirl her under his arm, then he pulled her close again.

Joy filled her. He was so much fun.

He frowned. "Why haven't we been dancing all week?"

"We were avoiding each other."

He pondered that. "Ah. That's right. Shame that we missed all the fun we could have had dancing in the wine-tasting room."

It was. Not just because the break would have been nice but because she'd missed him. Missed his laugh. Missed his great smile. Missed the romance of being with him.

She held back a wince. All those were dangerous thoughts. She was having a child with this man and a smart woman would keep her wits about her. There were agreements to be struck and arrangements to be made.

The music changed, slowed down and Rico pulled her so close she melted against him with a sigh.

Her head filled with questions, she glanced up and their gazes caught. His eyes filled with longing. They were staying apart because of an issue greater than their attraction. All that seemed logical and right, except they were still in a grace period of a sort. Their baby hadn't arrived yet. They had plenty of time to come up with a visitation schedule—

Plus, he was supposed to be her vacation fling. But they'd spent most of the time keeping their distance.

Being held in his arms, gazing into his dark eyes, it suddenly seemed like a night for forgetting everything and being happy.

CHAPTER SEVEN

RICO DIDN'T LET her out of his sight all night. If he wanted to be persnickety, he could pretend to himself that he was concerned about the child that grew within her, but the truth was he liked her. He enjoyed her company and loved the sound of her laughter.

Was it so wrong to want to indulge himself?

He did not think so.

He persuaded a bartender to pour club soda into a wineglass so it would look like she was drinking wine.

She glanced at the soda, peered up at him, then glanced at the soda again. "That was really sweet."

"Just trying to make a smooth transition."

She smiled. "It's still thoughtful."

"I know. That's part of my charm." He grinned sexily. "Would you like to dance?"

"Absolutely."

This time when he pulled her into his arms, he let himself enjoy her the way he had when he'd first met her. She was soft and beautiful, and her lovely lilting laugh held just a hint of her Southern accent. He knew this was a moment stolen out of time, but he was taking it.

Right before midnight, the bride and groom took the microphone from the lead singer in the band, thanking everyone for helping them celebrate their good fortune in finding each other.

"We're leaving for the airport and our honeymoon. Thank you all for celebrating with us."

Rico glanced around. Lorenzo and Juliette had everything under control. Just like at the engagement party, he knew they'd close the room with Gerard when the time came.

He caught Marietta's hand and kissed the knuckles. "Wanna go upstairs?"

Her eyebrows. "To your room?"

"Or yours."

She didn't even hesitate. She leaned and brushed a light kiss across his mouth. "I'd love to."

As Rico turned to lead her out of the ballroom, he noticed Juliette watching them.

"Don't look now, but I think Juliette saw that kiss."

She laughed. "She notices everything."

"That's kind of my point."

"In a couple of months, I'm going to have to tell her that I'm pregnant. This way she might be surprised but she won't be shocked."

If he'd been drinking something, he would have spit it out on a big laugh. They eased out of the ballroom, along the corridors and to one of the elevators. The second the doors closed, he took her into his arms and kissed her. The spark that always ignited between them didn't waste time flickering. It burst between them fully formed.

He slid his hands from her shoulders, down her arms, enjoying the feeling of her soft skin, and she stepped closer, deepening the kiss before the elevator stopped and the doors opened. They kissed going out of the elevator and down the hall, not caring that anyone on the floor might have seen them.

But when they reached her door, he pulled back. "You're sure? I mean there's a lot of stuff—"

She opened her door, caught his hand and pulled him inside. "We're dynamite together. And let's face it. I can't get any more pregnant."

She said it with such joy that Rico shook his head and laughed. But as soon as he closed the door behind them, he reached for her, kissing her so hard and so long that he felt lost, bewitched. But when she inched back a step, he woke up and instantly reached for the zipper of her dress. As it puddled at her feet, he shrugged out of his jacket and shirt.

She crawled onto the bed and after he rid himself of his shoes and trousers, he joined her. There was something about being with her that combined passion and happiness. He'd say it was contentment but that was too dull for what he felt. It was as if she brought sunshine into the room, into their passion.

He touched and tasted every inch of her. At a certain point, she nudged his shoulder. Catching him off guard, she tumbled him to his back, and she returned the favor. Little fires lit everywhere her lips grazed. When the sizzle between them hit a fever pitch, he took her by the shoulders and rolled her to her back, joining them in the process.

The heat was luxurious, perfect.

In a moment of unexpected sentiment, he knew he'd remember that feeling for the rest of his life. Then her fingernails scraped down his back and intensity roared through him, quickening his pace, tumbling them over the edge to oblivion.

Once again, Rico awoke alone in Mariette's bedroom. Another note told him she—again—had an early flight.

He rolled out of bed and dressed in the tux he'd worn the night before. He stuffed his socks in his jacket pocket and slid his feet into his shoes, then poked his head out of her bedroom door, glad when he didn't see either Juliette or Lorenzo. Though he had no idea why they'd be in the hallway, Rico didn't have the best luck when it came to Marietta.

He wasn't sure if she was a step ahead of him or if he was somehow looking for something that wasn't there. But no one ever felt more like Cinderella than he did searching that silent hall before he sneaked out of her room and headed for his own. Except for having both shoes, he was as off-kilter as poor Cinderella had been when she had to race out of a palace with the clock striking midnight.

For once, he'd like to know what it would feel like waking up next to her—

But that was a fool's thought. Once their baby was born, there would be nothing between them but the memories of how good they were together. In the same way that he'd never let himself imagine what it might be like to have a family, he wouldn't let himself, let his feelings for any woman, go too far. People who did that only invited loneliness into their life when the relationship died. He'd had his fair share of being alone as a child. He'd never invite it in again.

He made his way to his room, showered and dressed for breakfast. Only GiGi sat at the big table.

"Good morning, Rico."

He reached the table, bent down and kissed her cheek. "Good morning. How did you sleep?"

"Like a log." She sucked in a satisfied breath. "Riley and Antonio took the jet to Paris last night. Juliette and Lorenzo are sleeping in. It's just you and me."

Maybe it was his thoughts when he woke alone, again, but an unexpected sensation stopped him halfway to his chair. With Antonio and Riley pairing off and now Lorenzo and Juliette, he was the extra person, again. The person who didn't fit.

He shook off the feeling and smiled at GiGi as he sat across from her. "I know. I got a note saying Marietta also had an early flight."

GiGi peered at him. "You did?"

"Probably a text is a better way to put it," he lied because GiGi was as perceptive as Juliette was eagle-eyed. "I just assumed everyone got it."

GiGi picked up her spoon and slid it into her oatmeal. "I'll have to check my phone later."

When, hopefully, he would be long gone.

He smiled. "I should probably jet back to London this morning."

"What's your rush? Maybe enjoy the day?"

"I missed a lot of things last week. I need to go home and get on my computer."

She sighed. "Everyone's always busy. Did you know Marietta will be taking over the US end of Riley's business?"

"Yes."

"She's a lovely girl."

Rico hid a smirk. GiGi was always matchmaking. "Yes. She is."

The cook came into the room and asked what he'd like for breakfast. He didn't even have to think about it. He was hungry for pancakes. Blueberry. The cook nodded and left the room.

"You two seemed to get along."

"I'm sorry...what?"

"You and Marietta. You seemed to get along."

"We did."

"There was just something about you two..."

And in another day GiGi would probably figure it out. Though she didn't know it, her intuition wasn't about matchmaking. She simply sensed something was going on between them. Everyone had seen them dancing and laughing, enjoying each other's company. So GiGi knew they weren't hiding their romance. Pretty soon she'd realize that. Once she did, she'd probably ask Juliette what was going on. Rather than guess, Juliette would approach Marietta.

GiGi was smart. Juliette had eagle eyes. He and Marietta were not going to be able to keep the pregnancy a secret for long. Rico would have to remind Marietta of how astute Juliette and GiGi were and suggest that she tell at least Juliette before it became an issue…or, worse, a guessing game among the bridal party.

Rico flew back to London knowing he would be calling Marietta. But as he stepped into his house, all thoughts of Marietta disappeared. He suddenly saw his home with a fresh perspective.

Marietta had told him at least ten times that he needed to think through his involvement with their child. Where he lived was a big part of that. He thought about his house—six bedrooms, plenty of room for a child, and close to Hyde Park. He was squarely in the middle of London's old-money sophistication, infused with new money from guys like him, who moved there to enjoy the luxury and convenience of it.

He could see a child here. *His child.*

His heart tumbled with emotion that mixed and mingled with confusion. He'd never even considered becoming a father. Somehow or other he would have to figure out what a dad did with a baby, a toddler, a child—a *teenager*.

This time his confusion was overshadowed by a sense of incompetence. He knew nothing about having a family or caring for a child. Of course, he could get a nanny. Actually, he'd *have to* get a nanny, even for short visits, because entertainment aside, he had no idea about feeding times, bedtimes, playtime.

He wondered how Marietta would feel about her son or daughter having a nanny, in a swanky house in a luxurious part of London, then realized he didn't know her well enough to answer that.

They hadn't spent a lot of time together before the wedding. And even when they were together, they might have talked a bit about their pasts but in some ways that left him with more questions than answers.

In the warm sunlight of his beautiful home, it became very clear to Rico that he didn't need to examine his living arrangements to see if a child fit his life and lifestyle. He needed to get to know the mother of his child.

That realization hit him so hard and so fast that he had to sit. But as he sat, he pulled his phone out of his pocket and called his pilot.

"I want to go to Manhattan."

"Now?"

Rico winced. Technically, he'd just gotten off his plane. Still, he said, "As soon as we can."

"Oh." There was a pause. "I'll get things rolling."

"If we have to hire another team to fly me there, that's fine."

"Okay."

He thanked his pilot, then walked into the foyer where he'd left his luggage. He was so confused about this whole baby deal that he'd raced to check out his home before he even took his baggage upstairs. But now he knew what to do. He didn't need to call Marietta to warn her about GiGi. He needed to talk to her. Face-to-face. Because he needed to get to know her. The woman who would be raising his son or daughter. He couldn't negotiate visitation or child support or anything with someone he didn't know.

Why had it taken him so long to recognize that? That was Negotiating 101. Know your opponent…or partner. In this case, they'd be parenting partners.

He carried his luggage upstairs, dumped out the clothes from the week before and repacked. This time jeans. T-shirts. Sweaters. Then he pulled his Lamborghini sports car out of his garage and onto the street.

With his confusion gone, worry about GiGi thinking

things through fell into place. He had taken the wheel of his life, so to speak. True, he would have to be careful of Marietta's feelings, but he finally felt like himself again.

Despite the fact that she'd arrived in Manhattan on Sunday morning—the time difference worked in her favor returning to the States—Marietta went right to bed and only got out for water or food.

Monday morning, she woke feeling refreshed. She wasn't sick. The pregnancy wasn't exhausting her. She'd had a long week and a time difference dragging her down, but after some sleep, she felt great again.

She dressed for work and was at her desk before anyone else arrived. She'd started her job as the general manager of the US arm of Riley's proposal planning company the week after Riley's engagement party. But for some reason or another, with Riley now married and a resident of Florence, everything felt official.

She held a Monday morning staff meeting, sealing the deal that she was now in charge, and returned to her office strong and in control. With the stress of the wedding and telling Rico about the baby gone, energy and confidence infused her.

Her phone buzzed. She hit the button to activate the intercom. "Yes?"

"There's a gentleman here to see you. Rico Mendoza?"

Her heart stopped, then jumped to double time. She didn't even let herself wonder why he might be there or what the heck he wanted. Damage control became the priority.

"I'll be right there."

She bounded out of her chair and up the hall to Sissy's desk. When she saw him, her breathing stuttered and happiness tingled through her. She couldn't believe it had only been a day or two since she'd seen him. If she closed her eyes, she could remember the pure joy of lying in his arms.

Reminding herself of damage control, she stopped those thoughts.

"Rico!" With a smile, she faced Sissy. "Rico was the best man in Riley's wedding."

Sissy smiled, her gaze shifting from Rico to Marietta and back again.

Trying to make it appear they had business to discuss, she held out her hand for Rico to shake. One of his eyebrows rose, questioning her without saying a word, but he shook her hand.

"It's nice to see you again, Marietta." He nudged his head toward the hall. "Can we have a minute alone?"

Still working to throw Sissy off track, she said, "Oh, do you want us to plan a marriage proposal for you!"

His already confused face shifted again. "No. But there is business we need to discuss."

She motioned for him to follow her down the hall. "I'm guessing that means you have vendor names for me?" she all but shouted, hoping to give credence for why he was at their office.

They walked inside the nice-sized room with the white blinds and bleached wood desk, and she closed the door.

He didn't waste a second. "GiGi is going to figure this out."

She eased over to her desk. "Figure what out?"

"That we're pregnant."

She fell to her chair. "I don't see how."

"You know how Juliette's got the eagle eye?"

"Yes."

"Well, GiGi has instincts, intuition. At first, I thought she was trying to matchmake us at breakfast on Sunday morning. Then I realized it was more. I could all but see the wheels spinning in her brain."

"But we did nothing for GiGi to suspect we're sleeping together!"

"This isn't about sleeping together… It's about her sensing something unusual going on between us. Once GiGi starts pondering, her brain will veer off in the direction of wondering why you were tired the day she insisted we all stay at the villa. After jet lag, pregnancy is bound to be one of her options."

Marietta sat back in her big chair.

"If we force her and Juliette to guess, we become gossip. If we tell them, we control the narrative."

"Spoken like a true businessman."

"Sometimes it's good to handle things like a businessperson rather than two people who really like sleeping together. Telling them ourselves, we can take out the emotion of our situation and deal with facts."

She thought about that. "I like that."

"I do too. I'm not good with secrets."

"You can't keep a secret?"

"I don't like secrets. It's one thing to hold back information on a new product until you beat your competitor to the market. It's another to not talk about a child."

Her breath froze in her lungs. Of course he felt that way. His whole life was a mystery. A secret. Something he didn't know and might never know.

She swallowed. "Okay. I'll make an announcement."

He glanced around. "Here?"

"Juliette and Lorenzo are coming back to Manhattan tomorrow. If I know Juliette, she won't even take a nap to adjust to the time difference. She'll take a car from the airport to the office."

"We can tell her then."

She frowned. "I hadn't pictured you being in on the announcement."

"Why not?"

"Why?" She rose from her seat, walking around the desk

and leaning her butt against it to speak frankly with him. "Rico, I'm running Riley's company, but I still do some managerial things for Juliette. I need the conversation to be professional. I don't want us to look like two kids telling their parents they gave in to their urges and made a baby. For me, this child is the chance of a lifetime. If I tell Juliette myself, I can make her see that, and also call upon her own memories of having Riley…working through her pregnancy and while she had an infant at home—"

"And with a guy in the room, you can't?"

"No. I just don't want to look like two teenagers confessing to their mom."

He snorted. "You have some strange ways of looking at life."

She gaped at him. "Really?"

"You might say things through that cute little accent but that doesn't make them normal."

"You mean you can stick your boots in the oven but that don't make 'em biscuits?"

He laughed. "Sort of." He sucked in a breath. "I have a deal to propose."

"I'm listening."

"You tell Juliette. I'll tell Lorenzo."

She pondered that. "What are you going to say?"

"That we're having a child and we're thrilled, and then I'm going to suggest he and I have a shot to celebrate."

She frowned. "Are you thrilled?"

"I looked around my house when I got back to London, and I realized there was plenty of room for a child. And I had some…feelings."

"Feelings?"

"Okay, at first it was fear. I never had a dad, and my memories of my foster dads are vague, except for the bad ones. So, a little panic set in. But this is also *my* child, not just yours. And no one knows as well as I do how much a kid needs parents."

She squeezed her eyes shut. "Yeah." She popped them open, then said, "Meaning you want to be a part of our child's life."

"Maybe a big part."

She could picture him at their baby's birthday parties, baseball games and even reading to him or her, and warmth filled her. But she squelched it. All her warm, fuzzy feelings for him were supposed to stop after the wedding. This was never supposed to be a long-term relationship. She'd been married. She knew it wasn't right for her. Anything between them had to be platonic, which meant she had to set some boundaries.

She shoved herself away from the desk with a heavy sigh. "Don't forget, you live on another continent."

"As you already pointed out, I have a plane."

"Your work is in Europe."

"My coffee company headquarters are in Europe. I hired a CEO to run it. I'm primarily an investor. With the internet and conference calls, I can carry on business from anywhere."

Realizing she wasn't going to dissuade him, she looked at the ceiling. "We really weren't supposed to have these kinds of conversations until we talked to our lawyers."

"I don't think there's any harm in discussing the basics. It might even be good to have a few things decided before we drag the lawyers into it."

"You're missing my point. I'm not *ready* to talk about any of it."

"Yeah, well, I wasn't ready to hear you were pregnant the first day we arrived for the wedding. I was expecting five days of wine and romance. I might not have handled it well, but I handled it. Now, it's your turn to adjust."

CHAPTER EIGHT

MARIETTA STARED AT Rico and he held her gaze. He was not backing down. No matter how cute she looked in her comfy work clothes and how badly his sizzling attraction to her wanted to be given free rein. They were about to be parents. Getting to know each other was more important than attractions or legal issues.

Though right now the attraction really, really wanted to take over. He'd give half his portfolio if he could kiss her.

He sucked in a breath and put his mind on their discussion. This was the one he really needed to win. "And here's another little something for you. I think our next step is getting to know each other."

Her face fell. "I think we already know each other."

"No. I'm talking about getting to know each other as parents. No matter how this shakes out, we have to trust each other. And trust requires that we know more about each other than whether our ribs are ticklish."

She rolled her eyes.

He wasn't offended. After their kitchen chat in the middle of the night, he understood why she was so protective of her independence. But he could not raise a child with someone he didn't know.

Neither could she and eventually she'd see that.

"I'm here to spend time with you." He paused a fraction of a second. "What do you want to do tonight?"

She groaned. "Seriously?"

"Yes."

"Fine." She glanced at her calendar and frowned. "I can't do anything tonight. I have plans."

He raised his eyebrows. "Date?"

"With a real estate agent. One of the things that kept me from panicking about the baby was knowing I could now afford my own apartment."

"Okay! I'll come with you. There's no better way to get to know someone than to see how they choose a house."

She looked as if she wanted to argue but relented, crossing her arms and saying, "Fine," again.

He rose. "Text me where you want to meet and the time. I can come to your current apartment or meet you here."

She winced. "Neither. I'll text you the address of the first condo I'm looking at. You can meet us there."

"Okay." He smiled. "See you then."

She sighed as if put upon. "See you then."

He left her office realizing that while he would have been very happy to take her to bed and let this discussion be pillow talk, she'd erected some barriers. Again, he remembered her bad marriage. She wanted a platonic relationship and he understood all her reasoning. He really didn't want anything permanent either. All the same, they did have to get to know each other—which was why he was in Manhattan. To get to know her.

Surely, they could fight off one little sexual attraction.

Stepping out into the cold morning, he realized he had most of the day to kill. This wasn't like being in Florence. She had a job to do, and it was important to her that she do it right. She couldn't play hooky with him. Their time together would be limited to evenings.

He glanced at his watch, then went back to his hotel, pulled out his laptop and began researching a potential investment.

Around four o'clock, his phone pinged with a text. He was to meet Marietta and her real estate agent at six thirty at a condo building. He answered that he would be there and immediately began researching the area in which she was considering purchasing a condo.

It wasn't bad. It certainly wasn't anything like his house in Connaught Village. But it was typical New York. An old brick building near a coffee shop, newspaper stand and tiny convenience store. He wouldn't criticize. He knew how expensive real estate could be.

He met Marietta and Artie Rosen outside the unremarkable front entry for the building. There was no elevator, only stairs to the fourth floor. But it was clean.

The agent unlocked the door. "Tenants just moved out and the owner decided to sell rather than rent it again. You're the first to see it."

He opened the door and Marietta sighed with surprise as she stepped inside. "Wow. It's bigger than I thought."

"Two bedrooms. Just what you asked for."

The kitchen, dining space and living area were all one big room. Rico walked in slowly. "Everything needs to be painted."

Artie grinned. "That's why they're selling rather than renting again. Buyer will have to paint…but isn't that what you want?" he asked dreamily. "To make it your own? To put your stamp on it."

"Will the price be lowered to accommodate that?" Rico asked, slowly examining the big room.

"Let's have a look at the two bedrooms," Artie said, craftily ignoring Rico's question. Meaning, there probably was no wiggle room on the price.

They eased over to the first door. Artie opened it on a decent-sized room. The closet was tiny.

Marietta nodded with approval. Rico said nothing.

The second bedroom was only big enough for a twin bed. That closet was smaller than tiny.

"You're going to need cabinets to compensate for the size of the closets."

Artie smiled.

Marietta frowned. "I already have one…from the apartment I'm renting now."

"Buying is so much smarter than renting," Artie said, always the salesman. "You're building equity and New York real estate prices never fall. They always rise. No matter when you buy, in ten years you can expect to make a profit when you sell."

The single bathroom was in a corner off the kitchen. It was so small only one person could fit at a time. Marietta nodded. Rico held back a grimace.

When they'd seen the entire space, Marietta sighed happily. "This is lovely." She glanced around the open floor plan approvingly. "But I'm not making any decisions until I see a few places. Let's move on to the second condo."

The second condo was smaller than the first and more expensive.

"Exactly how much money do you have to spend in this city to get a decent space?" Rico asked Artie as they clamored down the five flights of stairs leading to the entryway that Artie had the audacity to call a lobby. "Something that doesn't need to be painted and has a bathroom bigger than a steamer trunk and an actual lobby. Maybe a doorman."

"For two bedrooms in a more secure building you have to come up with at least—"

He said a number that made Marietta look sick, but she pulled herself together. Totally ignoring the idea of a more expensive condo, she said, "Let's move on to condo number three."

Number three was a slight improvement. But all three

condos had very little closet space, small bathrooms and a second bedroom that was barely large enough for a twin bed.

Because it was close to nine o'clock, Artie told them he had three other places lined up for them to see the following evening.

Marietta said, "Thanks. Let me have a look at my schedule and we can arrange to meet."

Artie turned right and walked away.

Rico sighed. "We need to regroup."

"We?"

"Marietta, if you were getting a condo for yourself and you liked to paint and you could use the second bedroom as a closet, I'd be cheering you on right now. But you're going to be carrying your groceries and a baby up four flights of stairs. There are logistics to consider."

"Money is a bigger issue." She sighed. "Maybe I should rent?"

"Or maybe I could help you with the purchase price. If you let me add enough money to double your budget, I'll bet we could get you something with an elevator in a better part of town."

She gaped at him. "This is a great part of town. You're just accustomed to fancy things like the Salvaggio villa."

"Don't insinuate I'm a snob. I was perfectly content in that little hotel we stayed at in Florence."

She glanced away, then glanced back. "I knew this was going to happen."

"What?"

"You're not letting me be me. Any one of those three places would have been okay. But you have so much money that you forget that this is how the rest of us live." She huffed out a sigh. "My probably also unworthy apartment with my friends is just around the corner." She shook her head in dismay. "That's why I wanted to move into this part of town. I like it here." She turned away. "I'll see you tomorrow."

She left him standing on a street that was well lit and had enough foot traffic that he wasn't worried she'd be mugged walking around a corner. But he discreetly peered around the building to see where she went. She entered an older brick building and disappeared up a set of steps.

The condos he'd insulted were exactly like where she currently lived. No wonder she'd been so upset.

He hadn't meant to sound like a snob. He also hadn't meant to disparage the way she lived. What he needed to do was view this area in the daytime. He'd probably see that it was safe and perfectly acceptable.

He'd certainly lived in worse places. He of all people should understand.

Except this was where his child would live. And he did think it would be more convenient for a woman with a baby to have a building with an elevator. That wasn't snobbery. That was common sense.

He pulled out his phone to call a cab. He could plead ignorance of the real estate market in New York and apologize the next day. But right now, he wanted to get back to his hotel, order room service and investigate other condos being offered in the city.

The last thing he would ever do was lord his money over anyone. Yet somehow that was exactly how she'd taken it. While he absolutely wanted to help her with her house hunt—financially as well as with his negotiating expertise—he would have to be very careful how he proposed anything.

He supposed he should be happy that the first crack in their relationship came over a piece of real estate rather than how they'd raise their baby—

Except technically this was a disagreement over how they'd raise their child. He wanted a say in where she lived.

And with her independent streak, he had a feeling that things were going to get ugly. Because he could be as stubborn as she was.

Marietta stood back the next day as Juliette returned to hugs and happiness from her staff. It wasn't that the employees of Juliette's home nursing agency and Riley's proposal planning company didn't like Marietta. It was more that everyone adored Juliette. And everybody wanted to talk about the fun and fabulous wedding they'd attended in Italy. Half of them had never expected to leave the continental United States in their lifetime. Getting to go to a villa in Florence? That had been a dream come true for most of them.

It was after five o'clock by the time Juliette worked her way to Marietta's office. She flopped into the chair in front of Marietta's desk.

"Things look like they are running smoothly."

"They are," Marietta assured her. "You have a great staff. They rarely come to me for anything. And managing Riley's proposal company is like a dream. I love the creativity of it."

Juliette sat up. "Oh, no. You said that so fast that I know there's a *but*! Marietta, if you found a better job, I swear I will pay you anything you want to stay."

Marietta laughed. "I haven't. I'm not even looking for another job. But I am looking for an apartment. A condo to buy. I set my budget and looked at some condos last night, but I think I set my price too low."

"Well," Juliette said. "We also haven't discussed your raise for taking over Riley's company and managing the office for both of us."

"This isn't a ploy for me to get more money," Marietta quickly assured her. She pulled in a breath and chose her words carefully. "I love this job. *Love it.* Juliette, I waited my whole life to find a job like this. I may never leave you and Riley."

Juliette laughed. "Thank you. But I did come to your office to discuss your new salary." She named a figure that made Marietta sit back in her chair. Not relaxing, but sort of in shock.

"That's a great number."

"Marietta, our situation works because Riley and I spent a lot of years establishing our companies. Now, both of us want to have more free time. Your knowing our businesses so well makes that possible. You've earned this raise."

Marietta swallowed hard. "Thank you. It's good to feel appreciated."

"You are appreciated, and Riley and I are very happy. This situation works."

It suddenly seemed like the best time to tell Juliette she was pregnant, even as it seemed like the worst.

Could she piggyback a complication onto a compliment—a vote of confidence? Wasn't that like taking advantage?

She sucked in a breath.

Juliette shook her head. "Okay. Before you have a heart attack, I know there's something else going on. I sensed it the week before the wedding. So just tell me."

Remembering what Rico had said about GiGi and Juliette guessing and speculating, Marietta knew what she had to do. "I'm pregnant."

Juliette's mouth fell open. "I thought you couldn't have kids?"

"Turns out I can." She laughed. "I mean, I haven't been to a doctor yet, but I took four pregnancy tests and all of them were positive."

Juliette winced. "Those tests are pretty accurate. But you know what? Maybe don't do anything drastic until you go to your doctor."

She laughed and almost said that's the same advice Rico's lawyer gave him. But she caught herself...then wondered why. Somewhere in Manhattan Rico was probably telling Lorenzo right now. That was the deal they had made.

"You're happy?"

"Juliette, it's the most amazing feeling to have something you believed could never happen suddenly happen."

"I feel that way about Lorenzo. I honestly thought I'd never find real love. Oh, I knew I could have romance and boy-friends, but I thought love was something that I wasn't meant to have. And when Lorenzo and I clicked, it was like the world opened up for me and everything changed."

"That's exactly how I feel! So different. So happy." She paused, then grinned. "I'm going to be a mom."

Juliette laughed. "It's a lot of work being a single mom."

"I'm ready."

"I think you are."

"You trust me to run this place and be a mom?"

Juliette rose. "I *created* this place while I was raising Riley. All you have to do is run it. So yes. I trust you."

She turned to leave but Marietta stopped her. "Wait. There's one more thing."

Juliette faced her.

"Rico is the baby's father."

Juliette returned to the chair so she could sit. "Oh, my goodness."

"Yeah. He's kind of irresistible."

"I can imagine."

"And he's adjusting to the news."

"I'd hope so."

"And we're seriously trying *not* to make too many plans or decisions until the pregnancy is further along."

"I'd say that's smart."

Marietta studied Juliette. She'd expected shock. But once

that wore off, she'd thought Juliette would start rattling off advice. Since she hadn't, Marietta worried something was wrong. "Now, I know there's something *you're* not saying."

Juliette said, "Okay. You're right. I've heard stories about Rico from Lorenzo and Antonio." She sighed. "He's such a playboy."

"That's fine. I don't want to marry him. I'd also probably like it better if he'd let me raise this child alone—"

"He's not going to do that."

"He hasn't figured out yet what he's going to do."

"Trust me. Rico might be a runaround, but once this pregnancy and baby become a reality… He's going to want a part in things. Lorenzo told me he was raised in foster homes. It will be difficult for him to have a child and not be involved in his life."

Remembering his mood the night they'd talked in the kitchen—talked about his mother abandoning him—she knew that was true. Suddenly his unexpected appearance in Manhattan made sense.

"You're going to have to play this right. He works in Europe now because it's what he's accustomed to. But his 'work' is investing. He can do that from anywhere."

"You're saying I need to set boundaries?"

"No. I'm saying you need to establish a friendly, amicable relationship now, before the baby is born, so that when you start negotiating child support and visitation, you'll know each other well enough to be fair."

"He *is* here in Manhattan because he said we need to get to know each other."

"Exactly. He's finding his way. He might not know how he fits, but he knows he's going to want to be part of all of this. And if you're smart, you'll let him in. Show him he can trust you. So he doesn't have to move next door or file a lawsuit to get to see his child. Things like that will make you bitter enemies. Raising a child will go a lot easier if you're friends. He's looking for trust." Juliette rose. "Marietta, you are the most trustworthy person I know. Riley and I both adore you. You can make him trust you too."

Marietta sat up. "I can."

"Yes, you can." She headed for the door, but stopped and faced Marietta again. "And no sex. Seriously, your situation now is very delicate. Don't muddy the waters with a romance that will disrupt any good parenting things you set up."

When Marietta didn't respond, Juliette said, "You said you don't want to marry him."

"I don't want to marry anyone. Ever. Not ever again."

"Then do yourself a favor, do Rico a favor, do your baby a favor…and walk away from the romance."

CHAPTER NINE

RICO CALLED LORENZO and suggested they meet. Now that Lorenzo lived with Juliette in Manhattan, he didn't have to fly to Italy. He could meet him somewhere in town.

Twenty minutes later, he found the Irish pub a few streets up from his hotel that Lorenzo had suggested. Marietta hadn't texted with the addresses for that night's condo viewings, so he was fairly certain he might have lost his real estate privileges with her.

He pushed on the heavy door and walked into a room that could have been located in Dublin. The wood of the bar and surrounding tables was dark and heavy. Pictures of Ireland and commemorative plaques hung on the walls. The place smelled deliciously of beer and bread.

Lorenzo already had a table and waved him over.

Removing his jacket, Rico sat with a sigh.

"What was so important that you had to see me?"

He didn't waste a second with platitudes or greetings. That wasn't the kind of relationship he and Lorenzo had. He jumped right in. "Marietta's pregnant and the baby is mine. At least I think the baby is mine. She said she hadn't been with anyone in a while…so though my lawyer thinks I need to wait for DNA I'm inclined to believe her."

Lorenzo absorbed all that. "Marietta doesn't date much. At least she hasn't in the time I've been living with Juliette. But more importantly, she's a very honest, genuine person."

He laughed. "And funny. Don't get me started on the accent and metaphors about putting your boots in the oven or how you can be all hat and no cattle."

Rico couldn't help it. He burst out laughing. "I've been warned about putting my boots in the oven, but I hadn't yet heard the one about the hat and the cattle."

Lorenzo shook his head. "So? You okay?"

"I'm gobsmacked. Apparently, her first marriage fell apart because she couldn't get pregnant, so she's thrilled about becoming a mom. I, on the other hand, know nothing about being a dad."

Lorenzo batted his hand. "I raised Antonio alone. I know you can handle it."

"You do?"

"Piece of cake."

Rico ran his hands down his face. "I hope you're right."

"Of course I'm right. And if you get into trouble, you can always ask me questions. Or GiGi. She's a font of advice. You'll be fine."

"Okay."

"So…shots to celebrate or maybe a little champagne?"

Before Rico could reply, his phone pinged with a text. "It's Marietta. She sent me the address of the next condo we're looking at."

"The next condo you're looking at?" Lorenzo's eyes narrowed. "You're moving in together?"

"No. She wants to leave the apartment she shares with three other people and purchase a place with a second bedroom."

"And are you buying it for her?"

"I wish. She wants something she can afford so she's looking in some rather sketchy places."

"Let me call Juliette and tell her to up Marietta's raise."

Rico rose and plucked his jacket from the back of the chair.

"Do not do that. I might not know Marietta well, but I can tell you she's wildly independent."

"A bad marriage will do that to a person."

Realizing Lorenzo knew that all too well because of his own bad marriage, Rico hid a wince. "Which is exactly why I've stayed away from serious relationships."

"It's also why you should step back a bit from Marietta. If you want to be involved in your child's life, you need to prove to her right now that she can trust you. And part of that is being as neutral as possible."

"Neutral?"

"Don't be her best friend and for God's sake, end anything romantic. With only your parenting relationship between you, you can be open and honest and even debate the best things for your child. Romance just messes everything up. Stay neutral. It took a long time to get to a good place with Antonio's mom after our divorce. It wasn't until I dropped any sort of attempt to be friends with her and dealt with her only as Antonio's second parent that I could win arguments with her and do what was best for Antonio."

"Okay." Everyone knew Lorenzo's first marriage and his relationship with Antonio's mom had been difficult, so obviously his advice was solid.

Rico walked out of the pub, into the freezing cold January night, realizing that married people might be able to be romantic and raise their children because they had a commitment. Not just to each other, but to their family. But two strangers? Raising a child? Neutrality really did seem to be the best way to go.

He hailed a cab and arrived at the location of the condo Riley would be looking at. Surprised, he got out of the cab, peering around at the white brick building with a row of terraces up the center of the front wall.

Huge glass doors opened for him as he stepped up to the

lobby—with a doorman who nodded as Rico walked into the open space furnished with modern decor.

Wearing a pretty white wool coat and a pink beret, Marietta met him in the center. "Well?"

"It's great!"

She laughed. "Juliette made my raise official tonight. But I also realized that you'll probably want to pay child support and the condo for our baby would be the best place to spend it. So I had Artie shift gears and look for a place more like what you suggested." She glanced around happily. "Do you like it?"

"Yes! Yes to child support and yes to this building!" Relief swamped him. "Let's go see this place." He almost put his arm around her shoulders to guide her, but remembering what Lorenzo said, he stopped that thought. He didn't let himself dwell on how cute she looked in a beret. Didn't let himself notice or react to anything about her.

No matter how difficult it was.

They met Artie on the way to the elevator—or, bank of elevators. There were actually three. Two for regular residents and one that went only to the penthouse. The little car took them smoothly to the fourth floor. They walked out into a wide, clean, carpeted corridor and passed two doors before Artie jangled some keys and granted them entry to the condo.

Marietta looked around at the open floor plan—kitchen, living room and dining area—with a sigh. Rico examined the space more carefully. The building was relatively new. Everything had recently been painted.

She turned to him with a happy smile. "There's a view!"

Artie motioned to the three-paneled glass door to the terrace. "As you can see, there will be a lot of light in the daytime."

A pale sofa and two chairs sat in front of a sage green tiled fireplace. A print area rug pulled the mishmash of colors and styles together.

Marietta turned from the living space toward the white kitchen. "This is lovely."

Rico said, "It really is."

She laughed. "Don't gloat."

"I'm not gloating but I might be giddy."

"With relief, I hope." She walked toward the kitchen. "I simply didn't have a good handle on finances last night. Today, I do."

He desperately wanted to hug her. Not just for pulling everything together in her mind and realizing her next step, but because she was cute, proud of herself and gloriously happy. That expression always made him want to kiss her.

Remembering Lorenzo's advice, he knocked that idea out of his brain and kept things neutral. "Let's get a look at the bathroom and closet space."

"There are two bathrooms," Artie happily announced. "One for guests and a private bathroom for the primary suite." He led them down the hall, showing them the guest bathroom, which had been recently updated, and then walked them to the primary suite. "The closet's not amazing, but it's big enough." He laughed. "Certainly bigger than what we saw yesterday."

Artie showed them three more places, all in the same neighborhood. The streets were well lit. The buildings had elevators and a doorman. Each had a primary suite with a private bathroom. Two had fireplaces.

Marietta could have chosen any one of them, but she didn't want to make a quick decision. She thanked Artie, told him that any of the four they'd seen that night would be perfect, but she wanted a day or two to consider all her options.

He saluted and left her and Rico standing on the street.

Watching him go, Rico said, "Did you tell him who I am?"

She shook her head. "He didn't seem concerned. He could

have thought you were my boyfriend or my brother." She shrugged. "He's only interested in selling me something. Not my private life."

Remembering what Juliette had said about establishing trust, she waited a beat, then said, "What did you think?"

"Exactly what you did. That any one of the condos we saw tonight would be perfect." He smiled congenially. "You choose."

An odd suspicion tingled up her spine. She knew he was a nice guy, but he was also a bossy guy. A lot like Juliette, who didn't hesitate to give her opinion about everything. Still, Juliette was also usually right. When she said this was a time for her to let Rico know he could trust her, Marietta recognized that probably was the thing to do.

"I'm going to take a day or two to think through the advantages and disadvantages of each condo. Then I'll talk to my banker."

"I could finance it for you," Rico said, then he winced. "Sorry. I don't want to be pushy. I also know that getting a mortgage will help your overall credit score. You do what's best for you."

Her suspicion that something was up with him grew. Of course, he could have realized that he'd been out of line the night before and simply be pulling back because he'd learned his lesson.

But maybe that was part of how they were building trust? Making and fixing mistakes. Trying things. "Okay. I'll need a few days. I'll call you when I decide."

He shook his head. "This will be *your* home. You don't have to call. I trust you to make the choice that's best for you."

Aha! It *was* about trust. Once again, Juliette's observations of the situation were right on the money.

Before she could say anything, her stomach rumbled loudly. Rico took a step back. "You know what? You're hungry and we're done looking at condos. I'll let you go so you can get dinner."

He turned away quickly and started striding down the street. But as she blinked in surprise, he faced her again. "Actually, I'm returning to London tomorrow." He obviously worked to appear casual. "I have some business to take care of and…you know—"

No. She didn't know. For a split second, she'd actually worried that he would insist on buying her dinner when her stomach rumbled, and she would have to talk her way out of it. Sweet, considerate Rico would have done that. Now, she didn't know what to think. Plus, wasn't he the guy who was in New York so they could get to know each other?

Yes. He was.

Now, suddenly, he was bolting?

Going back to Europe?

It wasn't as if he was just going across town. He was going across an ocean.

Still, in the grand scheme of things, if they were only parents together, nothing more, the reason for his returning to London wasn't any of her business. Technically, they weren't even friends. She had no right to probe.

Sadness filled her but she mustered a smile. "Okay." He was clearly setting boundaries. Which was good—

She supposed.

But hollowness echoed through her. She said the only thing she was allowed to say. "Have a good flight."

He smiled stiffly. "Okay."

He turned and walked down the street, away from her. As he pushed through the crowd, his charcoal gray overcoat began to disappear in fragments until all she saw was a piece of his shoulder and then he was gone.

She swallowed, wondering why she felt so empty when the night before she'd wanted to kick his behind for butting into her business. She turned up the collar on her white wool coat and slid the strap of her big purse up her shoulder and headed down the street.

She told herself she should call a cab, but she wanted the frosty air nipping at her cheeks and appreciated the chance to burn off the energy of everything she was feeling. As Juliette said, they should establish trust, end any thoughts of romance and be friends—

But wouldn't a friend have suggested dinner when her stomach growled?

Something was definitely up with him.

Worse, though, she hated this feeling that now lived between them. Their relationship had always been fun. Now, it was nothing.

Two weeks later, Rico returned home after a quick trip to Stockholm. Normally, he wouldn't have asked to meet the owner of the company in which he planned to invest, but he'd been nervous and antsy since leaving Marietta on the street that cold night.

She was an adult who'd lived in New York City for years and knew how to navigate the hustle and bustle and even the cold. He hadn't been worried for her safety, especially not in the part of the city of her potential condos.

She also probably had a deli that she frequented for sandwiches or salads when she came home late. All the weird emotions he'd experienced since that night couldn't be concern for her welfare. He trusted her to be smart and take care of herself.

Still, something had bugged him about leaving her that frigid night, and for two weeks he'd paced his downstairs, gone to plays he hadn't wanted to see, visited Antonio and Riley and by extension GiGi, who was over the moon about his baby. Lorenzo hadn't been told to keep it a secret so now a good portion of Italy probably knew he was about to become a dad.

The word was out, and everyone had congratulated him, been happy for him. He was adjusted enough to the idea of becoming a dad that he was happy for himself.

So what the hell was wrong!

He picked up his phone and automatically checked for a text from Marietta, as he'd done a million times in the past two weeks. Because she hadn't reached out to him, he'd assumed she hadn't chosen a condo, but surely by now she had.

Unless she'd changed her mind and decided not to get one of the four that were so perfect—

But wouldn't she have called him?

Actually, he'd told her that she didn't have to. Going with Lorenzo's advice that they should work toward a parents-only relationship, he'd told her she didn't have to call him.

Now, that seemed like a bad idea.

It *was* a bad idea.

And weren't they nearing the time when they could get a DNA test?

Yes. Yes. They were.

So why hadn't she called him?

Because he'd told her not to.

Lorenzo's whole advice wasn't wrong, but maybe Rico had overinterpreted it? Even if he and Marietta only saw each other as parents, they still had to communicate.

He scrolled through his contacts and found her number.

He was calling her. Consequences be damned.

CHAPTER TEN

MARIETTA HALF SAT, half sprawled across the sofa in the living room of the condo she shared with her three friends. They'd been thrilled she was pregnant, sad she was leaving them for her new digs, and now they were out celebrating with their new roommate, a pretty twenty-two-year-old blonde who could have a margarita.

Not that Marietta was upset about not being able to drink alcohol. It was more that her life seemed to change on a dime. Her support systems were crumbling. Her friends wanted different things out of life—

Except Riley. She and Antonio were ready and eager to have kids. She wanted nothing more than to be pregnant at the same time as Marietta.

Unfortunately, she now lived in Florence. Even if she got pregnant tomorrow, they'd have to video call to share the pregnancy experience.

She had a new job.

She was now the boss.

People who had been her work friends were now her staff.

Her life was suddenly so different.

She refused to let herself add Rico into the list of ways her support systems were crumbling, and her life was changing. So, he'd made dividing lines? She respected that. They needed boundaries that would allow them to be together for the sake of their child, but didn't involve intimacy.

Though one would think they should be allowed to communicate. Wouldn't they have to communicate to raise a child?

Of course they would.

Still, Juliette's advice must have been right on some levels. As soon as they'd both pulled back and stopped acting like lovers or even friends, the choice of a condo went smoothly.

She should be glad he wanted nothing to do with her—

Except she missed him. She even missed the guy who forced his way into the decision to buy the condo. Sure. Sure. He was a bit of a nitpicker. But in the end, he'd been right. An elevator was a good idea. So was a second bathroom. And she had gotten a bigger raise than she'd imagined. Adding child support to that, she could afford accommodations that fit having a child.

Her life was great.

Great.

Really great.

No. It wasn't. This whole thing with Rico was off. Wrong. Not that Juliette was wrong. Juliette was never wrong.

Marietta herself simply might have misinterpreted things.

Her phone rang and she bounced up off the sofa, half from surprise and half from eagerness to talk to anyone, rather than sprawl across a piece of furniture trying to sort her changing life.

When she saw the caller was Rico, her heart stopped, then revved up.

She took a minute to calm herself. She would not let him hear relief or eagerness in her voice. Technically, she didn't know this guy. And his behavior had made it clear that he wanted to be involved in their child's life, but not hers.

It was all very logical. Very much what Juliette had also told her. And she had to accept it.

She hit the button to answer the call, calmly saying, "Hello, Rico."

"Hello, Miss Boots-in-the-Oven-but-That-Don't-Make-'em-Biscuits."

She laughed. "If you can't appreciate a good ol' Southern explanation of truth, you're missing out on a lot of fun in life."

"I'm definitely missing out on a lot of fun in life. Your condo for one. I don't even know if you got one. How you're feeling for another. And if you've seen a doctor yet. And just plain you. Apparently, I like hearing about boots and ovens."

She laughed, but happy tears sprang to her eyes. "I like telling you about boots and ovens."

She sat back on the sofa, enjoying the shuffle of relief that softened her muscles and calmed her nerves.

"So how are you?"

"Good. No problems so far. And, yes, I did see a doctor and, yes, I'm pregnant. For honest to God real now."

"You're telling me I should see my lawyer and set up child support payments?"

"Do you want me to get the DNA test first?"

For a few seconds he didn't say anything. "Honestly, I believe you when you say the baby is mine. One of the first things you told me after we made love was that it had been a while for you."

"I coulda been talking about two weeks."

He laughed. "You were too eager. Either that or I swept you off your feet."

"Oh, you swept."

He laughed again and everything inside her bubbled with joy. This was what they needed to do. Communicate. Not avoid each other. She wouldn't forget Juliette's advice about keeping some distance. She would simply modify it.

"What have you been doing?"

His voice became businesslike. "Wheeling and dealing."

"Buy anything good?"

"I'm investing in a corporation that's working on establishing a crypto currency system."

"Isn't there already one?"

"Sort of. We're searching for a way to keep everyone honest. Something like the New York Stock Exchange, but for crypto. How about you? Did you buy a condo?"

"We're in escrow. We should close in two weeks."

"Which one did you get?"

"The first one we saw on the second night."

"I liked that one."

"So did I. Now I'm thinking about getting a cat."

Rico sat up on his sofa. "A cat? You're about to have a child! What do you want with a cat?"

"Pets are very good for children. Plus, I always had a cat back home in Texas. Had to leave Sophia Maria Lolita Conchita Chequita Banana behind when I left for New York. Didn't let my ex have her though. My mom took her in. We video called once a week until she passed."

She paused and he heard her suck in a breath, as if she was preventing herself from crying.

He swallowed hard. For as funny as she tried to make the story, he could feel the love she had for her pet and understand that she missed her. All the same, he kept the mood light.

"That's a lotta names for a something that probably didn't weigh twenty pounds. Was she named after relatives?"

"No. She just showed up at our door one day, so we didn't know her family. But she was a big personality. Too many good things about her for her to have only one name."

"She sounds like fun."

"She was. She was a warrior princess who kept the rodents

away. Not just for our property, but the neighbors' too. That's why I want another cat."

He winced. "For rodent control?"

She laughed. "No! For company. But I need a cat who's not accustomed to being outside."

"Okay, but any cat isn't going to like being stuck in your condo all the time. If you chose a dog for a pet, you could walk it."

"I can get my new cat a leash and walk her too."

He laughed. "I would pay to see that."

"Well, you could come out to see that once I get settled."

He missed her enough that he wasn't sure he could wait that long. "How about if I come out and help you move?"

"There's not much to move. Our furniture was shared and there's an unwritten rule that if a roommate leaves, they kiss the furniture goodbye. I'm even leaving my big closet-like cabinet."

"Okay. How about this? What if I come out and help you celebrate your new home? We can go out to dinner or see a show."

There was a pause. A long one. Eventually, she said, "You mean like a date?"

The concept flummoxed him for a second. He'd never taken the mother of his child on a date. And now, he wasn't supposed to. There were lines that couldn't be crossed.

But he'd missed her. And it didn't seem right to have a child with someone and treat them like...

He wasn't sure what Lorenzo's "neutrality" meant. How could he treat this woman who was giving him a child like... nothing?

Screw it.

"Yes. Like a date."

"Really?"

"What? You don't like me?"

"I like you fine. It's just that…"

"You think there are lines we shouldn't cross?"

"Yes."

Everything began to fall into place in his head. Her talking to Juliette. Him talking to Lorenzo.

"Because of something Juliette said to you?"

She paused long enough to confirm his suspicion. But she sighed and said, "Rico, this is about more than Juliette's advice. A child binds us. We will be going to birthday parties and dance recitals and graduations and planning a wedding for this baby when the time comes."

"And?"

"And I love all that. But I want all those times we're together to be cordial. Which means there probably shouldn't be anything more between us. We had a fling. We like each other enough that we could have probably kept that fling going for a while. But things end. Even marriages that start out good can end. I know things about marriage that you don't know—"

"I never asked you to marry me."

"I know. But while Antonio and Riley have an innocence that will carry them through a long happy life and Lorenzo and Juliette are so perfectly suited they'll complement each other forever. You and I are neither innocent nor Legos."

"Legos?"

"The little blocks that fit together."

"I know what they are. I just don't think anybody wants to be described as a block."

She sighed. "And I don't want to get into another bad relationship. Or ruin what we have. Our child has to come first."

"Agreed. But if we both don't believe in fairy tales," he said, even though the Cinderella comparison kept slapping him in the face because right now he felt like one of the stepsisters who didn't fit into the shoe, "maybe we could have something better."

He could hear the skepticism in her voice when she said, "Something better?"

"Trust?"

"Trust?"

Things Lorenzo said began to piece together in his head. "My parents, the people I should have been able to trust, didn't want me. I grew up in a system that I only trusted enough to acknowledge that everyone was *trying* to do their best for me. The first chance I got I bailed, believing I could take better care of myself than the government could. I trusted myself. And when your marriage ended and you moved to New York City, you trusted yourself."

"I did."

"Because you've been hurt. And I've been hurt. And we know life's not easy. Trust is more important than anything else. So what if we trusted each other?"

"To do what exactly?"

"To be honest. To admit it when whatever romance we have is over and let each other go without anger. To do the best we each can do for our child."

"That's an interesting concept. It sounds like the opposite of marriage vows. Rather than the promise to stay together, you're proposing we promise to let each other go peacefully."

In spite of the negativity of her reasoning, he knew she got the concept. "It's how I've lived my life. I trust someone or a situation until the trust is breached. Then I walk away. But I don't walk away angry."

"You shake the dust from your feet and start over? No hard feelings?"

"Yes. No hard feelings. If we both promise to be honest, both promise that neither one of us will cheat or stay in the relationship past the life of our feelings—"

"Then we can be romantic?"

"Yes. For as long as it lasts."

"It's about trust?"

"And honesty. Do you think we could do that?"

She didn't really know what she thought. What he'd said seemed too good to be true. But she supposed if there was one thing she could promise him it would be honesty.

After all, what choice did she have? They would be together in some way, shape or form for at least eighteen years. They had to get along and they also needed to figure out what to do with their attraction. Maybe letting it run its course before the baby was born would be the end of it?

"Okay. We'll try your way."

They talked for another twenty minutes about her condo and his insistence that he should be there to help her set up her home. She couldn't talk him out of it, so she knew he'd be arriving the weekend she took possession of her new place. The condo would have no furniture. She'd planned on buying a sleeping bag and sleeping on the floor until she got everything set up.

Just for the heck of it, she decided to buy a second sleeping bag to tease him. She knew he'd probably get a room at a fancy hotel while he was in Manhattan, but it would be funny to make him think she expected him to sleep on the floor.

The following evening, Marietta left the office sliding into her white wool coat. She buttoned it in the elevator and said good-night to Fred the doorman as she walked through the lobby to the street.

The temperature felt as if it'd dropped a million degrees. With a deep breath, she joined the crowd of commuters heading toward the subway entrance. But she didn't get four feet before someone fell in step with her.

"Hey."

His accent sent shivers through her blood. She stopped. "Rico?"

"I said I missed you."

She laughed. "Oh, you billionaires. Drop one hint and you land on our doorstep."

He eased her out of the crowd, to the entryway for another building, pulled her to him and kissed her. She let herself fall into the delicious kiss, the warmth, the passion, all the while thinking of the weird promise they'd made to each other.

She hated to look at this wonderful kiss as step one of letting their attraction run its course, but considering this little fling of theirs to be anything other than temporary was ridiculous. Plus, if they really wanted to have a solid friendship as they raised their child, it was smart to get the sexual attraction out of their systems.

He pulled back. "There. I feel better now."

She allowed the little jolt of happiness that formed to ripple though her. "I suppose I missed you too."

He slid his arm across her shoulders and led her onto the street again. "Just what a guy wants to hear." He stopped in front of a big, black SUV. "I rented a car."

She eyed it skeptically. "Looks like a minibus."

"It could easily get us to your apartment where you could pack a few things for tonight and work tomorrow morning… maybe tomorrow night and work the next day—"

She gaped at him. "How long are you staying?"

"I can only stay two days. Well, two nights. Plus, I promised you a date and things will be too rushed tonight. It would probably be better to get Chinese food delivered to my hotel room."

"I could eat Chinese."

He opened the SUV door. "Good. Punch your address into the GPS and we'll get this party started."

She smiled as he closed the door behind her, but as he

rounded the SUV's hood, she prayed they were doing the right thing.

She didn't want to get her heart broken, or break his, but there was no future for them. She had to keep reminding herself of that.

Because if anybody could tempt her into falling in love it would be Rico. She had to be smart, keep a little distance, guard her heart. Or she'd ruin everything. Not just their parenting together, but the life and confidence she'd built after her disastrous marriage.

She could never go back.

CHAPTER ELEVEN

HIS ROOM TURNED out to be the penthouse suite of one of the best hotels in the city. Because they ordered their Chinese food in the car on the drive from her apartment to his hotel, it was waiting for them in the kitchen area of his room.

Walking inside, he shrugged out of his overcoat. He tossed it on the back of a white sofa and used a remote to bring the fireplace to life. "It's cold out there. The fire makes it cozy."

"Yeah. Cozy." Pulling her small wheeled suitcase behind her, she looked around. This was very different from the cute hotel they'd stayed at in Florence. Very different. "Wow."

"I usually stay in this suite when I'm here for business." He pointed to their left. "There's a conference room back there." He pointed at the small area with a refrigerator, stove, microwave, dishwasher and sink. "A little kitchenette. A huge bedroom suite." He huffed out a breath. "It's very convenient."

Convenient?

It was huge. And gorgeous.

"Convenient for doing business?"

He walked over and pulled her to him. The move was so natural she didn't have time to think, only react by melting against him.

"For doing anything I want." He kissed her quickly. "But right now I'm starving. So let's eat."

A little dazzled, she stepped away from him. "Let me take my bag to the room."

"Okay, you do that. I'll dish the food. I'm warning you though, if there's an extra egg roll, it's mine."

She laughed and headed to the double doors at the end of a short corridor. She opened them on an exquisite bedroom. Lush with the textures of silks, weaves and wood in lamps, chairs and bedside tables, the simple beige-and-white room took her breath away.

She slipped out of her coat and hung it in a closet before hanging her two work outfits beside it. She put her makeup in the bathroom, telling herself she wasn't stalling—just in awe. It was the first time since she met Rico that she saw his wealth. Sure, she could have seen it in the Bentley, but lots of people had nice cars. He dressed well, but usually casually. Though he wore a white shirt and tie today, he'd covered them with a leather jacket. Not a suit coat.

She'd never seen how he lived.

She glanced around. She'd bet his house in London was a lot like this. Which was why he was so comfortable here and why she was taking everything in, touching silky lampshades and shiny wood surfaces.

Yet another reason it was a good thing their romance had a shelf life. She did not belong in this world and even with her new condo he'd be slumming any time he visited her.

Needing to relax, she took off her work clothes and slipped into sweatpants and a big T-shirt.

When she arrived in the kitchenette, where he sat on a tall chair beside the island that acted as a table, he laughed.

"I wanted you to get comfy, but now I feel overdressed."

"Yeah." But he looked great. Leather jacket off. Sleeves of his white shirt rolled to his elbows. Tie loosened.

It didn't matter what he wore or how he wore it, he managed to look sexy and yummy.

She slid onto the chair beside his and dug into her chicken

fried rice with a groan of contentment. "I didn't realize how hungry I was."

"What did you have for lunch?"

"Salad."

He grimaced. "You might have to add a sandwich to that while you're pregnant."

She peered over at him. "How would you know?"

"I've been reading up on pregnancy."

"Oh." She wasn't sure if that was good or bad but remembering what Juliette had said about how he would want to be a part of his child's life, she understood.

"In addition to gaining weight, your feet are going to swell. Your back will hurt. And don't even get me started on bladder control."

She shook her head. "Such a sweet talker."

"And this whole time nothing will happen to me."

"Humph. It would be interesting if something did happen to fathers. You know, a guy couldn't deny paternity if he threw up every time his pregnant girlfriend did."

He laughed. "Yeah. Evolution wasn't really fair about that." He paused. "Though if you think about it, fathers might have been created to miss out on trouble so they could ward off predators and hunt for food."

"I suppose it all goes back to caveman days. I'm glad we've evolved past that, and I can earn my own living, make my own way."

His expression changed. He almost looked disappointed, but he said, "I'd like to think I would be handy with predators."

"How are you with a crossbow?"

He laughed. "Yes. Your point is taken. We have evolved and I am useless."

She didn't want to insult him or leave him out. They were supposed to be establishing trust. "You're not useless!"

"Really?"

"Hey, I agreed to child support. I took your advice about a building with an elevator. I even understand your stance on enjoying our romance while it lasts and moving on."

"Meaning, I'm your idea man?"

"Yes." She took advantage of the silence that followed to dig into her chicken, but she suddenly wondered about his parents. She knew his difficult start in life was what dictated his reactions now. He wouldn't leave his child to fend for itself—or with only a mom. He would be a part of this. He wouldn't just take responsibility. He wanted to help raise this baby.

"Do you ever wonder about your parents?"

"I used to." He lifted his dish from the center island, rinsed it and put it in the dishwasher. "But when I was about seven, I realized there wasn't much point in trying to guess who they might have been or why they didn't want me, and I stopped."

"That's too bad because there are a lot of angles a seven-year-old kid might not have explored. For instance, what if it wasn't your mom who left you but your grandmother?"

He gaped at her. "How is that better?"

"I'm not looking for *better*. I'm looking for alternative origin stories. Being left in that train station might have been the best thing that could have happened for you."

He crossed his arms on his chest. "This I've gotta hear."

She would have laughed at the skepticism in his voice, but this was important, serious. "What if your parents had died and your grandmother couldn't support you? What if she was trying to give you a better life? Or what if your mother was the one to leave you and she did it to protect you from an abusive dad."

His face changed, softened. "That would have been awful for her."

"Yes. Or you could be the heir to the throne in a country that overthrew its monarchy, and all royals were executed."

His lips twitched with the effort not to laugh.

"Okay, maybe not a monarchy but a crime family. What if your mom wanted something better for you than the vicious cycle of that kind of life? Then she wouldn't merely have saved you, but also your child…" She pointed at her stomach. "*This* child…would have been born into that life if she hadn't gotten you out."

He uncrossed his arms and studied her for a few seconds. "A seven-year-old is definitely too young to consider things like that."

"There might not be a million reasons why a mother would believe she was protecting her child by letting him go, but there are a just enough for you to realize you might have been loved so much, that your mom believed she had to take you out of your circumstance to save you."

He looked stunned, as if unable to take it all in. "That's amazing to consider."

"You always believed you weren't wanted. But what if you were loved so much your mom made the ultimate sacrifice."

He rubbed his hands down his face. "You're asking me to shift my entire life's beliefs."

"It's not your entire life. Your work won't change. Your friendships won't change. Considering a different reason your mom left you only broadens your horizons a bit. It's not like you're going from an armadillo to a turtle. You're simply considering that maybe you shouldn't believe the worst about your beginnings. After all, not knowing for sure and not being able to know for sure, means you can believe the best if you want."

He sucked in a breath. "That's a bigger shift than you think it is."

"Hey. You should be pregnant." She tossed her napkin on

her now empty plate. "It feels like my life changed completely in the time it took to snap my fingers."

He snorted, but raised his gaze to the ceiling, then brought it back to her. "Is this your way of telling me I'm asking a lot of you?"

"By having our baby? No! I want this child! I can't wait to be a mom. And I'm happy to do the shifting. I'm just saying some of the hardest shifts are the ones we're forced to make. Or the ones we *need* to make when circumstances change."

He thought about that. "You're saying that I've focused for so long on the bad reasons someone would abandon me and never considered that I might not have been abandoned but rescued."

"Like Moses in the basket."

He walked over and sat beside her. "You might think I don't know that story, but I do."

"Of course you do." She leaned in and gave him a quick kiss. "In order to make good investments, you study. Probably a lot. It makes you a well-rounded person and that might be another gift your mother gave you."

"Being well rounded? You think having to learn everything on my own made me well-rounded?"

"I know a lot of people who went to university, but they didn't really learn practical applications. Your entire life is practical applications. I would bet you could do anything you want."

She tried to shift away, but he caught her shoulders and kept her right where she was. He gazed into her eyes as if mesmerized, then he kissed her, long and deep. The emotion of it tripped something in her heart, but she caught it before it could fully kick in.

She knew the kiss was an expression of his appreciation of her take on his life and she stood by it. With her own child growing in her belly, she could clearly see the lengths she would go to protect a baby she hadn't even met yet. The love that radiated through her filled her with strength and resolve.

That's the feeling she got when she pondered Rico's mom leaving him. Strength and resolve and a protectiveness she'd never felt before.

That was also why she'd never take away his right to be part of his child's life. Maybe this baby was his opportunity to experience emotion so strong that he could finally come to terms with his own beginnings?

He broke the kiss but barely moved away from her, whispering, "Wanna go back and see the bedroom suite?"

She laughed. "I already saw it."

"I have new things to show you."

She didn't doubt it for a second.

He kissed her again, easing her off her stool to stand. She let herself enjoy the feeling of him as she slid her arms up his forearms to his biceps and the sensation of pressing against him when she moved in to deepen their kiss.

She'd never felt this way with anyone. While she knew that might be because she'd begun dating her ex when she was young, she wouldn't downplay all the wonderful sensations and even the closeness she felt with a guy she barely knew.

CHAPTER TWELVE

THEY KISSED THEIR way back to his room, then, like an old married couple, they broke apart to remove shirts and pants. They could have come together in a storm of passion. Everything about her made him hot and hungry. And happy. But he knew about the temporary nature of life. Even her possible origin story of his mother protecting him proved that moving on was a part of life. She had a bad marriage and wouldn't risk her sanity again. He didn't have to get married to know that the best way to move through life was unencumbered. Ultimately, they would drift apart. But tonight, she was his and he intended to enjoy that.

They rolled across the bed, kissing and touching, then she began the tasting. He loved the feel of her tongue as it slid across his chest, down his belly. But he'd missed her so much in the past few weeks, that the pleasure pain intensified to the point that he had to stop her. He caught her shoulder and rolled her to her back, joining them and taking the sensations to the next level until they both cascaded over the edge of reason with a groan of delight.

He fell asleep holding her. Content in a way he'd never felt before. But, better, when he woke up, she was still there. In his bed.

The most wonderful emotion fluttered through him. He watched her sleep for a few minutes, then remembered how she'd been starving the night before and went to the kitchen to make her breakfast.

When the eggs, toast and bacon were ready, she ambled out and stood by the center island. Fully dressed. She probably thought she could race out the door, but she'd clearly underestimated the power of crispy bacon.

He answered the questions in her eyes when she glanced at the food on the center island. "Every other time we've been together, you've ditched me."

"Ditched you?"

"Maybe that's a little too negative. But I always woke alone. Today, I did not. So, I thought I'd surprise you with breakfast, give you a reason to always want to stay the night."

She eased her way to one of the stools. "For a man of the world, you don't seem to understand the simple realities of normal people with jobs."

He motioned for her to take a seat. She set her purse on the chair beside her, and he slid breakfast in front of her.

"I have time for the eggs, but I'll take the bacon and coffee to go."

"Yes, ma'am." He wrapped some bacon for her and poured coffee into one of the paper cups supplied by the hotel for busy businesspeople who would be jetting off to meetings and taking their morning coffee with them.

She ate the eggs and toast so quickly he wasn't sure if she was late or starving, but either way, he'd fed her, made sure she didn't leave the house hungry.

Pride swelled in his chest.

When she rushed out for work, the penthouse suite echoed with quiet, but it was good quiet. Still, after an hour of researching prospective investments on his laptop, he got antsy.

He picked up his phone and texted his mentor, Ethan O'Banyon, asking if he wanted to meet for lunch. Within seconds, he got a return text suggesting a restaurant. Two hours later they were sitting in a quiet dining room with white linen tablecloths and waiters in dark trousers and white shirts.

Ethan ordered a martini. The waiter scampered away.

Rico said, "So, how's retirement?"

"What retirement?" Ethan, a short balding man, who still looked like a tycoon in a suit and tie, laughed. "You know people like us don't retire."

Rico shook his head. "I guess not. But I would like to think that by then I'll be putting the bulk of my money into something safe, something I don't have to watch as much."

"Oh, now where's the fun in that?"

Rico laughed. "I have to think a little more responsibly now. I'm about to have a child."

Ethan's face filled with joy. "Rico! And you let me order a martini when we should be drinking champagne?"

"Eh. You wasted a couple of bucks." He hailed the waiter. "Get us a bottle of champagne."

The waiter nodded and left.

Ethan sucked in a long breath. "I cannot believe you're having a child."

"Technically, my…" He fumbled over what to call Marietta. She was too interesting and he liked her too much for her to be something as pedestrian as a girlfriend. "My baby's mother is having the child."

"You're not married?" He paused. "Of course you're not. You would have invited me to the wedding. So what's up with this?"

"Neither of us believes in marriage. In fact, we're doing the opposite. To stay on good terms for the sake of our baby, we've promised to split amicably when the romance dies."

Ethan just stared at him. "What?"

"We don't want to mess up our kid's life with our bad behavior, so we're ending things before they get ugly in order to stay friends."

Ethan continued to stare at him. Then he shook his head as if trying to think it through and failing. Ethan was older. His values and views on some things were dated. Rico never questioned him about his choices or beliefs. He respected him. And Ethan never pushed Rico into things that weren't right for him.

The champagne came. The waiter opened it and poured two glasses. As the young man walked away, Ethan raised his glass. "Congratulations."

They touched glasses. Rico said, "Thanks."

"With the exception of the romance being a bit off, you seem happy."

"I am happy."

"Then I am happy for you," Ethan said. "So what's she like?"

Rico said, "Funny. Interesting." He laughed. "She's from Texas and has an odd way of looking at life."

"Ah, Texas. Cattle. Oil. Money. The money almost got me to settle there myself, but I like city life."

"I do too."

Ethan took a sip of his champagne and set his glass on the table. "So, you like her because she's different?"

"She's not different. She has a different take on things that sort of fascinates me. Last night, she suggested that I flip my beliefs about who left me at that train station and why."

Ethan's face contorted. "Flip it to what?"

"Instead of thinking my mom left me because she didn't want me, Marietta suggest that I consider that my father was abusive, or a career criminal, and my mom was trying to get me out of that life."

Looking oddly relieved, Ethan pulled in a breath and picked up his champagne glass. "You'll never know."

"That's what I thought! It's pointless to think about it. But I could tell that's not how she feels. She called whatever I believe about why I was abandoned my 'origin story.'"

Ethan laughed. "Like a comic book hero?"

"I don't know."

The waiter returned and they ordered lunch. Their conversation turned to some upcoming investment possibilities Ethan wanted Rico's opinion on and Rico suddenly realized that their roles had reversed. Rico had always been the one asking for Ethan's opinion. Now, Ethan didn't merely trust Rico. He depended on him.

They finished lunch and walked out into the sunny—but cold—February day.

"I'm thrilled about your child," Ethan said, hugging Rico. "But I want you to promise me one thing."

"Sure. If I can."

"Keep an open mind."

"About?"

"About life."

"I've always had an open mind about life."

Ethan made the odd face again. "Yes and no. I just don't want you to ruin the experience of having a child because you're hung up on other stuff."

"You mean my origin story."

Ethan shook his head. "Yes. Forget all that. Focus on your child. Or maybe focus on your baby's mom. She sounds lovely. Like somebody you might want to keep around for a while."

"Ethan, we'll be in each other's life for years...decades."

"Yes, well, it sounds like she's more to you than the mother of your child. Thinking about things like that silly origin story might keep you from seeing that. Love is a surprising thing. Not always what we think it is."

"We're not going to fall in love. Neither one of us wants that."

"Whatever."

Rico smiled at Ethan's sarcastic, "Whatever," before the old man said, "Goodbye," and walked away.

Rico watched him go. He'd already promised Marietta that they would let their relationship dissolve when it was over. And that's what he intended to do. After all, that had been *his* idea.

But packing his things to return to London the following morning after Marietta left for work, Ethan's words popped up in his brain again.

Love is a surprising thing. Not always what we think it is.

He batted his hand in dismissal. He'd already made his decisions and if the two days he'd just spent with Marietta were any indicator, he'd made a good choice. They'd had fun. They always had fun. If they handled their relationship correctly, being a parent with her would also be fun. He did not want to risk their good relationship on something as fleeting as love.

He knew from experience that love did not last. And if he ever thought it did, all he had to do was remember being left in a train station—

Except, what if what Marietta said was true? What if he hadn't been abandoned but rescued, saved from something like an abusive home or a life that was more of a prison than a life?

Then he hadn't been left at a train station out of selfishness. He'd been left out of love.

Real love.

The possibility nearly floored him.

He drove his SUV to the airport and tossed his keys to an employee with instructions to return it to the car rental office, then he climbed aboard his private jet.

But as he walked into the cabin, he looked around with fresh eyes.

Would he even have any of this if his mother hadn't loved him enough to rescue him?

Feeling silly happy, Marietta ordered two sleeping bags, which were delivered the Thursday before she took possession of her condo. Friday night, Jake the videographer and Layla the new photographer helped her cart her boxes of clothes from her apartment to a car she'd rented.

At the condo, as if they'd been given instructions from Juliette not to let her lift anything, Layla put all her boxes on a bellboy's cart and Jake held a sleeping bag under each arm as they rode the elevator to her floor.

She unlocked the door and presented her new home to her friends. The open floor plan. The white kitchen. The fireplace. The view from huge sliding glass doors on the wall in front of the terrace.

Layla said, "Oh, my goodness!" She spun to face Marietta. "It's gorgeous!"

Jake shrugged, saying, "It's nice." High praise from a guy who didn't talk a lot.

Marietta laughed. "It's perfect for me and a baby. That's what counts."

Jake rolled the bellboy's cart down the hall to the main bedroom and Layla began ripping the packaging off the first sleeping bag.

Marietta stopped her. "It's fine. I can do that."

Layla held the sleeping bag away from her. "You have eight boxes to unpack once we're gone. Let me unwrap this."

"Okay. Fine." She glanced around. "I don't even have water to offer you."

Unraveling the long strand of plastic around the sleeping bag, Layla said, "Then why don't you run down to the convenience store and get a few things, while I unwrap these and Jake unloads the cart in the bedroom."

"That might not be a bad idea."

"Or maybe you don't need to." Rico walked in the door they'd left open. He held out two bags. "I got bottled water. Some bagels and cream cheese for morning." He walked over and kissed Marietta. "And wine."

Layla stared at them. Her eyes round and curious.

Marietta laughed. "This is Rico. Baby's dad."

Layla's eyes lit. "*This* is Rico?"

He pointed at his chest. "Baby's dad."

"You know you're going to have to drink that wine out of the bottle because I don't even have glasses."

He shrugged out of his overcoat. "That's fine. You weren't getting any anyway." He looked around. "So…no furniture. Probably no bedding."

She winced. "I do have towels. And sleeping bags." She grinned at him. "I've got to warn you. If you're going back to your fancy hotel, you're going alone."

He glanced at the sleeping bag Layla was unwrapping and then at Marietta. "You can't sleep on the floor."

"Of course I can. This is my first night in my new home. I want to experience it. Sleeping bags and all."

He groaned and shook his head.

Marietta said, "Go help Jake unload the boxes in the bedroom so Layla and Jake can go home. I appreciate their help getting my boxes here, but I don't want to keep them all night."

Rico walked back through the hall to the bedroom and Marietta and Layla unwrapped the two sleeping bags and unrolled them.

"Let's put them in front of the fireplace."

Layla laughed. "Are you really going to make that good-looking guy sleep on the floor?"

"Hey, this is my first night as a homeowner. If he wants to be part of the experience, then he's sleeping on the floor."

They laid out the sleeping bags. As they finished, Jake and Rico walked up the hall.

Jake said, "Everything that can be done is done. Boxes are off the cart. Technically, you need to go through them to see where to store things. Though it's not like you have a dresser. Just a closet."

"Doesn't matter. It's all clothes," Marietta said. "I have to go online tomorrow and order things like glasses and dishes."

"Or we could take the SUV to a shopping center." Rico pulled out his phone. "There's got to be one around here somewhere."

Layla said, "Maybe Jersey."

Marietta frowned. "New Jersey? Go the whole way to New Jersey for dishes?"

"And sheets and towels and furniture."

"I'm with Marietta. Just shop online," Jake said, walking into the living space to peek at the fireplace. "You'll pay for delivery, but it's worth it to have somebody else have to cart your sofa into the service elevator and get it up here."

Rico said, "Maybe we start online and go to brick-and-mortar stores for things we can't find."

Layla lifted her coat from the center island. The only flat surface in the apartment to store anything. "Makes sense." She hugged Marietta. "I'll see you on Monday."

Jake waved. "See you on Monday."

And then they were gone. Closing the door behind them, they left Marietta and Rico alone in the echoing condo.

Rico said, "I love it. You did a good job choosing a home."

She glanced around proudly. "I did."

His gaze collided with the sleeping bags in front of the fireplace. "So, you're really going to make me sleep on the floor?"

"Yes."

"Marietta, there's nothing here. Not even a television to amuse us. Let's go back to my hotel."

She walked over and began unbuttoning his shirt. "I can think of something to amuse us."

He laughed. "There is that." He frowned. "Except I have

an idea." He knelt down before the first sleeping bag. "Let's see if this works." He unzipped it and spread it out. Then he tugged the second sleeping bag over and unzipped it. He laid it on top of the first one like a blanket.

"Oh, so we can cuddle."

"Now, wait. I'm not done." He found the zipper for the first bag and then the second, fusing them together.

She laughed. "You're making one big sleeping bag."

"The events of my childhood did give me some interesting skills."

"Well, this one looks like fun. But there's one more thing." She raced into the kitchen, opened drawers until she found what she wanted and pulled out one of the many manufacturers' instruction sheets for the appliances. She rifled through them until she found the one for the fireplace. "Here it is."

She ambled back to Rico, reading the instructions, then hit the button that brought the flames to life. She smiled at Rico. "It's gas."

"That's handy." Then he patted the sleeping bag.

She smiled and knelt beside him. Crazy feelings bombarded her, mostly tingles of arousal. But also great joy. She had a home now. Soon she'd have a baby. And she liked her baby's dad.

She couldn't remember ever being this happy. He kissed her and for sure she knew she'd never been this happy. Bubbly. Content.

But relationships were temporary. Not permanent. Her baby and her new home had to be what filled her with joy. Rico might be part of it but she'd been in a marriage. She'd watched love fizzle, then die, then turn into something awful.

She would never again go that route. She'd enjoy him while he was with her, but when the baby came she would insist they focus their attention on being good parents.

CHAPTER THIRTEEN

RICO SLEPT BETTER than he had in years. The fireplace was warm, but so was the sleeping bag, especially when he was snuggled against Marietta. Without opening his eyes, he reached for her, but she was gone. The condo smelled different too.

Hearing her in the kitchen, he said, "What are you doing?"

"I put the bagels you bought in the oven."

Still not opening his eyes, he mumbled, "But that don't make 'em biscuits."

"Hold that thought," she said, her voice moving away.

He groaned. "What now? I've already slept on a floor in front of a fire. That's all the down-home stuff I want to do this weekend. If there's no bed here by six o'clock tonight, we sleep in my hotel room."

The sound of her moving around in the kitchen echoed in the open space. "Or we could sleep in my mom's guest room."

He bolted up, positive he hadn't heard right. "What?"

"My mom called this morning. The condo impressed her, but she might have—actually, she totally did—seen you sleeping in front of the fireplace."

His eyes bugged. "Your mother saw me?" His eyes widened even farther. "I'm naked!"

"You were covered. She saw nothing…just that there was a man sleeping in my condo…" She winced. "With me."

"Damn it."

"Haven't you ever been caught with a woman?" She laughed. "You're in your thirties. You're an adult. You're the sexiest man alive. People know you're not celibate."

He ran his hand down his face. She handed him a toasted bagel, slathered in cream cheese.

"Oven toasted. I have my unusual skills too."

Too hungry to be picky, he bit into it and groaned. "Okay. That's delicious."

"Anyway, go back to your hotel and pack a bag. My mother wants to meet you."

"Today?" he asked incredulously. "You want to go to Texas today?"

"Today is as good of a day as any because... I also told them I'm pregnant and they're curious about you. And I want you to go so my parents can see you're a normal, nice guy."

Horrified, he glanced around. "Okay, remember how we said we'd build our relationship on trust and honesty?"

"Yeah."

"Well, I'm going to be honest and say I'm not ready to meet them. And meeting them also shouldn't be spur-of-the-moment. Let's plan a weekend to go. That will give me a chance to pack appropriately and your parents time to adjust to us being pregnant."

She frowned. "I guess."

"I *know* and we are sleeping in the hotel tonight." He slid out of the sleeping bag. "But first, get your computer. We have some shopping to do."

"Okay, but really there's nothing for you to worry about meeting my parents. My mom is cool. My dad's even cooler. You're going to love them."

Hundreds of reasons that couldn't be true filled his brain. He was an orphan. A confirmed bachelor. He'd gotten their daughter pregnant. He made a point of never meeting anybody's parents. But he supposed this situation was different.

Partially because Marietta believed she couldn't have children. Maybe the baby was a point in his favor? And maybe by the time they actually went to Texas all of that would have sunk in for them?

He hoped.

But for now, they were staying in her condo and there was shopping to do.

Slowly but surely, furniture began to arrive in Marietta's new home. Even though Rico flew to Manhattan every Friday night to watch her condo take shape, she spent those two weeks doing Valentine-themed proposals and he spent Saturdays and Sundays alone.

But that also meant they couldn't go to Texas until the first weekend in March. Which really did give him time to adjust to the idea of meeting her parents.

They slept in her new bed that Friday night and woke Saturday morning for the flight to Texas. Everything went smoothly and a few hours later, he was driving a rental car up a small incline when her family home came into view. The brown brick one-story house seemed to stretch forever.

Though he'd been calm the whole time, the hair on the back of his neck suddenly began to prickle. He had never been in the situation of meeting the parents of the woman who would be having his child. It all seemed so normal in Italy, London or Manhattan where people were sophisticated and suave. But here—in the country, the home of cowboys and hardworking folk—he wasn't so sure anymore.

They drove down a long lane to the house. Rico glanced around. Just as with the Salvaggio vineyard, there was nothing for miles except green grass and fences surrounding outbuildings. One was clearly a big barn.

He got out of the SUV they'd rented at the airport, looking around. "Your parents own all this?"

"It's a ranch."

He knew that. "I just hadn't expected it to be so big or so green. And where are the cattle?"

She laughed, making her curls shimmy as she got out of the SUV. "It might not be what you pictured in your mind, but you're going to love it here. Trust me." As soon as her car door closed, she said, "When we get to the house, let me do the talking."

"Protecting me?"

"No. I just know how to make my dad see that me having a baby is a dream come true."

"Should I be worried?"

"I'm a grown woman who has lived away from home for five years. My parents don't get a say in how I live my life." She winced. "But my dad will react."

She headed up a stone path toward the front door.

He gaped at the space she left behind, then he raced after her. "Your dad will *react*?"

She reached the door. "This *is* Texas. And I'm his baby girl. He's going to…have some thoughts on that. And he's probably going to tell you all of them."

"And you never told me this because…?"

She shrugged. "It never came up. Besides, he'll be fine once he gets it all out. I told you he's cool." She waited for him before opening the house door. "Come on. It's not going to be bad. And you'll like my family. Actually, I think you'll love my two brothers."

They stepped into a foyer that was open to the general living space. He could see shiny white tile floors in a cream-and-beige living room and dining room and an all-white kitchen.

As she walked toward the kitchen, she called, "We're here."

But she hadn't needed to. Everybody seemed to have congregated around a big center island with gray, black and white granite counter tops. His gaze swept the room, then stopped on Juliette and Lorenzo.

Juliette and Lorenzo?

As Marietta hugged and was hugged, he walked up to Lorenzo. "What are you doing here?"

Juliette laughed. "Cole's roasting a pig. They called earlier in the week, said it would be fun for us to jet on down since you and Marietta were going to be here. What took you so long to get here?"

Rico wanted to say, how do you know the Fontains? But he didn't get the chance. A big guy in a cowboy hat opened the sliding glass doors and entered. "Going to be hot for March."

Marietta seemed to take that as her cue. She caught Rico's arm and turned him toward the guy in the cowboy hat and a red-haired waif who Rico assumed was her mom.

"Mom, Dad, this is Rico."

The waif threw herself at him and hugged him. The big guy gave him the once-over.

Adding the hug to the way everyone was in jeans and a T-shirt, even Lorenzo, Rico suddenly felt overdressed and totally out of place.

Still, as a former foster child, he wasn't a stranger to being the odd man out. As Marietta's mom released him, he approached the big guy with his hand extended. "It's a pleasure to meet you."

Her dad still eyed him suspiciously. "That's what everyone says."

Marietta beamed with joy. "My dad's really well loved in the community." She hooked her arm with his, clearly proud of him. "He's head of the cattleman's association."

Her dad finally took Rico's extended hand and shook it. "Have been for thirty years."

He suddenly realized that the eyes of ten strangers were on

him. Two guys. Could be her brothers. Two women. Could be her brothers' wives. Six kids.

Six kids?

Marietta pointed to the first man. "That's Danny and his wife, Tonya, and their four kids."

Rico shook Danny's hand. The kids waved shyly.

"That's Junior," she said, pointing at the second brother, "his wife, Cindy Lou, and their two daughters."

One of the daughters hid behind her mother.

Discomfort crept up on him. Not because they were staring at him but because he suddenly realized how odd he must look to them in his chinos and golf shirt.

Plus, to them he probably spoke weirdly.

And he was the father of Marietta's child.

A child everybody believed she couldn't have.

Sheesh. He might as well be from Mars because to these people he was an alien.

The kitchen began to fill with conversation and laughter. Marietta's mom, Sheila, told him to get their bags while Marietta caught up with everyone.

Grateful, he left the noisy kitchen, brought their overnight bags into the house and met Sheila in the foyer.

Wiping her hand in her apron, she said, "Guest room is back this way."

The entire house had the shiny white tile floor, protected by big, colorful area rugs. Furniture was natural wood, not stained, a little rough, weathered. Paintings of buffalo hung on every wall. Two of the clocks were wagon wheels.

The home somehow managed to pay homage to the Old West past, even as it had a modern appeal.

"Your house is lovely," he said, following Sheila down a long hall.

"Oh, thank you. Decorating this was how Cole and I

learned to compromise." She laughed. "Remodeling it, we learned how to compromise even more."

He laughed. "Marietta and I did some compromising around her purchase of a condo."

She paused. "Really? She let you help choose her condo?"

"Sort of. I went to see a few with her and gave her my thoughts. She made the actual decision."

She studied him. "That's still more opinion than she lets other people have." She laughed. "She's headstrong."

She opened the door on a big, airy bedroom. Sliding glass doors showcased a patio area. Off to the right, he could see a pool with a tall sliding board.

The doors were so big and everything was so close, he felt like he'd be sleeping outdoors.

But he said nothing. When Sheila guided him to the patio where everyone had congregated, he'd been given a beer and shown the refrigerator in the outdoor kitchen so he could help himself—like family, Sheila had said.

Like family.

He understood that because of how the Salvaggios had welcomed them into their life, but this felt different. First, there were about four times as many people. Second, there were kids and adults. Neighbors.

Danny and Junior joined him. "So. I hear you own a Bentley."

He shrugged. "Yeah. It's my favorite car."

"You probably have a sports car, too."

"Lamborghini."

"Oh, sweet."

The conversation shifted from cars to investments, and he realized that the big ranch that didn't seem to have any cattle did very well for itself.

"The clincher," Junior said, "was putting in the meat-packing plant."

Danny pointed behind them. "It's the biggest outbuilding off on the horizon. Now we control every step of the process. It's also a way to eliminate a middleman and cut costs."

Rico said, "I hear that," glad that they'd made a connection. Her brothers might dress more casually, but the business principles they operated on were the same Rico way guided his own investments.

He took a slow, happy breath. Just as Marietta had predicted, he did get along with her brothers.

But looking around, taking in the ranch and the people, watching Juliette and Sheila laughing as if they were longtime friends, knowing they had to have met because of Marietta, he realized something odd.

These people could have afforded to buy Marietta a condo. Yet she'd lived in an apartment with three roommates.

They adored her. One of her brothers almost always had his arm slung across her shoulders. Too many times to count, he'd seen her mom glance at Marietta with love in her eyes.

Yet she'd left them and lived virtually hand-to-mouth for five long years.

Her mother had said she was headstrong, but combining everything he was learning here to his own dealings with her, he had a sense she was a little more than headstrong.

The sun grew hotter, as Cole had predicted it would, and the kids put on swimsuits and filled the air with screams of delight as they splashed in the pool.

When her brothers left him, Marietta came over and sat by him. "Sorry, I sort of stranded you."

"I've been having interesting conversations with your family."

She winced. "Ouch. I can only imagine what they said."

"Nothing bad." He caught her gaze. "In fact, you seem like the favorite child."

"Oh, I am," she admitted without hesitation. "I'm the only girl."

He snorted.

"Hey, where we come from, dads and daughters, brothers and sisters?" She shrugged. "It works in my favor."

He glanced at her father again. He stood by an odd patch of land that not only had smoke meandering out in puffs, but also was covered in big leaves. He was the only one of Marietta's immediate family that Rico hadn't had a conversation with.

"Hey, Marietta," Juliette called. "Get over here and solve an argument—"

She glanced at him. He shook his head with a laugh. "Go. This is your family time."

He rose from the chaise lounge at the same time she did. "I think I'll get another beer."

Strategically, he got two and walked over to her dad and the patch of land that seemed to be on fire but no one cared.

He handed the beer to her dad, who said, "Thank you."

"You're welcome." He glanced around. The weird feelings about Marietta living in a cheap apartment haunted him. He understood that she was stubborn, but he couldn't see this big, brawny Texan letting his little girl live below their means. Given that he couldn't come right out and ask, he decided to edge his way to that with simple conversation.

He pointed at what looked to be dry leaves. "This is interesting."

Cole gave him a confused frown. "There's a pig in the ground, son."

Okay. That was odd. "A pig in the ground?"

"You've never had a piece of pork that was roasted this way?"

He just looked at him.

"Seasoned with garlic and simmering in the ground for twelve hours… Mmm. You are in for a treat."

Dear Lord, he hoped so.

A few seconds went by, then Cole said, "You seem to really like my little girl."

Seeing his opening, Rico sat on an available lawn chair and Cole sat on the one beside it. "I do. She's smart and funny." He didn't mention her cute accent since everyone in the family seemed to have one. "And strong. One of the strongest people I know."

Cole sniffed. "Yeah. She's smart and strong all right."

"You don't think so?"

"Took her a while to leave that jackass she was married to."

Rico held back his surprise. He absolutely wouldn't mention that Marietta had told him the jackass had left her. She might have let it appear that way to save face.

"But I will give you that she's strong. Took a lot of guts to move away. Wouldn't take a dime of our money. Insisted she would make it on her own."

"And she did."

And her dad let her.

He still couldn't quite come to terms with that.

Cole gave him the side-eye. "I heard you paid for half the condo."

Feeling oddly like that was a condemnation, Rico said, "It's my child too and I wouldn't let her get a condo where she had to walk up four flights of stairs."

Cole laughed. "I'll bet that was an argument."

"Not really. I sort of gave her enough time to think it through and she realized I would be paying child support anyway and that meant she could afford something nicer."

There was respect in Cole's voice when he said, "It *is* a nice condo."

Rico held back a wince wondering if this guy had also seen him sleeping on the floor in front of the fireplace. Deciding it was best not to ask, he said, "Yeah. She did a good job picking it out."

"You give her space?"

Realization struck him. Rico had easily seen the end result of her bad marriage was an unbridled need to be independent. But he would bet her family had needed a little more time to figure it out. And that they'd made some mistakes in the process. "You don't?"

"Oh, we do now. At first, we weren't so smart about how we dealt with her. Her ex was a piece of work. She never saw it. When she did, it was too late. He'd all but ruined her. She was shy. Hesitant. Afraid of her own shadow." He huffed out a breath. "She'd needed to go away. Sheila calls it finding herself. Made me promise not to interfere." Cole peered over at him. "You seem to be good for her."

"I think her job, Juliette's trust and Riley's friendship probably were better for her than I've been."

"Interesting. So you're saying you found her at just the right time."

He laughed. "Maybe."

Cole patted his knee. "Nope. I think you did. It all feels right to me." He pulled in a breath and hoisted himself out of his chair. "Pig's going to be done in about an hour. If you weren't dressed so fancy, I'd let you help get him out of the ground."

He wasn't sure what getting a hot pig out of the ground entailed, but Cole had made it sound like a compliment or an honor to be part of things. "I have a T-shirt and jeans in my overnight bag."

"Well, go get 'em on, boy. I'm starving."

CHAPTER FOURTEEN

A WEEK LATER, Marietta was overseeing a proposal in a coffee shop near her condo. The proposer was a nervous investment banker who'd met his girlfriend in this very coffee shop when they both reached for the same chai tea latte.

Trevor Martin wrung his hands in distress. "I'm sorry she's late. I swear. Her friend *is* bringing her here."

"No worries," Marietta said, brushing her hands along his shoulders and straightening his tie. "It doesn't hurt for you and me to have an extra minute to run through what's going to happen."

"You have the guy dressed up as a big cup of chai tea latte?"

"Absolutely." And he'd paid dearly for it, but apparently there was a running joke between him and Eloise about the talking latte. Marietta didn't have to understand people's inside jokes. She only had to fulfill their wish for a perfect proposal.

He glanced outside through the big glass storefront. "Here she comes."

Marietta said, "Places, everyone!"

The prospective groom raced to the counter and ordered two chai tea lattes.

The barista giggled. Everybody behind the counter tittered in anticipation.

Marietta slid into the background. The soon-to-be bride's parents waved at her, and she waved back. Friends and family of the happy couple filled most of the tables. It had also cost the groom a pretty penny to clear out the coffee shop for the fifteen-minute proposal so that all the tables were filled with friends and relatives.

The door opened. The two women entering chatted happily. The unsuspecting future bride innocently bopped inside. The friend who had lured her to the coffee shop winked at Marietta, who had blended into the crowd in the back of the room.

The bride walked up to the counter. "Chai tea…" She looked around. "Hey, this is the coffee shop where I met Trevor."

The man dressed in a huge coffee cup costume with "Chai Tea" written across the front said, "Did someone say chai tea?"

Everyone in the crowd laughed.

The bride-to-be finally saw her prospective fiancé. "Trevor?"

"That's my chai tea," Trevor joked.

Everyone laughed again.

The bride suddenly noticed that everyone in the room was someone she knew.

Trevor got down on one knee, opening a ring box. "I promise to always let you have the chai tea if you'll marry me."

She pressed her fingers to her lips. Her friend stepped back to get out of the pictures Layla was taking and the video Jake was filming.

"Yes! Yes! I'll marry you!"

The big cup of chai tea began to dance. Friends and relatives got up from the tables and approached to congratulate the happy couple.

Marietta stayed in the back, but she smiled. Another good proposal in the books. She watched them hug their parents and siblings, so happy, each had tears in their eyes. They were both in their midthirties but Marietta saw only their innocence. They naively believed that this happiness would last forever. But wait until the first time she burned his toast.

For some reason or another the bride's mother suddenly morphed into her mom. The bride's dad into her dad. She remembered her proposal with stunning clarity—

Her stomach soured. Her ex might have planned the most wonderful proposal, outside, spring birds chirping, family and friends laughing and weeping with joy, but the marriage had been a disaster.

Painful.

Filled with anxiety and depression.

Marietta gulped in a quick breath. She'd done at least a hundred proposals in the past year and not once had she had this kind of reaction. Remembering her own proposal? Superimposing her own family over the bride's? What was that—

The answer hit her quickly. *That* was the result of seeing Rico with her family. Once he and her brothers had clicked, there was no stopping him. He swam with the kids, helped get the pig out of the pit and absolutely charmed her mother by making blueberry pancakes for breakfast Sunday morning.

He fit with her family as if he belonged there.

Her chest tightened. All the air seemed to disappear from the room.

Not just because she didn't want to get married again, but because Rico fitting in lent a certain permanence to their situation.

Or made her the bad guy if she didn't want him coming to Texas with her or if she tried to put some distance between them.

"Marietta?"

At the sound of Jake's voice, she shook her head and brought herself out of her confusing thoughts. Rico had his own life. He had no intention of taking over hers.

"What's up?"

"We're done and the coffee shop owner says we have five

minutes before our time is all used up. He wants his space back."

"You have the video and Layla has the pictures. The happy couple is laughing. I'd say our work here is done." She handed her clipboard to Layla. "Just let me say our goodbyes to everyone."

She walked toward the newly engaged couple but stopped suddenly, facing Layla and Jake again. "You two can go back to the office if you're ready."

Jake said, "Okay," and headed for the door. Layla followed him. In seconds they disappeared up the busy Manhattan street.

Marietta approached the future bride and groom, shaking her head. It was weird that she'd zoned out like that. Not just imagining her family but also forgetting to dismiss Layla and Jake. It wasn't like her to get distracted. People who wanted to keep their jobs stayed focused. And she could not afford to lose her job, her independence.

It would never happen again.

When Rico called her that night, as he did most nights, she even more clearly understood why all those strange things had happened to her that day. She and Rico were getting too close. Close enough that their situation reminded her of her first marriage, and close enough that worry about Rico edging his way into her life had sounded through her brain like a warning.

Maybe it was time to put some real distance between them?

When he called the following night, she didn't pick up. He left a message, and she didn't return his call until late that night when she knew he'd be fast asleep in London. She told him she was extremely busy and suggested that he not come to Manhattan that weekend.

"I'll be doing two proposals a day. It's springtime. Everything's starting to bloom so people see the nice scenery as the perfect chance to have a beautiful setting for their proposal."

She disconnected the call feeling odd. Not like a liar…because she did have many proposals to oversee that weekend. The odd feeling was more like confusion. Telling him not to visit was the right thing to do—

So why did she feel horrible?

Rico had no problem with not going to Manhattan that weekend. He almost wondered how they'd gotten into the habit of spending so much time together—except he had a plane and a very uncomplicated life. He could pretty much be anywhere he wanted to be anytime he wanted to be there. He'd simply taken advantage of his freedom.

But after replying to his phone messages with texts all week, she begged off the next weekend and the one after that. Though he hated that they were talking through technology, not to each other, Rico refused to let himself be suspicious. She had a job. It was spring, April now. Her weekends were full of proposals and her weeks were filled with planning those events.

Respecting her workload, he didn't call her at all that week and, taking a page from her book, Friday afternoon he didn't call but texted about coming to Manhattan that weekend. Seconds later, he sighed as he read her text that she was too busy again for him to visit, but as he tossed his phone to a nearby table, it rang.

Hoping it was Marietta saying she'd changed her mind, he scooped it up, then frowned when he saw it was Antonio.

"Hey, Antonio. What's up?"

"GiGi's throwing a party tomorrow afternoon. It's last-minute, outside in the big entertainment area. It's not warm enough to swim but it will be fun to get together with all our friends. You can come, right?"

He thought of his disappointing text from Marietta and sighed with relief that he had something to get his mind off that.

"Yes. I'm totally free." So free he was excited over an unexpected invitation? To stay at the home of his friend's *grandmother*? That was so wrong he almost couldn't believe what he was feeling.

Or maybe he couldn't believe what he'd been doing. He'd thrown himself so far into Marietta's life that it had taken him weeks to realize she didn't want him there.

Glad he'd caught himself before he did something really off the wall, he called his pilot, packed a bag and was in GiGi's social room a few hours later, holding a glass of wine. Antonio was already there with Lorenzo and Juliette. The party was scheduled for the next day in the outside entertainment space, but it was good to be with his friends and feel normal again. Not like an unwanted guest—

Though Marietta had never made him feel unwanted and she'd been thrilled the weekend they'd visited her parents. Her family had loved him.

None of it made any sense.

Riley suddenly burst into the room, as if she'd run to get there.

She sat in the big chair with Antonio, and he kissed her cheek. "Okay, now?"

"Sure." She smiled weakly. "I'm fabulous."

GiGi said, "Rico, this is why we're glad you could come a day before the party."

Lorenzo and Juliette sat up weirdly, as if coming to attention. Antonio grinned. Riley said, "We're going to have a baby too!"

Rico blinked. "What? That's amazing! Marietta will be so thrilled!"

He rose to shake Antonio's hand as Riley said, "Oh, she was thrilled. She's talking about video calling and making tons of visits so our kids will know each other."

Though it gave him a weird jolt to realize Marietta had

known about this baby before he did—known and hadn't told him—he hugged Riley.

But after a quick embrace, she pulled away and fell to her chair again as if dizzy. "I may have to miss dinner."

Juliette raced over to check on her.

Antonio said, "She has terrible *morning* sickness…that lasts all *day*."

"Marietta hasn't really been sick at all." Rico felt like a fraud saying that. How did he know Marietta hadn't been sick? He hadn't seen her in weeks. Sure, January and February seemed to go okay. But he'd barely seen her in March. What if she'd been keeping him away because she didn't feel well?

"Yeah, she's amazing," Juliette said. "You wouldn't even know she was pregnant. She's like a busy bee. She wanted to be here but apparently getting engaged in April has become a thing in Manhattan."

A weird sensation passed through Rico. He hated hearing about the mother of his child secondhand, from her boss.

But that was their life, the way they'd decided to live—

No. It wasn't. They'd decided to continue their romance until it ran its course. They'd promised to be honest when their feelings dimmed or died.

But if her feelings had dimmed or died, she hadn't said that. She'd used work as an excuse to get him out of her life and—damn it—he was not accepting that. If she wanted out, she had to say it. That was their promise to each other.

The reverse marriage vows.

Still, he couldn't leave the Salvaggios when they were having a party for Antonio and Riley to announce their good news. But Sunday morning? He was out of here.

Marietta had some explaining to do.

CHAPTER FIFTEEN

HE LEFT FLORENCE so early that with the time difference he arrived in New York just after sunrise. It took an hour to get from the airport to Manhattan. Coffee shops and newspaper stands were open and doing business on the warm Sunday morning, giving him an idea. If Marietta wasn't awake when he arrived, he could make breakfast. The scent of bacon would wake her slowly and she'd be fully conscious by the time she came out into the kitchen. He would not surprise her.

Just to be sure, he sent her a text before he opened her apartment door with the key she'd given him the day she'd moved in. He'd been taken aback by the gesture, but she'd said that as their baby's dad, he should have access to the house, just in case.

He wasn't sure what "just in case" entailed, but he knew what she meant. Still, that made her refusal to see him the past few weeks even odder.

He carried the bacon, eggs and bagels that he'd bought in an open convenience store to the center island, not hearing a sound from her bedroom.

Shrugging out of his jacket, he headed for the stove and found appropriate frying pans, but before he even lit a burner, she came up the hall yawning.

"What are you doing here?"

Her voice sounded so wonderful that he couldn't turn from the cabinets. He needed a minute to get control of the emotions that burned through him. Need for her collided with the knowledge that she hadn't wanted him here. And he knew today would be the day he would confront her about forcing him to stay away. They would make decisions. Most of them not in his favor. And God only knew when he'd see her again.

His heart stuttered as he said, "I'm about to make breakfast. I sent you a text."

"I saw it. But aren't you supposed to be in Florence?"

His pain increased with the reminder that she knew things about him because of the Salvaggios and the Salvaggios knew things about *her*, about his baby, because of Riley.

The horrible feeling of being left out, being that foster kid who didn't belong anywhere, rumbled through him like a thunderstorm. He wasn't angry with Marietta or even the Salvaggios. It was more that he was tired of life treating him so shabbily…like an afterthought.

He turned to find her standing on the other side of the island, dressed in a T-shirt and yoga pants. Her hair billowed around her like a red-blond veil—then he saw it. Her stomach. The shirt, big as it was, had somewhere to fall, something to fit.

His heart stuttered. "You're showing?"

"Not really." She ran her hands down her belly, making the little bump obvious. "I have grown out of most of my pants, but I don't think I look pregnant."

He laughed. "Oh, you do. Just not to other people yet." He walked over and put his hands on her shoulders. "But I've seen that tummy flat as a pancake." His hands fell from her shoulders, down her arms and to the hem of her shirt. He slid them under the soft material to the swell of their child.

"Oh, my God. It's…" He felt the softness of her skin that protected their child and the bump that was their child. "Amazing."

Emotion overwhelmed him and he pulled her to him, hugging her. "Are you sure you're okay? Riley's throwing up and looks like death warmed over."

"I'll tell her you said that."

Even though the rumor mill that passed between all the women who worked at Juliette and Riley's companies annoyed him, right now it made him laugh. "Seeing her made me worry about you."

He hugged her again, feeling things he could neither define nor describe. She looked fine, hail and healthy, but that was a blessing. Their baby was a blessing. Marietta was a blessing, and he couldn't stop hugging her.

If they were breaking up today, he wanted one last chance to be with her.

A hug had never felt so good to Marietta. She hadn't seen him in a month. Hadn't let herself actually speak to him. Only listened to the sound of his voice in his increasingly short messages. And she knew he had grown weary of her avoiding him.

To have him here, holding her, made her want to weep. She melted into him, unable to stop herself, as tears filled her eyes and the sense of rightness billowed around them.

But she told herself it was pregnancy hormones, even though she allowed herself to stay right where she was enveloped in his arms, happy for the first time in weeks.

The joy of seeing him collided with the cold, hard fear of losing her independence, being subject to someone else's wishes and will, and formed a lump in her chest. As good as he felt, as desperate as she was to hold him, she knew the consequences of their staying close.

He very quietly said, "So, food first, or should we go back to your bedroom and say hello properly?"

She wasn't as hungry as she was desperate. Half of her had longed to see him. The other half kept shouting warnings. Still, the warnings acted as a reminder that all of this was temporary. And she would know to be strong in the bad conversation that was to follow.

She stepped back, caught his hand and led him to her bedroom.

He stripped off his T-shirt the second they stepped into her room. His jeans followed. But when she reached to remove her T-shirt, he caught her hands.

"Let me." He laughed. "It's like unwrapping a present."

Guilt filled her. He liked this. Liked her. But she would have to put an end to it before she got in too deep...or he did. That was her real fear. She always knew to hold back, but he sometimes tumbled over into emotions because he didn't have a bad marriage in his past to show him how dangerous they were. With little to no knowledge of family, he was the wild card.

He lifted her shirt over her head, tossing it away before he bent and kissed her breasts. His lips then followed a path to her stomach. They smoothed over her baby bump reverently. Then he looked up at her and smiled. "This is amazing."

She agreed. It was amazing. And she was going to shatter when he had to leave her as a companion and only connect with her as their baby's dad. But it was the right thing to do, better than losing her independence.

He eased away from their baby bump and rose to kiss her. Wrapping her arms around his shoulders, she allowed herself the pleasure of feeling him, memorizing the texture of his skin and the shape of his shoulders. He slid his hands to her bottom and rid her of the yoga pants before he eased her onto the bed with him.

He went slow. Tasting her. Teasing her. Sending electricity through her and regret. But she knew the right thing to do. Let him go. She took her turn enjoying the feel of him under her lips and fingertips and straddled him to complete their union. He took advantage of her position to cruise her skin, as if memorizing the shape of her. But that only increased her need until one final movement sent her over the edge.

They didn't drift apart. She couldn't. Knowing they were about to create those dividing lines for their relationship killed her. She rolled over to nestle against him as he laid his head on the pillow. His hand fell to her back and stroked softly.

"There is something we need to discuss."

She squeezed her eyes shut. For every bit that she knew this was necessary, it still hurt. "Yeah?"

"We made a promise to each other. I thought that meant we wouldn't play games or hedge when it came to our relationship. I thought we were supposed to be honest when we no longer wanted to be romantically involved."

She took a long breath, not sure what he was saying. But before she could think of a reply, he added, "I don't understand. To me, it seems like our romance is alive and well. I mean, I know that attraction fizzles eventually, but I felt like we had a good year ahead of us before we tired of this."

He made a motion with his hand, sort of encircling them both, and her heart stuttered. She'd forgotten their deal. He hadn't. Even if he was having thoughts that went beyond raising the baby together, he didn't intend to act on them. He still wanted their deal. The one that assured they would walk away, wouldn't cling, wouldn't try to possess the other. The one that guarded her independence.

She said, "You give us a whole year?" Buying time as her brain continued to process the fact that he wasn't going to pressure her into something she didn't want.

"You don't? I mean, correct me if I'm wrong, but you seemed to have missed me."

She all but purred against him, as everything he said

soaked into her emotion-filled brain and brought her to the conclusion that she'd misread him, misread what was happening between them. "I did."

"Then what was the cold shoulder about? You wouldn't even answer a phone call, let alone let me visit."

"I was busy." Not a lie. She was busy. And she felt foolish for jumping to the conclusion that Rico had changed his mind about their relationship. Then there was the matter that she hadn't fessed up to those fears or confronted him. She'd backed away—

A leftover from her awful marriage. Keith could never handle the truth. Avoidance became the way they communicated.

She suddenly realized how wrong that was. And that Rico was an honest guy who didn't want hard feelings between them. He wanted honesty.

Oh, God! The only way they could ever raise a child together would be if they were honest and she'd blown the first test!

She should have told him she worried he was getting too close.

"So is spring proposal season over?"

She laughed. A sense of lightness filled her. Rico would never trap her as Keith had. She could relax. Enjoy.

"I'm afraid spring proposal season is in full swing and when it ends summer proposal season will start."

He snorted. "That's some job you have."

She nestled against him and traced a circle on his chest. "Actually, it's a fabulous job. Layla may be leaving us when she graduates NYU. But we're training Jake to handle proposals on his own."

"The videographer with the long hair who's always in jeans?"

"Yes. We can hire another person to video the proposals.

But he's seen so many in the past two years that he could oversee the simpler ones. As he gets better, he could plan and oversee more complex ones."

Still skeptical, he said, "The guy in the jeans?"

She laughed and playfully punched him. "Yes. You don't have to be romantic and bubbly to fulfill someone else's wishes. You have to listen. He does. You have to do what they want. He follows directions wonderfully. And you have to show up. No one is better at showing up than Jake is."

"Okay. Jake it is… Does this mean you're going to have free time?"

She nodded. "By summer…yes."

"That's great!"

"I'm going to have this child in late September. I'll need a few months off, time to establish a routine and hire someone to watch the baby once I go back to work."

"I'll help."

Unafraid now that she knew he didn't want anything permanent, only wanted to let their attraction run its course, she smiled at him. "You know, if you wanted to…you could be here during the months I'm off."

"I think I'd like to be here a few weeks *before* you have the baby. You know…to make sure you get to the hospital. That kind of stuff."

She laughed and angled up to kiss him. "I'll know to get myself to the hospital."

"What if there's a complication?"

"Eh. Maybe it would be good to have you here."

He rolled his eyes. "Other women would be thrilled if the father of their child took this much interest."

Seeing the disappointment on his face, she sobered. She shelved the sassiness that always helped her keep her distance and was honest with him, the way he wanted her to be.

"I am thrilled. I love that our child will have both parents. And I'll help establish a routine for you in London if you want."

"You'd be okay with me taking the baby to London?"

"Well, it might be better for you to visit here for the first year. But after that, our child should know how you live too. He should see your world, find his part in your life."

He nodded. "Makes sense."

She nestled against him again, totally relieved. They'd planned out an entire year. Technically, she'd made the dividing line. He wouldn't "live with" her for the full year after the baby was born, but she wouldn't stop him from having long visits if that was what he wanted. But after that year, everything would change. Their child would be able to visit him in London. There'd be no need for him to spend weeks or even weekends in Manhattan.

They now had an ending.

And she could relax and enjoy their relationship until that time came.

CHAPTER SIXTEEN

RICO HAD NEVER been happier. With the proposal planning business being what it was, he decided to go to London on the weekends and spend weekdays at her house. He got into the habit of picking her up after work, and because he had a car, he found himself carting her and Jake to venues for nighttime proposals.

But he didn't mind. He enjoyed feeling like part of her life. He got to know Juliette better. He watched Jake go from being a kid in blue jeans who took the videos to being the guy in dress slacks and a white shirt *overseeing* the kid who took the videos.

Watching him in the back corner of a restaurant where a doctor had just proposed to his girlfriend and a string quartet was entertaining the crowd of well-wishers and other restaurant patrons who'd loved seeing the proposal, Rico faced Marietta. "You have a good eye."

"Because I knew to train Jake?" She shrugged. "I can't take credit. Riley suggested it even before she and Antonio got engaged. After that both of our worlds became a whirlwind, so it took us until now to implement that plan."

The string quartet stopped. Patrons went back to eating. The doctor and his new fiancée took their seats again.

Jake walked over to where Rico stood with Marietta.

Marietta hugged him. "That's it. That's the last proposal I'll supervise you. You did great. You're on your own now."

He said, "Thanks," and immediately loosened his tie.

"And you don't have to dress so formally for proposals. You can go back to wearing jeans, as long as you stay in the background."

"I always stay in the background. No one wants their proposal planner in their videos," Jake said.

"Which is why I mentioned you being able to dress down," Marietta said with a laugh. "Any way that you want to dress is fine. Actually, going back to your jeans might be a good idea. Guys relate to you. It's fun watching how you can so easily get them talking about what they want."

Jake snorted, then shook his head. "I've got to admit, it's a skill I never would have believed I have."

"Good."

Rico dangled his car keys. "Need a lift somewhere?"

"No. I'm going back to the office. You and Marietta can head home. I'll walk."

He said goodbye and left the restaurant. The happy couple who'd gotten engaged also left, snuggled together, happy, settled.

Watching them, an unexpected longing for that kind of contentment rippled through Rico. He was sort of dating, sort of living with, definitely having a baby with a woman who was very happy when he was around. She'd whisper the naughtiest suggestions to him when they talked on the phone the weekends when he was in London. She was openly affectionate.

But she was happy with things the way they were. She didn't want anything permanent. Even suggesting they should make some kind of commitment would probably send their relationship into a tailspin.

And what did it matter? He was happy too. He didn't need to muddy the waters by wanting something permanent. He was a grown-up with a very good life. The life he wanted—

That thought brought him up short again. Not because he hadn't thought that before, but because right now, in this moment, the simple idea that he had the life he wanted seemed to take on a deeper, richer meaning.

This really was the life he wanted.

Staying in Manhattan on weekdays, instead of weekends, he met Ethan O'Banyon for lunch every Wednesday. He'd bought an SUV to keep in the hangar he'd rented for his plane. He slept with Marietta, made her breakfast, took her to work—

Good Lord. He was putting down roots. He was doing happy couple things. His subconscious was pointing that out because changing their life without even realizing it was how people got hurt—

Except he couldn't see it ending in hurt. He couldn't see them ending at all. They fit. He fit into her life. She hadn't had to change a thing to add him into her world. And he'd found his place there. They *were* living as a happy couple.

As Marietta collected her things to leave the restaurant, the realization coalesced. He didn't have the sense that he should protect himself. After years of guarding his heart, keeping his distance, he'd found the place he wanted to stay.

Forever.

But he didn't dare tell her that.

The following night, they were proposal free, so they left the office a little after six and got into his SUV.

"Dinner?"

She shrugged. "It's early. Besides, I'm tired. Maybe we order a pizza?"

He glanced down at her increasing belly. She was heading toward six months along now. Only about ten pounds heavier. But he noticed that she tired easily. And he also noticed that he liked taking care of her, as they casually lived their lives like two people who belonged together. Even though neither one of them acknowledged that.

He started the SUV. "Pizza it is."

She relaxed against the seat with a sigh. "Good." She took a breath, then faced him. "My mom's birthday is next week so Dad's having a party on Saturday."

"Oh…"

So much for having the perfect life. With their living arrangements the way they were, he didn't know if she was telling him she'd be in Texas or asking him to go with her.

"I realize you like spending weekends in London because of my work schedule, but I know she'd love it if you'd come."

She'd love it if he'd come. Her mom. They weren't just a couple. Marietta made him sound like family.

But he didn't think Marietta realized how casually she'd included him. Which totally baffled him. Unless she was growing out of her fear of a commitment? They were happy. Their life was easy. Maybe she was changing her beliefs the same way he was changing his?

Still, this wasn't the time to ask. He wasn't even sure of his feelings yet. And the last thing he wanted to do was push her to the point that she kicked him out of her life again.

"Is your dad roasting a pig?"

"Now, don't get spoiled. He doesn't do a pig for every party." She laughed. "But he is for this one."

"Sweet."

She laughed again and took out her phone to order a pizza. By the time they got to her building, it had been delivered. They gave a slice to Tony, that night's doorman, along with a tip for accepting the order for them.

They ate the pizza in front of the TV and when they crawled into bed she fell asleep almost immediately.

He lay beside her watching the slight rise and fall of the covers as she breathed. A sense of comfort stole through him.

Peace like he'd never known. And the final piece of the puzzle tiptoed through his brain.

He belonged.

Not just with her family. Not just in her life as a helpmate. But with her.

With her.

The absolute surety of it stole his breath. He'd never had a thought like that. Never. He'd always been so sure there was nowhere that he belonged. No one he belonged to or belonged with.

But he belonged with her.

He loved her.

Holy hell. He loved someone. He'd never felt this way about anyone or anything…but his instincts told him this was love.

They flew to Texas that weekend and arrived at the ranch house like family, not visitors. He knew the way to the room where he took their luggage. Her mom kissed him hello. Her dad slapped his back and told him to come outside and sit by the pig with him.

He soaked in the sense of belonging. He knew it was an extension of his feelings for Marietta. But he also knew that while his feelings with her family were dependent on his feelings for her, his feelings for her weren't dependent on outside forces.

He loved her. And if keeping her in his life meant never mentioning that, that was a sacrifice he'd make.

It killed him to recognize that it was the right thing to do. He'd never felt this kind of love or the urge to tell her, to act on it, but the last thing she wanted was a commitment.

He and her father stepped outside to a blue sky that allowed an unrelenting sun to bathe them in warmth. Guests began arriving with Jell-O salads, three-bean salads, cookies and cupcakes—and gifts. What looked like hundreds of gifts piled on a table to the right of the buffet that also grew with every guest. The air shimmered with heat and friendship.

Rico sat back in his Adirondack chair.

"So, baby in a couple of months?"

The question came from her brother Junior, who had come over to join Rico and Cole. Even before he answered, Danny walked over too.

Accustomed to her family's way of talking, shortening sentences, eliminating verbs sometimes, he said, "Yes. In a few weeks, we'll start putting together a nursery." Talking about the baby, he could see his and Marietta's life together stretching before them in a never-ending wave. He wasn't going to quibble over the word *commitment*. Sometimes actions were better than ceremonies.

"You gonna move from London?"

That question was a little trickier. He'd probably never sell his house in London, but he'd be living with Marietta. It would happen naturally and continue forever. He had absolutely no doubt of that.

His gaze found her in the crowd, laughing with her mom and sisters-in-law. She looked at him and smiled.

Yeah. They would be together forever. Just without the rings.

"I'll be keeping the house in London. But I also intend to help Marietta raise the baby. I'll be in Manhattan a lot."

As if she could read his mind, her pretty smile grew.

Dear God. He really loved her. The feeling was so amazing it nearly overwhelmed him.

Breaking the spell, he shifted his gaze to her dad. "I can work from Manhattan, but, you know, I've been in London for over fifteen years. I don't want to get rid of that house. A person can have more than one house."

Cole batted his hand. "Billionaires. You guys kill me.

You've gotta have a house everywhere. Tell me something. Do all your houses feel like home?"

Rico chuckled, but the question fit with all the thoughts he'd been having. He'd never actually had a home. He'd had foster homes that gave way to living under a bridge that gave way to living in crappy apartments that gave way to better apartments that eventually became the London house—

But none of them had ever felt like home. They were symbols of where he was financially. Stepping stones.

Living with Marietta felt like home.

Living with Marietta *was* home.

The conversation slowed and her two brothers drifted away to get their kids out of the pool or greet new guests.

Cole pulled in a long, content breath. And why not? His house was filled with happy friends and neighbors. His wife loved him. His sons worked the family business. They all adored Marietta. They were a family.

"Are you ever going to make an honest woman out of my daughter?"

Rico almost choked on his beer at the abruptness of the question. He would like nothing better than to marry Cole's daughter, but he knew life didn't always give a person everything they wanted. He would be content with what they had.

"She wouldn't be happy to hear you ask me that. Besides, that's an outdated attitude."

"Yeah. Yeah. I know. You and Marietta are very hip."

Rico snorted at Cole's use of the word *hip*.

"Come on. Sell that house. Move to Manhattan. I know you want to."

He did.

But he also respected Marietta's wishes. Meaning, he also wouldn't discuss them with her dad.

"My house in London is home base."

Cole's face scrunched in confusion. "What does that even mean?"

"It's…you know…if someone wants to find me that's where they look."

"Or they could call your cell phone. You don't have to have a home base anymore. People can reach you from anywhere anytime," Cole said with a laugh, but he sobered suddenly. "All joking aside, Rico, I've never seen Marietta this happy. It's as if her past didn't happen. I don't know you well, but I can see you're happy too. Not sure what kind of sign you two think you have to get to tell you that you need to make a commitment, but you do. You and my daughter created a child, and kids need security. They need to know you are going to be around to keep them safe and make their supper." He rose from the seat. "I know I sound like a meddling old man right now…but in Texas a dad's got the right to say his piece. That's mine. My daughter loves you. Intentional or not, you started a family. Make it official."

Cole left and Rico found Marietta in the crowd and joined her conversation, but Cole's words haunted him the rest of the afternoon. Not because he didn't like Marietta's dad's interference, but because deep down Rico knew he was right. He loved Marietta and when she snuggled against him in bed that night with a contented sigh, he knew she loved him too.

He didn't want to push her into something she didn't want. But was it really out of line to help her to see they belonged together?

It might not be. He looked at their relationship as evolving and if her dad was to be believed, being together had changed her too.

Still, he didn't know that for sure.

Driving to the airport the next day, Rico sneaked a peek at her. He felt things for her he had never believed existed, but they also had a deal. Still, that might actually be the way to approach this. From the vantage point of their deal.

He suddenly had a flash of guilt for wanting a commitment with someone who'd made it clear she didn't want one.

Worse, he had no idea what he would do if she said no.

The last time she'd thought they were getting too close she'd kept them apart for almost a month.

That was the risk he was facing.

But the other risk was that they'd fall apart or drift apart. There were too many ways they could drift apart if they didn't at least have a commitment conversation, and he didn't want that. He wanted to grow old with her.

He really and truly wanted to ask her to marry him.

The conclusion surprised him so much he could have wrecked the car, but it was right. He knew it was right.

CHAPTER SEVENTEEN

THE FOLLOWING WEEKEND, with Rico in London, Marietta's condo echoed with silence. She reminded herself that a baby would fill her house with noise and happiness, but her thoughts took a horrible turn.

She began imagining herself as an abject failure as a mom. Most of her thoughts were based on the horrible insults her husband would hurl at her when she couldn't get pregnant.

You can't do anything right.

You're worthless.

You're weak.

She wasn't weak. She was strong.

She was strong enough that she hadn't had thoughts like these in years. Literally years. They could have been from normal fear as her due date approached or maybe pregnancy hormones, but realistically she knew making two trips to Texas so close together had probably brought them back. Memories of dating Keith and getting married in her parents' backyard had risen from her subconscious, but being pregnant seemed to make them worse.

Like it or not there was a connection between a baby and her ex. The baby she couldn't give to him. His anger and outbursts. That was when the insults would fly. Normally, a person would think that being pregnant should end all her doubts. After all, her getting pregnant pointed to the idea that perhaps Keith was the one who couldn't conceive. Instead, being pregnant seemed to bring back her insecurities.

And that was wrong.

That was also why people had friends. Riley would remind her that she was fine. Better than fine. She was pregnant. She had a new job where she was a leader. She had a home. A condo she'd purchased.

She walked back to the soon-to-be nursery, which currently housed a table for her laptop and a comfortable chair. She ambled to the comfortable chair and hit a few keys on the laptop to video call Riley.

She answered on the first ring. "Hey!"

"Hey! I didn't expect you to answer so quickly."

"I was working on my computer… I'm thinking about adding a new arm to the business."

"Are you up to that? I know you've been sick."

Riley studied her friend. "I was. That's mostly gone now, but we'll talk about that in a minute. Your eyes are tired. Are you not sleeping?"

"I'm fine. I'm just…having some thoughts."

"Thoughts?"

"Yeah. Remembering things my ex-husband would say when we couldn't get pregnant." She batted a hand. "You know what? It's foolish stuff. Things that I know aren't true. I'm fine."

"You aren't fine, or you wouldn't have called me. Just talk about it. You'll feel better."

She sucked in a breath. "Okay. Honestly, I know being pregnant affects people differently. And I know going to Texas twice in the past few weeks has…you know, brought some things to mind. But every time Rico goes to London, the quiet in the condo leaves an opening for thoughts to creep in."

"Makes sense," Riley answered casually. "That marriage

was harder than you let on. You kept a lot inside and while another person might believe getting pregnant would prove once and for all your ex was wrong…reminders are a weird thing."

She blew her breath out on a sigh. "So, you agree that's it? That I'm just being reminded of things?"

"There are a lot of connections going on. Getting pregnant. Going to Texas. Thinking about being a mom. How could you not have a flashback or two from all those years you tried to get pregnant and couldn't?"

That was exactly what the thoughts were. Flashbacks. Not current or even applicable to what was happening now. Just old memories.

She laughed. "You're right."

"Tell the thoughts to take a hike," Riley said. "They're just thoughts. Just things a miserable man said to make you feel like you were to blame. We all know that you weren't."

She ran her hands down her face. "You're right. And seriously, the only time I think about these odd things is when Rico's in London."

Rico arrived at the Manhattan condo, using his key to let himself inside. He hadn't waited until Monday morning to leave London. He'd flown out early. He liked the daily ritual of taking Marietta to work. And, thanks to a long conversation with proposal planner Jake the week before, he also had a plan to ease changing their deal—committing to each other—into a discussion.

He'd actually met with Jake to arrange a proposal. He'd considered every possible way for him and Marietta to have the talk about making their relationship permanent and they all seemed blah. Worse, all of them gave her a way to push the discussion to another time. But watching one of Marietta's proposals, he'd realized that emotion always won the day at those events, and if he asked Marietta to marry him among friends and family, with him being sincere and vulnerable, their emotion would overwhelm them, and they'd hug and kiss and everything would be decided.

When he'd said it, Jake had winced.

"First of all, I think you two belong together. So getting married is a good thing."

Glad Jake agreed with him, Rico waited expectantly, until Jake said, "But you can't take her to Central Park and spring the idea of getting married on her. From what I hear, her first marriage was a mess, and she also likes to be in control."

Rico sniffed. "Yeah. I get that. But I'm out of ideas. We never even considered marriage when we got together. In fact, we sort of vowed we wouldn't do it. Now, I don't know how to bring it up. I thought maybe proposing in a really great way might get her to see we should get married."

Jake shook his head. "No. If she sprung a proposal on you that would work, but you proposing to her would be better if it happened naturally. And I think that's why you're out of ideas. I think life's trying to tell you to wait for the moment when the time is right. Be ready. Have the ring. Have the words. And wait for your moment."

Deep down, Rico knew all that. But he'd hoped Jake could come up with an adorable proposal that would somehow get around all the stuff they needed to handle. When he hadn't, Rico knew he was back to square one.

But, as Jake had said, he was ready. He was now on the lookout for the right time, and he'd bought a ring in London.

The silence in her condo confused him until he walked down the hall, heading to the bedroom where he would leave his suitcase, and he heard Marietta talking.

Then he heard Riley's reply. "Maybe the thing to do would be not have Rico go back to London every weekend."

Rico stopped in the hall, just short of the open door. He

didn't want to eavesdrop, but it sounded like the discussion was breaking in his favor.

"Oh, no. No. No. No. I was just thinking exactly the opposite. The only way I'll adjust to the quiet condo is if I experience it more."

He bobbed his head in silent agreement, seeing her logic. But her not liking the quiet of her condo could mean that she missed him a lot more than she let on.

Another point in his favor. Another way to start a conversation where they could reevaluate their relationship.

"Look, you can adjust to the quiet later. Right now, you have to get through this pregnancy. If having Rico around helps with that, I say solve today's problems today and handle tomorrow, tomorrow."

It wasn't just the quiet? She'd had a problem? When he was away? What kind of problem?

"It's just a bunch of wayward thoughts. Ideas planted by a person who wanted to hurt me. Logically I know that. The best way to handle them is to learn to blot them out."

"Yeah, but I think there's more to your feelings when Rico's not around. I think you miss him."

"I do."

Riley laughed. "Because you like him."

"I do! I like him a lot."

Rico smiled. Things were definitely breaking in his favor.

"Honestly, Marietta, I think you two need to get married."

His heart about jumped out of his chest. He fingered the ring box in his jacket pocket. Everything Jake had said seemed to be taking shape. This really was beginning to feel like that spontaneous moment they needed.

Then he heard Marietta say, "We're fine as we are."

"You're not fine. You're in limbo. And you're not the kind of person to live in limbo. You make decisions. You take action. That's why you're feeling funny. You *want* the next step."

Rico stifled a sigh of relief. Things were back to looking good again.

He waited. If Marietta could work through all this on her own with Riley, the discussion of amending their deal and getting married would go a lot easier for him.

"I disagree about us getting married. And you should too! We were just talking about what a creep Keith was. I don't want to get into that again."

Riley immediately came to his defense. "Rico's not like that."

"Not now."

His face scrunched in confusion.

"Just wait until things go wrong. Wait until he can't have his own way." She sucked in a breath. "I've seen the bad side of a great guy."

"Keith was not a great guy."

Antonio's voice calling for Riley came through the computer.

Riley said, "I'm in here."

"GiGi and I are waiting for you to come to dinner."

She winced. "Sorry. I must have been working longer than I thought."

Marietta shook her head. "No. I'm sorry. I didn't mean to keep you."

"Are you kidding? I love talking to you! And we can pick this up later if you want. We'll talk about something happier than your horrible ex."

Marietta laughed. "Okay. Maybe I'll call tomorrow."

Riley said, "Sounds good," then she disconnected the call.

Rico stood outside the bedroom door, his thoughts scrambled, his mind whirling. He didn't even have the brainpower to get himself away from the door. Just stood there as she walked out of the room.

Her eyes widened. "Rico!"

"I'm not that guy."

"What?" She studied him for a second and he watched recognition change her expression. "You heard our conversation."

"Only the last two minutes. I would have walked by the door, but Riley said something about you having a problem and I stopped. I wanted to hear it so I could help you."

She pulled in a breath. "I'm sorry if what you heard offended you."

"It didn't offend me. It confused me. I'm not your ex and I'm glad. I've heard nothing but crap about him every time I went to Texas. Your marriage didn't fall apart because you couldn't get pregnant. It fell apart because Keith was a narcissist."

"No. My parents like to think everything was Keith's fault, but there were issues. He started off a nice guy and our issues ruined him."

"Is that really what you believe?"

"Yes and no. I get it that he was self-centered and when things got complicated, he couldn't handle not getting what he wanted."

He released the ring box, let it fall from his hand and nestle into the soft material of his pocket.

This was not his moment. Not even close.

"But in the beginning, he was a good guy."

"You are more generous with him than I would have been. But what's interesting is that you gave him the benefit of the doubt. But you won't give me the benefit of the doubt. You're sure I'm going to become just like him."

"Maybe you're right." She took a breath. "But it doesn't matter. You and I have already been through this. We made a plan. We're going to have a baby and raise that child happily because we aren't going to let arguments and different needs get in the way. We're going to work together."

He watched her eyes for a few seconds because it was his turn to draw some conclusions. Their pact didn't just protect her from their relationship souring. She saw it as a wall. Something that completely separated them.

"And you think us getting too involved, or even liking each other too much, risks what we have?"

"It's not the 'liking' that's the risk. It's expectations that cause friction. We won't have that."

He stepped back, as the full force of what she said hit him. "No. If we're not supposed to like each other, or care enough about our relationship to try to straighten out points where we disagree, then we won't have any emotion at all."

"We'll have love for our child."

He nodded but his heart splintered into a million pieces. They couldn't go forward because she couldn't stop looking back, building barriers that prevented them from repeating what she saw as mistakes. He didn't question what she was saying or how she felt. Having been disappointed by love, he'd also shied away for years. But knowing her had changed him. Falling in love with her, thinking he finally understood love, those things had changed him.

But falling for him hadn't done that for her. Her disappointment with relationships didn't merely linger. It informed what she believed about love. It still colored how she looked at life. How she looked at *him*.

If the strength of what he felt didn't even make an impression, everything he believed he was experiencing was a mirage.

The sense of belonging.

Having a place.

Being in love.

Those had all been illusions.

He turned and headed toward the door again. This time was different—given that he had an expensive suitcase in hand, not a trash bag of his belongings as he'd always had when a foster home didn't work out—but the feeling of being let down was the same as he took the familiar long steps to get away.

It was the story of his life. Nothing was permanent. Especially not emotion. Or love.

She called after him. "You're going?"

"I think I'll stay uptown tonight and head home tomorrow."

"Wait!" Her voice was incredulous, not filled with fear or sadness. Only surprise that their discussion was causing him to leave. "You don't have to go."

He stopped, turned. "I think I do. At first, I thought we were on the same page about our relationship, so I couldn't believe you didn't see we were changing. But now I understand. We're looking at our situation two different ways. I sort of edged myself into your life, but you haven't even tried to fit me into yours." He sniffed a laugh. "I also see why. While I was finding things in common with you...making a connection, you were always holding back, keeping me in the place you thought I fit, keeping your world as close to what you wanted as you could." He turned back toward the door, but quickly pivoted to face her again. "I get it. I do. No one wants to wake up one day and find themselves in a bad relationship. I understand. You just don't feel for me what I feel for you."

He took a breath. "Call me if you need anything. But no more visits. In fact, when the baby's born, I'll get a nanny so I can have time with him or her on my own. We don't have to see each other again."

With that he left. He stepped through the door, into the

hall and stopped only long enough to take another breath to shift gears.

He wished he was angry. But he wasn't. He was familiar with rejection. He'd handled the hurt of it, the stinging pain of realizing he was on his own, hundreds of times before.

He would handle it again.

But this would be different. Maybe for the first time in his life, he had let himself love someone and she'd rejected him. Before, he could always say that as long as he held himself back the rejection wasn't personal, but this time he'd loved. He'd felt the joy of it. Now he felt the wave of pain.

And, again, even as it made him understand why she held back, it made the heartache immeasurably worse.

CHAPTER EIGHTEEN

MARIETTA WOKE ALONE—AGAIN. Only this time she knew it was permanent. She tried to tell herself that while being alone, being hurt, feeling empty was what she'd been trying to avoid, she couldn't escape the inevitable reality that she had landed here anyway.

Because that's what happened in relationships. People got hurt.

She rolled out of bed, showered and dressed, talking to the baby, who was active now. Twice she swore he or she had tried to punch her.

Sadness hit her. She didn't even know if her baby was a boy or a girl. They'd decided not to learn the sex of the baby because they'd wanted to be surprised together in the delivery room. But what fun would it be to be alone when she got the news?

Telling herself not to think about that, she took the subway to work and hurried to her desk. She told herself she wasn't hiding from the heartache of losing Rico and knowing she'd broken his heart. She simply had a lot of planning and budgeting and supervising to do. Luckily, the complexities of accounting would keep her so involved that nothing else would have a chance to sneak in.

The first week that Rico was gone, she'd convinced herself she was upset because she'd hurt him. The second week, when Marietta had fallen into full-fledged depression, she couldn't be so detached. She missed him. With lots of time to think through everything he'd said, she realized he could see their future as something more than them being polite to each other while they raised a child. He saw them sharing a house, bouncing their little boy or girl on their knee, fixing dinner, putting this child to bed, then sharing a bed.

She'd believed he was being dreamy or starry-eyed. But after another two weeks without him, she could see his vision and realize that it all sounded right.

Not because she hated being alone. That was just a symptom of a bigger issue. She loved him. Somehow love had sneaked by her defenses and she'd fallen. Almost accidentally.

When she'd come to that conclusion, it had knocked everything else out of her brain. They'd spent months together. It should not shock her that she'd developed strong feelings.

But as he'd said, she'd kept him at a distance. He'd eased his way into her world. She'd stayed out of his. As if she wanted no part of him. No wonder he'd been hurt.

She ran her hand across her forehead. He probably hated her.

If he didn't, he should.

She hadn't given an inch in their relationship.

That was supposed to protect her from this pain, but it hadn't.

Jake knocked on the frame of her office door. "I have last month's hours for you to approve."

She forced herself to look happy and chipper. "Need me to authorize overtime?" she teased.

His face reddened. "Actually, I'm not taking money. I'd like two mornings off to compensate for two of the nights I worked last week."

She took the spreadsheet he handed her. "Doctor's appointments?"

He winced. "Dates."

"Oh."

Embarrassed that she'd inadvertently delved into his personal life, she put her attention on his spreadsheet. Looking over the entries, she almost signed it. Then she saw *Mendoza=canceled*.

"Mendoza is Rico's last name."

His face reddened again. "I know."

Just the mention of his name sent longing through her. But Mendoza was a common name. She should have recognized that it could have been any one of the other hundreds of thousands of Mendozas in the greater New York area and let it alone. But something pushed her.

"Did he come to you for a proposal?"

"I don't feel right talking about it."

She arched one eyebrow. "I'm your boss. You're supposed to talk to me about every aspect of your job."

He winced. "Okay. He did want a proposal. But he canceled it."

Her heart sank. He was thinking about proposing to her?

"Actually, I should have taken it off my work page. The whole thing was a nonstarter. He came to me because he wanted a proposal, but I talked him out of it. The entire conversation wasn't more than fifteen minutes."

Common sense told her to end the discussion, as it was a moot point, but some Texas longhorn devil pushed her forward. "*You* talked him out of it?"

"Marietta, I told him he shouldn't spring a proposal on you. But I also told him you wouldn't want anything public. I told him a proposal to you should be intimate."

Her heart stuttered. She could picture it. "Oh."

He started to leave but turned back again. "My conversation with him ended with him agreeing and nothing came of it. I should have erased him from the sheet."

The thought of marrying Rico should have scared her silly,

but with four weeks to think about how much she missed him, and realizing he'd been hinting for more from their relationship, a personal, intimate marriage proposal sounded nothing but romantic.

She tried to bring herself back to reality with a reminder of her ex, but all she remembered was Rico telling her he wasn't that guy. He wasn't her ex. He wasn't like her ex.

Even thinking that he was, was insulting.

No wonder he'd stood his ground.

She'd insulted him.

A week later, she went home to a nursery that was filling with boxes of furniture that she would have to put together, or call her dad to put together.

But she couldn't think about her dad without thinking about how much he'd liked Rico. She leaned against the wall and slid down to the floor. How had she missed all this? How had she missed the signs of how perfect they were for each other?

Because she'd been falling for him, and she'd gotten scared. So she'd protected herself, refusing to see it.

He'd been moving forward, and she'd dug in her heels like a Southern belle on a rampage.

And she'd lost him because of it.

Weeks flew by like minutes for Rico. The only communication he'd had with Marietta was by text. She told him about doctor's appointments, setting up a nursery and hiring a nanny as neutrally as if she'd been telling him the weather.

It did not faze him. The final nail in the coffin of him believing in love had not only been pounded in; it was secure.

He'd always believed he was meant to be alone. The failure of his relationship with Marietta had proved it. He'd reached deep down into his memories and found the strength to go back to being the kid who understood that and made a good life anyway.

He scheduled six weeks off. The last two in September when the baby was due and four weeks in October to have time with his new child. But he wasn't staying with Marietta. He would get his usual hotel suite.

He arrived in Manhattan that sunny September day to find a car waiting for him. That was another thing he'd done. No more owning a vehicle when he was in the city, as if he belonged there. He didn't. He would have a driver at his disposal.

The chauffeur opened the door. He got in, got settled. With an hour's drive into the city, he opened his briefcase and began to work.

His phone rang.

He sighed, picking it up to dismiss the call. But he saw the caller was Juliette and he answered, "Hey, gorgeous! What's up?"

"Rico, I don't know where you are, but you need to get here. Well, not the office, the hospital. Lorenzo and I are on our way out now."

He sat up. "Did something happen with Marietta?"

"Her water broke. Ambulance just took her to the hospital."

"Which hospital?"

She gave the name.

"I just landed at the airport. I'll be there in a few minutes."

"Lorenzo and I will see you there."

They disconnected the call. And for the first time since they'd decided to call it quits, he let himself think of Marietta. Her pretty smile, her wild hair, her stubbornness. He closed his eyes, remembering touching her, loving her.

He shouldn't have feelings for her. If anything, he should think of her like poison ivy and just want to stay away. But worry that something had gone wrong filled him. He had to get to her. He had to help her. He would let himself be neutral again after the baby was born and everything was fine. Because the baby would be okay and so would she. He wouldn't accept anything else.

But right now, she needed him and he would be there.

What felt like an eternity later, he got to the hospital and was directed to the maternity ward. After the typical hustle and bustle of racing through groups of people and riding an elevator, he experienced an unexpected quiet and calm when he arrived on her floor. He went to the desk and once again had to present ID.

Luckily, Lorenzo stepped out of one of the rooms and walked over to the nurses' station. "This is the father of Marietta Fontain's baby."

The nurse nodded. "Go ahead and show him down the hall, Lorenzo."

As they walked away from the nurses' station, Rico said, "Lorenzo? You're on a first-name basis with a nurse?"

He laughed. "It might be like Fort Knox to get in, but once you prove you belong here, the ward atmosphere is very friendly."

They walked into a room where Juliette stood beside Marietta's hospital bed. When she saw him, she stepped back, revealing the see-through bin in which a very tiny baby slept.

He just stared at Marietta and the baby.

Juliette eased Lorenzo out of the room. "We'll give you some privacy."

He walked closer to the bed.

Marietta's lips trembled when she said, "Don't be shy. We are fine and your son wants to meet you."

"I have a son?" Tears filled his eyes. He didn't know what to process first. The baby or the feeling of seeing Marietta again after weeks and weeks apart.

Knowing her feelings about him, though, he held himself

together, didn't give in to the emotions that swamped him. "You're okay?"

She made a strangled noise. "It seems I might lean toward spontaneous deliveries."

"Spontaneous deliveries?"

"My water broke. Juliette called an ambulance. I got to the hospital quickly and by the time they wheeled me up here, Henry was making his way into the world."

He stepped closer. "Henry?"

"Okay. Maybe not Henry. How about Neville?"

He inched closer and peered and across the bed at the red-faced baby. Everything suddenly felt real, not wooden, not the neat little package of strength he had wrapped himself in to protect himself. Wave upon wave of emotion flooded him.

"Oh, my God. That's our baby."

"Remember how you thought it was amazing that my stomach was growing?"

He remembered clearly. It was his first time of truly understanding that they were having a child, and probably the first time he realized that his feelings for her were inching beyond their deal.

He tried to fight those feelings now, but love for her hit him full force. He eased closer to the bed. "I remember."

"Well, holding the baby is a hundred times more amazing."

He didn't doubt that for a second. He had so much trouble struggling against his longing for her that he knew once he held his child, he'd be overwhelmed.

He bought himself some time to pull himself together. "I don't like Neville either."

She laughed. "Yeah. You're right. It sounds very Broadway play to me. How about Stewart?"

His emotions began to click with reality. The baby. Being beside Marietta. Talking like normal people. Even though they were far from normal.

Standing so close to her, he couldn't deny that she was everything he'd always wanted. And maybe he should have fought for her.

But honestly, he hadn't known how. As broken as he was, she was worse. Raw and vulnerable. Leaving her had been the right thing.

Still, they both had to deal with the fact that he would be in her life while they raised their child. "I'm sorry I missed his birth."

She caught his hand and squeezed. The softness of her fingers wrapped around his nearly did him in. "You could have been right next door to the hospital, and you would have missed the birth. It wasn't worth the price of a ticket. He all but bounced on the diving board and jumped out."

He laughed, realizing how much he'd missed her Texas way of looking at life. All the reasons he'd fallen in love with her coalesced, reminding him of why he'd been so willing to take the risk on love when it had done nothing but treat him shabbily.

Still, that was the past. He had to deal with her differently now. Everything was about their child.

"I suppose I have a lot of things to apologize for."

She frowned at him. "Really? Like what?"

"Being so distant these past few weeks." It killed him that he'd stayed away. But standing here now, so close to her, he understood why he'd had to do it. He longed to love her, even more than he had before.

But she didn't want him, and he had to accept that. He had a child now to fill his life. He would make that enough and be grateful. "I was thinking maybe we should name him Cole."

She frowned. "After my dad?"

"I like your dad."

She smiled. "I like him too. And he'll be thrilled for a namesake. But what about Rico Cole."

"He sounds like a soft drink."

She laughed. "How about Cole Michael?"

"Cole Michael?"

"Like Michael the Archangel… If you don't like angels, Michael's simply a very nice name. Strong. But also cute." She frowned. "Oh, shoot. I can see my daddy calling him Mikie."

He tried out the name. "Mikie." He caught her gaze. "I like it."

Her eyes filled with tears. "I do too." He looked so good that her heart hurt. She'd also missed him so much that he could have been covered in dirt and wearing sackcloth and she'd have been happy to see him.

He headed toward the see-through bin in which little Mikie lay. He was finally going to meet his son. And it was her fault he hadn't been here for the birth. He'd wanted to spend the weeks before with her. Then she'd driven him away.

"Now I guess it's my turn to say I'm sorry."

Bent to pick up his son, he raised his head and glanced at her questioningly.

"That argument we had that ended us? That was all on me. You were right. I was afraid. I was judging you by my ex's behavior. I was wrong."

He looked away, not answering. Instead, he reached in, lifting the baby.

She understood why he wouldn't want to talk about that day and changed the subject.

"Rub your cheek against his," Marietta suggested. Though she tried to stop it, her heart swelled seeing him holding their son. "He's like velvet."

He brought their faces together and laughed. "Oh, my God, he's so soft."

This was it. Despite what had happened between them,

he wanted to be part of their son's life and she had to do the right thing. "And he's gonna need a daddy hanging around."

"You might need dynamite to keep me away." He cuddled the baby again. "I almost can't believe it."

"Me neither," she said, her heart stuttering. Though she loved seeing Rico with the baby and knew he didn't want to talk about their argument, she couldn't just let things stand. She'd hurt him and he deserved to know how wrong she'd been. If she left out the argument, there was only one way to show him.

For all her bravado, she wasn't sure she had the chops for this. But she took a long breath and said, "I love you."

He peered over at her. "Do you want me to give you Mikie?"

She shook her head. "No. I wasn't talking to Mikie. I was talking to you." She paused only a second. "I do love you, you know."

He stared at her as if he didn't know what to say. Then the shattered look came to his eyes again and she was lost for a way to fix it. She'd made such a mess of things that she knew she had to be the one to make the first moves, say the right thing, rid them of the awkwardness.

She remembered the way he'd been thinking about proposing to her and knew just how much she'd probably broken his heart. In a world where very few people got a chance to make up for the wrongs they'd done, she actually had one. He might not have asked her to marry him, but she knew he'd wanted to.

And she really wanted him in her life again. Not as the father of her baby. As her everything. He'd seen it before she had, but now that she'd realized it, she also prayed they weren't permanently broken.

This was her chance, her moment. If this didn't set things right, nothing would.

She held his gaze. "I told you I love you because I want to marry you."

* * *

Rico stared at her. He'd stomped down his feelings for weeks, but the second he'd seen her, they had all come storming back. If she hurt him again, he wasn't sure he could survive it.

"Do you think this is the best time for you to be making a life decision? We're both a little overwhelmed right now."

She laughed. "Oh, honey. Sometimes the truth only stands out clearly when we're bombarded by other emotions."

He snorted. "You Texas people have a weird way of looking at life."

He cuddled his son. The click he'd felt the day he'd decided he wanted to marry her returned. The silly, happy emotion of it. He remembered her father's words about a child needing security, but it was the way she made him feel when he was with her that flooded him.

"I'm not saying yes."

Her eyes grew sad. "Okay."

"You're getting this all wrong. I do want to marry you, but I want to be the one to propose."

She peeked up at him. "Really?"

"Yes. And there are some things we need to talk about first. You know, we're going to fight sometimes, right?"

She laughed. "Probably not knockdown, drag-out fights, but yeah we'll disagree."

"And you still want to marry me?"

"Yes. But without the big to-do… I want what we have to be about us. Not how we look to other people. I want us to be honest and fair and talk about things. I want us to be together forever."

His heart melted. He knew what it had cost her to get to this point, but she'd gotten here, and he wouldn't make an issue of it. "That sounds good to me. I watched other people have families my entire life and fought the urge to want one myself. But you made me feel normal. Like I belonged. That's what I want."

"I think we just wrote our marriage vows."

He laughed. "Or maybe we just took the real vow that's going to keep us together. Though I wouldn't mind a small ceremony at the Salvaggios' vineyard."

"Oh, in the summer when we can use GiGi's new outdoor space."

"And all your friends and employees get to fly to Italy again."

She smiled. "They will love that."

Rico stood there, waiting for more. Technically, she'd just agreed to marry him. He was holding his son. The woman who'd changed his entire view of life was his.

He knew it in his heart.

He felt a click, something that felt like surety, like surrender, but in the best way possible.

He returned the baby to his little bin and eased himself onto her bed. "I love you."

Her eyes filled with tears. "I love you too. Ridiculously. I'm sorry it took me so long to see it."

He leaned down and kissed her. But the brief kiss wasn't enough and their tongues twined as he let his hands slide along her arms.

"Someone should call your parents."

She pulled back. "Juliette probably already has." She gasped. "Our condo's too small for them to stay with us. We need to make a reservation at a nice hotel for them. That way they can stay for weeks and we'll all remain sane."

He laughed. It was the kind of problem he'd never thought he would have. But today it was like music to his ears. He'd buy some good bourbon and invite Lorenzo and they'd sit on the terrace of the condo, watching the traffic on the street below, talking about life.

It didn't compare to Texas longhorns, but this was their home now. Manhattan. They might be frequent visitors of Texas and Italy, but this would always be home.

His life really did stretch out before him as happy, content.

He had all the things he'd told his sixteen-year-old self didn't exist.

But now he knew they existed. In abundance. With the right person.

EPILOGUE

THE DAY BEFORE Rico and Marietta were supposed to fly to Italy to help GiGi prepare for their wedding, Rico got a call from Ethan, asking him to meet him at the coffee shop. He thought it odd, considering that Ethan would be seeing him in a week for the wedding celebration, but Ethan insisted.

Twenty minutes later he and Marietta left Mikie with the nanny and walked into the coffee shop that smelled like fresh blueberry muffins and strong beans for brewing.

They got their coffee at the counter and sat across from Ethan at a small table.

Ethan slid a manila envelope across the table to him. "I wasn't ever going to show you this."

Rico frowned. "Show me what?"

He took a breath. "Long before I met you, I was a doctor."

A little surprised, Rico cocked his head. "How did you end up being an investor?"

"I invented a little instrument that became essential in open-heart surgery. Made a mint. Quit work. Became an investor." He paused. "I was a doctor in *Spain*."

Odd feelings clenched Rico's stomach at the way Ethan accented the word *Spain*, but Marietta frowned. "I know you're going somewhere with this, sweetie, but we're not picking up on it."

Ethan drew in a long breath. "One extremely cold night, when I was closing up, a young woman came into my office.

She was already in labor." He shook his head. "No. She was delivering the baby. I barely got her to a table. The whole thing took a minute and a half. I cared for her, wrapped the baby in a towel and left the room to call an ambulance to take her to a hospital and when I got back she was gone."

"My mother." Rico's voice fell flat. The words felt heavy, wooden.

Marietta eased her hand over to his.

Ethan sighed. "I'm fairly certain, you were the baby I delivered that night. A week later, there was a story that went around town about a baby left in a train station. The station with in a village was twenty miles north. So it apparently took a week for the news to filter down to us, but the timing worked."

Mariette gasped. "You really think that was Rico?"

"Yes."

"So you knew my mother?"

"No. I didn't know her, and she never gave me her name. She also never named you. She was gone when I returned to fill out the birth certificate. So, I don't know much more about you than that your mom was no older than fifteen. She could have been fourteen for all I know. She'd told me that she'd hidden her pregnancy from her family... That was why she didn't want to go to a hospital. That's probably also why she ran away and couldn't take you home."

"Her parents didn't want me?"

"Her parents didn't know about you. She was a very scared, very young woman who believed she'd made a huge mistake and was trying to fix it."

"So my dad's not a mobster or in a gang?"

Mariette snorted, but Ethan chuckled. "Not that I know of. But your mom held you as if you were a precious jewel when I handed you to her. I could see in her eyes that she loved you."

Rico nodded. He'd been a father for nine months. He'd

never before felt the emotions he had when he held Mikie. He couldn't imagine leaving him, but he also wasn't fifteen, afraid, probably broke. In the eyes of a teenager, letting him go might have seemed like the best option. Just as Marietta had speculated.

But his entire body rattled. Knowing who he was, or who he might be, filled him with emotions so strong, he didn't know how to process them.

"I had a friend in the foster care system. I kept track of you." Ethan laughed. "Until you moved to London. Then I lost you, so I had a private investigator find you for me."

"All those rides I gave you where you taught me about investing? Was that to make up for me being abandoned?"

"And to get to know you." He shrugged. "I wasn't a hundred percent sure you were the baby I delivered that night. And I never felt comfortable telling you the story."

"Until now."

"I've never known you as anything other than an ambitious young man. Struggling. Pushing. Now, you're stable. I thought you could handle the information. Especially since I don't believe you were unloved or unwanted. Your mother looked at you with such love. But she was a kid, who for some reason couldn't tell her parents. She was young and her decision was rash because she was desperate."

Ethan nodded at the big envelope. "That paper has all the information I'd filled in for the birth certificate. That gives you the date and time and the place you were born. But no names. Still, a good private investigator might be able to find your mother."

"It would screw up her life."

"Maybe. Or maybe she's been waiting for you."

He said, "Yeah. Maybe," then folded the envelope so he could stuff it in his big jacket pocket. He would hire a private detective and make a few discreet inquiries, but if he found his mother was happy, he probably wouldn't disturb her. He had a good life, a life rich with people and purpose. Everything he needed.

* * * * *

If you missed the previous stories in
The Bridal Party trilogy,
then check out

It Started with a Proposal
Mother of the Bride's Second Chance

And if you enjoyed this story,
check out these other great reads
from Susan Meier

Fling with the Reclusive Billionaire
Claiming His Convenient Princess

All available now!

CINDERELLA'S FESTIVE FAKE DATE

KARIN BAINE

MILLS & BOON

With thanks to Helen for sharing her pottery skills.

For Sheva xx

CHAPTER ONE

'NOPE. NO WAY. Absolutely no chance in hell. N-O!'

Evie didn't know how else she could say it. There was no way she was going to go home to spend the evening with her stepfamily when she'd done her best to avoid them as much as she could for the past few years.

'Don't you go home every year for the annual switching on of the family Christmas lights? I mean, according to you it's a six-foot plastic tree with some fairy lights strung round it, so I don't know what the big deal is, but you usually participate.'

Ursula, Evie's studio assistant, rested her head in her hands, elbows on the workbench, watching her at the pottery wheel.

'Under duress, and it's the only time I usually visit. This is different. It's not just putting on a happy face and gritting my teeth in front of Courtney and Bailey. This is to celebrate their engagement. How am I supposed to get through that without bawling, or finally telling them that they're two-faced back-stabbing traitors who don't deserve to have me in their lives?'

The anger she'd been suppressing for too long seemed to work its way through her body and out of her fingertips, until she was strangling the clay vase she'd been lovingly and delicately shaping until then. The clay wobbled and collapsed, leaving her no option but to take her foot off the pedal to stop the wheel and scrap her work. She tossed it into the bucket with the other remnants for recycling later, and it landed with a satisfying wet slap. What she wouldn't do to toss her stepsister and ex-boyfriend in there along with it.

'I vote for the second option. It's been a long time coming. Honestly, I don't know how you've stayed in contact at all. I would've flipped my lid by now.'

Ursula lifted a ball of new clay and plonked it in the centre of the wheel for her, though Evie knew it was pointless trying to work now. It would be impossible to concentrate on lovingly creating something beautiful to sell at the potters' Christmas market coming up when she was so full of pent-up rage.

She wiped her hands on her apron and turned off the wheel. 'It wouldn't achieve anything. I'd be accused of being overdramatic and selfish. I'll just seethe in private.'

If it had been anyone else, she would've severed all ties and got on with her own life. To some extent she'd probably done just that, setting up her own studio in the heart of Belfast and focusing on her work. However, Courtney, her stepsister, was the only family she had left, other than her stepmother. With no one else in her life apart from Ursula, and her other, hairier, studio assistant, Dave the golden retriever, abandoning her family didn't seem like a viable option.

Besides, she'd promised her father on his deathbed to keep their family together, to be tolerant of her stepsister, who, even fifteen years ago, had been a princess, someone incapable of taking anyone's feelings into account other than her own. Evie's father had obviously witnessed some of her stepmother's favouritism towards her own daughter, over the one she'd inherited with her husband. Perhaps he'd hoped it would lessen over the years, that they would grow closer, never imagining that his child would be treated as a lodger, a burden, in the wake of his death.

When she looked at it like that, Evie wondered why she did bother keeping in touch at all. Deep down, she knew it was only because they were the last connection she had to her father, and she had a promise to keep.

None of which would make it any easier to stomach a return to 'celebrate' this painful engagement, and reminder of betrayal.

Ursula screwed up her face. 'It's not healthy bottling everything up. What you need is closure. Wave them off on their life together, and walk away.'

'Which is all well and good in theory, but I don't want to end up a teary, snivelling mess in front of the smug twosome.'

Even thinking about it was making her stomach churn. Her stepmother fawning over the pair, Evie feigning happiness for them, and feeling outnumbered. On her own. As usual.

'Hmm. If you want, I'll come with you and give them a piece of my mind.'

The thought of firecracker Ursula letting rip and telling Courtney and Bailey how vile they were for treating her friend so appallingly did cheer Evie up. However, she knew it wasn't the solution. It would just be seen as spiteful on her part for putting a stranger up to it.

'I don't think that would be a good idea. Besides, I'm sure you have other, more exciting plans for a December weekend than watching fairy lights on a plastic tree being switched on.'

Her friend was the extrovert Evie wished she could be, who lived to the beat of her own drum and didn't give a hoot what anyone else thought.

'Well… I do have a hot date…'

'Naturally.'

There were very few Saturday nights when Ursula didn't have plans with a handsome man or, at the very least, a glamorous girls' weekend away somewhere expensive and indulgent. She was lucky she had Mummy and Daddy to fund that lifestyle, and a bulging little black book full of phone numbers from adoring men who couldn't seem to get enough of her.

All things elusive to Evie, who'd had to work hard for everything she did have. Although she wasn't in the market for any kind of relationship after Bailey had broken her heart. These days, the only man in her life was Dave. He wouldn't leave her for another woman. At least for as long as she kept cooking him sausages.

'I know! Why don't you join a dating site? You could take a man with you and stick two fingers up at Bailey and Courtney.' Ursula began scrolling through her phone. No doubt she was signed up to every dating app going. That was probably why she was never stuck for a date.

Evie, on the other hand, was averse to most modern

technologies. She loathed social media in general but was forced to engage, posting content and selling online so her business could survive. Therefore, the idea of soulless dating apps based entirely on a person's appearance was her idea of hell. If she couldn't trust someone she'd known for years, basing a relationship on her attractiveness to a person didn't seem like a positive step forward.

'I don't think so. It'll be awkward enough without taking someone on a first date to witness my humiliation.' And she didn't know why she was beginning to talk as though she was actually going to acknowledge this engagement in person…

Undeterred, Ursula thrust her phone in front of Evie's face, forcing her to look at the list of dating sites and apps available. She was about to bat it away when something caught her eye.

'Fake date register… What's that?' she asked the expert.

Ursula frowned, tapping away at the screen. 'Exactly what it says. Apparently, you can "engage in a mutually beneficial arrangement with no strings or expectations". How boring.'

However, Evie's interest was piqued. 'So I could get someone to pretend to be my date, and all I'd have to do is be their "show girlfriend" in return? It might be a possibility.'

At least she wouldn't have to degrade herself by paying someone to do it. If she decided she was desperate enough to go down that route. It would certainly wipe the grins off some faces if she turned up at this engagement with a Bailey replacement, as though what had occurred was of no consequence to her whatsoever, and hadn't completely turned her world upside down.

She heard the familiar sound of a camera shutter as Ursula snapped a photograph.

'What are you doing?' a self-conscious Evie asked, aware that she wasn't wearing make-up, her hair had been tied up in a very messy bun and she was likely covered in clay as usual.

Ignoring her, Ursula continued tapping on her phone, the odd ping of notifications breaking her silence. Eventually she smiled and held up the screen for Evie to peer at.

'I've set up an account for you.'

'You've done what?' Evie grabbed the phone off her, staring in horror at the profile picture, every bit as hideous as she'd imagined. 'I look awful. Who the hell is going to want to date that mess? Besides which, I never agreed to anything. I was simply investigating the possibilities.'

Ursula pouted. 'I'm only trying to help. And you look adorable. There are several men who seem to agree.'

Before she could wrestle the phone back off Evie she saw for herself that there were some potential 'fake dates' in the mix. Perhaps this wasn't a completely off-the-wall idea after all.

'What do you mean, I'm unapproachable?' Jake barked at his sister, Donna, who also doubled up as his business partner. They ran Hanley Film Studios in Belfast's Titanic Quarter, which had become a thriving area for the television and film industry over the last fourteen years or so.

Although born in England, he'd completed his business degree in Belfast and, after a brief enterprise in London working in television, he'd made the move back to Northern Ireland to capitalise on the opportunities here. Donna had moved over to join him a year later, after her relationship ended and she needed a fresh start.

The petite blonde didn't look anything like him, and had a completely different disposition—one that had made her the friendly face of the company, rather than him. He didn't tend to make friends easily, and he didn't want to. Growing up as an army brat, he'd learned not to lean on anyone because they'd be out of his life soon enough.

Something he'd unfortunately carried over into his love life too. To the point he'd left the love of his life to focus on work. Now he was being told he should be 'nicer' to the people he paid.

'This,' she said, waving a hand in his general direction. 'You're spiky. And, if you haven't noticed, we have a high turnover of staff in the office. You're great at your job, but you're single-minded and it doesn't make for a great atmosphere. I'm telling you this for your own sake, to make life easier for you, and for everyone else here. Poor Patty is going to have a nervous breakdown if she has to come into your office to ask you for another training budget. Be kind.'

His mouth twitched into an almost smile. Timid Patty in Accounts was definitely not someone he wanted to lose, but it was true, she didn't stand up to him the way Donna did. He'd admit he wasn't always in the mood to discuss another ex-employee, or the fact that they needed to interview more potentials.

Jake relaxed his frown, took a deep breath and attempted a calm voice. 'What would you suggest?'

'It's coming up to Christmas. I know you don't like parties, but I do think you should attend something with your staff to get to know them better. So they can see that, behind the expensive tailored suits and perma-scowl, you are actually human. That those rumours you were created in a lab under a full moon aren't actually true.' Donna batted her impossibly long eyelashes and smiled a sickly-sweet smile.

Jake raised an eyebrow. She was dancing on thin ice here. Especially when she was sitting on his desk, on top of his paperwork, not showing an ounce of respect for anything. It was just as well she was important to him here as a liaison between him and the outside world or he might take exception to his little sister telling him what to do.

'Again, I ask: what would you suggest I do to make *friends* around here?'

There was a heavy dose of sarcasm in the request. He didn't need to make friends, but he could do with fewer interruptions in his working day. If it got Donna off his back, and his workforce could toil independently of his input, it might be worth a try.

'Well... I've heard about this place that does something called a pizza, prosecco and pottery night.'

'Sounds like my idea of hell,' he grumbled, imagining a room full of drunk women chucking clay around. He had no idea how that was going to improve working relations, and he wasn't about to reenact any romantic cinematic pottery scenes with his employees in order to gain some fans.

Donna slapped him not so playfully on the arm. 'It'll be fun. And I don't mean you pay for the evening and disappear. You'd have to stay and participate.' She whipped out a business card from her pocket and handed it to him. 'Here's the address.'

Clearly, she already had this planned out, and if he wanted rid of her so he could get on with his working day, he would have to at least make it seem as if there was a possibility of arranging this.

'Okay, okay, I'll think about it. Now, shoo. I have work to do.' He took the card and waved her out of his office.

Donna took her time getting up from his desk, brushed off her black and red body-con dress and narrowed her eyes at him. 'See? You need to be nicer to me. I'm not some household pest; I am an asset to you, Mr Grouchy-Pants. Without me, you'd just be some recluse all the local kids are scared of. I am the only thing standing between you and a midnight procession of villagers with torches at your door.'

With a swish of her hair, Donna left his office.

How could he argue with any of that?

It was late, as usual, when Jake finally left work. The place was dark and empty. Sometimes he preferred it that way. Just like the city streets at this time of night. At least when he went home at this time he missed the rush-hour traffic, and the ensuing madness of everyone trying to get home at the same time. All he had to worry about here was driving on a dark, rainy December night.

As he waited at the traffic lights for the imaginary pedestrian who apparently needed to cross the road ahead of him, he happened to glance up at the building on the side of the road, an old converted mill now housing all manner of business units. He wondered why the street name seemed familiar, then he realised it was the address of the pottery place Donna had been so insistent about. On a whim, he clicked on his indicator and as soon as the green light flashed, he swerved onto the side road and into the car park in the grounds of the old mill buildings.

A quick glance around showed that many of the units were still open—a gym, a dance studio and oh, the pottery studio. A small sign attached to a heavy metal door proclaimed 'Evie Kerrigan's Ceramics Studio' was upstairs. He could see that the lights were still on and, after some hesitation, Jake decided to unbuckle his seatbelt and investigate the place for himself.

Upon hauling the heavy door open he was faced with a stone spiral staircase surrounded by whitewashed walls, a cold, unwelcoming entrance that spoke of the original building, but eventually gave way to a brightly lit corridor and more modern-looking facilities. He noted the business names on the doors until he came to the one he was looking for. With the door already open, he knocked and walked on in.

It took him a moment to see past the wooden workbenches and shelves laden with an assortment of wares, but eventually he focused his gaze on the figure at the right-hand side of the room. Head down, humming away to the songs on the radio, she clearly hadn't heard him enter the room. Jake took in the sight of her in her muddied apron and glasses while he waited.

Some snuffling at his feet alerted him to what

seemed like a huge shaggy carpet laid before him. Then the creature raised its head and presented a half chewed, sodden teddy bear. Tail wagging with obvious excitement at sharing his prize with the stranger, he wasn't much of a guard dog.

'Dave! Come away! Sorry, I didn't hear you come in.'

'Dave?' Jake peered at the retriever type canine with amusement, ruffling his fur and setting the tail wagging at full speed again.

The bespectacled brunette wiped her hands on an already dirty rag before getting to her feet to face him. 'Yes. He's my studio companion. It can get quite scary in here at night, and the place is rumoured to be haunted by a lady in white who apparently threw herself to her death from the top of the building. Mind you, I'm not sure Dave would do much to save me if I ever found myself in danger.'

'No, I don't think he'd be capable of scaring anyone away.'

Even Jake, who wasn't usually a fan of any four-legged friend, was becoming increasingly enamoured of the lumbering furry cutie who was now lying on his back expecting tummy rubs. More startling than that was the fact that Jake was kneeling on the dusty floor in his suit, obliging.

A pair of crusty old trainers began to move towards him.

'I thought you'd changed your mind about coming here tonight. If I'd known, I would've made myself more presentable. Although I know this isn't a date date.'

'Pardon me?' Jake stood up again in time to see the

pretty potter shaking her long hair free from its elastic confines and wiping the clay from her glasses.

'I suppose you were a bit nervous, like me. It's not the norm for either of us, I guess. Although, I have to say, you don't look gay. I mean, I know that's the wrong thing to say…not very PC, but I'm sure you could've found someone you know to do this for you.' The woman was rambling. He was frowning, and wondering why on earth she would've assumed he was gay.

'I'm sorry? It was my sister, Donna, who suggested this.'

'Oh. So you were talked into this too? I have a friend like that. What is it with the hideous profile pictures they insist on setting up? Yours doesn't look anything like you. You're more handsome than I thought. Although your fur baby was covering most of your face so it was hard to tell.' She rattled on nervously, making no sense whatsoever to Jake. His head was spinning, trying to make sense of what she was saying.

'I'm sorry, I have no idea what you're talking about. Thank you for the compliment, but the rest of that was lost on me. What's a fur baby? And where is it you think you've seen me before?'

Jake watched her cheeks pink. 'Your dog, Princess. She was in your profile picture. That's what drew me to you on the Fake Date site.'

'Fake Date?'

Now her cheeks were scarlet as it began to dawn on her that he probably wasn't who she thought he was.

'The app. For matching people who need a pretend girlfriend/boyfriend for the night. You're not Olly Leadbetter, are you?'

'No, I'm Jake Hanley. Not on any dating sites that I know of. I don't have a dog called Princess, and I'm definitely not gay.'

But he was amused by the whole situation. There was something adorable about this woman, and it wasn't just the streaks of clay on her face and in her hair.

It was the fact that he was so at ease in the midst of her chaos.

Usually, he needed everything neat and orderly around him to feel comfortable, no doubt a throwback to his father's army-style parenting methods. It wasn't as though he wasn't used to highly strung women either. Patty from Accounts had her nails bitten down to the quick on a regular basis, and Donna only ever sat still if it was on top of his desk in the midst of his working day. But this was different. He was enjoying being in this woman's world, which seemed such a long way from his, and he was curious about what the hell was going on with her.

'Evie Kerrigan,' she said, then buried her face in her hands. 'I'm so sorry. I just assumed you were the guy I was supposed to meet tonight. Then he cancelled, and you showed up, and I just put two and two together.'

'And came up with a closeted gay dog owner?' He supposed it was an improvement on the village monster, and something which would make Donna cackle at the very thought.

'Ugh. Sorry. Again. Can we just forget about that? What can I do for you, Mr Hanley?'

'Jake. I actually came to see about arranging one of those pizza and pottery nights for my employees, but please, tell me more about this fake date thing, Evie.'

He pulled over a high stool and sat down, waiting for her to spill the details.

Her laugh, a mixture of embarrassment and hilarity at her own faux pas, made him chuckle too, something he didn't do a lot of these days. Hell, he didn't even realise it was in his repertoire to do so.

'I can't. It's so unprofessional. And, may I say, uncharacteristic for me.' She bent down to cuddle the dog, buried her head in his fur, and eventually ended up lying on the floor with him.

He liked this crazy Evie woman.

'I haven't actually employed your services yet, and I do think you owe me some kind of explanation...'

Evie sighed and stretched flat out on the floor.

'My friend signed me up to this site so I can take a fake date home. Where my stepsister is getting engaged to my ex-boyfriend. That's sad, right?'

She rolled over onto her side and leaned on her elbow.

Jake considered the scenario, which seemed harsh for someone who appeared so nice. 'Practical, I'd say. Though I don't know why you'd want to be involved in that at all.'

'It's complicated. They're the only family I have, and I made a promise to my dad that I'd try and keep us together.'

'I'm sure he didn't mean for you to stick around to be walked over. These people screwed you over.' He was assuming she'd made the vow on her father's deathbed or something when she seemed so tied into the idea.

Evie winced and flopped back over onto her back, with a concerned Dave lying beside her. 'I know, I know. For the past fifteen years I've been treated as though I'm nothing more than a nuisance. Ursula thinks I need closure. They broke my heart, but I picked myself up and started my own business. I shouldn't be lying here thinking I'm a failure because the people I loved most in the world broke my trust. And why is this beginning to feel like a therapy session?'

'Should I get my notebook and pen?'

'I'm sorry. None of this has anything to do with you. You only came in to book a session. Which I'm going to have to heavily discount now if there's any hope of you coming back. I swear I'm not usually this much of a mess.' Evie got back onto her feet with another sigh, which seemed to come from the depths of her very soul.

'So this is about revenge?'

'More a case of not wanting to humiliate myself further. Although asking a stranger to pretend to be my boyfriend isn't exactly the dream scenario.'

'Sounds practical to me.'

Evie cocked her head to one side. 'You don't think I'm crazy?'

'I never said that.' He grinned. There weren't many strangers who were willing to even approach him, never mind share such a personal story on a first meet. He supposed it was only because of a case of mistaken identity, but he got the impression from this brief interaction that Evie Kerrigan wore her heart on her sleeve. Something which, in the circumstances, was probably going to set her up for another fall with these horrid people in her life.

At least he'd managed to make her smile.

'Well, thank you. I think.'

'Honestly, I think it's a good idea. I have a…thing to go to. It would be easier if I had someone to accompany me. No strings, no complications or expectations.' The cogs were beginning to whirr now with the possibilities of this kind of arrangement.

Evie's eyes were as wide as saucers. 'Wait. Are you actually considering doing this with me?'

'Yes, I am. My mother's getting remarried and I'll be expected to take a plus one. I don't want the hassle of asking someone who'll read more into it.'

Plus, Evie was sweet and amiable. She could probably act as a barrier between him and a legion of people he didn't really want to talk to. Including his parents.

'Okay…but I don't know anything about you. At least with Olly I had an idea of the person I was going to be taking home with me.'

Despite being the answer to her prayers, she was now eyeing him suspiciously, her arms folded defensively across her chest, as though he often spent his nights trawling old buildings in search of women going through an emotional crisis.

Honestly, he was offended.

'My name is Jake Hanley. I'm thirty-four, an army brat who moved from country to country with his parents, and who now also runs his own business and is too busy for "normal" relationships. I only came here because my sister, Donna, suggested I needed to bond with my workforce. Apparently, I'm too…unapproachable. Something about villagers chasing me with torches and pitchforks if I don't make an effort.'

He wasn't sure any of that information would help her to believe he wasn't a danger, but it was the truth.

It had been a day for uncomfortable truths.

Evie was smirking by the end of his introduction. Arms unfolded. Ice broken.

'Okay, I believe you, and I can see we both need each other. We will also have to get our stories straight if we're ever going to convince anyone that we're a couple. But it's getting late. Why don't we meet up to discuss the details some other time?'

'It's a date.' He couldn't resist getting one last rise out of her before walking away, her side-eye putting a little pep in his step.

Today had been full of surprises, but the biggest one had been meeting someone who took his mind off everything except her.

Donna would be impressed. Exactly why he wasn't going to tell her anything about Evie Kerrigan.

CHAPTER TWO

'YOU DO GET yourself into some terrible messes, Evie Kerrigan.' She took a sip of her luxury hot chocolate, keeping her eye on the door of the coffee shop for her 'date'.

Fake date, she reminded herself. Though she still couldn't figure out exactly how this had happened. One minute she was happily working in her studio, the next she was lying on the floor spilling her guts out to a complete stranger. Who, by all accounts, had serious issues of his own. And she'd just agreed to take him home with her in an attempt to convince the people who'd broken her heart that she was happy.

This didn't have disaster written all over it at all!

She was on the verge of texting Jake back to say perhaps this wasn't a good idea when he swept into the coffee shop. He looked completely out of place among the groups of chatting mothers, phone obsessed teens and crossword-filling pensioners. With his slicked-back hair, long wool coat and his handsome dark looks, he looked as though he'd just stepped out of an aftershave advert.

Even her heart gave a little gasp at the sight of him, and she knew why he was here. To concoct a fake relationship because he was too busy to entertain the idea of a real one. Not exactly the stuff dreams were made of, but what she needed right now.

'Jake!' She raised a hand to get his attention, then quickly dropped it as every pair of eyes in the place suddenly swivelled towards her, as if to ask why on earth this perfect specimen of masculinity was here to see *her*.

He strode over towards her table. 'I need coffee.' Then did an about-turn towards the counter.

Evie gulped her chocolate, wishing for something more than cream and marshmallows to steel her for this encounter. He looked even more handsome and out of her league in daylight and she wondered how the hell they were going to fool anyone into thinking they were a couple.

It wasn't long before he was back, clutching a small cup of espresso. 'Thanks for coming on such short notice, but I'm a busy man. As I'm sure you're a busy woman.'

Evie nodded, though she was sure throwing cups and vases wasn't as draining as whatever he did for a job. At least she got to sit down, listen to the radio and drink as many cups of tea as she could manage. She could picture him shouting into a phone at the stock market, or something equally stressful.

'I wasn't expecting to hear from you so soon, but I suppose we have a lot to sort out.' Despite their agreement last night, his text this morning had come as something of a surprise. Needless to say, she'd spent the couple of hours since brushing her hair, putting on some make-up and making herself presentable.

'Yes. In all the excitement, I forgot to ask when this engagement party was.'

'Saturday.'

He almost spat his coffee in her face. 'So soon?'

'Yes. Sorry. I completely understand if you can't make it.'

'No. We made a deal. I'll just swap a few things around in my schedule.' He took out his phone and started tapping, making her feel special that he was even giving her the time of day, never mind committing to a whole evening with her family.

'Hopefully, we won't have to stay too long. Just dinner and a couple of drinks to toast the happy couple.' She tried and failed to keep the sarcasm and bitterness from her voice. Only time would tell if she'd be able to overcome that over the course of the following few days.

'Where is it?'

'Bangor. County Down,' she said, for reference. The supposed moneyed part of the country. Yet where she'd grown up virtually having to fend for herself financially once her father died. It was funny that her stepsister had never been expected to get a menial part-time job, unlike Evie, who'd worked in retail and hospitality to fund her time at university. Yet even now she didn't know how Courtney earned the money to keep her in the lifestyle to which she'd become accustomed. No doubt banker Bailey had a lot to do with that.

'I'll drive. What time?'

'I haven't told them I'm coming yet.'

Jake glanced up from his screen to give her a look of disapproval.

'I'll confirm tonight. It'll probably be about six-ish, and home no later than ten, I imagine.'

'I'll need your address to pick you up. Which I assume will be around five o'clock.'

She nodded, feeling slightly as though she was being interviewed in a speed date fashion, where every second and word counted. He wasn't wasting either on small talk, and she was beginning to see why his sister had pushed him into being more sociable. This work version of Mr Hanley wasn't smiling and teasing like out of hours Jake who'd turned up unexpectedly in her studio last night. Though she supposed that was a good thing for her personally, so she wouldn't be blinded by good looks, and potentially hitch her wagon to yet another wrong horse.

'In terms of our story…where should we say we met?'

She needed something plausible and it was going to be obvious to everyone that they didn't move in the same social circles. He looked like someone who'd just walked out of a catalogue, and she looked like someone who simply stroked the pages lovingly, wishing she could afford the contents.

Though in this instance no money had changed hands. He wasn't an escort and she wasn't desperate, or rich, enough to pay for his services. She was sure Jake Hanley would be an expensive investment, though probably worth it…

When she realised the full lips she was staring at were moving, those cool blue eyes staring at her, she had to refocus.

'Sorry. I didn't catch that.'

He huffed out an exasperated breath. 'I said we

should stick as close to the truth as possible so we don't trip up.'

'You mean tell them you came to book a class and I mistook you for my gay fake date, before launching into details of my romantic trauma?'

'Hmm, we can probably skip that part. We'll just say I stopped by to book a class and things went from there. It's early days though, so that should cover us for not knowing everything there is to know about each other.'

'Good idea. Courtney and Bailey would laugh themselves into a coma if they knew the truth.'

'And that would be bad because…?' The twinkle was back in his eyes that she'd seen last night.

Evie preferred this warm, funny Jake, as opposed to the efficient, no-nonsense Mr Hanley who'd first come through the door. She was all about the nonsense.

'Because I don't want them to know they hurt me so badly I don't even want to risk being with anyone else.'

She didn't want to bring the tone back down again but she wanted to be honest with him. Ironic, in the circumstances. But it was important he knew how big of a deal it was going to be for her to face Courtney and Bailey again.

'I get that.' He nodded, but what else could he say to that other than telling her to man up and forget about them? Ursula had tried the tough love approach with her and it hadn't worked so far.

'So, tell me about your event. What do I need to know?'

He sat back in his chair, looking uncomfortable before he'd even opened his mouth. Evie was glad this was a two-way deal so she wouldn't feel vulnerable on her own, opening up like this with someone she hardly knew. Clearly, Jake had his personal problems with his family too.

'Mum's getting married soon to someone I hardly know. She moved over here after Donna and I did, and met Gary. He's one in a long line of boyfriends since she and my dad divorced. They're still friends, so he'll be there too. I'd rather not be. They're not the advert for good parents, or relationships, but I don't want to cause a drama. I just need a buffer. That's where you come in.'

So now the price she was going to have to pay for his assistance was becoming clear. If his family were half as scary as he had a tendency to be, Evie wasn't sure she'd be the partner he needed for the occasion.

'Your dad's ex-army, right?'

'Yes, but don't worry, he probably won't stick around long. He never did.'

There was a poignancy to his words that made her think he wasn't as indifferent to his parents as he was making out. He'd clearly been hurt too.

'Is this going to be a fancy "do"? Will it require me wearing something not covered in clay?' Clearly, she was going to have to get a new outfit but she wasn't sure what level of couture would be required, and if she needed to remortgage her flat so she could afford something suitable.

'I imagine so, but I'll cover any expenses.' He whipped out a credit card and slid it across the table.

'You trust me, a stranger, with your credit card?' She could do some serious damage with that if left unsupervised. Like pay off all her bills and buy a new spray gun for her glazes.

'Well, there's a chance you could empty my bank account and flee the country, but I get the impression you want to see this engagement party through. And you seem to like your work so...'

'Right on both counts. Where do you want to go?' She didn't imagine he did much shopping in the charity shops or discount stores she usually frequented. There wasn't much point in wearing expensive clothes in her line of work when they ended up covered in clay and glaze. She dressed for comfort, and warmth, to limit the possibility of freezing to death in that draughty old building.

Jake frowned. 'I'm not going dress shopping with you. That's why I'm giving you the card. I don't really even have time to be here.'

'Of course. It's just... I'm not sure what's appropriate. It's okay. I'm sure I'll figure it out.' What was she expecting? That he was going to do a Richard Gere and take her shopping on Rodeo Drive? This wasn't some romantic fantasy; it was an attempt to survive her heartbreak.

'I'm sure you'll be fine. You look lovely today. Better. Than last night,' he stuttered, showing that even the seemingly unflappable Jake could get flustered.

Evie didn't know which one of them was blushing more at the unintended compliment. Yes, she was ignoring the follow-on comment because he'd said she looked lovely. It wasn't an everyday occurrence for her to hear that. Not only because she didn't dress to impress on a daily basis, but because usually the only people she ever saw in her studio were Ursula, customers and, of course, Dave.

Then again, she'd actually made an effort today, knowing she was seeing Jake. She'd wanted to look nice for him, and to feel good about herself after making such a crazy first impression on him. So she'd donned her prettiest winter dress, emblazoned with holly berries, tied neatly at her waist, and teamed with a dark green cardigan. There was no way she was letting him take that back. Not now, when her heart was beginning to flutter. A miracle when she was sure Bailey's antics had all but killed it.

'I'll ask Ursula for advice. She goes to enough of these things to know what I should wear.'

Other than not turning up in white, Evie didn't know a lot about wedding attire etiquette, or high society functions. Her studio assistant, on the other hand, seemed to live her life in a whirlwind of parties and socialising. Probably why she'd hired her. Ursula was better at the people side of the business. When she thought about it, Jake would probably have been better off taking Ursula to this thing. Although she didn't want to lose him when she was just getting used to the idea that she was going to have someone to support her through this difficult time.

Jake's ringing phone prevented him from having to concern himself with the small matter of her wardrobe. He tossed back his coffee and got up from his seat. 'Great. I'll see you on Saturday and we'll talk about it then.'

Focused now on whoever was calling, he disappeared out of the door, clearly a busy man. Evie considered herself lucky he'd spared her these few minutes of his precious time. He must've really wanted backup for this wedding when he'd agreed to grant her an entire Saturday evening.

Now Evie had more to worry about than showing herself up in front of just her ex and her stepfamily.

The screen flashed on her phone with an incoming call.

'Speak of the devil,' she muttered, seeing her stepmother's name.

For a moment she considered not answering, but she knew she'd have to face up to the inevitable. Especially now that Jake was rearranging his busy schedule to accompany her to the event of the year.

'Hey, June.' She'd never been able to bring herself to call her 'Mum'. That role had been taken long ago, even if Evie didn't remember her mother, who'd died of peritonitis when she was little more than a baby. Not that June would've wanted that anyway.

She hadn't been the maternal figure for Evie her dad had probably hoped she'd be after raising his daughter alone until her teenage years. In contrast to her own daughter, whom she'd showered with praise and money, June had treated Evie like a lodger at best. At worst, a skivvy around the house, doing the chores neither she nor Courtney were prepared to do, as if Evie had a duty to earn her keep in the house she'd grown up in long before they'd come on the scene. It had always been just Evie and her father for as long as she could remember. Her mother was nothing more than some faded photographs. And even they'd been hidden away once June arrived.

Still, they were her only family, and they did still include her in these get-togethers. Even if she didn't always want to be there.

'We haven't heard from you about your sister's engagement. You are coming, aren't you? I know there was some unpleasantness some time ago, but that's all past us now.'

Speak for yourself.

'Yes. I'm coming.'

'Alone?' It was such a loaded word. A question not only about her relationship status but also her mental state. Was she going to cause a scene with her bitterness, or just celebrate with the happy couple?

Neither, but at least she'd have Jake there in her corner.

'No. I'm bringing someone with me.'

'Oh, good. I just want you to be happy for your sister.'

Evie was twitching at the fact she was still being painted as the one in the wrong. Though that was always going to be the way between the two of them where her stepmother was concerned. Her precious little Courtney could never do any wrong. Even if she had slept with her stepsister's boyfriend behind her back.

'I'll be there.' That was as much as she could promise.

'And who's this young man you're bringing? Tell me all about him. Courtney will want to know the details.'

Eve's stomach somersaulted at the mere mention of her date. Goodness knew how she was going to get through a whole night with him in their company without breaking cover. The idea of Courtney analysing their every move made her want to throw up. Evie was neither a good liar nor a great actress. Two things her stepsister apparently excelled at. Ironically, she might be able to spot the fake.

'His name's Jake. We're not long together, so take it easy on him.'

She tried to make light of it, though she knew there was no chance they weren't going to sit through an interrogation about their 'relationship'. She only hoped she could withstand the intense questioning. As for Jake, she wasn't sure which side of him would be better suited to this meet-the-family scenario. Though she preferred the Jake who'd turned up at her studio last night, and he would certainly charm everyone, today's cool customer might be more to her advantage. He wouldn't give anything away, and probably make everyone else feel insignificant and inferior. Yet she would feel more comfortable with the relaxed Jake who'd actually seemed interested in her problems. The man she could actually see herself being with.

'Is he handsome?'

'Yes.' The answer to that one came easily.

Trust June to be so shallow when it came to a suitable partner. The next thing she'd be asking would be about his annual income. Evie wouldn't put it past her if she tried to matchmake with Courtney if she knew the truth. Jake was a much better prospect than cheating Bailey.

'Ooh. Can't wait to meet him.'

'Well, I have to get back to work, but we'll see you on Saturday.'

'Oh, yes, I'm sure those teacups won't make themselves.' The sneering was there as always when it came to talk of Evie's career.

It didn't matter that she had a degree and ran her own business, as far as her family was concerned, she just played with clay for a living. Which to some extent was true, but she also thought she deserved some level of respect for making a success of it.

Evie hung up before June could ask any more questions about Jake which she probably wouldn't be able to answer, or insult her any further, feeling as though she'd mentally just gone ten rounds in a boxing ring.

It occurred to her that their getting-to-know-one-another meeting at the coffee shop this morning hadn't achieved much other than the confirmation that he hadn't changed his mind about the whole thing. She didn't know any more about him. Not enough to withstand any intensive questioning. They were going to have to wing it. It wasn't exactly the ideal plan when trying to convince her family she was in a committed, loving relationship. Only time would tell if it was inviting more pain and humiliation into her life, but at this point she didn't have anything left to lose.

CHAPTER THREE

'I CAN ONLY apologise in advance for anything anyone does or says.' Evie was getting in early, absolving herself of any responsibility, as they drove to her family home.

Jake smiled. 'It's fine. I have a good idea of what I'm getting myself into.'

'You have no idea…'

'Families are all a nightmare. You'll be returning the favour soon enough.'

It was another hint that he had some deep-seated issues with his parents which didn't sound as though they'd be resolved any time soon.

She couldn't help but push a little on the matter so he'd remember the reason they both needed this to work.

'Is your mother a shallow, passive-aggressive nightmare too?' she asked, batting the false eyelashes she was worried weren't going to survive the night before she ripped them off.

'Worse.' Jack pursed his lips together. 'She's a romantic.'

The unexpected horror on his face at the revelation made her laugh hard. 'How terrible for you.'

Jake took his eyes off the road for a moment to narrow them at her. 'You have no idea. She falls in love every five minutes. Only this time she's apparently making it to the altar. I have no idea how she and my father ever thought it would work between them when he's so...grounded.'

'Maybe she's just an optimist.' It didn't sound so bad having a mother who apparently saw possibilities in everyone. A definite contrast to her family, who thought she was a lost cause.

'She's that all right. I seem to spend my whole life defending my decision to focus on work instead of "settling down". Be prepared for a barrage of questions about when we're having babies when it's time for you to return the favour.'

It took a moment for her to remember to laugh at the absurdity of that when her mind had taken her somewhere unexpected and erotic. A wistful wondering about what her and Jake's babies would look like had quickly taken her to the conception. Her imagination was conjuring up pictures of him in a state of undress, what was hidden behind the designer suits and the very efficient exterior. Meanwhile, her body was already reacting to the idea of what he would be like in the bedroom. Warm and engaging, or efficient, wasting no time in getting to a successful conclusion? Either way, her interest was piqued way beyond someone she was only with to convince her family she was over their betrayal. Perhaps she was finally getting over it, and some day she might be able to get back on the dating scene for real. This was certainly the first time since Bailey she'd felt anything like this for another man. Probably only because this was the closest she'd ever let herself get to one, through fear for what was left of her self-esteem as well as her heart.

Evie shifted uncomfortably in her seat, the confines of his car, where she could feel his body heat, and smell his intoxicating cologne, suddenly becoming stifling.

'Can we turn the radio on?'

She fiddled with the console before he'd even had time to give an answer, needing a distraction, something to create the illusion of distance between them at least, the only consolation being that they were almost at their destination. It said a lot about her current state of mind when she was thinking of her family as the lesser of two evils, ready to face their certain disapproval and disregard over whatever she was beginning to feel for Jake. A man she didn't know, and wasn't supposed to actually be involved with beyond this deception.

'There is a weather warning across the province, with snow showers predicted later this evening.'

The weather forecast on the radio didn't do anything to ease the tightness in her chest.

'Should we be worried, do you think?' It was one thing feeling as though she should put in an appearance as a show of good will, but quite another if they were endangering their lives to get there and back.

'I checked the forecast before we left and it looks as though the worst of the snow will hit the area overnight, so we should be okay if we only spend a couple of hours. The motorways and main roads will be gritted anyway. I'm sure we'll get back.' Jake's confidence was reassuring, because she knew there was no way he'd risk taking extra time out of his life for such a non-event.

'It'll be a good excuse to leave early, at least. Dinner, drinks, and out of there as soon as possible.' That was the plan and if they stuck to it, hopefully, there wouldn't be time for them to be rumbled, or for Evie to suffer too many barbed comments.

'I won't be drinking. Driving, remember?'

'I wasn't talking about you,' she muttered. Not usually a big drinker, she knew she'd need some Dutch courage to get through this. Or at least a few glasses of wine.

'No being sick in the car. That's my number one rule.'

'Yes, sir.' She saluted him, but understood why he wouldn't want the pristine interior of his sleek ride sullied by her inability to function normally around her family.

'Stop worrying. I'm here for you, okay?' He pulled on the handbrake as they arrived outside their destination and turned to her, his intense blue eyes filled with a genuine concern for her that she wasn't used to.

She bit her lip as she nodded, trying not to burst into tears and make a fool of herself before they'd even set foot inside the house.

'Let's do this.' She took a deep breath and got ready to face the firing squad, all the while wondering why she felt like she was the one who'd done something wrong when all she was guilty of was being too trusting. And, after today, of faking her happiness with a new partner. It wasn't as though she'd got caught in bed with her stepsister's boyfriend and gone on to become his fiancée.

The anxiety must've been coming off her in waves as they crunched across the gravel driveway in the dark as Jake reached out and took her hand, giving it a squeeze as she rang the doorbell and offering her a smile as they awaited admittance. Enough to remind her she had his support, and he actually cared about how she was feeling. Enough for her poor wounded heart to give one last gasp before it threw in the towel altogether. Perhaps she wasn't completely done with men altogether if there were still nice ones like Jake Hanley out there, capable of making her feel safe, even for a couple of hours.

Her pulse picked up an extra beat with the sound of every stiletto step towards the front door.

'Evelyn!'

'Evie,' she mumbled as her stepmother gripped her by the shoulders and delivered two air kisses.

'And this must be your beau.'

Evie cringed as Jake was swamped by June's enhanced cleavage in a more demonstrative hug than she'd ever received.

'Jake,' she corrected.

'You must come and meet everyone, Jakie.' June grabbed for his hand, forcing Evie and Jake apart.

Even though he wasn't actually hers, Evie felt the loss immediately. He managed to flash her an apologetic look before he was dragged further into the house in front of her. She was left to close the door as he was spirited away to be introduced to the awaiting crowd, whilst she was an afterthought. As usual.

Evie hung up her coat and bag, checked her reflection in the full-size hall mirror and took a deep breath before entering the fray.

The lounge was packed with people, and the room full of chat and laughter, a full assault on the senses when combined with the smell of food and expensive perfumes. Not to mention the mouthful of wine from the glass she helped herself to from the buffet table set up at the far side of the room.

'Mummy thought we should celebrate at the golf club, but we thought we should keep things low-key. Intimate. It didn't seem right to have a huge party.' Courtney was nursing a glass of her own as she approached Evie, insincerity oozing from every make-up camouflaged pore.

'How considerate.' More likely they couldn't afford to put it on at the exclusive venue, or Bailey had put his foot down. He wasn't one for splashing his cash around, which made their match even more baffling. One thing was certain, they weren't doing any of this for Evie's benefit.

Courtney was dressed in a gold and champagne lace mini dress, her honey-coloured hair swept up at the sides and secured with a diamond barrette, leaving soft romantic waves falling to her shoulders. She looked sufficiently beautiful, and expensive, to make Evie feel inadequate. When Evie had put on her wine-red velvet wrap-over dress and done her make-up and hair, she'd been pleased with her reflection, along with the appreciative look Jake had afforded her at the door. Now, however, she was reminded why she hadn't been enough for Bailey. At least by bringing a fake date she didn't have to worry that history might repeat itself.

'Thanks for coming, Evester. We appreciate it.' Bailey's obnoxious nickname was equally as aggravating as June's insistence on using her full name.

'Bailey.' She couldn't bring herself to do anything other than acknowledge his presence. Though in her head she was chucking her drink in his face and mashing some of that fancy salmon mousse in his face.

'Honestly, we didn't think you'd show your face here again after all the histrionics.'

A smug Bailey slid his arm around Courtney's teeny-tiny waist as though he was claiming his prize, leaving Evie feeling as though she was the loser in all of this. It was mind-boggling to her now what she'd ever seen in him, or why she'd been so bothered about them being together in the first place, other than their sneaking around behind her back. They were welcome to each other.

Evie considered going home now that she'd apparently made peace with the situation and done her duty by giving them her blessing, when she felt a pair of strong arms wrapping around her.

'Sorry, babe. June wanted to show me around. I missed you.' Jake hugged her close against his hard body, his face pressed against hers so she could feel the rasp of his stubble on her face and his hot breath in her ear.

She almost let out a squeal, giving the game away,

then she remembered they were supposed to be a couple and this level of intimacy should be the norm. Doing her best to relax into the embrace, she leaned back and stroked the side of his face.

The flare of Bailey's nostrils and clenched jaw only made her want to act up more.

'I missed you too, sweetie. I was just telling Courtney they shouldn't have downsized their celebration on my account. We're all good.' Bolstered by scoring a point over them, she spun around and planted a kiss on Jake's lips.

The gruesome twosome soon lost interest and wandered back to the rest of their guests, leaving Evie to deal with the consequences of her actions.

Her face was flushed, and not just from the wine. Jake still had his arms around her, their bodies packed tightly together, and she could still feel the impression of his surprisingly soft lips on hers.

'Sorry,' she whispered, aware that kissing her hadn't been in the brief, but she'd taken his cue and run with it. All the way out of both of their comfort zones.

'It's okay. I think we did a good job of convincing them.' He sounded as breathless as she felt.

'Ladies and gentlemen, can I have your attention, please?' Her stepmother called everyone together and once Evie and Jake realised they were still clinging on to one another they sprang apart.

The general hubbub subsided until Evie was sure the only sound that could be heard was her heart, jolted back to life with the electricity from spontaneously kissing her unsuspecting date.

'I just want to thank everyone for coming to celebrate my beautiful daughter's engagement to my favourite future son-in-law, Bailey.' June raised a glass to the couple basking in glory in the centre of the room.

There was that vomit feeling coming that had Jake so concerned about the integrity of his upholstery.

Evie half-heartedly clapped along with everyone else so her urge to barf wasn't blatantly obvious.

'It hasn't been an easy time since I lost Len, but I know he'd be proud of his daughter. I just wish he could be here to walk you down the aisle. He was the only father you ever truly had, and I know you were the daughter he always wanted, Courtney.'

Another round of applause, but Evie couldn't join in this time as her hands were now clenched into fists.

'Just breathe.' Jake leaned in and though his close proximity didn't do anything to ease the tension in her body, it did manage to divert her attention away from the verbal assault going on.

Evie was the one he would be proud of, because she'd made something of her life, and had done it without any help, or managing to hurt anyone. Apart from anything else, *she* was his daughter. That wasn't something else June and Courtney could just take away from her because they felt like it. It wasn't her fault that Courtney's real father had never wanted anything to do with her, and it didn't mean they could just steal hers. Yes, he'd loved Courtney, but he would not have been happy to see them try and erase Evie from history. The only saving grace was that he wasn't here, and she wouldn't have to suffer further indignity watching him walk Courtney down the aisle to marry *her* ex-boyfriend.

On Jake's advice, she took deep breaths and waited for the rage to subside. Only for Courtney to take centre stage.

'Thanks, Mum. I'm so grateful to have you and Bailey in my life, and lucky that we're going to be one big happy family soon.'

'Honestly, it's like I don't even exist sometimes,' Evie muttered under her breath.

Jake reached for another glass of wine and handed it to her, adding fuel to her fire.

'Like every couple, we've had our ups and downs. And kissed our fair share of frogs along the way.'

Jake's hand was on her arm now, as though he was ready to restrain her should she suddenly lunge at the blushing bride-to-be.

'But we've finally found each other.'

Ha! Evie had found him first, and Courtney and Bailey had known each other for quite some time before they'd decided to betray her.

'And I'm so lucky you took a chance on me.' Now it was Bailey's turn to increase the ick factor. 'My life had no meaning before you were part of it.'

'I've heard enough,' Evie fumed quietly to Jake, setting down her drink and making a sharp exit from the room.

It was one thing making an appearance, and getting some closure, but something different listening to her only meaningful relationship be dismissed so casually. As though she, and it, had meant nothing, when the brutal end of it had caused her so much heartache. Clearly, these two had no crisis of conscience about what they'd done to her, but she didn't have to stick around to hear them rub her nose in it. It wasn't jealousy fuelling her ire, but the injustice. They'd hurt her, betrayed her trust, and irrevocably changed her life. Yet neither of them seemed to care what they'd done to her. As always, her feelings were irrelevant here, and she'd been brutally reminded of that.

What made it worse was that it was happening in front of Jake in real time, opening his eyes to the loser she was, and likely always would be, at least in the eyes of her family. If she'd harboured any notion that he would come to like her in any romantic fashion, this debacle had poured cold water all over that. Everything about this party said that she could never be enough for anyone.

Evie fled the room before the tears fell, or she actually did punch someone and irreconcilably damaged the relationship she did have with her family. Bailey was going to marry Courtney and be a part of her life and she was going to have to get used to that. For now, though, she needed a little breathing space, and sought solace in her old bedroom.

Surprisingly, June hadn't altered it at all. Probably because the boxroom wasn't considered grand enough to use for anything other than an unwanted stepdaughter. However, right now, it was a familiar sanctuary for Evie to hide away for a while. The boy band posters on the wall and sketches she'd done herself pinned to her noticeboard spoke of the naïve teen she'd once been.

Although the celestial themed navy and gold bedcovers had some other more unpleasant memories of the naïve adult she'd remained until her heart had been spectacularly demolished.

Her attempt to slam the door shut like all overemotional teens was halted by a shiny leather loafer as Jake stepped into the room behind her.

'Are you okay?' he asked, handing her a handkerchief. She hadn't even known that men still carried those—something she'd thought dreamed up solely for handsome men to dish out to distressed heroines in period dramas.

'I'm fine,' she insisted, then blew her nose noisily on the white cotton.

'They're idiots. You know that?' Jake looked ridiculous perched on the end of her bed, too big to fit comfortably in here.

'Then why am I letting them get to me?' She threw herself dramatically onto the mattress beside him.

'Because you're normal. You have feelings and emotions, which these people don't seem to possess. Sorry, I know they're your family.'

'You know this is where I caught them? On my bed. As though they wanted me to find them. Courtney has her own princess bed in a room twice the size of this one, but no, they decided to have sex in my bed, and act shocked when I walked in.' The image was burned onto her eyeballs for ever, indelible scars left on her heart.

'There are people in this world who get off on inflicting pain on others. It's not a reflection on you, it's on them.'

'I think Courtney wanted to prove she could take him from me. To prove he didn't love me any more than she or June did.'

'As I said, they're both idiots, and you're better off without them.'

'So why can't I get over it?'

'You will. It's hard when you think you're going to spend the rest of your life with someone, only to realise you're better off on your own.' He kicked off his shoes and stretched out flat until his head was lying on the pillow beside her and his feet were hanging over the edge of the mattress.

'There speaks a man of experience.' She couldn't imagine anyone cheating on Jake, and thinking there was a better alternative, when he seemed like the complete package to her. Good looks, financial stability and compassionate—a woman would be lucky to have him as a life partner.

He sighed. 'I was with someone for a long time. Lacey. We lived in England together.'

'What happened?'

'Me. Work. You have to remember I spent my whole life moving from country to country with my parents. At least until my mother got sick of it, and decided my father wasn't the romantic hero she'd imagined, never around for any of us. Anyway, I met Lacey when I lived in London with my mum, and eventually we moved in together. We both worked at the TV studios there, but I wanted to go into business myself. I saw the opportunities here when big movie companies started to come here for filming. I realised there was a need for studios and wanted to buy some land to build my own. It was a huge opportunity and I had to take some big risks with investors but I knew it would be worth it. It made sense to move here, and since I'd gone to university in Belfast, I knew the city well. I had faith that I could really make something of myself here.'

'And she didn't want to come with you?'

He shook his head. 'She wanted to stay in London and raise a family, and that wasn't something I was ready to commit to. I didn't want to let that kind of business opportunity slip through my fingers on the basis that we might be the one couple who'd live happily ever after. Life's not like that. Mine certainly isn't.'

'Do you regret it?' Perhaps Jake wasn't the perfect man she'd imagined if he couldn't even commit to someone who'd obviously loved him.

'Honestly? No. I think it proves we weren't meant to be. I'm happy with my life, and I think she did get married and have the babies she wanted in England. My point is, you don't have to stay in a relationship that clearly isn't right just for the sake of it. Sometimes you're better off on your own, and as far as I can see you're doing all right. Much better than any of these morons are giving you credit for.'

He seemed to have the knack for making her smile even when she was at her lowest.

'You don't think you'll ever settle down with anyone?'

It was a depressing thought to imagine herself alone for ever, but these feelings Jake had seemed to awaken in her gave her an inkling that she hadn't completely given up on the idea of love and being with someone. She just had to make sure it was the right person. Someone who loved her as much as she loved them, and wouldn't jump into bed with her stepsister the second her back was turned.

'Never say never, but I've learned not to get close to anyone because you'll inevitably end up on your own anyway. What about you? Has this put you off relationships for life?'

'I hope not. I'd like to have someone other than Dave to cuddle in bed.'

'You don't need a loser like Bailey in your life for that. Come here.'

She scooched over and Jake put an arm around her, gathering her close. Head leaning on his chest, she listened to the steady, reassuring sound of his heart beating and the tension began to leave her body.

'What do you want to do now?' he asked, and she had to tell herself he was talking about the situation beyond this room, not what usually happened when two adults got into bed together.

'Can we just stay here for a while? Until everyone else has gone home?'

'Sure.'

Evie snuggled into him and closed her eyes, enjoying this sensation of safety in his arms. When she was here, Courtney and Bailey didn't even enter her head.

CHAPTER FOUR

IT WAS PITCH-BLACK when Jake opened his eyes and it took a few seconds for him to remember where he was. At the same moment he realised he was spooning Evie, and his body apparently didn't know this wasn't the time to react to being pressed tightly against a beautiful woman's behind. He moved away to compose himself, but Evie's little moan as he did so didn't help his painful predicament.

He stared at the ceiling, at the sparse bare bulb hanging there, wishing away what a lot of men would pay good money over the chemist's counter to have.

Evie was upset and vulnerable, and his arousal was inappropriate on so many levels. The least of which being that they weren't even on a real date. However, the more time he spent around her, the more he liked her, and the more he felt as though he should protect her. Especially from those she considered family but who, as far as he was concerned, were toxic.

As they'd belittled her, and her achievements, in front of friends and family, it had taken a great deal of control not to come out swinging, or sweep her up into his arms and carry her away from it all. He supposed he had one thing to thank his father for. The disciplinarian had instilled in him the importance of self-control when it came to emotions. Whilst it hadn't been all that useful in terms of relationships, at least it prevented situations like this from escalating.

It hadn't been beyond him to provide Evie with some comfort though, and she'd obviously needed it. He'd surprised himself, not only by offering it, but in how much he'd enjoyed simply cuddling her on the bed. Due to their arrangement, he didn't have to worry about what happened next or either of them getting too attached when this was a temporary setup. So he'd been able to reap the benefits of holding her close without having to deal with any of the potential complications. He had to admit it was nice to wake up with a woman in his arms again, someone he knew more about than simply a first name. On the occasions he had shared a bed with anyone since moving to Belfast, he'd been sure to keep things casual and uncomplicated, which had suited him until now. He simply had to remember that this was where it stopped with Evie, because she was the sort of woman who needed, and deserved, more than she'd been afforded in her relationships to date. Despite their similarities, he wasn't the man to give her that. Relationships simply weren't for him. No matter how attractive a prospect Evie was to him right now.

'What time is it?' she mumbled in the darkness.

Jake grabbed his phone and the screen lit up the room. 'It's eight o'clock.'

Evie scrambled to sit up. 'What? How did that happen?'

'We must have both fallen asleep.'

He went over to the window and opened the curtains, his heart sinking when he saw the thick blanket of snow sparkling in the moonlight. His was the only car still parked out front, almost completely covered in the white stuff.

Evie appeared beside him. 'Oh, no. How are we going to get out of here?'

'Maybe your stepmother has a shovel in the garage. Everyone else seems to have managed to get out.' Though any tyre tracks away from the property had been long since hidden with another layer of snow.

They made their way downstairs and into the lounge, where June, Courtney and Bailey were cleaning up the remnants of the party.

'Oh, you've decided to show your face again, then?' Courtney sniffed.

'Why didn't anyone wake us?'

It was the first time he'd seen Evie look angry. He guessed she really wanted to get away from here, and he couldn't blame her after what he'd witnessed so far.

'We thought you were having one of your temper tantrums and we should just leave you to it. I told you we didn't want a scene.' Evie's stepsister turned her back on them and proceeded to gather the empty champagne glasses and walk away to the kitchen. They'd apparently missed the toast and he was thankful for Evie's sake she hadn't had to go through that at least. They both might well have choked on the champagne.

'We didn't want to disturb you, dear.'

June was more diplomatic, though Jake got the impression they'd been happy to have Evie out of the way for the remainder of the party, lest she would say anything incriminating about how the happy couple came to be together.

'How are we going to get out of here?' Evie demanded.

'Do you have a snow shovel, Mrs Kerrigan?' Perhaps he could make some sort of road out of here.

She shook her sleek blonde hair. 'Even if I did, you wouldn't get out at the bottom of the lane. It's treacherous down there, by all accounts. Everyone else left before the snow began. I'm afraid you're stuck here for at least the night.'

He could only imagine how that news was going to go down with Evie when he felt physically sick at the prospect. After witnessing their ill-treatment of her, he knew she wouldn't want to spend a second longer in their presence than necessary. They were toxic, and damaging, to someone who deserved better.

He wanted to get her away from these people, but he was also worried about the consequences of this enforced stay in her company for him too. For someone he was supposed to be pretending to like, he'd had some very real feelings towards her today. And not just the physical ones he'd experienced after waking up beside her in bed. Jake already cared enough about Evie to not want to subject her to any more 'family time', a development he hadn't anticipated, or wanted, when he deliberately steered away from this kind of emotional drama. He'd made the decision years ago to only worry about himself. It was safer than getting close to anyone. But Evie had managed to slip past those defences and make him feel protective towards her. Along with everything else.

'We can't be stuck here. We can't stay here. Jake has to get back. This wasn't the deal.'

In her panic, she'd almost let the details of their arrangement slip. As expected, the news had sent her into
a tailspin and if her detractors had any inkling of their
'relationship' they'd tear her to shreds. He didn't think
she could take much more. Her vulnerability was so
startlingly obvious it was no wonder they saw her as
easy prey. Jake felt it was part of his role as her partner, fake or otherwise, to support her. To let her know
that he was there for her, regardless of his own mis-
givings about their situation. They were powerless to
do anything anyway.

He slipped his arms around Evie's waist and gave
her a hug to reassure her that they'd survive this together. 'It's okay. I've nothing to rush back for. As long
as we're together it'll be all right. I promise.' He did
his best to reassure her they'd survive an overnight
stay here, even though it was likely both of their night-
mares come true.

Looking up at him with big, trusting brown eyes,
Evie nodded. He knew in this moment he was the only
person she had to rely on. Whilst it wasn't a position
he wanted to be in, he wasn't going to let her down.
Not today at least.

'Such a drama queen,' Bailey snipped, earning a
dark look from Jake, and a wish that he could knock
him out. But he was here to calm troubled waters, not
whip them up into a storm.

'Where are we going to stay?' she asked quietly.

'Your room, of course. You seemed quite cosy there
earlier. Courtney and Bailey will be in her old room. I
really don't see the problem, dear.'

She wouldn't. Evie, on the other hand, was looking

at him in such a state of panic he was beginning to feel it himself. That bed was tiny, and torturous. It was one thing falling asleep atop the covers by accident, but quite another being expected to share it for the night. Still, to make a big deal over it would raise suspicion and blow their cover. The last thing Evie needed.

'I'm sure we'll manage.' He rubbed her back reassuringly and felt the muscles beneath his fingertips begin to un-bunch.

'If we're all here for the night, why don't we play some board games to pass the time?'

Courtney's suggestion was met by a chorus of groans but she pouted until she got her way and everyone agreed.

So it came to be that five of them set up in the lounge, Evie and Jake against the rest, in a battle of wits, and wills. It only served to highlight the differences between Evie and her stepsister. Her general knowledge was far superior to Courtney's, much to her and Bailey's frustration. When it came to team games, guessing one another's drawing clues, Jake and Evie seemed to be in tune. Their high fives to one another was a stark contrast to the blank faces on the other team, and Bailey's frequent insults to Courtney's intelligence. In the end, with Courtney on the brink of tears, and the engagement almost over before it began, they agreed to call it a night on the game night fun.

'Why don't I make us all a nice cup of tea?' June suggested as Bailey shoved all the game contents roughly back into the boxes.

'That would be lovely, thank you.'

Jake hoped this would signal the end of their forced

proximity for the night. They'd been conciliatory and sociable, and at one point he and Evie had even seemed to be enjoying the games. Probably because they'd won most of them, causing Bailey and Courtney's moods to darken considerably. He didn't care about that, only that Evie seemed more relaxed.

Of course this wasn't where he wanted to be tonight, especially overnight. He had business to tend to, and he had some concerns about how involved he was becoming in Evie's life. However, if it helped her to be more at ease with herself, and events beyond her control, it would be worthwhile.

Perhaps not wanting to be left alone with Bailey and Courtney in the living room, Evie headed into the kitchen, with Jake following close behind. He didn't trust himself not to speak his mind to those who'd betrayed her so cruelly if they should say anything more derogatory about her in his presence.

'Can we do anything to help?' Evie had already busied herself getting the china cups and plates from the cupboard as June stirred the teapot.

'Perhaps Jake could carry the tray in? We'll put those big muscles to use.' She was teasing him but he swore Evie was blushing more than he was at the mention of his physique. It was sweet that she was embarrassed on his behalf, but he was also wondering if there was more to it. If perhaps he'd become more than a convenience to her too.

Whilst it was a complication he didn't need, it at least validated that the bond between them wasn't just all in his head.

'Evie, you take in the plate of sweet stuff,' he heard

June order her behind him, noticing it wasn't often Courtney was called to do anything too taxing. Evie would oblige for the same reason she'd offered to help in the first place, because she was kind-natured, and that was the main difference between her and her family. When they spoke to her as though she was somehow inferior to them, all he wanted to do was gather her in his arms and protect her from the vitriol. Although probably not before giving them a piece of his mind first. He only held back because he knew that wasn't what she wanted. His role here was to be visibly present, and quietly supportive. Hopefully, he'd remember that and didn't manage to widen the chasm between Evie and her family even further.

Bailey and Courtney were lying nauseatingly entwined across the full length of the settee, letting June pour their tea for them.

'Would you like something to eat?' Evie offered them the plate of chocolate-covered teacakes and mince pies.

He couldn't bear to see her pander to them just to keep the peace. She was a better person than he was, that was for sure.

Courtney screwed up her nose. 'Are you trying to make me fat? I have to watch my figure. You keep them for yourself, Evie. I know you like the sweet stuff.'

Now Jake knew they were being mean to her just for the sake of it. Evie had curves in all the right places and he would rather have that than a clearly unhappy person who could only get their kicks putting other people down. Specifically, this woman whom he'd become very fond of in such a short space of time.

'I'll take one. Life's too short to count calories.' He helped himself to a teacake and popped it whole into his mouth.

To his delight, Evie copied him and they stood, laughter dancing in their eyes, munching down the sweet treats. Courtney tutted.

'Can you two sit down? I can't see the TV past you.' Bailey waved them out of the way, even though the volume had been turned way down and Jake doubted he had any real desire to watch Z-list celebrities dancing to Christmas songs. He just didn't like to see Evie happy.

With Bailey and Courtney taking up the entirety of the sofa with no attempt to make room for anyone else, Jake and Evie were forced to share one armchair. He sat in the seat and she was forced to perch on his lap. Uncomfortable for all concerned.

'Tell us where you two met.' June made an attempt at conversation even though he hoped she wouldn't probe too deep into their so-called relationship.

'We…uh…' Under the spotlight, Evie seemed to struggle with the idea of telling the story, so Jake took over.

'I popped into the studio to see about one of Evie's classes for my employees. We hit it off, and things just progressed from there.' He stayed as close to the truth as he could for now, not wanting to make Evie feel any more uncomfortable about this ruse.

'What classes?' June asked, showing she didn't know much about her stepdaughter's life at all.

Evie cleared her throat. 'I…er…run pottery and pizza evenings. I show groups how to throw their own pot, then they can order a pizza and have a drink afterwards.'

'Putting that degree to good use,' Bailey sniffed.

'The classes are very popular.' He felt the need to defend her when she had absolutely nothing to be ashamed of. On the contrary, it was apparent to Jake that Evie was a success despite her family, and had made it all on her own.

'I have to run a few different classes and things to pay the studio overheads, but I do my own range of ceramics and take commissions too.'

It was a shame Evie felt the need to defend how she made her living when it was clear to him how much she enjoyed it.

'You should be proud of her. She built a business up on her own and made a success of it. Trust me, it's not easy to do in this day and age.' He made a point of celebrating her achievements because it was about time someone did. If that meant shaming her family into finally recognising what an amazing woman Evie was, then so be it.

'I am proud of her,' June spluttered into her tea.

'Spending all day playing in the dirt just seems a little…provincial.' It was Courtney turning her nose up at Evie's career now, and he felt her tense in his lap.

'And what is it *you* do for a living?' He couldn't help himself. They were so busy putting Evie down he doubted they had any time for self-reflection, or self-awareness.

'I'm a personal shopper at a very well-known department store, but I don't see what that has to do with anything.'

'So you spend other people's money for a living? Very admirable. I guess we're all just making our way in this world, and no one has the right to criticise how we do that. Especially if we make other people happy and get tremendous satisfaction from our work. We shouldn't let anyone try to take that away from us.' It was the closest he could get to telling them all to leave Evie alone without actually saying the words.

'I think it's probably time we went to bed. Hopefully, the snow will have cleared by the morning and we can be on our way first thing.' Evie jumped to her feet, giving Jake a pleading look to come with her.

It was obvious she wasn't happy with him for saying what he had, but he regretted none of it. At least he had peace of mind in knowing he'd stood up for her, given her some support in the face of her family, and that was what she'd wanted him there for. Although perhaps she'd seen him in more of a non-speaking role...

'I know you've done very well for yourself, Evie. Your father would be proud of you.' Finally, June made some attempt at praising her stepdaughter. Enough to bring tears to Evie's eyes.

'Thanks. I hope so.' Her voice cracked as she reached out a hand to Jake. 'Bed?'

For a heartbeat he'd forgotten this was for everyone else's sake and took her hand, ready to sweep her off to bed. Then he remembered where they were, that this wasn't real and he wasn't going to actually spend the night how his wide-awake body was hoping.

'Oh, look. You're under the mistletoe. Isn't that sweet? A goodnight kiss before you leave.' Courtney threw one last spanner in the works before they could make their escape.

Jake looked up to find the troublesome sprig of white berries hanging from the chandelier, then at Evie, who seemed frozen to the spot. They were under scrutiny now, and though he wanted to kiss her passionately and eliminate any doubts in her family's minds that they were a couple, he was reluctant to do so. Firstly, because it wasn't something they'd discussed and he didn't want to do something as intimate as that without her permission. Also, because there were certain parts of him that didn't need any more encouragement when it came to this woman.

He leaned in, watched her eyes flutter shut and her lips part. Mustering all the strength he could find, he simply gave her a peck on the mouth, not wanting to linger there in case all of his self-control disappeared in the taste of her on his lips.

'Goodnight, everyone,' he said, not hanging around for a score on his performance, knowing it would be found lacking. However, he was willing to let his ego take a hit rather than let himself get too carried away in his role as pretend boyfriend.

None of this was real. It wouldn't do for him to start thinking there was more to this than physical attraction, and a promise to help.

Evie needed to get out of this house now more than ever. It was bad enough being stuck here listening to her family's insults and put-downs, but now she had to lock herself away in that tiny boxroom with Jake for the night.

This evening had been emotionally overwhelming. Jake standing up for her had given her mixed feelings in that she appreciated someone doing that for the first time in her life, but confronting her family like that about their behaviour was something she'd never done. Whether he meant what he'd said or it was all part of the act she'd never know for sure. Especially when that kiss seemed to have been purely for display purposes.

If she was honest, it had been an anticlimax. When she'd known he was going to kiss her, her heart had raced in anticipation. However, the reality had been rather lacklustre, to say the least. A thin-lipped, closed mouth, hard kiss which hadn't rocked her world at all. She'd expected a lot more when she'd often let her thoughts drift in that direction. The lack of passion was disappointing, and she supposed he didn't harbour any attraction towards her in the slightest. Not his fault, but it did make a mockery of the feelings she'd been having towards him when it turned out to be one-sided.

Now she had to spend the night with him, all the while knowing it was a chore for him when every touch or kind word was enough to send her pulse rocketing.

'Will you slow down.' Jake was bounding up the stairs after her and reached the bedroom just as she was closing the door.

'Sorry. I just wanted out of there.'

'It's easy to understand why. I'm so sorry you have to put up with that.'

'And you didn't help, stirring things up like that. They'll probably be ten times worse now. Don't forget there'll be a wedding to go to after all of this, and you won't be there as backup.'

The thought was disturbing. At least tonight she'd had someone to lean on. He'd been her place of sanctuary, and she knew her current attitude was a reaction to the realisation that he wasn't going to be there for ever. Nor did he want to be. That much was apparent in the awkward kiss.

'I'm sorry. I couldn't just stand back and listen to them talk to you like that. You deserve better.'

'You can stop pretending you care, Jake. There's no one to see your performance except me.'

He frowned. 'What are you talking about? I didn't say anything I didn't mean.'

'Ah, but you do kiss women you don't want to.'

She hadn't meant to address the matter at all, but it had been bugging her that he'd clearly felt nothing in that kiss, when it seemed to Evie that she'd been waiting for it from the moment they'd met.

Another frown. 'What makes you say that? I mean, I know kissing wasn't part of our deal, but it would've looked weird if we hadn't in the circumstances. And who says I didn't want to?'

She was beginning to wish she hadn't gone down this route. Now she had to hear him say out loud that he didn't want her. Not only that, she'd have to spend the night with him in this tiny room with nowhere for either of them to hide.

'You. Your body language.'

'Trust me. I wanted to kiss you, Evie.' Standing on the other side of the room, hands in pockets, he wasn't making a convincing argument.

'Really? I'm not sure we convinced anyone with that demonstration. Don't get me wrong, I know there are men out there who don't know how to kiss properly. I just didn't expect you'd be one of them. Though I suppose when you look the way you do, you don't have to try with women...'

She was trying to reconcile what he was telling her with the experience and it just didn't add up. There had to be some reason he hadn't lived up to expectation, yet he was insisting it wasn't because of his partner. The only conclusion she could come up with was that perhaps that was simply his kissing style. Flat. Unexciting. And such a shame.

Rather than look embarrassed, shocked or angry by her review, he wore a determined expression as he crossed the floor towards her in one long stride.

'I know how to bloody kiss.'

Jake moved swiftly, cupping her face in his hands and planting his lips on hers. His mouth was firm and demanding at first, but as she relaxed into the kiss he softened against her. A tenderness which had been missing previously, and apparently had the capability of melting her bones.

He traced her bottom lip with the tip of his tongue, before dipping inside to meet her. She was lost to him, to the sensation of this kiss which was exceeding all previous expectations.

A little 'Mmm' of satisfaction slipped out that she knew she'd come to regret later. When she remembered every second of this encounter, and how she'd enjoyed him like an ice cream on a hot summer's day.

Then it was over as quickly as it had begun. He'd proved his point. And then some.

Jake took a step back so she could breathe again.

'When I kiss someone it's a promise of more to come. I didn't think either of us was ready for that.' His voice was husky, his face dark, and Evie's knees weak.

'Yeah, you were probably right.' She collapsed onto the edge of the bed.

He gave a half smile. 'It definitely wasn't anything to do with you, or my…technique.'

'I believe you.' Evie could certainly verify that last part of his statement. There was nothing wrong with his technique except for the need it awakened in her to do it again.

However, by challenging him like that, forcing him to kiss her like he meant it, she'd made things even more awkward for them.

'I don't want to make things complicated between us when the whole idea of this was to make things easier. I still need you to be my fake wedding date.' His grin went some way to helping the truth go down easier.

He was right. She was a mess. This absolutely was not the right time or place to get involved with anyone, much less the man posing as her fake boyfriend. Since he'd upheld his end of their contract she could hardly back out when he needed her to step up for him soon in return.

'Of course. Let's just put it behind us and get this night over with.'

Then they could go their separate ways until the wedding at least. A little distance and perspective would help her realise this had been nothing more than a lonely woman reading more into a kiss than was intended. It was Jake's ego at work here, not his pent-up lust for her. She'd challenged him, and he'd more than stepped up to the plate to prove himself. Now she had to get over it.

And perhaps take Ursula's advice to get back on the singles market if she was so het-up over one little kiss.

'Where do you want me?'

She studied Jake's face for signs of amusement, convinced he was trying to rile her further, but no, he was being serious. She was the one with issues, immediately picturing him in her bed, carrying on where that kiss had left off.

'I…um…'

It would seem churlish to ask him to sleep anywhere other than the bed, given they'd shared it only hours earlier. However, she knew she was going to find it difficult lying so close to him now, her body acutely aware of how he could make her feel. The only problem was there weren't a lot of choices available in such a tiny space.

'I can take the chair if you toss me one of the pillows.' Thankfully, Jake's gallantry saw him provide the solution, no doubt at the price of his own comfort.

The egg-shaped wicker chair in the corner of her room had never been the most comfortable item of furniture in the world, but it was going to have to do for one night.

'If you're sure?' She did her best to provide some padding to soften the impact of the hard surface, kitting the inside of it out with some scatter cushions for him to sit on.

'It's fine. As soon as the snow clears, we'll be out of here anyway.'

Seeming as anxious as she was to leave, Evie imagined him sitting watching out of the window all night for the first sign of a thaw so he could get the car revving for their getaway. Which wasn't a bad thing, considering tonight's events.

Evie hunted through her old chest of drawers and pulled out an old, shapeless nightshirt with cartoon dogs plastered on the front. She wanted to be comfortable enough that she might actually be able to sleep and forget about this evening, as well as keep her clothes semi-respectable to wear again in the morning. It was doubtful she had anything in her teenage wardrobe that would fit her, or be suitable for a woman now in her late twenties. This veritable sackcloth wasn't in the least bit sexy, so any idea of passion would be killed stone dead as soon as she donned it. Maybe then they'd both be able to put all thoughts of that kiss out of their heads.

'I'm afraid I don't have anything suitable for you to wear. Unless you'd be comfortable sleeping in a pair of yoga pants and a crop top, because I'm pretty sure that's all I left in that wardrobe.' Despite the teasing, the idea of seeing him in such tight, revealing clothing was tempting.

He tightened his lips in faux outrage. 'I think I'll pass, thanks.'

Instead, he took off his jacket, undid his tie and opened the top few buttons of his shirt. He kicked off his shoes and sat back in the chair. Still pretty much clothed, Evie wondered how he managed to make it seem as though she'd just been given a strip show. It had been equally, if not more, erotic unbuttoning that formal exterior than if she'd had a greased up male exotic dancer giving her a lap dance.

She quickly disappeared into the bathroom, clutching her nightie like a shy virgin who'd just caught a glimpse of her first naked man.

A splash of cold water on her face and a change into her nightwear brought her rising temperature down a little, but it wouldn't stop the indecent thoughts she kept having about him. It was only when she exited the bathroom and his cool gaze followed her across the room that she realised how short the nightdress was on her adult body now. It appeared the attraction went both ways.

She didn't think the effort he'd put into that kiss was entirely an act to salve his fragile ego. Still, taking things any further than one kiss wasn't a good move for either of them. They needed each other for more than the short-lived pleasure she might gain from a fling, because he'd made it clear he didn't do relationships. Though Evie wasn't ready to get into any sort of serious commitment either, she doubted anything casual was going to do her any good.

If she ever ventured into sharing her life, or her heart, with anyone again, it would have to be with someone she knew was going to be there for her. A man who thought she was enough, and wouldn't need to look elsewhere. Someone she could trust not to let her down and break her heart. Jake had been upfront with her about the kind of man he was. A workaholic who'd been prepared to give up a loving, long-term relationship for a business deal. There was absolutely nothing to be gained from thinking about him in any sort of romantic scenario.

So why couldn't she stop?

CHAPTER FIVE

JAKE WOKE EARLY, having spent half the night replaying events in his head, and squirming in the most uncomfortable chair he'd ever had the misfortune to sit in.

Evie, on the other hand, looked quite content sleeping in her bed, and he was reluctant to wake her. She deserved that tiny bit of peace.

Slowly and carefully, he picked his way across the floor to the window, trying not to wake her. He took a peek outside. It was beginning to rain now and hopefully by the time Evie stirred they'd be able to make tracks through what was left of the snow. He eased the door open, taking one last look at her lying there, hair mussed and that damned nightshirt riding high on her thighs. The very reason he had to get out of this room.

He'd inflicted a special kind of torture on himself by kissing her like that last night. He could pretend he was making a point, defending his honour and reputation, but that hadn't been his main motivation. It was simply the excuse he'd needed to kiss Evie the way he wanted, without an audience. Now he was going to be plagued for ever with the knowledge of how she felt in his arms, tasted on his tongue and responded passionately to him in return. Everything he didn't need to know if he was going to be able to go ahead with this wedding date charade.

Goodness knew he wasn't looking to get any more involved with Evie and her family than he already was. He had to stick to the plan. No strings. No complications. No kissing.

Evie had obviously had her heart broken and was carrying way more emotional baggage than he needed in his life. The last thing she would be ready for was a man whose work was his priority, and who had no idea of settling down. She wasn't going to have her heart mended by him, a man who'd left her in bed to come downstairs and catch up on the work he'd missed out on. Because that was his life, the only dependable thing in it that no one could take away from him.

Jake made his way into the kitchen and made himself a coffee. He liked this time of morning when everything was still. As if the rest of the world was yet to wake. Even the birds were still in their slumber. It helped quieten his mind for a little while. Until his thoughts were consumed with work and ensuring that he, and everyone working for him, had a secure future.

Taking his coffee to the kitchen table, he sat down and video-called Donna. Like him, she'd be awake and raring to go. Another crossover from life with an army parent who'd made sure they did their chores before they even left the house for school in the mornings.

The call had barely connected before Donna's face appeared on the screen. She was already dressed, hair perfect and make-up immaculate. Jake was definitely slacking today.

'Hi, bro. Where are you? I know it's Sunday but

you're usually in the office by now. It's a bit rich expecting me to come in if you're not going to be here.' She was peering behind him, trying to figure out where he was, clearly miffed that she'd had to give up her Sunday morning lie-in for this important meeting they had with a film company. Unfortunately, it was the only day Jake had been able to make work.

'I know. I got snowed in. I'll get there as soon as I can, but I need to get home and shower first. Can you manage things until I get there?'

It was a rhetorical question. He knew as well as she did that his little sister was every bit as capable as he was of running the business. She simply chose a life over work. Sometimes he wondered if she had the right idea, working to live rather than living to work. He imagined if Evie was in his bed every morning, he might find it harder to leave the house.

'Of course. Wait… You haven't been home? You dirty stop-out.'

'It's not like that. I was doing a friend a favour and I got trapped because of the weather. Otherwise, I would've been home and we wouldn't be having this phone call.'

'A friend, eh?'

Her grin was nauseating, but he knew she was only teasing because he never let her meet anyone he spent the night with. Apart from the fact his private life had nothing to do with her, he didn't want her to know about Evie and get the wrong idea. It wasn't as though they'd actually slept together. At least not in the way his sister would probably imagine. A scenario he was trying to avoid.

'Yes.' He adopted his serious, don't-mess-with-me boss face, ignoring the fact he was wearing yesterday's wrinkled clothes and hadn't washed, shaved or brushed his hair today. Something which was blatantly obvious, seeing himself on the screen. He looked like he'd spent the night half sleeping in a chair wondering what new mess he'd got himself into.

'I hope you'll be bringing this "friend" to the wedding so I can meet her.'

Jake just knew he was never going to hear the end of this. It was such a novelty for him to be caught on the hop like this, Donna was going to use it against him at every given opportunity, like any little sister would.

'Listen, I need you to host my nine o'clock meeting. You have all the facts and figures there. Just tell them I'll catch up with them when I'm back at my desk.' He chose to ignore the teasing and try to refocus her on the more important business at hand. His absence was unprofessional, and it didn't sit well with him, even if it was a source of amusement for Donna.

'Sorry. I didn't realise you were down here. I thought you'd left without me.' A sleepy Evie walked into shot in her tiny nightdress and completely blew all pretence of credibility for him with his sister.

'I'll talk to you later, Donna.'

Jake ended the call. Too late for him to possibly have any valid excuse for why he'd spent the night here with Evie. Not least because she was going to be his plus one at the wedding. He supposed it gave his story more credibility, but he didn't want Donna to think he was distracted from his job.

Evie's hand went to her mouth. 'I'm so sorry. I didn't

know you were on a call. I can go back upstairs if you like?'

'It's okay. I was just letting them know I'd be late into the office this morning. I didn't want to wake you. I would never have gone without you.'

As tempting as it might have been to get in the car and drive far away from the situation he'd got himself into, Jake would never have done that to her. He didn't want to be another one to let her down and break the trust she'd shown in him by even bringing him here.

'Do you need to go now? Sorry, I didn't realise you'd be working today. I can throw my clothes on.'

She still had that dreamy look on her face, her hair a tangled curtain around her pale face. He could see she needed a little time to come round before they made a hasty exit.

'It's okay. Donna is going to take care of things until I get in. Take your time and have some breakfast. You didn't have much to eat last night.'

Neither had he, but he was used to working through the night on meagre sustenance. Evie should take the opportunity to have some food without every morsel being analysed and commented on. At least she might be able to enjoy it without a critical audience.

'I am hungry.' Evie hunted in the cupboards looking for something to eat, and finally settled on a box of cereal.

Jake did his best to look away when she stretched up to get a bowl, her nightshirt revealing even more of her soft thighs and the curve of her backside, and failed.

'Would you like some?' She turned to meet his gaze.

He blinked, then realised she was talking about breakfast. 'No, thanks.'

Okay, so maybe he would chivvy her along after she'd eaten, and get back to real life. Where he wasn't tempted by half naked women distracting him from work.

Evie brought her breakfast over to sit at the table with him.

'Was it an important call? I know you're a busy man. Sorry you're stuck here.'

'I had a meeting this morning, but Donna's going to take care of it until I get there. These things happen. It's no one's fault.'

If anyone was to blame, it was him. He should never have lain down on that bed with her. He'd crossed the line between being an anonymous fake boyfriend and being someone who cared about her. Now he was suffering the consequences.

'Your sister's very pretty.'

If Evie had time to see Donna, that meant in all likelihood she'd spotted Evie too. At the very least she'd heard her. Jake groaned inwardly, knowing the teasing and one hundred and one questions he'd face when he got home.

'Pretty annoying,' he answered back, in that childlike tone siblings always adopted when talking about one another.

'Yet you work together?'

'I didn't say she wasn't good at her job. She knows me better than anyone, and compensates in areas where I'm apparently found lacking. Hence the suggestion for the pottery night in the first place. Apparently, I'm intimidating and distant.'

Evie didn't contradict him.

'Donna likes to think she's the friendly face of the company. I don't know what that says about me.'

'You do have a certain...do not approach vibe. But I know beyond that there's a very caring man, willing to stand up for someone he barely knows in front of her family.'

He didn't know how to cope with the unexpected praise, so he quietly accepted it.

'Donna moved with me when I was setting up the business. Said there was nothing keeping her in London any more. I think she'd just split up with her latest boyfriend. She's another romantic, I'm afraid.'

Although Donna's attitude towards relationships was slightly different to his. She wasn't afraid to get involved with anyone, but she had a habit of moving on quickly when it didn't work out. A product of their nomadic upbringing, he feared.

'At least you get along, are there for each other. I often wonder what it would've been like to have had a full sibling. You know, someone who didn't mind that I was part of their life.'

Jake took Donna for granted, both as a sister and as a valued member of staff. He couldn't imagine being without her, or her treating him the way Courtney treated Evie. Naturally, they teased each other, like all siblings, but it was usually in good humour. She was really the only person he had in the world to confide in, to lean on. The only person he could rely on in life. Evie didn't even have that with her stepsister. It was no wonder that she was lonely.

'You won't want to hang around much longer then, will you?' Although he'd told her to take her time, now Jake was beginning to think they should get on the move as soon as possible. Not that he was looking forward to facing Donna, who wasn't going to let this matter drop, but at least he and Evie could get some distance between them again.

'I'll get dressed. I'd prefer to get out of here before anyone else gets up. I'll leave a note.' Evie rinsed her dishes and put them back in the cupboard, before going back upstairs to get changed. With any luck they'd be on their way soon and be able to put all this behind them.

Jake only hoped by the time the wedding came around they'd have forgotten all about what had happened. That he'd have put it from his mind how it felt to share a bed with her and forget the outside world existed.

'So…?'

'"So" what?' Jake ignored Donna, hovering in his office doorway, and went straight to his desk and logged on his computer.

'Who is she?'

'Who's who?' He played dumb, not wanting to place any significance on the woman he'd been with, and give Donna ammunition.

She rolled her eyes at him and followed him over to his desk. Clearly, she wasn't going to let the matter drop.

'The woman you were obviously with last night. The woman I saw wearing next to nothing on the call this morning.'

'Why are you so interested? I don't quiz you on your love life.'

'Because, dear brother, I have never known you to be late for work on account of a woman. Never mind stay over at their place.'

'I told you. We were snowed in,' he said weakly.

'Uh-huh. And are we going to meet this mystery woman at any point? Will she be going to the wedding?'

This was exactly what he'd been dreading. That Donna was going to put two and two together and he was going to end up with a wife.

'Yes, she's going to the wedding, but don't get too carried away, okay? We've just met.' There was little point in denying everything when he was supposed to be convincing people that they were a couple for the wedding. He just didn't want anyone thinking they were in a serious relationship.

'What's her name?'

'Evie. Now, how did you get on without me this morning?' He did his best to change the subject now she'd got as much information out of him as he was willing to give.

'Fine. Although they probably won't believe anything until they speak to the *real* boss. Now, back to more important matters… When will I get to meet this Evie?'

Jake let out a frustrated breath. 'At the wedding.

Don't make a big deal out of it, please, Donna. I just like her company.'

That much was true. Well, there was a lot more than that which he appreciated about her, but he needed to downplay it for this conversation.

'It is a big deal. I don't know the last time I even saw you with a woman, and the fact you're bringing her to the wedding...'

'Don't read anything into that. It's just to stop Mum matchmaking with every single woman within a hundred-mile radius for me.'

'I'm just happy for you, Jake.'

To his horror, she rushed around the desk and grabbed him into a side hug. He eventually managed to shrug her off.

'Yes, I'm happy for me too. Now, can we get back to work?'

He gave up trying to deny anything else when Donna was as stubborn as he was at times. The only way to get rid of her was to tell her she was right. It did the trick.

'Okay, bro. If you're not going to tell me anything else I'll get back to work. I'll just have to get to know Evie at the wedding.'

Why did that sound like a threat?

His thoughts turned to Evie at the wedding and being ambushed by his sister. She definitely wasn't ready for that. Even though he'd left her less than an hour ago he found himself calling her number. He had to warn her, right?

As he waited for her to answer, he realised he'd been in the office ten minutes and he hadn't opened his emails or checked his calendar. He was definitely changing already and Donna wasn't the only one he needed to be careful didn't carried away.

The only reason he was calling Evie now was so she didn't get caught out in their lie at the wedding. It would be humiliating for both of them. He would give her some warning about what she was in for, then leave her alone until the wedding. Once that was over, their arrangement done, they never had to see each other again. It didn't have to be the crisis he was anticipating simply because he'd enjoyed kissing her.

'Hello?' The sound of Evie's voice immediately soothed his troubled mind.

'Evie? It's Jake.'

'Is everything all right?' Her concern was palpable and he felt better that she worried for him the way he'd done about her last night.

'Yes, I just wanted to give you a heads-up that since catching a glimpse of you this morning, my sister is very eager to get to know you. Don't worry, I'll try to head her off as much as possible at the wedding but I thought I'd prepare you.'

Silence.

'Evie? Did you hear me?'

'Yes,' she answered quietly. 'About the wedding... I'm wondering if it's a good idea at all for us to go together.'

Jake's stomach dropped onto the floor. He'd clearly crossed the line somewhere when she was backing out already. It could be down to the fact he was already phoning her after just having dropped her off home, or it could be because he'd kissed her when there was no call for it. He hadn't realised how much he'd been looking forward to seeing her again already until it might not be a possibility at all.

'Is something wrong?'

What did I do?

'It's just a lot. I'm not very good at social situations, as you've seen for yourself. I don't know what to wear, and I'm likely to embarrass you as much as myself. You'd be better going without me. Which reminds me, I still have your credit card. You're going to need that back. Maybe I can courier it over to you.' She was tripping over her words in her haste to get them out. It reminded Jake of that first night in her studio when she'd charmed him into agreeing to this ridiculous situation in the first place.

'It's fine. I have plenty of others. Hold onto it in case you change your mind. I would really like you to be with me, Evie. Listen, if it's the dress code that's bothering you, maybe I can make time to go with you to find something suitable if you like? We could grab some lunch too. What do you say?'

Jake couldn't quite believe he was offering to go shopping with her, and completely slacking where work was concerned. Yet at the moment it seemed more important to have her onside for this wedding where he'd have to face his parents. He was beginning to think it was more about having the support than convincing his family he was happily settled with someone. Being there for Evie last night seemed to have made a difference and helped her get through a difficult evening, and he was hoping for the same.

If all it took to get Evie to accompany him was to

play hooky from work for a couple of hours and get her a dress, it would be worth it.

The silence on the other end of the line seemed to go on way too long. Until eventually she offered an unenthusiastic, 'Sure.'

It was enough to satisfy Jake for now. Though if Donna found out he'd never hear the end of it.

Evie didn't know how on earth she was going to stomach lunch when her whole body was tense and tied in knots. Including her head. She'd decided against going to the wedding with Jake even before he'd called to warn her that his sister would likely give her the third degree over their alleged relationship.

It had been a week since the engagement party but, unable to get that kiss out of her head, or the way she'd caught him looking at her that morning with undisguised lust, she'd thought better of seeing him again. But here she was, already going against all common sense to meet up with him only days later.

After dealing with Courtney and Bailey her emotions were in turmoil, and this attraction she was feeling towards Jake wasn't helping. She thought he might have been glad to get out of their arrangement and used her outfit as a lame excuse to call things off. Jake had called her bluff, apparently still keen for her to accompany him to his mother's wedding. How could she let him down when he'd done so much for her?

There was also the matter of her wanting to see him again. Usually, she was more than happy holed up in her studio, avoiding the world outside and anything, or anyone, that could possibly hurt her. However, she knew part of the tension inside came from the anticipation of spending more time with Jake. The only person in a long time who'd stood up for her, worried about her…taken care of her. Perhaps she was mistaking that for something more that had been missing from her life since she'd found out that Bailey was cheating on her, but she enjoyed being with Jake. That feeling had been missing for too long in her life, and even if it only lasted until his mum's wedding was over, she would take it.

As Evie turned the corner onto Royal Avenue an icy wind blasted, her long padded black coat proving scant protection from the cold. She pulled her scarf up over her nose and mouth and strode against the blustery weather. When she saw Jake standing on the pavement ahead waiting for her, her temperature shot up a few degrees.

'Hey. Thanks for coming.' He greeted her with a kiss on the cheek and his warmth, though short-lived, helped to thaw her a little more.

'I should be thanking you. You're the one who'll be paying,' she teased, trying to keep this about fulfilling her promise to him by attending his mother's wedding.

'I thought we could try a few boutique shops I've heard Donna talking about. Failing that, we can get a personal shopper to help us.'

He was scrolling on his phone, clearly having researched some suitable stores. It was touching that he'd taken it upon himself to come with her when he could easily have sent someone in his place. He was a busy man after all. Perhaps he just wanted to make sure she wouldn't back out again.

'As long as it's not Courtney! I'm happy to have a

look first. I'm not sure how comfortable I'd be with a personal shopper.' Apart from the expense involved, the idea of a polished, sophisticated store assistant measuring her up, and bustling into the changing room with her, wasn't something she'd look forward to.

'I'm no expert but I can give you my opinion, as well as my credit card.' Jake grinned and linked his arm through hers.

It might well have been a tactic to stop her from running away, but Evie relished the close body contact, regardless that it was how he made her feel that had given her second thoughts about the wedding. The experts always said treats in moderation didn't do a body any harm…

'I like that one on you.' Jake's eyes lit up when Evie stepped out of the changing room wearing a multicoloured mid-length dress which nipped in at her waist and had a daring plunging neckline.

'You're no help. You like all of them.' She rolled her eyes and smiled.

'Exactly. You look good in anything, so just pick the one you feel most comfortable in.'

Clothes shopping was usually a chore, even when it came to choosing for himself, but he'd enjoyed sitting here having his own private fashion show. Evie was shy about her body, probably as a result of her ex's betrayal. The rejection she must have felt would undoubtedly have had an effect on her self-esteem when she was such a sensitive soul. But she had absolutely no need to worry on that score. She was beautiful, inside and out. Bailey was an idiot for ever letting her go.

'Well, it's not this one. I'd be too afraid of falling out of it.' She was tugging at the two strips of fabric currently covering her modesty.

'We can rule that out then. Next.'

He sat back and waited, hoping she was secretly enjoying this as much as he was. It was probably a long time since anyone had treated her to anything, judging by her family. Anything she had, she'd worked for herself. Much like him. She deserved a little spoiling. Goodness knew he wasn't averse to splurging money on himself when the mood took him.

'I'm not sure about this one either...' She opened the curtain tentatively and stepped out, taking Jake's breath away in the process.

The blush pink silk skimmed the curve of her hips, and the slit at the side showed off her long lean legs when she moved.

'Stunning,' he said, once he remembered to close his mouth.

'It's very tight though. One canapé too many and it might burst at the seams. It shows everything.'

She had that right. Under the air-conditioning he could see that the cold was reaching her extremities. The last thing either of them wanted was to have people staring at her hardened nipples. Including Jake.

'What about the first one you tried on? We both liked it.' Anything to take his mind off her perky breasts and stop him feeling like a voyeur.

'Give me a second.' She hitched up the skirt and waddled back into the cubicle, re-emerging with a smile on her face.

'Yes. You look beautiful in that too.' It was a modest white sheath dress emblazoned with a cobalt blue trailing leaf which reminded him of the Willow Pattern china his mother used to have. Nothing special on its own, but it showed off Evie's figure without being too revealing. The most attractive feature was the beaming smile she was wearing with it.

'I think this is the one. Though I'm afraid I might be too cold. It is December after all.'

As if by magic, the shop assistant appeared with matching accessories. 'We have a bolero-style jacket or a stunning blue cashmere pashmina, which will go perfectly with that.'

'Oh, that's beautiful.' Evie stroked the pashmina with longing, and the assistant launched into her sales spiel.

'You can wear it as a shawl or a wrap.' She draped the fabric around Evie's shoulders and she snuggled into it.

'It's so soft,' Evie sighed, clearly in love.

Not about to waste an opportunity, another assistant arrived with a matching clutch bag, shoes and hat. The pair set to work kitting Evie out in the full outfit, and she was beaming in the midst of it all.

'Sold,' he said, much to everyone's apparent glee.

'We also have a matching tie.' One of the sales women ran off to fetch a silk tie for him to co-ordinate with his wedding date.

'Yes. Fine. Add that to the bill too.'

'Oh, Jake. Let me get that for you. It's the least I can do,' Evie pleaded, taking the tie for herself.

'There's no need.' He knew she was probably on a

limited budget which likely didn't include expensive silk ties.

'Please. I want to.' Those pleading eyes were too hard to resist. He knew this was more about the gesture than the cost.

'If you insist.'

'I do.' She disappeared back into the changing room to take off the outfit before he could argue any further.

As the sales assistants carried her purchases to the till, Evie cradled the tie in her hands as though it was the most expensive item in the store.

Jake appreciated that she wanted to do something for him. Too often people took it for granted that he would pay for a meal or a taxi, because of who and what he was. Although he didn't mind covering any bills, he did mind when people expected it from him. When they didn't appreciate him for who he was, and thought more about what they could do for him. Evie was different. This was her way of saying thanks, and showing him that they were in this together. Even though she was the one doing him a favour by attending the event of the year.

'So…lunch? Where would you like to go? There's a good tasting menu on at the hotel I usually take my clients to for dinner.' At least he had plenty of experience when it came to impressing people with good food and fine wine. He reckoned they deserved it after a busy morning of shopping.

To his astonishment, Evie turned her nose up at the idea of a posh meal in a fancy restaurant.

'Could we get something on the go? The Christmas Market is on at City Hall and I never get the chance to go there. They have loads of food stalls there. I'd love to have a walk around and soak up the atmosphere. Unless you'd rather not? I don't want to keep you from anything more important.'

'There's nothing that can't wait.' Presently, he couldn't think of anything he'd rather do.

They put their purchases in the car and walked the short distance to City Hall, where the grounds were alive with Saturday Christmas shoppers and the air was filled with amazing aromas coming from the food stalls. The Salvation Army band outside the gates was playing traditional Christmas carols, adding to the whole festive atmosphere.

'I think I'll get a hot chocolate to try and warm up. Can I get you one?' Evie stopped at the first log cabin style stall selling all manner of hot beverages, including mulled wine and spiced cider.

'I'll take a hot chocolate too, thanks. You can have a shot of whiskey or brandy in yours to really warm you up. If I wasn't driving, I might have been tempted...'

Evie frowned. 'And spoil the taste of my hot chocolate? No, thanks.'

She ordered their drinks, which arrived quickly, and they carried their takeaway cups with them as they browsed the other stalls. A variety of sweet treats, wooden and knitted crafts, artisan soaps and personalised Christmas decorations, there was plenty for everyone. There was even a mini funfair in the grounds for small children to enjoy.

'I had no idea there was so much here.'

'Have you never been before?' Evie asked, sipping her hot chocolate.

He shook his head. 'Too busy. Besides, Christmas was never really a big deal for me.'

'Why not?' Evie was looking at him as though he'd committed a crime.

'We were never in one place long enough to really get excited about the build-up to it. There were no family heirloom ornaments to decorate a tree, although I think my mother would've liked that. She goes a bit overboard now when she's decorating for the season. I think she's overcompensating. Dad didn't like us having too many unnecessary "things" because it would've made moving around more difficult. He was what you would call a minimalist.'

That was putting it mildly. He and Donna had known better than to get attached to anything because their father would've got rid of it in time for the next transfer. Therefore, Christmas presents were kept to a minimum too.

'That's awful. I can honestly say it's the one time of the year I always felt happy. Dad made such a fuss. Even June was a bit more human around Christmas. Although there was always a distinction made between Courtney and me in terms of gifts, obviously.'

'Of course.' That was how people like Evie's stepmother liked to keep control, keep her stepdaughter in her place. He could imagine her being treated as a second-class citizen next to her stepsister because he'd witnessed it for himself. He was only glad she had some good memories of her father to hold on to.

'I still have some of the tree decorations Dad and I bought before he remarried. June thought they were tacky, but her loss was my gain.'

'I suppose you're one of these people who've had their tree up since the start of December?' He was teasing, but he liked that she still had some of that child-like wonder about the season which he'd never been allowed to cultivate.

'Try November,' she said with a laugh. 'Usually. Except I've been so busy with commissions this year I haven't had a chance to get one yet. Otherwise, it would look like Santa's Grotto at my place.'

Jake didn't doubt it when she'd forgone an expensive meal out to revel in the festivities here, despite the noise and crowds. It was nice to see her happy and relaxed, simply being herself, without having to prove herself to a family that clearly didn't deserve her loyalty.

'I don't usually bother.'

'That does not surprise me.'

'Donna makes an effort in the office for the employees' sake, and she deals with corporate cards and gifts. Otherwise, it hardly registers on my radar.'

Evie was shaking her head. 'You poor, poor man. You've missed out on so much.'

'Like what? I'm usually force-fed a huge Christmas dinner by my mother, and partake in the exchanging of gifts under duress. I think that covers all the bases.'

'You make it sound like a chore. Don't you know it's the most wonderful time of the year? I suppose you don't line up all your favourite Christmas movies to watch, or eat an entirely chocolate based diet for the month?'

'Um…no.'

'When it was just the two of us at home, Dad made Christmas magical. There were so many lights on the house you could probably have seen it from space! He paid just as much attention to the inside of the house too, with decorations everywhere and our stockings hanging on the mantelpiece. It looked like a Christmas card scene. Then there was the food… My goodness, he baked gingerbread and cookies along with Christmas cakes. He read me Christmas stories every night and we used to drive around to look at everyone else's light displays. I loved that. He must have scouted those places out first because he seemed to know where the houses with the best displays were. We'd be driving in complete darkness, drinking hot chocolate, then, all of a sudden, the skies would be lit up with these amazing scenes. I don't know if he was trying to make up for Mum not being there, but he made it a special time for me growing up.'

'It does sound idyllic, but I'm guessing it didn't stay that way?' Jake saw the dip in her shoulders when other, probably more unhappy, memories were brought to the fore.

'June didn't like the tacky decorations and Courtney thought all of our little traditions were childish. I suppose they were, but that's what made it fun. Dad always made me feel like a little girl at Christmas. Until he remarried and I guess he had other priorities.' Despite having every right to feel bitter about the change in the family dynamic, Evie simply sounded sad about it.

'And you like to recreate that kind of Christmas atmosphere to remember your father.' It was a mark of Evie's resilience that she'd been able to cling on to some of those happier memories rather than focus on the negative ones her stepfamily had created.

'Yes. I know it sounds sad when I'm on my own and there's no one else to benefit from the over-the-top decorations and traditions, but that was a happy time for me. It's all I have left of my father.'

'Maybe one day you'll get to share those traditions with a family of your own.' For her sake, he hoped she would when it was clear she was desperate to recreate that happy family that had been taken away from her. He had no such inclinations.

She shrugged. 'In an ideal world, probably. But I can't see me ever wanting to get close enough to anyone for that to be a possibility. It's hard for me to trust these days.'

'I get that, but don't rule it out completely. Christmas might not be my thing, but you seem to revel in the festivities. It seems to make you happy.'

'It does.' She gave him a beaming smile. 'You don't know what you're missing out on, Jake.'

For the first time he could remember, he did actually wonder. He imagined it could be a magical time with someone like Evie. If he ever decided it wasn't just an excuse to do as little work as possible. Nothing much changed for him in that department, except his workforce and input dropped. He used the time to catch up on paperwork or prepare for the forthcoming business plans for the next year. It never entered his head to lie around like a couch potato, gorging on snacks. Although if Evie invited him to do so with her, he might be tempted.

His father hadn't been the type to encourage those whimsical notions that most children were allowed to indulge in at Christmas, or any other time of the year.

But hearing Evie recall those memories with her father and seeing her smile showed how happy it made her. He wouldn't want to take any of that away from her.

'We'll have to agree to disagree on that one.'

They explored a little more around the market, sampled a few of the exotic foods available, and indulged in some sweet Dutch mini pancakes dusted with icing sugar and topped with cream. She really was a bad influence. But he was having fun.

He couldn't remember the last time he'd kicked back like this and just let himself enjoy the moment. A whole month of this with Evie was something he couldn't possibly comprehend, but he was sure he could probably come around to her way of doing things if given half a chance. Here, neither of them was worrying about work or family, or the expectations people put upon them. It seemed a simpler, happier way to exist.

Evie's phone rang then, and she moved over to the side of the grounds to answer it. He watched her face turn into a mask of concern and immediately knew something was wrong.

'Ursula? Calm down. What's wrong? Is he okay? Where is he? I'll get there as soon as I can.'

It was frustrating hearing only one side of the conversation, knowing something had happened but powerless until she hung up and recounted the conversation, which was clearly disturbing her.

Eventually she ended the call, visibly upset.

'Evie, what's wrong?'

'It's Dave—my dog. Ursula was looking after him in the studio, but he got out onto the main road. He's been hurt... I need to get to him.'

She dumped her takeaway cup in the nearest bin and rushed towards the exit.

'Evie, wait. Where is he? I can take you.' He expected her to protest that she didn't want to impose any more on him, that she would let him get back to work.

Instead, she simply said, 'At the vet's. Thank you.'

It showed how much her pet meant to her when her entire focus shifted onto his welfare.

'We'll get there as soon as we can,' he assured her as they hurried back to his car.

She was unusually quiet and he knew it was likely because she was imagining the worst, worried she wouldn't get to her dog in time. As they buckled into the car and he typed the address into the sat nav, he reached across and gave her hand a squeeze, forcing her to look at him.

'It'll be okay.'

It was a big promise, but he was going to be there for her whatever happened. He knew how important her canine companion was to her and, as far as he could tell, she didn't have anyone else in her life to give her the kind of emotional support she needed right now.

Despite his previous reservations about getting too close to her, he was willing to set them aside in order to provide a shoulder for her to lean on over the next few hours.

CHAPTER SIX

'EVERYTHING WILL BE all right. I'll be here when you wake up.' Evie kissed her best boy's golden fur, his little whimpers breaking her heart.

'We'll phone you as soon as he's out of surgery. Hopefully, it will be straightforward but, as you know, there are always risks with older dogs when they're under anaesthetic.' The vet was as sympathetic as she could be, but Evie knew she still had to outline any possible complications.

'Thank you,' she said, doing her best to hold the tears back.

By the time she and Jake had arrived at the surgery, Dave had already been X-rayed and they'd discovered a small fracture in his back leg. She'd excused Ursula, who was almost as distraught as she was over the accident, and Jake had sat with her until the vet had come out to update her on Dave's condition. Now it was a waiting game.

'Where do you want to go now?' Jake asked gently. He'd been so kind. Not only had he bought her those beautiful, expensive clothes, and indulged her trip to the Christmas market, but he'd been there to reassure her from the moment she'd heard about Dave getting hit by a car.

They'd been having a lovely morning up until that phone call. Even though she'd pushed him out of his usual schedule, and comfort zone, he seemed to have enjoyed it as much as she had. It reminded her what it was like to have a partner to do nice things with. She hadn't had that since Bailey, and even now those memories seemed tainted by his betrayal, as though he'd been play-acting all those times they'd been happy together, and had secretly been wishing he was with Courtney.

Maybe if she could get past those intrusive thoughts, those fears that someone else would hurt her the way he had, she might be able to be happy with someone else. One day she might be ready to share her life again, and revel in those joyful moments. However, even today she knew they weren't real when Jake was only in her life because of the deal they'd made. He wasn't a potential life partner, he was simply an extended fake date, with her because she owed him.

'I don't want to go home. I need to keep busy, so I think I'll just head back to the studio. Sorry for dragging you into this, Jake.'

'It's fine. I'll stay with you until they call you.'

'You don't have to do that.'

Whilst she appreciated the offer, she didn't want him to feel obliged. Especially when he'd already gone so far out of his way today to accommodate her.

'I know, but I want to. You shouldn't be on your own. Maybe you could put me to work and I can make myself useful.'

She knew there was little he could do in the way of her commissions, but she wasn't in the right head-space to do anything of any real importance. Although it might be fun to show him how to use the wheel, per-haps give him a pottery lesson while they waited. It would certainly help take her mind off her poor boy lying on the operating table.

'You're very welcome to stop by, but if you need to go at any point I'll understand.' That at least gave him an out if he found it was eating too much into his work-ing day. Then she wouldn't have to feel guilty about keeping Jake from his work, as well as leaving Dave this morning.

'I want to make sure the old boy is okay as well,' he said, showing that he'd already become attached to her furry companion in the short space of time he'd had with him. She assumed he was a doggy person, even though his immaculate clothes suggested some-one who would avoid contamination of animal hair on his person at any cost.

'I wouldn't have had you pinned as an animal-lover.'

'I don't suppose I ever had the chance to find out. Obviously, we weren't allowed pets growing up, and I'm so busy now it wouldn't be fair to have a dog I didn't have time to take care of.'

'I was lucky. Dad was a dog-lover and we had a lovely big Bernese mountain dog called Bran when I was growing up. I was devastated when he died, but then Dad met June and she was allergic to animal hair, so we never had any more pets after that. The first thing I did when I left Bailey was go to the rescue home and pick Dave so I had someone to come home to every night.' It was a shame Jake had never had the companionship of a pet growing up when his childhood sounded so disruptive.

'I'm glad you have him, and he's a lucky dog to have found a home with you.' Jake was so understanding, when Evie knew a lot of people would find her distress over a dog over the top. Despite never being a pet owner himself, he seemed to relate to her attachment. She supposed that was simply down to his compassionate nature, but having someone she could talk to so freely without fear of ridicule made her well up all over again.

'It must seem silly getting so upset over a pet, but he's more than that. He's a friend, a companion, and I don't know what I'd do without him.' Perhaps it was because she felt as though she was in a safe space with Jake, free to express her emotions, but the tears began to fall in earnest now.

'I know how much he means to you, and I'm sure he's going to be all right.'

When the words came from him, Evie was inclined to believe it. Jake was a steadying presence in her life, remarkable for someone who'd apparently gone through so much upheaval in his. She only hoped she could offer the same support to him some day.

They pulled up outside the studio, and when they reached the top of the staircase she almost expected to hear the pad of Dave's paws across the floor to meet her. Unfortunately, behind the door was her cold, empty studio. She'd told Ursula to go home for the day, and now she was glad Jake had insisted on coming with her.

The first things she did was turn on the radio to interrupt the silence she was worried would set her off again when she was so used to hearing Dave wrestling with his toys or appealing to her for attention.

'So, what can I do?' Jake asked, clasping his hands together as he surveyed the room.

'Um…first things first, you'll need to put an apron on.' She was worried even being in this room would ruin his suit so she lifted one of the long aprons and hung it around his neck, leaving him to tie it around his waist.

'What are you working on at the moment?'

'I have a few orders in for bespoke dinner services, and I'm trying to get some stock together for upcoming Christmas markets.'

'And obviously you want a few Jake Hanley originals in there to increase the value.'

'Obviously. Would you like to try your hand at throwing a pot?'

If she wasn't going to be able to focus on getting her work done today, she might as well try and have a little fun. It had to be better than sitting around moping, staring at pictures of her dog and wondering what she would do if the worst happened to him.

'Let's not call it a pot in case it ends up more of a modern art sculpture,' he joked, following her over to the wheel.

'Okay, put your legs either side. Like that.' She fetched one of the balls of clay ready for working with and handed it to him. 'I want you to smack that down in the centre of the wheel.'

Jake did as instructed, hitting the target and centring the clay perfectly.

'You'll need plenty of water to help form the clay.' She scooped water from the bucket beside the wheel to saturate it.

'Do I need to keep my hands wet?' he asked.

'Yes, and the wheel. If you just lean your foot on the pedal, we'll get a nice steady pace for you to work at. Good.' Now came the tricky part.

'Lean your arms on the tops of your legs to stabilise them. Lock them in. Yes, like that.' She made sure he was comfortable with the positioning before she moved onto the next step.

'Now, with both hands around the clay, keeping it centred, we want to raise it up until it resembles a traffic cone.'

Slowly, Jake pulled the wet clay up into a questionable shape which made him snigger as the tip wobbled unsteadily.

Ignoring any attempt at childish innuendo, Evie carried on with her instruction. 'Using the flat of your fist, push it down until it looks like a hockey puck shaped disc.'

She had to admit Jake was very good at following the steps, his strong hands already commanding the clay when other students were hesitant at first. He had a confidence that would likely make him a very good potter if he ever thought about taking it up on a more permanent basis.

'More water?' he asked, pausing for her consent before dousing the wheel again.

'Using both thumbs, I want you to push down slightly into the middle, careful not to go right through the bottom.'

Jake tentatively opened up a divot in the clay and, with her hands covering his, she gently guided him, pulling the walls out and up until it resembled a bowl shape. She tried not to think about the strong hands that had held her not so long ago, or what they would feel like on other parts of her body. Though this impromptu pottery lesson was definitely helping take her mind off other matters.

'It's actually starting to look like something.' His enthusiasm was touching as they drew the sides up and gave the bowl some shape. He looked at her with eyes aglow and a smile on his lips. Evie wished he took more time to enjoy the smaller things in life when he'd got such pleasure from simple things today. She wondered if he was afraid to stand still in case he realised, like her, that outside of work his life was quite empty.

Evie understood that perhaps he too was afraid of opening himself up because he'd been hurt in the past, but he had so much to offer, and deserved more than being a slave to his job.

'We can keep going, bringing more height to it, but that means thinning the walls more and risking collapse.'

'No, I think I'll quit while I'm ahead.'

She handed him the cutting wire. 'Slide this under, keeping it taut.'

With one swift movement he brought the pot to the

edge of the wheel and Evie gently lifted it onto a board to dry.

'It's a little on the wobbly side,' he mused, head tilted to one side as he studied his creation.

'Rustic, we call it. It's handmade, not moulded in a factory, so it's going to be unique.'

'Very diplomatic.' He grinned. 'I can see why you'd make a good teacher.'

Evie blushed at the praise. 'I'll put it with all my other students' work, ready for firing. Maybe you can come back in and glaze it yourself before the second firing.'

'I'd like that,' he said with a smile which made her blush all over again.

'I should really get on with some work…' She might have managed to distract her thoughts from her poor dog, but now she needed a new diversion away from this man who made her feel things she hadn't felt in a very long time.

'Of course. Maybe I can help with cleaning up or something that'll keep me out of your way.'

Evie directed him towards the dirty utensils at the sink and left him to wash up whilst she set about throwing some plates and pots for firing later. They settled into a busy, quiet contentment. Every now and then she became aware of him watching her, but tried not to let it affect her concentration lest she lose any work.

As the light outside grew dim in the late afternoon her phone rang, and sparked both of them into high alert. Bile rose in her throat, knowing that she might hear some news she wasn't ready for. Jake rinsed his hands and dried them, before lifting her phone from the counter and handing it to her as though he knew it was the only way she was going to answer it.

'Hello?' It wasn't only her voice shaking, her entire body trembling with fear.

Jake came and wrapped his arm around her shoulder, centring her just as he'd done with the clay. As long as she had him to support her, the news would be easier to take.

'Hi, it's Jan here at the surgery. I just wanted you to know that everything went well. Dave came through his operation well and is sleeping off the anaesthetic. We want to keep him in overnight for observation, but you should be able to come and pick him up in the morning.'

Evie managed to mumble her thanks and hang up before bursting into sobs of relief. Jake folded her into his arms and she cried into his chest.

'Your clothes are going to be absolutely ruined,' she managed to joke through the tears.

'I don't care. Do I take it Dave is okay?'

In her relief she'd forgotten to share the good news.

'Yes. Sorry. They're keeping him in overnight and I can collect him in the morning.'

'I'm so pleased for you, Evie.'

He rested his chin on the top of her head and held her tight. They rocked together with the soft strains of the radio playing in the background, like the slow set at the end of a wedding disco, clinging to one another, not wanting it to end. She was drawing too much comfort from his warmth, his strength, and his understanding.

'Thank you so much for staying with me.'

She reluctantly pulled her face away from his chest to look up at him, but neither eased up on the hug, as though they both still needed that contact and letting go would move them on from a place they weren't ready to leave just yet.

'You're welcome.' Jake sounded as choked-up as she was by the whole situation.

For a few moments they simply gazed at one another, and she knew he was thinking about the next move as much as she was. Eventually, they both seemed to come to the inevitable conclusion at the same time. She tilted her face up to meet Jake's as he dipped his head towards her.

The kiss when it came was as sweet and tender as it was passionate. A voice in the distance was telling her to put a stop to this now, that she was vulnerable and not in the right headspace to make rational decisions. Probably why she had no intention of stopping. She was enjoying it too much. Evie reached up and wrapped her arms around his neck, pulling him down further into the kiss. His lips were soft, meshing perfectly with hers, and his teasing tongue drew a satisfied sigh from deep within her.

She needed this moment of happiness. To feel wanted and cherished. There'd be time later for recriminations and regret, but for now she would relish every second of this. Because she'd wanted it since the last time he'd kissed her. After spending the day shopping together, enjoying the market, and killing time waiting for news from the vet, this had seemed inevitable. It was clear they liked each other. There was an attraction they'd given into twice now. Perhaps it was about time she started thinking about dating again. Specifically, Jake, if he was agreeable. He certainly seemed to be, and they couldn't keep kissing each other and pretending it hadn't happened. That would tear her up as much as if he deliberately hurt her like Bailey. Maybe, just maybe, she was ready to take the risk of being with someone again when this felt so much better than being on her own.

Her phone rang, the outside world bleeding into their little haven and making them face reality. One in which they weren't a couple, and shouldn't be doing this.

'You should get that.' Jake stepped back, setting her free from his embrace, and she could already sense the shutters coming down again.

If she wasn't afraid that it might be the vet getting in touch to say something had happened to Dave, she might have let it ring out. Instead, she left Jake so she could answer it. When she saw it was Ursula's number on the screen she swore inwardly that her friend had interrupted the moment. Then immediately felt bad because she knew Ursula was only phoning out of concern.

'Hey, Ursula.'

'How is he? How are you? I'm so sorry. I only took my eyes off him for a second when the postman came and he slipped right out past us. He can move quick when he wants to.' Her words spilled out on top of each other until she burst into loud tears on the other end of the phone.

'He's fine, Ursula. I'm okay too. Honestly. It's no one's fault.'

Out of the corner of her eye, Evie could see Jake take off his apron and put his jacket back on. He was getting ready to run.

She waved at him to stay put.

'I've been so worried about you both. I wouldn't blame you if you sack me for gross incompetence or something.' Her friend's melodrama made her smile. At least she wasn't the only one prone to sentimentality over a dog. Or catastrophising.

'I'm not going to sack you, Ursula...'

Jake opened the door and she frowned at him, hoping to portray a look which said *Don't you dare go anywhere*. Apparently, it didn't have the desired effect as he gestured towards his watch and shrugged.

Ursula was rambling on about making every cup of tea in the studio until the end of time if Evie forgave her. Something she would hold her to, but wasn't the most pressing thing on her mind at the minute.

'Ursula, I'm going to have to go. I'll call you later.' She hung up. 'Where do you think you're going?'

'I have to get back to work. I'm glad everything's okay.' He had the audacity to actually walk away, but Evie followed him into the corridor.

'We're not actually going to discuss the fact that we keep kissing each other?'

Jake hung his head. 'I'm sorry. It's an emotional time, but I don't think it's a good idea for either of us to take things any further. I can't be the man you need, and to promise you any different would be a lie.'

With that, he turned on his heel and walked away, Not even giving her the chance to put up an argument. To tell him she didn't need promises of for ever. That for now she was content to be reminded that she was wanted. He was in too much of a hurry to get away to hear a word of it.

Something told her it was the last she'd see of him until the wedding. If he even still wanted her there.

CHAPTER SEVEN

'HAVE I TOLD you that you look beautiful?' Jake whispered to Evie as they sat waiting for the bride to appear.

'Yes. Several times.' She blushed in that adorable way that made him think people hadn't told her that enough.

'Well, you do.'

'Thank you. You look good too. I like your tie.' She nodded towards the coordinated tie she'd bought him when they'd gone clothes shopping together.

The conversation the whole way to the register office had been the same. Awkward. Stilted. Making it feel as though they'd never shared anything other than a car here. He knew that was his fault. Since that afternoon in her studio, he'd cooled things off between them. To the point he was surprised she'd even agreed to still come to the wedding. Perhaps she'd only done so out of misplaced guilt over the outfit he'd bought. Either way, he was lucky Evie was still speaking to him.

It seemed the more he enjoyed spending time with Evie, the more he freaked out over it. Having the whole day together, investing in the welfare of her dog, not to mention kissing her again, had taken him to a place he wasn't ready to be in. He'd felt like part of a couple, waiting for news about her dog. Shared her happiness and relief when everything had turned out okay, and let himself give in to the temptation to take her in his arms again. All of which would've been perfectly normal to anyone else, but to someone who knew not to get close to anyone it spelled disaster.

He didn't want to hurt Evie by leading her on when nothing could come of it. Settling down wasn't on the cards for him, and it was clear that was what she wanted in a partner. When today was over it was probably best to make a clean break so neither of them got caught up in this fantasy of being a real couple.

The lilting music from the harpist at the front of the room marked the bride's entrance, along with the creaking of chairs as everyone turned to take a look. Jake didn't. It felt weird being here to witness his mother getting married to someone he barely knew. Gary, his soon-to-be stepfather, was just one in a long line of boyfriends in his mother's quest for love. The difference being that this one was prepared to make a public commitment. Not that Jake thought it would last. It never did.

'You look like your mum,' Evie whispered.

She apparently had opted to sneak a peek at the bridal party currently making its way down the aisle.

'Yeah,' Jake mumbled, hoping it was sufficient.

Now that this was really happening, he was beginning to feel that familiar tensing in his body. As though he was the only one who could see disaster coming and no one else would listen. Instead, he was supposed to sit and smile and agree with how romantic it all was, knowing it was a car crash waiting to happen. And that was before his dad even made an appearance. Something else he wasn't looking forward to.

He drew some comfort from the fact Evie was here with him. Despite all the ways he'd messed things up, she was still supporting him. Maybe if he'd had someone willing to do that earlier in his life, he wouldn't be so reticent about being with anyone now.

His mother and sister were level with him now. Donna managed a sly wave to him and Evie and he knew she was busting to speak to his plus-one.

The nervous groom, who couldn't have been more than ten years older than Jake, turned to meet his bride, the romantic moment somewhat sullied by the sound of Jake's father sighing and checking his watch, letting everyone know he had better places to be and giving every appearance that he was so busy they were lucky he'd made time to come at all. Anyone else might have wondered why his mum had invited her ex at all, except for Jake, who suspected she still held a candle for him. Both of his parents were lost causes. And the very example of how relationships went wrong.

He nudged Evie and nodded towards the end of the aisle opposite. 'That's my dad.'

She leaned around him to see for herself. 'Huh. He doesn't seem so scary.'

That right there was the reason he'd brought her here today. Whether it was showing him it was fun to get his work suit covered in clay or reminding him that his father was human, Evie had a way of bringing him back down to earth.

Jake zoned out as the vows went on. They were nonsense anyway. In his experience, they were empty promises, impossible for a couple to keep. No one knew for certain what the future held and vowing to stay together for ever seemed naïve at best, and a lie at worst. If sickness or poverty became an issue they couldn't weather together, or one half of the partnership didn't want to settle down in one place, it wasn't a realistic notion. Which was why Jake didn't believe in marriage. It was the ultimate commitment and, as far as he could tell, the ultimate heartbreak waiting to happen. That was why he was happier being single, and free from expectations and responsibility. Wasn't he?

He glanced at Evie sitting beside him, already dabbing at her eyes, truly caught up in the romance already, thoughts of their day together running through his head like a movie montage. Sharing a hot chocolate together, Evie showing him how to throw a pot, hugging when Dave got the all-clear, and kissing when temptation proved too much. Had he really been happier these past days without her than those few hours he'd spent in her company? Not according to Donna, who'd likened him to a bear with a sore head lately.

It begged the question: what was so bad about the idea of getting more involved with her than he already was? Okay, so things might not work out. 'For ever' was not always a possibility. But was she worth at least opening his heart up to the idea of something more than her being his fake date?

As his mother said 'I do' and exchanged rings with her new husband, Jake realised he only had today to decide what he was going to do. If he was prepared to let her walk out of his life for good in just a matter of hours. After the reception she was under no obligation to him so he had to make that decision that might just go against everything he'd been telling himself about relationships for years.

Not an easy task against the backdrop of his parents and the dysfunctional relationships at play here today. He only hoped there was a pivotal moment which would help him take that leap of faith because, deep down, he knew he didn't want to lose Evie for good.

The whole day was overwhelming for Evie. She'd never felt so welcome and included as she did by Jake's family and friends, who all appeared delighted she was there. It was difficult to get used to when she'd spent her teenage years being treated as an inconvenience.

Jake seemed just as uncomfortable with the attention, though for different reasons. She was beginning to wonder why he'd invited her at all when he'd been so reluctant to introduce her to people, or talk about their 'relationship'. He might as well have come on his own if he didn't want people to believe they were together.

They'd got caught up at the register office for a while as guests rushed to meet his 'girlfriend'. At one point she'd thought they were getting more attention than the bride and groom. They'd both protested when the photographer had asked her to be in the family group photos, but his mother and sister had insisted. Something they might come to regret when they saw the dark expression he'd been wearing in most of them.

As she shuffled away from intruding further upon the wedding party she had absolutely nothing to do with, Donna grabbed her by the arm.

'I can't tell you how happy I am to see you with

my big brother. He's been so grumpy these past days, even more so than usual. I was worried you'd broken up already.'

Evie smiled politely. 'I'm Evie. It's nice to meet you.'

'Donna. You have no idea what a big deal it is for him to bring someone with him to this sort of thing. I hope I get to talk to you more at the reception.'

'I don't know if I'm going…' The way she was feeling at the minute it seemed like a pointless exercise if it was just going to make her and Jake even more uncomfortable.

'Of course you are. You're practically family now.' Donna gave her a wink before she walked away, just in time for Jake to catch the end of the conversation.

'We should probably head on to the hotel for the reception now.'

Evie didn't think it was possible for Jake to look even more disturbed by today's events but she'd been wrong. As if she'd gatecrashed the wedding and announced herself as the next Mrs Hanley.

She managed to hold her tongue as she teetered over to the car behind him, struggling to keep up with his long deliberate strides in the heels she wasn't used to wearing. It was only when they were safely ensconced away from everyone else, the atmosphere tense and uneasy, that she said her piece. At this point there was nothing to lose.

'I'm not going.'

'Pardon?'

'To the reception. I'm not going. So you may as well drop me back home.' She put her seatbelt on and sat, hands in her lap, ready for him to drive.

'But the deal…'

'I came as your plus-one. Say I'm sick or something. I'm sure no one will notice.' It was a lie. Donna was sure to have a hundred questions about why she hadn't accompanied him to the reception dinner, but that would be for Jake to explain. It wasn't Evie's problem any more.

He still hadn't started the car and she was stuck here until he did.

'But I need you there.'

She looked at him in disbelief, surprised to find an anxious face looking back at her.

'Why? So you can take your bad mood out on me, Jake? You've made it clear you don't want me here. It's like you're embarrassed to be seen with me.'

'Never.'

His insistence didn't erase his attitude the whole time his family and friends had stopped to talk to them.

'I don't know why you wanted me to come if you didn't want people to think we're together. I don't understand you, Jake. What I do know, though, is that I don't have to be a part of whatever is going on with you. I've had a lifetime of feeling as though I'm not wanted. That I don't fit in. I don't need that in my life any more. Especially with someone who's not going to be around after tonight. I'd rather cut my losses now. Thank you for being there when I needed you but I'm sorry, I have to put my own feelings first for a change.'

It was kind of cathartic to actually say what was on her mind for once. A speech she'd often rehearsed saying to her family but had never had the courage to voice in person. Ironic that it was Jake who'd probably given her the confidence and safe space to do so. Weirdly, she was confident enough around him to say how she was feeling.

'I'm sorry. You're right. You don't deserve any of this.' He started the car, but Evie still wanted an explanation.

'Then tell me what's going on, Jake.' She reached across his lap and turned the key, switching the ignition back off.

'I thought by having someone with me it would stop the judgement. Then everyone would stop quizzing me about why I don't have a partner, like I'm some freak of nature. I didn't expect you to have this impact. Everyone's so happy for me. But none of it is real.' His hands were still gripping the steering wheel as he spoke.

'But this was what you wanted.' It was so confusing to her. Goodness knew what was going on in his head.

He finally let go of the wheel, letting the circulation back, his knuckles no longer a deathly white. 'I know, I know. I guess it's just opened my eyes to how different things might have been. If my unstable childhood hadn't had such an effect on me, perhaps I would've settled down with someone. I could've been happy.'

'And you're not?' Evie would've imagined someone in his position, with money and a successful business, was content with his lot, but Jake certainly didn't sound happy.

'I thought I was, but now I'm wondering what I'm missing out on. My parents splitting up, my breakup with my ex…all confirmed that relationships don't last. They're just painful. I told myself I didn't need anyone else in my life who could hurt me in the future.

Then I stumbled into your studio.' He gave her a lop-sided smile, reminding her of that bemused stranger that night who'd listened to her strange tale of needing a fake date to impress her family and agreed to do it for her.

Though she didn't know how she'd changed his view of relationships when she was just as afraid of being in one. On that account they were on the same page. Long-term commitment meant heartache down the line.

'I haven't asked you for anything, Jake. Nor do I have any expectations beyond tonight, or even this minute. I came because I owed you a favour, and okay, yes, I like you. I don't think we'd keep kissing each other if the feeling wasn't mutual. But I'm not looking for anything more, if that's what you're worried about. Bailey hurt me too much to consider another relationship. If, however, you still want me to accompany you to the reception—'

'I do.'

'If you promise not to be moody—'

'I do.'

It was beginning to sound as though they were making their own vows. Ironic, when he wanted the opposite to 'till death us do part' where she was concerned.

'Then I will go with you. On the proviso that we just go and have a good time, and forget all this other stuff you're currently overthinking.'

Evie knew she was asking a lot, but she didn't want to spend the rest of the night regretting not walking away now. He'd made it clear he wasn't interested in pursuing anything with her, so she needed to put all thoughts of it out of her head too. If this was the last time they were going to be together she simply wanted them to enjoy it, so she'd have a memory to look back on fondly. A nicer one than his blatant unease at people thinking they were a real couple.

'Done. I'm sorry that I made you feel uncomfortable. That's totally on me. I'm the one out of my depth pretending to be part of a couple. It was easier doing it at your home, with people who didn't know me beyond anything we told them was the truth. This is a deception involving my parents and my sister I probably should have thought over a bit more.'

'I'm beginning to think that myself,' Evie joked, well aware they couldn't go back and change things now. They simply had to press on as well as they could, and hope for the best.

At least lying, and the consequences of it, weren't something he did easily. Jake had a conscience. Unlike Bailey, who'd lied and cheated on her for months without a second thought of what it would do to her. Evie was sure that part of what was troubling him was how upset everyone would be once they found out the truth. Something she selfishly hoped would never come to light, so they wouldn't think badly of her either.

'So, we're going?' He was leaving the final decision down to her, then she only had herself to blame when she was left bereft at the end of the night, knowing she'd never see Jake again.

'Y-e-s.' She said it slowly, almost questioning her own answer. As well as her sanity.

Jake was mindful of Evie every time someone approached them to say hello. He didn't want her to end up resenting him for bringing her here, so he was doing his best to be sociable. Something that didn't come easy to him when he was used to doing only things he wanted, with only his own feelings to take into consideration. He supposed that was a selfish kind of way to live, but it was how he'd protected himself all these years. It was only Evie being so honest and upfront about how his actions were making her uncomfortable which made him take a hard look at himself. Perhaps there had been a transition in him at some point where he'd changed from the wounded party into the transgressor, and the thought didn't sit easily with him.

Other than his sister, Evie was the first person to hold a mirror up and ask him to look at his behaviour. He didn't want to be someone else in her life making her miserable or feeling as though she was somehow inferior, because it wasn't true. Nor was he happy to make anyone else feel that way. Whatever his personal feelings surrounding the day, or the people he interacted with, he was determined to play nice. Otherwise, they were all going to wonder why the hell someone as lovely as Evie would ever want to be with him.

'Hello, son.' The appearance of his father in the hotel lobby as they reached the reception venue was going to be a serious test of his new vow.

'Dad.' There was an awkward few seconds' silence as the three of them stood staring at one another, sipping the complimentary glasses of Buck's Fizz they'd been handed on arrival, whilst the rest of the guests mingled and chattered around them.

It was Evie who broke the silence and held out her hand. 'I'm Evie. It's nice to meet you.'

'John Hanley. So, are you two together then?' As expected, he got straight to the point, not wasting time on small talk.

Evie took a strategic sip of her drink, leaving him to answer that one.

'Yes.' He could be equally efficient with his words.

'Hello, Father dear. Talking the ear off our latest member of the family, are we?' Donna appeared and rescued them all, as she kissed their father on the cheek.

They'd always had a better relationship than Jake and his father had ever had. Most likely because she'd still been young when their parents had split up, hadn't experienced his absence, or moved around as much. Growing up with their mother, in a settled home, had been a much calmer experience and Donna had obviously benefitted from it. Jake mused that the emotional, and perhaps psychological, damage of his father's behaviour had already been done to him by then.

'Hi, sis. You look amazing.' Jake gave her a quick hug, pleased to see her more than ever.

'I know, but look at you two. Twit-twoo. And Dad, you're immaculate, as always.'

She looked them all up and down, and Jake knew he should take a leaf out of his little sister's book when it came to successful mingling. Always ready with a compliment and ease of conversation, she was always the most popular person in the room. Though he reminded himself that her openness came at a cost too. She was the one who got her heart broken over and over again, a glutton for punishment when it came to love, but as she'd told Jake, she'd never give up trying to find the right 'one'. He admired her tenacity, even if she shared their mother's fatal flaw of romanticising life. One thing his father had taught him was that it was tough and not something you simply floated through. You had to make a path for yourself and not wait for life to happen to you.

'You have to make an effort, don't you?' Jake's father straightened his perfect tie.

He always dressed smart. Shoes shined, trousers freshly pressed and not a hair out of place. Jake supposed that was something else he'd had ingrained in him. Perhaps that was why he'd enjoyed that day at Evie's studio. There was something liberating about getting clay on his clothes, an act of rebellion in a way. She'd shown him he didn't always have to be immaculately turned out, and it didn't matter if he wasn't. The world hadn't ended because he'd got a bit dirty.

Evie helped him relax. He wasn't the tightly wound ball of stress he usually was around her. That was probably why he'd wanted her here with him in what he knew was going to be one of those stress-filled situations. Though all he'd managed to do so far was instil that sense of anxiety-induced propriety that he'd grown up with. Hopefully, a few drinks and dancing would help them both relax a bit more.

'I'm afraid it's a bit of a waste of time in my line of work. That's why it's nice for me to have a chance to dress up for once.' Evie joined in the conversation, though he knew it would spark more interest from his sister.

He was right.

'What do you do for a living, Evie?'

'Ceramics. I have my own studio, and I run some pottery classes.'

Donna's mouth dropped open and she stared at Jake. 'You dark horse.'

'Yes, Evie runs the pottery nights you told me to enquire about,' he conceded.

'So you booked Evie for the team bonding, then you asked her out for some one-on-one bonding?' his sister teased, mischief in her eyes as she watched him over the rim of her glass, waiting for a reaction.

'Not exactly. As I recall, you didn't actually book anything.' Now Evie was getting in on the act, making him look bad.

'I must've been distracted...' He reminded her that she was having some sort of existential crisis when he'd walked in and hoped that would be enough to end that particular topic of conversation.

'Well, you might have solved the issue of your desolate love life, but you still have to sort something out for your employees. He needs to work on his personal skills on more than just the tutor.' Donna was openly laughing now, and Jake couldn't help but smile.

He'd definitely taken her advice when it came to being more accessible, but only when it came to Evie. Even then he had a tendency to blast her with that cold front when it felt as though she was breaching his defences.

'I'll arrange something. Don't worry.' There was still time, although things were bound to be booking up this close to Christmas. Perhaps they'd have to take a look at a New Year's get-together instead.

'I still have room in my schedule. I could put something in the diary if you want to book a session?'

Now Evie was putting him on the spot he was having to think about whether or not he wanted to make another arrangement to see her again. Although the answer was a definite yes, he still had to question if it was a good idea. Though he didn't think *I'm afraid I'll like her too much* was going to be a suitable excuse to his sister if he had to explain why he hadn't booked after all.

'Sure. I assume you'll be there too, sis?'

'With bells on. I am not going to miss you up to your elbows in clay, swearing when the wheel fights back.'

'As a matter of fact, Jake's quite a dab hand at throwing.' It didn't matter that Evie was bigging him up when he saw the dark look on his father's face.

'Sounds like a waste of time to me,' he grumbled.

Evie's stricken look was reminiscent of that evening at her family home when she'd been the object of unfair criticism there too. Jake immediately felt that same need to protect her.

'Sometimes you need a bit of fun in your life, Dad. And actually, Evie is a very skilled ceramicist as well as a tutor. So I'd appreciate it if you respected that.'

There was something liberating in speaking his mind instead of keeping it bottled up. He could see why Evie had let loose on him earlier. It was possible if he'd been so bold when he was younger that the dynamic between him and his father might've been different now. It was that overwhelming need to defend Evie that had finally prompted him into action now. She was changing his staid life in so many ways it should've been scary for someone so reluctant to change. However, Jake was finding each small concession to his usual composure refreshing. Mind-blowing. A relief.

'I, for one, am looking forward to your class, Evie. Now, I suppose we should go in and find our seats for the meal.' Donna changed the subject quickly and motioned towards the rest of the guests, who were filtering into the dining room. She'd always been the one to defuse any tension when it came to Jake and his dad. Some things never changed.

'I'm at the top table, but I'll catch up with you later,' Donna promised with another round of cheek kisses before disappearing into the room in a swirl of chiffon.

'It looks like I've been stuck at the table with the distant cousins and barely known acquaintances.' His father bemoaned his lot, though Jake hadn't expected him to stay beyond the ceremony. Perhaps his mother hadn't either and that was why she'd seated him at one of the far tables.

'Why wouldn't your mother sit you together?' Evie enquired as his father went looking for his seat. Jake wouldn't put it past him to try and swap with someone else in a more prominent position.

'She knows better. Probably trying to avoid any sort of scene. Also, I think she originally wanted me at the top table. She asked me to give her away, but it wasn't something I was keen to do.'

He didn't want to be a part of something he didn't believe in, but he'd agreed to attend once he'd known Evie would be coming with him. That concession had kept everyone happy. Though he hadn't expected the idea of bringing a plus-one to cause so much excitement in the family.

'How did she take that?'

Jake shrugged. 'As well as could be expected, but she knows I'm not into the whole marriage idea. Bringing you was the sweetener.'

'Ah, I see. Well, at least we're sitting together.'

She took his hand and he let her lead him to the table closest to his mother and her new groom. Far enough away from his father that he didn't have to be on guard, waiting for him to insult Evie again, forcing him to react. At least now they might be able to do some of that relaxing and having fun she'd talked about.

The dinner and speeches had gone well, although Evie hadn't eaten much of her meal, nerves getting the better of her. She already felt out of place and it hadn't helped when Jake's father had looked down his nose at her choice of career. The only reason that she hadn't let it get to her too much was the fact that Jake had stood up for her. Again.

She knew she shouldn't rely on him to ride in and save her every time she was in distress, but it was nice to have someone there willing to do so. In contrast, his sister Donna seemed lovely, and very friendly. Though Jake had warned her that his mum and sister were keen to have him paired off and in their heads they were probably already making plans for their nuptials, making her wonder even more why he'd gone ahead with this.

It had taken a lot of courage for her to speak out in

the car back at the register office, but it had needed to be said. For her peace of mind, if nothing else.

'Sorry I haven't got talking to you before now, Evie. I don't remember being this in demand on my first wedding day.' Jake's mother came to join them at their table once the hotel was getting things ready for the evening entertainment and an influx of new guests who hadn't been lucky enough to get an invite to the actual ceremony.

'That's okay. It's your big day. You and Donna look beautiful.'

It was easy to compliment her when she was glowing. The elegant bride, who Evie estimated to be in her early sixties, was wearing a tasteful ivory lace dress with a faux fur cape, and looked every bit as happy as she hoped to be some day.

'Thank you. So do you. Now I know who's behind the change in my son recently.' She gave an embarrassed Jake a shoulder squeeze.

'I don't know about that.'

Now it was Evie's turn to squirm. She didn't want to take any credit for anything Jake-related when she was nothing more than his fake date. After tonight she wasn't going to be anything to him. Unless he wanted her to, in which case she'd left the door open for him with the whole pottery class setup.

'You got him to come here, so I'm grateful for that. Now, I have a whole floor of rooms reserved for family. I hope you're staying the night.'

Before Evie was forced to make some feeble excuse to his mother, Jake stepped in.

'I'm afraid not. I'm driving Evie back so I won't be drinking. I don't need a room.'

Evie supposed that was mainly who they were for— guests who partook of a little too much alcohol over the course of the day's celebrations. She knew Jake couldn't wait to get away so would be leaving as soon as he'd done his bit here as the dutiful son.

'Well, the room is there should you want it. Evie can always get a taxi if she needs to. Right, I must get back to my new husband. Do try to get to know Gary, son. I promise he's not like all the others. Save a dance for me.' She kissed her fingers and touched Jake's cheek, a gesture Evie was sure wasn't a one-off. He didn't seem the type to go in for public displays of affection and she wondered if this was his mother's only way of getting to express her love for him.

Once again, Evie felt a surge of love and empathy for the young Jake, who perhaps hadn't been used to a tactile family. His father certainly didn't seem the type to go in for kisses and cuddles, much like her stepmother.

Perhaps they were both victims of their dysfunctional families and damaged relationships, but they were old enough to make a change themselves. Break that pattern.

It could be that started with a simple thing like dating again. She didn't know how Jake would feel about that, but she was beginning to think she was ready to dip a toe back into that pool at least.

'Your mum's right. I can get a taxi if you want to stay here tonight. It's her wedding day, you should be celebrating with her.'

Evie didn't want to stand in the way of him making

any progress where his family were concerned. Both Donna and his mum had commented on his improved mood, and the fact that he'd agreed to come here at all seemed to be heralding some sort of emotional change. It could be down to the time he'd spent with her family, and realised his wasn't all that bad in comparison. Or he'd realised how lucky he was to have people who genuinely loved him. Whatever was drawing him closer to them, she didn't want to throw a spanner in the works now and interrupt any progress.

'I might have a couple of drinks. I'll probably need them. We can still get a taxi. I know you're off the clock come midnight.'

'Midnight? That's pushing it. I think you only managed a few hours in my family's company before we did a disappearing act.'

Evie liked to needle him every now and then to keep things light. Sometimes Jake needed reminding that not everything had to be serious. After meeting his father, it wasn't surprising.

'You know you're free to go any time, Evie. I'm not holding you hostage.'

She gathered up her bag and pretended to leave. 'In that case…'

Jake reached out and grabbed her wrist, a genuine look of panic in his wide eyes. 'Please don't go. I need you.'

Evie plonked back down in her seat, her knees weak and her heart sore for him that he worried so much about being left alone. No doubt a throwback to his childhood, when he'd been forced to follow his father's military career around the world, never having a stable home environment.

'I was only joking.' She took his hand across the table. 'I'll see you through whatever happens tonight.'

After that, she wasn't sure. It was down to Jake to decide if he was willing to venture into anything more than a fake relationship with her.

He gave her hand a quick squeeze then got to his feet. 'I think I'll go and see about those drinks.'

She watched him up at the bar whilst she made small talk with the friends of the groom they'd been seated with during dinner. Jake was drawing admiring glances from a lot of people in the room, not that he seemed to notice. As he stood at the bar waiting for their drinks, he was approached by a couple of women he seemed to know as he hugged them on sight. He was smiling and nodding, engaged in conversation, and appeared to be enjoying this interaction, as opposed to any he'd had with his family so far. Even more than he had with her.

She couldn't take her eyes off what was happening, a burning sensation rising inside her that she recognised as jealousy. The absurdity of feeling territorial over a man who was uncomfortable with her as his fake date made her either want to laugh or weep. Later, in the privacy of her own empty home, she might indulge in both. Because it was becoming increasingly apparent that she didn't just want to try dating again. There was only one man she wanted to try it with. Jake.

When he started walking back towards her, drinks in hand, smile on his face, she was almost giddy with the anticipation of him coming back to her. She hated herself. Fan-girling certainly wasn't the way to convince Jake that she was the girl for him. Nor was it the way to break herself back into dating if she was hanging on his every word and every second of attention that he afforded her.

She needed to slow this down, and take it one moment at a time. Otherwise, she was going to have her heart broken even sooner than expected. One minute past midnight, by all accounts. Unless something drastic happened between now and then, Cinderella would be going home in her pumpkin carriage and leaving the handsome prince behind for ever.

'A glass of wine for the lady.' He delivered her drink with a flourish, his mood clearly buoyed by his interaction at the bar.

Evie seethed.

'Thank you.' She bit her lip to prevent herself from saying anything else which would give away her irrational jealousy and raise all manner of red flags to him.

He sat down, still smiling about something. 'I ran into a couple of cousins I haven't seen in years. I actually forgot I have family beyond Donna and my parents because we see them so rarely.'

'That must've been so nice for you.' Captain Green Eyes was able to stand down.

'You know, it's easy to see all the negatives of family when you haven't had a particularly happy childhood. It's funny how something like this can reconnect you with some of the positives you've forgotten about.'

'Oh?'

Unfortunately, Evie couldn't relate when June and Courtney were the only family she had, and any good memories had died along with her father.

'They reminded me that I used to go to the under-eighteen discos with them when we were kids. Apparently, they have photographic evidence of my boyband haircut and penchant for skinny jeans. They were complimenting my improved taste in clothes.'

He shook his head, but Evie could see he was genuinely pleased to have reconnected with this part of his past. It could only be good for his future relations with his family. Perhaps he might look to cultivate more of a relationship with these cousins and have a more rounded view, not only of his family and relationships in general but also himself.

'I'm so going to need a copy of those photographs or, you know, at least see them.'

It dawned on her it would be weird to want photographs of a man she wasn't supposed to care about, or see again.

'I'm not sure anyone needs to see those…'

'Well, I'm sure it was good to see your cousins again.'

'It was. It really was.' Jake really seemed to be relaxing, becoming more open to the idea of being with family.

Evie wondered if he still needed her at all, but the truth was she was reluctant to leave anyway. She wasn't ready to walk away from him and the feelings he was reawakening in her. Jake Hanley was making her realise that her life hadn't ended when Bailey had cheated on her. The problem now was what to do about it.

CHAPTER EIGHT

JAKE DIDN'T KNOW if it was down to the alcohol, the fact that his father had left the venue or that he had Evie with him, but he was beginning to enjoy the evening. The pressure was off now that the wedding was over, the family had met Evie, and got over the novelty of him bringing a woman with him. They'd simply accepted her, and them as a couple. And why wouldn't they? Evie was amazing, and they made a good team. She'd be the perfect partner if he was ever ready to have one. But he wasn't. That didn't mean he wanted to say goodbye though. He just wished there were a happy medium somewhere so he wasn't under the pressure of expectations or commitment.

'Are you going to sit there brooding all night, big brother, or are you going to loosen that tie and come and dance?' Donna, who had been up on the floor boogying with the rest of the bridal party, grabbed his hand and pulled him from his seat.

'You know I can't dance,' he protested, shooting Evie an apologetic look for leaving her.

'You *don't* dance. There's a difference. Besides, it's the only chance I'll have to quiz you on Evie.' Donna twirled herself around his fingertips, forcing him into being her dance partner.

He knew it would be futile to try and avoid her questions. All he could hope for was that this song would end soon, along with his humiliation.

'What do you want to know?'

'Why you've been hiding her.'

'I haven't been hiding her. I simply haven't let you know about her. There's a difference.' He felt smug about using her quote against her until she pulled him into hold and made him dance with her.

'What's so bad about her, or me, that you couldn't tell me?'

'Nothing. It's called a private life, Donna. This is exactly why I didn't tell you about Evie. So you and Mum didn't get carried away and make a big deal out of it.'

'But it is a big deal. I can see she makes you happy, and that's all we want for you. Is that so bad?'

'I guess not.' He felt like a heel now, projecting his fears onto her. It was his idea to let people think they were together, so he shouldn't be surprised when they asked questions. Seeing him with a woman was unusual, so the fact that he'd even brought her to the wedding could easily be mistaken as a relationship.

'You don't want to let her slip through your fingers, so why don't you give her a good time, and show her what you're capable of?' Donna spun herself out of his arms and grabbed hold of Evie, placing her hand in Jake's, before going to find herself a new dance partner.

He knew she was talking about dancing, but her words applied to other areas of his life where he held back. Like loving someone, sharing his life and imagining a future with them.

'Sorry about this,' he mumbled into Evie's ear, knowing it was going to look odd if they didn't have at least one dance together now they were both on the floor.

'It's fine. I love to dance. I just don't get the opportunity to do it much.'

'You had lessons too?'

'Nothing as glamorous as that. I just used to dance in my room when I was younger. It was my outlet. Wait… You took lessons? You actually know how to dance?' Her eyes were wide with surprise, and perhaps something bordering on admiration.

Talk about giving himself away.

'Yeah. Mum insisted on it. She said a man needed to know how to dance if he wanted to impress a lady. Poor Mum thought everyone was a romantic like her.'

'No, she's right. I'm very impressed.'

'I haven't even showed you my best moves yet.' He couldn't resist the chance to deploy his secret weapon just this one time and perhaps give Evie a sample of his skills. Even if he was a bit rusty.

As the music changed to a slower tempo, more suitable for ballroom dancing, he switched up from gently swaying together and took Evie into close position, increasing their body contact with his right hand at her back, forcing her to wrap one hand around his neck as he clasped the other in his free hand.

'But I don't know how to dance.' The panic was there in her eyes as well as her voice that she'd make a fool of herself, but Jake wouldn't let that happen.

'It's okay. I'll lead.' The steps came flooding back to

him and she let him sweep her around the floor, eventually relaxing, a smile on her face as they spun around.

He'd forgotten how much he actually enjoyed dancing. His rebellion against it mostly born of his mother's insistence that he needed to learn to impress anyone. Now he was glad he was able to show off a little for Evie. He was probably holding her a little closer than usually permitted, holding eye contact when he shouldn't, because he wanted to enjoy her reaction. And he certainly shouldn't be feeling the way he was with her in his arms. Something that felt more intimate than those passionate kisses they kept indulging in.

He was sorry when the music stopped.

'I... I think I need some air.' Evie was barely out of his arms before she was running off the dance floor, leaving him staring after her, bewildered.

Jake had no idea what was wrong when she'd seemed so happy dancing with him only moments ago. What he did know was that he cared enough about her to find out and went after her, out through the doors and into the wintry night.

'Evie?' He found her in the little thatched summer house which, with its open front, provided no protection from the icy air.

Her features illuminated by the festive lights strung around the roof and heather-clad walls, she looked like a Christmas fairy sitting on the little bench inside.

'Sorry. I just needed to get some fresh air,' she said, moving up to make room for him.

'I think you've had a little too much. You're shivering.'

Without her pashmina she was bound to be feeling

the cold. Jake took off his jacket and hung it around her shoulders.

'Do you want me to go?' He didn't want to impose if she needed some time out. As long as he knew she was okay, and not about to freeze to death, he'd leave her alone if she needed some space.

'No. Stay.' She reached out her hand and placed it on his leg.

Enough contact to send all his nerve-endings into overdrive, the warmth of her hand resting on his thigh creating urges inside him it was becoming increasingly difficult to ignore.

'What's wrong, Evie? Was it the dancing? My family?'

He wanted her to tell him so he could fix it and make things better for her. It was obvious there was something bothering her. He just hoped it wasn't down to him, because he'd hate himself if he'd upset her when she'd done so much for him simply by being here today.

She shook her head and gave him a sad little smile that only made him ache for her more. 'It's me. I shouldn't have come here tonight.'

Uneasiness settled in Jake's stomach at the thought she'd felt pressured to stay. Obviously whilst he'd thought she was enjoying herself, it had all been part of the act she'd agreed to play in front of his family.

'I'm sorry. Do you want me to get you a taxi?' He pulled out his phone, eager to make amends, horrified with himself for not realising sooner that she wasn't comfortable. The fact that he'd been enjoying their turn around the dance floor together only made it worse.

'No. You don't understand.'

'Then tell me,' he begged, her feelings more important to him than he'd ever expected. Something that went far beyond the idea of a fake relationship.

'I don't want to leave. I don't want you to leave. I don't want tonight to end.'

Tear-filled eyes locked onto his and he was so lost in them for a moment it took a while to register what she was saying.

'That's why you're upset? Because tonight marks the end of our…arrangement?' After the way he'd been feeling, it was a relief to know that was what the problem was. That she liked him, not that she couldn't stomach playing the role of girlfriend for a second longer.

'I know this wasn't part of the deal, and it's not your problem really. Forget I said anything. I'll deal with it. You go back inside and be with your family.'

She was rambling again. It was a habit he recognised now when she was nervous, an adorable quirk that made Evie the woman she was. The woman who was making him question his attitude towards his love life.

For once he decided to act on instinct, and everything in this moment was telling him to kiss her.

When he didn't respond to her confession immediately, Evie started to spiral again. 'You know what? I'll go. Tell everyone I had a migraine or something. I'm sure you can come up with an excuse. I'm sorry for ruining things—'

Jake reached across and planted his lips on hers, kissing her not only to shut her up so he could try and think, but also to remind himself if it was as good as he remembered. It was. So much, in fact, that the idea of rational thought went out of the window. The only important thing in his world right now was tasting her on his tongue again.

He cupped her face in his hands and kissed her thoroughly, taking his time, unlike their previous lapses. As though he could afford the luxury now they'd both given permission for it to happen. It was clear she liked him as much as he'd come to like her. Never more so than when she wrapped her arms around his neck and pressed herself closer. Jake vaguely registered that his jacket had fallen on the ground in the process when he was so acutely aware of her body against his. Although they'd given into temptation before, this was the first time they'd leaned into a kiss. Really explored one another and how they were making each other feel in the moment. He didn't want to think of beyond now, the implications and complications of taking things further. Moving on to somewhere he wasn't sure either of them was ready for.

Despite the heat infusing his body, and the passion in their embrace, Jake could feel her body trembling. He wasn't vain enough to believe it was solely down to him, and realised that the cold was seeping its way into Evie's bones. As much as he was enjoying their time alone, they couldn't stay here for ever.

'We should probably go back inside before you catch pneumonia.' He picked up his jacket and draped it back around her shoulders.

'What happens now?'

'I have no idea,' he said honestly, his smile giving nothing away of the turmoil going on in his head, his body or his heart.

Well, he knew what certain parts of his anatomy

wanted to happen, but it was his head that had dictated his actions until recently. Right now, it was fighting with every instinct that told him to take the next step with Evie. Just because he liked her, wanted to be with her, it didn't change anything else in his life. He still didn't want a commitment. Nor did he want to hurt Evie. Yet he had this feeling they could have something special, and it was obvious Evie had the same intuition. Otherwise, they wouldn't be so reluctant for the evening, for this 'fake' relationship, to end.

'We could just let this night pan out and not think about what happens next,' Evie suggested with a twinkle in her eye. It was very tempting, and so was she.

'You mean spend the night together?' The idea had merits but he didn't know what was in it for Evie. She'd already been hurt once and he didn't want her to think they had a future together when he knew it was never going to happen.

'Why not? People do it all the time.' She shrugged nonchalantly but Jake wasn't convinced she had such a casual attitude towards sex when it was clear she hadn't been with anyone since Bailey, her long-term boyfriend.

'But not you.'

'Yeah, well, long-term commitment didn't work out so well. Not for me, at least.'

'So, what? A one-night stand?' Jake wasn't sure that was going to solve any problems for them either. It still meant they wouldn't get to see each other after tonight and, if anything, could make things worse. He doubted one night would satiate this thirst she'd created inside him.

'Why do we have to label anything? Or spend the whole night discussing terms and conditions, wasting precious time. We could be doing something much more fun.' Evie grabbed his tie and pulled him in for a kiss. She teased his bottom lip with the tip of her tongue, then tugged it with her teeth, teasing him with a bravado he hadn't realised she possessed.

Perhaps having fun and forgetting their troubles for a while was something they both could do after all. It was clear they both needed it.

Evie was shaking as she walked back into the evening celebrations to retrieve her pashmina and bag, whilst Jake checked them into a room for the night in Reception. The dance floor was crowded now so she was able to slip in and out unnoticed. Thankfully, she didn't run into any of his family members and be forced to explain why they were taking their leave so early in proceedings. She was out of her comfort zone enough without having to add more lies to her conscience.

'Everything okay?' Jake asked when she came to join him at the reception desk. She knew he was asking if she really wanted to do this. To spend the night with him.

She nodded and linked her arm through his. 'Yes. Take me to bed.'

Jake's face darkened, his jaw tightened, and she knew her seduction was working on him. In trying to be the confident, sexy woman who could sleep with someone at a wedding and not think twice about it, she hoped to convince them both it was enough for her.

Of course she wanted more, but Jake had made it

clear that wasn't on offer, and she knew she wasn't ready for anything serious either, waiting for that day when it would all come crashing down around her again. At least Jake was upfront about not being the commitment type. If Bailey had done that she would never have risked her heart, or her trust, being broken into a million pieces.

When Jake had danced with her earlier, making her feel special and cherished, it had been like a dream. Until the music ended and she was faced with going back to reality. Something she hadn't been ready to do. She'd thought the whole thing was over too when she'd spilled her guts to Jake outside, never imagining for a second he might have felt the same way. Now they were about to embark on new territory for them both.

'The room's just on the first floor so we…um…don't have too far to go.' Even he seemed a little nervous about what they were about to do as he waved the room key at her.

It occurred to Evie that she didn't have a change of clothes for the morning. Though that probably wasn't something a woman having a casual one-night stand worried about. Chances were that after the wedding she wouldn't be the only one doing the walk of shame in yesterday's clothes.

The short journey to the hotel room was silent, tense, and the atmosphere between them filled with anticipation. They both knew what they were here for, and Evie's pulse was in overdrive. She was sure there was an element of expectation as well as apprehension on both sides and just hoped that chemistry took over, as it tended to do between them, robbing them of common sense and self-consciousness, so that all that mattered was the passion which flared so easily to life when they allowed it.

'I upgraded us. I hope you don't mind,' he said, opening the room door.

It took Evie a second or two to realise he wasn't talking about their relationship.

'Not at all, but, you know, you don't have to seduce me. As I recall, this was my idea.'

Jake didn't have any reason, or need, to try and impress her. He did that anyway and, apart from anything else, it didn't take much to be an improvement from what she was used to with Bailey. His idea of a room upgrade would be booking somewhere that had a hairdryer.

So when she saw the vast suite Jake had booked for the night, complete with king-sized bed, bucket of champagne on ice and a hot tub, she could hardly believe her eyes. Or her luck. If they were only going to have one night together, Jake certainly intended to make it special, one to remember. That thrill of anticipation fizzed in her veins, thinking about what else he had in store for her.

'A hot tub. Now, that is fancy.' She walked over to the square tub sitting at the far end of the room, where there was also a selection of aromatherapy scents, fluffy white towels and robes.

'Not too cheesy?' Jake grimaced, viewing the scene himself for the first time.

'Well, if it is, I don't care. Though I don't have a bathing suit with me…'

'That's okay. For what we'll be doing, you aren't

going to need clothes.' He crossed the room towards her in a couple of strides and kissed her so hard and thoroughly it left her breathless.

When he eventually let her up for air, Jake reached down and turned the spa jets on so the tub was filled with inviting bubbles. Evie watched as he undid his tie, unbuttoned his shirt, and cast them aside to reveal his taut, solid body.

She bit her lip, trying to stave off the rush of arousal that coursed through her, when they had such a long night ahead of them. But goodness, he was beautiful. As he popped the button on his fly she couldn't take her eyes off him, until he coughed, forcing her to look at his face instead.

'I think it's your turn,' he said, making no further attempt to undress, apparently waiting for her to give him a show next.

In keeping with the light-hearted, sexy vibe of the moment, Evie kicked her heels off across the room. Then she slowly unzipped the back of her dress, letting it fall at her feet, and reveal her underwear. She'd never thought she'd be here doing this tonight so she thanked her penchant for pretty lingerie. It certainly seemed to have earned Jake's appreciation as he sucked in a breath watching her strip.

'Your turn.' She folded her arms and waited, wearing only her ivory silk bra and panties, and stockings.

At double speed, Jake undid his trousers and let them fall at his feet.

'Next,' he said with a grin.

Evie carefully rolled down her stockings, then held up each foot in turn for Jake to completely remove them. He called her bluff by tugging them off with his teeth and sending her temperature rocketing despite her current lack of clothing. There was something insanely erotic about a man tearing her stockings off with his teeth, the moment only surpassed when he tugged off his boxers and revealed his own impressive arousal.

Evie's cheeks were burning and it wasn't only because it was her turn to strip completely naked, revealing her body to him for the first time. Trying to ignore that little niggle at the back of her head telling her it hadn't been enough to keep Bailey faithful. As if picking up on her insecurity, Jake came to her.

'You're so beautiful.'

He held her close and kissed her so gently, so tenderly, that she forgot all her inhibitions. She could see for herself how much he wanted her.

'Hot tub?' Her voice was thick with desire as she made the suggestion, but she knew if they didn't get in now they never would. She didn't want to waste anything on offer tonight.

'I'll get the champagne.' It was nice to hear that desire reflected back in Jake's voice and know this wasn't necessarily the norm for him either.

Evie watched his perky little butt walk over to the bed to get the bubbly, then lowered herself down into the hot tub. The pressurised jets of water set to work kneading the knots of tension in her back, which had probably been there for decades. She lay back with a sigh of satisfaction and closed her eyes.

'Now, that's a picture.' Jake slid into the water beside her and handed her a glass of champagne. He dropped a kiss on her lips.

'It's so nice in here. I think I'll stay here for ever.' Evie let the bubbles inside and outside of her glass lift her body and spirits. It was nice to be pampered once in a while and she had to hand it to Jake, who seemed to know exactly what she needed.

'Maybe I'll have one installed in my living room.' Jake heaved out a groan of pleasure as he lay back and got his first taste of the bubbles too.

'You do that and you'll never get rid of me.' She'd meant it as a joke, but when the words fell from her mouth she snapped her eyes open to see his reaction, tension immediately taking control of her body again.

Tonight was supposed to be about seizing the moment, not threatening to cling to him for evermore.

'In that case, maybe I'll put one in every room.' His grin was every bit as good at massaging those knots in her muscles as the hot tub.

Another kiss. The taste of champagne from his lips. And a hint that this didn't have to end tonight. A heady mix.

Evie set her glass on the side of the tub and moved so she was straddling Jake's waist, arms around his neck to anchor her in the buoyant water.

'Now I'm definitely putting one in every room,' he growled as she began kissing her way along his collarbone to his neck.

'Hmm-mm? You have a place big enough?'

'You know it.' He buried his face in her neck and thrust his hips up so she knew he wasn't just talking about his house.

He ground himself against her so his arousal was pressed intimately between her thighs. Evie threw her head back in ecstasy, only for Jake to take one of her nipples in his mouth as her breasts bobbed on the water. He seemed determined to drive her crazy, bringing her to the edge of climax every time he touched her.

It was a surreal feeling being so turned on, so wild and spontaneous, when she couldn't remember ever being like this with Bailey. Even in the early days of their relationship they hadn't had this level of passion. Sex had been something expected, scheduled and, if she was honest, nothing to write home about. She'd believed that was how it was supposed to be with 'the one'. Not all about the excitement and ripping one another's clothes off, but sharing a life together. Perhaps that was what had been missing from their relationship. What he'd gone looking for elsewhere, and found with her stepsister.

If she'd known this was what it was supposed to be like maybe she would've ended things herself and not waited around believing a scrap of Bailey's affection was all she was worthy of. Given a chance, she would've swapped all those years thinking she had it all with Bailey for one night with Jake showing her what she'd been missing out on.

Only now she knew, she didn't think she'd be the same woman ever again. Would she find this again with anyone else? What if it was only Jake who could make her feel this way? She had no idea what the future held any more than she knew the answers to those questions. So all she could do was enjoy this while it lasted.

Kissing, petting, the waters swishing around their naked bodies writhing together, they could have been anywhere in the world. A newly married couple on honeymoon, bathing in the warm seas of the tropics, perhaps. Two people in the midst of an illicit affair, snatching whatever time together they could get. That was how intense the moment felt. Except she wouldn't have the luxury of extending her time with Jake beyond tonight.

'Let's take this somewhere more comfortable,' Jake said in a low voice in her ear, bringing goosebumps across her exposed skin.

He got out of the tub, water sluicing down his exquisite naked form, and held out a hand for her. The cold air only sensitised her more. She saw him take in the sight of her rising from the water, lingering on her ever-tightening nipples. Evie grabbed a towel and patted it over her body, giving Jake a glimpse of flesh every now and then, just to see the flash of desire darken his eyes.

By the time they both reached the bed they were both ravenous for one another. They didn't make it under the covers, their wet, naked bodies rolling around atop as they kissed and fondled, desperate to know each other intimately.

Certainly, Evie wanted to know every inch of him, so she could relive this moment over and over again. She let her hands roam over his chest, so solid and strong beneath her fingertips. Down to his hips, that indent at his waist, and that path of dark hair leading her further into temptation.

She dipped deeper to reach the epitome of his masculinity and grasped him firmly in her hand. There was a satisfaction in hearing him gasp, knowing she had some power over him. She thought it healthier for each partner to have some element of control, in the bedroom at least, if not in the relationship. In hindsight, Bailey had been the one who'd had all the power when they'd been together, playing with her emotions because he knew she loved him, much more than he'd ever cared about her.

Here, with Jake, they were attuned to one another's needs and wants, bringing one another to the brink of ecstasy, then pulling back because they wanted this to last. It wasn't a selfish race to one's own satisfaction. Although that build-up of arousal inside her was becoming too intense to bear much longer.

'Do you have any protection?' she asked, worried something was going to ruin the moment, and at the same time hoping to take that next delicious step with him.

'I think so. Don't go anywhere.' Jake dropped a swift kiss on her lips before going to retrieve his wallet from his jacket pocket and pulling out a condom.

Evie watched as he sheathed himself before coming back to her. Something had changed between them, their previous animal lust to touch and taste one another now replaced with a more tender, loving union. A soft kiss, his gentle touch as he traced the contours of her body with the back of his hand, as though marvelling at her softness and the feel of it against his skin. It didn't lessen the effect he was having on her body and she didn't shy away from letting him know, arching her body up off the bed with a frustrated groan, pressing her softness against the hard ridge of his erection. Until she broke his resolve completely.

Jake slid into her in one smooth movement, filling her full of him, and contentment. He kissed her again and moved slowly inside her, taking control of her body at the tilt of his hips. It felt every bit as deliciously indulgent as relaxing in the hot tub. With every thrust and grunt of effort, he pushed her closer and closer to that release she was desperately reaching for. Waves of bliss rippled through her, the ebb and flow becoming faster, unrelenting, until it was all-consuming. Evie cried out and clung to Jake's shoulders as her climax racked both of their bodies and triggered Jake's own, his guttural groan in her ear telling something of the primal urges lurking behind that gentlemanly exterior. Hearing him lose himself so completely caused her body to shudder again and again, until her extended orgasm left her thoroughly depleted.

How was she ever supposed to go back to real life when she'd just lived out the ultimate erotic fantasy? She had a feeling that being with Jake had changed her for ever, and not just because she seemed to have lost the power in her legs.

This was not where Jake had thought this was going to end up when he'd first walked into Evie's pottery studio. Not only physically, but emotionally too. He'd never expected to meet someone who would make him want to do something as corny as book a room with a hot tub at a wedding, just because he wanted to make their time together special in some small way. So it was more than just about sex. Even though that was exactly what it was supposed to be.

'Are you okay?' Clearly, Evie had noticed him lost in his own thoughts.

'Yeah. Sorry, just trying to get my breath back and

form a coherent thought again.' With a few words he was able to change her concerned expression into a smile.

'It was pretty intense, wasn't it?' Evie rolled over onto her side, looking up at him through long dark eyelashes. With her damp hair in tangles around her shoulders, and her cheeks pink from their antics, she looked adorable and sexy all at once.

'Amazing.' He reached over and kissed her again, something he never seemed to tire of doing.

'Do you think anyone has missed us at the reception?'

Jake shook his head. 'If they did, they'd have been up here cheering through the door.'

Evie laughed, a real unselfconscious belly laugh that only made Jake want to make it happen more often.

'I'm surprised they're not asking you for marks out of ten so they can improve my performance.'

Another chuckle. 'I have absolutely no complaints on that score. Ten out of ten. Would you like me to leave an online review? Five stars. Would come again.'

'That's good to know. Repeat business is always welcome.'

He liked her sense of humour as well as her cheeky grin. That was part of the reason he couldn't seem to simply walk away from her. There was an ease in being with Evie he'd never known before. Probably because he didn't hold back with her. When he'd been with anyone else, he'd kept that emotional distance from the start, wary of getting too close. The way their 'relationship' had started, he'd never had time to erect those barriers. Then he'd got to know her, realised how much they had in common, and by that stage it had been too late. Jake knew that tonight was about more than sex. He'd wanted to explore that connection with Evie before it was too late. Now he had, he knew it was too special just to let her go.

By their own admission, neither of them was ready for anything serious, but perhaps they could find a way to keep this thing going for a while at least.

'Do you mean that?' For a moment he thought Evie could read his thoughts, until he thought back to his last comment about repeat business.

He let out a sigh, wishing this was possible without all the complications. 'I told you I'm not looking to make a commitment.'

'Neither was I. But would it be such a bad thing?'

It was only natural after everything they'd shared for Evie to question his position on relationships. Especially when he was doing the same thing. Jake thought the least he could do was explain why he felt the way he did. If she couldn't handle that, then at least he'd been honest with her.

'You know we moved around a lot when I was a kid… Every time Dad was posted somewhere new, we had to pack up and go. That meant leaving behind all the friends and neighbours and relationships we'd built. I can't tell you how hard that is to do over and over again when you're little and don't really understand why. All you know is that it hurts.'

Evie scooted across the bed and placed her head on his chest and wrapped an arm around his midriff, providing him with that comfort he'd needed all those years ago.

'It must've been so lonely for you, and difficult to start all over again in new places.'

'Yeah. Most of the time Dad wasn't around and sometimes we didn't even speak the language. I was lucky that I had Donna, but we dealt with things differently. Still do. Donna jumps into relationships quickly. She doesn't waste time. Me? I'm the opposite.'

'You hold back.'

'Yes.' Though he knew Evie had come to know him better than most. 'I always leave in the end. Even the one serious relationship I had didn't last because I put myself first. I guess it's my way of protecting myself and I'm not going to change. I know you need someone who is going to be there for you the way Bailey wasn't, and I can't promise that.'

With a hand on his chest, Evie looked up at him. 'I never asked for that. I'm not sure I'll ever trust anyone enough to get into a serious relationship again. Can't we just enjoy this for what it is? Company, amazing sex, and a support group for victims of dysfunctional families.'

Jake chuckled. 'Well, when you put it like that...'

'We both have Christmas to get through. The present-giving, the awkward dinners, the parties... Then there's New Year's. The festive season is a minefield for hermits and workaholics.'

'You think we should carry on with our fake relationship into the New Year?'

The idea had its merits, though there was still that danger of emotional attachment getting wrapped up in the physical aspect of being together. Because he knew he couldn't go back to being together for appearances only. Not when he knew how dynamite they were together in bed.

'Why not? Nobody but us has to know that it's not real. That we're only together to satisfy one another's physical needs, and provide a little support when we have to deal with those awkward family situations. Let's face it, we're not going to see them much after Christmas anyway.'

Apart from Donna, but she wouldn't be surprised when he inevitably ended things with Evie. Even if she probably would be annoyed.

'But if either of us decide to end things before then—'

'No harm done. I think we're getting all the benefits of a real relationship without the hassles that usually come with it. If things start to get messy or complicated, then we'll call it off. We never even have to see each other again.'

Although that wasn't something that sat well with him just now, he could see the benefit of that if somewhere down the line he thought Evie was expecting more from him than they'd agreed on.

'Okay. I think in that case we have a deal.' He held out his hand and Evie shook it. 'Now, I think we should celebrate. Where's that champagne?' He left her temporarily to grab the bottle and brought it back to the bed.

'Now, what are you going to do with that?'

Jake held the cold bottle against her nipple, making her squeal. Then he poured a small amount of liquid into the cleft between her breasts and supped it up. He let a little trickle down into her navel and beyond. Following the river of bubbles with his tongue, he felt

Evie tense beneath him. Until he reached that vulnerable spot between her thighs and lapped greedily, and she went limp beneath him.

Jake lifted her legs over his shoulders and plunged deeper inside her, teasing and pleasing her with his tongue. He wanted her to feel as good as he did, perhaps in an attempt to keep this purely about sex for both of them. If he could promise her this every time they were together, then hopefully there would be no need for any emotional involvement at all. It certainly seemed to be the only thing on her mind as she writhed and moaned in ecstasy at his touch. And when Evie's orgasm hit them both he felt like a king.

He told himself this could work if they kept things purely physical. This could be the best Christmas ever, sharing it with Evie, as long as he remembered it wasn't real. Like everything else in his life, it couldn't last for ever.

CHAPTER NINE

'PIZZA'S HERE.' Jake walked into the studio carrying a tower of boxes, just as Evie was setting out the wine and plastic cups for tonight's pupils.

They'd finally scheduled his work's team-building class with Evie, and now they'd finished making their own wobbly pots it was time for refreshments.

'Are you having some, Mr Hanley?' one of his employees asked.

'Of course, and can I get some of that wine too, please?' He set the pizzas down in the middle of one of the workbenches and began to open them so everyone could help themselves.

Evie handed him a glass, assuming he was going to be staying at her place for the night if he wasn't driving. They'd spent most evenings together these past couple of weeks since the wedding. As a rule, they didn't go out much. That would've seemed too much like dating, she supposed. Not that she was complaining. Her sex life was the best she'd ever had and Jake had made her feel things she hadn't realised possible. As though he'd wakened this wanton inside her who couldn't get enough. She didn't know what would happen to that woman once this thing with Jake came to an end, but she didn't want to think about that when she was having such a good time with him.

Christmas wasn't that far away, time was running out on their 'relationship', and the thought saddened her more than she could have imagined. He'd become such a part of her life that it was going to seem even more empty once he was gone. Even now, watching him share his pepperoni with her dog, she knew she didn't want him to go. As much as she'd promised him, and herself, that she wouldn't become too attached, she hadn't been able to help herself. He'd allowed her to explore a side of herself she hadn't known existed but, more than that, she'd opened up her heart to him. Something she'd never thought she'd be able to do after Bailey.

If things had been different she'd be hoping for more than the casual fling they'd agreed to, but he'd been honest with her from the start that that wasn't what he wanted. It was her own fault if she was left broken-hearted once it was all over. He'd warned her not to fall for him. That bit had been entirely her own doing.

All she could do was keep this time with Jake as a happy memory that would hopefully help her when she did return to the dating pool. He'd made her realise that not all men were like Bailey, and that if she found the right man maybe she could think about settling down again, planning a future that might include marriage and a family. It was a shame that man couldn't be Jake.

'You know, Mr Hanley, you're not as stuffy as I thought you were.'

'No. You weren't afraid to get your hands dirty.'

'Thanks… I think.' Jake accepted the backhanded compliments from his staff in good humour. He'd certainly mucked in tonight, helping set up the wheels with Evie and portion out the clay, as well as helping those struggling with forming the pots.

'And you were so much better than us,' another commented.

'I think he's been having private lessons,' Donna mischievously added as she sipped her wine.

Although their families knew they were together, they hadn't made any blatant displays of affection in front of his employees. Evie supposed they had no need to, but it highlighted the fact that she still wasn't as much a part of his world as he was of hers.

'I'll fire everyone's pieces in the kiln, and glaze them. After another fire they'll be ready for you to collect in a few weeks. Or Jake…um… Mr Hanley can collect them for you.'

'Yes, I can get them. It's no problem.'

It was on the tip of her tongue to remind him they probably wouldn't be together by then, but resisted. Seeing him again might give her something to look forward to in the New Year.

Once they'd eaten their fill of pizza and downed the wine, the women began to pack up, ready to leave.

'We're heading on to a club if you'd both like to join us?' It was Donna who made the invitation, and Evie wondered how keen the rest really would've been to have their boss trailing along on a night out.

'That's very kind but I've a lot to do here.' Even if she hadn't, she wasn't one for going to clubs and getting drunk. She was more of a homebody. Especially if that meant being at home with Jake's body against hers. Heat infused her skin at the thought of another night of passion ahead with him.

'I think I'll stay and give Evie a hand. Have a good night.' Jake waved them off at the door whilst Evie began collecting all the rubbish for recycling.

'Don't work too hard,' Donna called back with a laugh, no doubt aware of what they'd planned to get up to as soon as everyone had gone.

Jake closed the door and walked back towards her, looking deep in thought. 'Donna's right, you know.'

'About what?' Evie began washing down the potter's wheels and workbenches so the clay didn't have time to harden on them.

'Working too hard. We've both spent all day working, then you tutored all my employees. We need a break. Something other than work and sleep.'

Before she could say anything, he was untying her apron, lifting it over her head and handing her her coat.

'What about Dave?'

'We can walk him back to your place then head out somewhere. If that's what you'd like?' He was checking with her, when she couldn't think of anything nicer to do on a December evening.

'Anywhere?'

'Within reason.' He added a disclaimer, probably in case she came up with something completely harebrained. Like gliding over ice, balanced on thin, sharp blades.

'What about ice-skating?' she finally plucked up the

courage to ask after they'd settled Dave at her place with food and water and his favourite toys to keep him company.

'Ice-skating?' As they passed under the streetlights she could see the surprised look on his face.

Well, if this erotic interlude in her life was going to be over soon, she thought she might as well add a little romance to the memory. There couldn't be anything more romantic than outdoor ice-skating together on a crisp winter night.

'They set up a rink down in the square every year. I've always wanted to try it but I thought I'd look tragic doing it on my own. Plus, I probably need someone to keep me balanced since I've never tried it before. What about you? Do you know how to do it?'

'I did it as a kid, but not for years. I can't say I ever felt the need.'

'And now?' Evie knew she was pushing his boundaries, but it had been his idea to come out, to move beyond the walls of a bedroom, and she was going to take full advantage of it. Perhaps in the hope that he'd begin to see the benefits of being in a real relationship and want to pursue something more with her, instead of ending things when all their Christmas-related commitments were over.

'If that's what you want.' He gave a laugh as if to say he thought it absurd but he'd go along with it for her sake. That was enough for Evie.

Like everything with Jake, she was sure he'd have fun once he was gently persuaded out of his comfort zone. It worked for her too. It occurred to her that they'd both been stuck in their own ways for too long, because they felt safe with the familiar. There was no chance of being hurt if they shut themselves off from the world. But she was beginning to learn there was a lot out there to be enjoyed. She was hoping to convince Jake the same. Then maybe he might be open to the idea of being with someone again too.

'It is, but I'll buy you a drink to say thanks. There's a beer tent somewhere nearby.'

'Ah, alcohol and sharp blades. What a mix.' Despite the mocking tone, Jake went with her to get their skates, and they sat on a bench at the edge of the rink to pull them on.

Evie watched the couples and families out on the ice having fun, wishing to be part of it. There was still that fake element to her time with Jake that wouldn't let her enjoy it completely. As though he was putting on a front to please her, the same way he'd agreed with Donna about putting on the pottery evening for everyone else's sake. He'd seemed to enjoy it in the end, but she wished he could just let himself go for once and really live in the moment. The only time he did that was in the bedroom, and she knew that was because there was no emotional element involved. There was barely even any talking. He felt safe there because she wasn't asking anything more from him than sex. Regardless that she wanted to.

'Don't be such a grouch. Come on.' She stood up, wobbled and almost fell over. Luckily, Jake was at hand to steady her. They weren't even on the ice yet.

'I can see why you wanted me to come. You're a danger to yourself and others.'

'Danger Evie. That's me,' she said with a grin, because this probably was the riskiest thing she'd done in a long time. Apart from agreeing to a casual fling with someone she already knew she cared about.

It was being with Jake that made her want to do crazy things. She wanted to experience new things and challenge herself, because she was happy around him. Safe. She knew that was ironic when their time together had an expiration date coming up, but she wanted to make the most of this feeling for as long as she could. Who knew if it would ever happen again?

Jake stepped onto the ice first, confident and steady. A stark contrast to Evie, who tentatively put one foot out and felt it slide from beneath her.

'It's okay. I've got you,' Jake said in her ear, wrapping an arm around her waist to hold her steady.

He supported her around the ice, just as he'd done from that first night in her studio. Going along with her crazy fake date plan, tackling her crazy family, and staying in her life even after their arrangement was supposed to have ended. It was a shame she hadn't managed to do the same for him, otherwise he might have wanted something more than a fling with her.

Though she supposed she should be grateful for now. This was a start, maybe the end for all she knew, but at least he was happy to be with her when they didn't have an audience. It said he might have some feelings for her beyond the purely physical when he was willing to do this with her. Unless he was just humouring her, and hoping it would ease the pain of their inevitable breakup…

As her mind drifted into not so happy territory, she wobbled and had to grab for the side of the rink. Jake still had hold of her, but she needed that extra support to centre herself again.

'Sorry. I'm holding you back. You probably would've done twenty laps of this place by now if you weren't lumbered with my dead weight.'

She watched the others skating past when she was still slipping and sliding all over the place like a new-born foal trying to find its feet.

In her romantic fantasy they'd be twirling around like Olympic gold medal-winning figure-skaters, instead of Jake trailing her around like a sack of potatoes. It was her fault for building things up in her mind. Again.

'Hey. I'm not here so I can show off. I'm here to be with you. Okay?' He tilted her chin up and planted a kiss on her lips, most likely a gesture of comfort and support, but, as it always did, it soon turned into something more. Until Evie felt herself blush, knowing they were putting on a very public display.

'We're going to get thrown out if we keep doing that.'

'Good. Then maybe we can get out of here and go back to your place.' The look he gave her, and the promise in his eyes, was enough to melt her heart right along with the ice beneath them.

More than that, it was the first time he'd kissed her like that in front of anyone. Usually they did that in private, where no one could see. It marked a change in their relationship, as had this venture out, and Evie couldn't prevent her heart swelling with hope. Maybe, just maybe, Jake was opening his life up to her too.

'What about that drink first?' As much as she was looking forward to their time in bed, as she always did, it would be nice to be with him in the real world for a little bit longer.

'Are we done here?'

'I think so. It didn't turn out quite the romantic experience I expected.'

It wasn't Jake's fault. He'd done everything right, but if she attempted to stumble her way any further around the ice she was in serious danger of landing face first. That definitely wasn't going to impress him.

'Oh? I didn't know that's what we were doing. Am I supposed to be romancing you?'

Jake escorted her back so she could change into more stable footwear and she wished she could change into a more stable human being at the same time. Then she wouldn't say such cringe-worthy stuff that caused Jake to look at her with suspicion. As if she'd tricked him into doing something awful.

'That's not what I meant. It's just…in all the Christmas films the couples are instant skating experts, tripping around hand in hand, as though they're not frozen to the bone. Not flailing around like a seal trying to make it onto dry land.'

'It was your first time. You did well.' Regardless of his praise, there was something hollow in Jake's words. The set of his jaw was not the usual smile she'd come to expect when they had quality time together.

Evie had a sense that she'd stuffed things up. That by making this into something other than an evening out, it had spoiled the arrangement. To assert some damage control, she led him over to the faux log cabin selling hot drinks.

'A beer, wasn't it? They do that hot German beer. I think I'll try a mulled cider. Do you want one of those instead? It might warm us up.'

'Just a beer, thanks.'

Yeah, he definitely wasn't happy.

'You know, that was just a joke back there. I didn't mean anything by it. I'm not trying to force you into a relationship you don't want, Jake.'

She decided it was better to tackle the subject head-on rather than let it fester between them. Perhaps if she and Bailey had talked more, she would have realised something was wrong long before she'd caught him with Courtney.

She'd been so wrapped up in the idea of settling down, having kids, creating the family she hadn't had in such a long time, that she'd ignored any problems, convinced herself all was well between them because she didn't want to lose everything. Looking back now, comparing what she'd had with Jake these past weeks to how things had been with Bailey for years, there was a vast difference. Perhaps she'd latched onto Bailey long after the initial spark between them had gone because she wanted that cosy family dream. She didn't want to make the same mistake with Jake.

'I know. Don't worry.' He smiled, but she still wasn't convinced by it.

Her worst fears were confirmed when she asked if he was ready to head back to her place.

'You know, it's been a long day. I might just head home tonight, if that's okay?'

'Sure,' she said brightly, even though she was dying inside. Her eagerness to push him into something he wasn't ready for was driving him away. The best she could do now was give him the space he needed and hope it was enough.

Gentleman that he was, he insisted on walking her back but he didn't come in, not even to see the dog.

'Thanks for tonight.' She hovered on the doorstep, feeling as though they'd just come to the end of a very awkward first date when it was obvious there wasn't going to be a second one.

'I had fun. I'll call you tomorrow.' The goodbye kiss was brief and perfunctory, not at all what Evie had become accustomed to.

''Bye.' She waved him off, her smile forced and her heart heavy. It seemed the final countdown had begun. If he was already stewing over being inadvertently romantic, they'd be lucky to see Christmas together.

Jake couldn't concentrate. The screen full of charts and figures was a blur today, his mind preoccupied with thoughts of Evie and last night, knowing he'd spoiled their evening. It had been his idea to go out and do something other than fall into bed, taking their relationship into the real world, where they weren't putting on an act for anyone else, simply enjoying each other's company. Or at least they had been, until he'd freaked out at the mere mention of romance.

Of course ice-skating at Christmas was romantic,

and he shouldn't blame Evie for pointing that out. But it had been so long since he'd been in anything resembling a romantic relationship he'd panicked. Evie knew the score. This thing between them was temporary and they didn't have much time left together. It wasn't her fault he'd started to have feelings for her, and run away—his usual self-defence mechanism.

It had all felt so normal, fitting in with the other couples and families out on the ice. Holding her in his arms. That was what had caused him so much concern. That it was becoming the norm, and he'd been content to keep pretending things between them were still casual. The trouble was, he didn't want to stop seeing her. As long as she wasn't expecting more than he was prepared to give, he hoped they could still enjoy the time they had left together.

His phone rang, Evie's number flashing up on the screen. This was the moment he had to decide if he wanted to keep on seeing her, or end things now before someone got hurt. He snatched the phone up without a second thought.

'Hello?'

'Hi. I hope I'm not disturbing you?' He could hear the uncertainty in her voice about contacting him and he was sorry he was the one who'd put it there. Evie had had enough of being made to feel uncomfortable in her life through no fault of her own and he didn't want to be another one on that list.

'Not at all. What can I do for you?' It wasn't as though he was getting any work done anyway.

There was a sigh on the other end of the phone, as

though she was building up to ask him a favour and really didn't want to. 'I was wondering if you were free for an hour or two to give me a hand with something.'

'Sure. What is it?'

'I need to pick up my Christmas tree. I swear I'm not trying to force you into some Christmas tree romance fantasy. I just need a strong pair of hands and a vehicle to help me with transporting it. Ursula is off for a couple of days and I don't want to leave it much longer or there's no point in getting a tree so close to Christmas Day.'

Overexplaining why she needed his help so much made him feel even worse that she thought she couldn't ask him for a favour without him turning it into a big deal.

'It's fine. I'm free now if you're ready to go?'

'That would be great, Jake. Thank you.'

'I'll see you soon.' He hung up with an increasing sense that things had changed irrevocably between them, and he only had himself to blame.

Jake closed down his laptop, grabbed his jacket and headed for the door. Running straight into Donna outside.

'Are you off again? You really are a changed man.' She walked away, shaking her head, a smile playing on her lips.

Leaving Jake frowning. She was right. Up until Evie had come into his life, he wouldn't have left the office for anything, work his sole focus. It was a big change for someone who was only supposed to be in his life on a temporary basis. If he'd changed, made room in his life for something other than work, then what was going to happen to him once the relationship ended? Everything he'd been afraid of since he was a child. Of being hurt, being lonely, and with a great big hole in his life where the people who meant most to him in the world used to be.

'Sorry about this,' Evie apologised the moment she got into the passenger seat.

'It's fine. Though I did take time to change into something more suitable for the occasion.' His red and black plaid shirt, worn jeans and tan boots did manage to raise a smile.

'Me too.' She clapped her gloved hands together, the same pale pink as her soft wool sweater and bobble hat. Even though they weren't going to be trekking through an actual tree farm, she was wearing jeans and boots too. At least they were dressed appropriately for any unexpected snowfall. It was certainly cold enough.

'I'm not sure if I'm the big city executive about to lose the girl, or the charming homebody who gives her her happy-ever-after, like in all of those cheesy Christmas films.'

Evie slid an amused gaze across at him. 'I don't know, but I never took you as the type to watch sentimental Christmas movies.'

Busted.

'Donna and Mum like them. I've caught a glimpse every now and then. I know the formula.'

That had been the one constant around the season. From November, those movies were always on the TV at home, no matter which part of the world they were living in at the time. They were a safe romantic fantasy where no one got hurt and they all lived happily ever after so he hadn't minded watching them. It probably helped that their mum had always made them hot chocolate with marshmallows so they could really get in the Christmas mood. He found something comforting even now about having them on in the background when he was at home. Not that he would admit that to anyone…

'Uh-huh.' Evie clearly wasn't convinced by his explanation, but at least the subject of his guilty pleasure had broken the ice between them.

'Are you telling me you don't watch them?'

'Not any more. Once you've had your heart so spectacularly broken it's difficult to watch things like that without crying a river or, you know, wishing a meteorite would hit Snow Falls, or wherever these annoying happy people live.'

'You should watch yourself, Evie. Hanging around with me is making you cynical.'

'Ach, I'm only joking. I love Christmas. Probably more than I ever loved Bailey. I'm beginning to wonder if I only stayed with him as long as I did because I thought he could give me the family I always wanted.'

Evie stared out of the window, and the longing in her voice would've melted most people's hearts. For Jake, however, it was another red flag.

'I didn't think you wanted another serious relationship.'

'I didn't. Maybe it's the season, and seeing everyone else with their little ones, but it's made me think I might be ready to start over with someone else. I always thought I'd have children and be content as a wife and mother. I know I've got my own business and that's great, but I just feel as though something's missing. I'm not saying it's going to happen any time soon, but I'm still hoping that some day I'll have the family I didn't have when I was growing up. It's not too much to ask, is it?'

It was for him.

'I can understand that. I'm sure you'll make a great mother.' Unfortunately, that was the opposite of what he wanted in the future.

'What about you? Didn't you ever want a family?'

'I can't say it's anything I've ever really considered. I've never been with anyone long enough for it to be an issue. In that respect, I suppose the answer's no.'

With his reluctance to get close to anyone, it wouldn't be fair on a child, or its mother. He was always going to be holding back, and if his father had taught him one thing it was that a child needed love. Something he found hard to give freely.

With both having voiced their very different views of the future, they lapsed into silence. It was clear they had no long-term future ahead, but they'd always known that. So why did Jake feel as though his supposed impenetrable heart had just taken a hit?

They pulled up to the Christmas tree lot, where the freshly cut spruces and firs were waiting for new homes.

'You know you can get plastic trees you can use every year, and they're cheaper.'

Jake had never had the pleasure of a real tree at Christmas. Though he realised he now sounded like his dad, who'd insisted they made too much mess, as well as being a waste of money. Jake wondered if that was the problem, or the fact that it might have brought the family some degree of pleasure, which it seemed he did his best to stamp out.

Evie held out one of the green branches. 'Just smell that. It smells like Christmas. You don't get that with a fake tree, and they're better for the environment. For every one chopped down here, another one is planted in its place.'

Jake inhaled the fresh scent and he had to agree the real thing was much better than the fake stuff.

'Maybe I'll have a look too. It might be nice to have a small one in the office.'

Donna would appreciate it, and it might brighten the place up a little. Perhaps a little of Evie's Christmas spirit was rubbing off on him.

Evie wasn't listening, wandering off to find a tree that was 'just right'. There was an incredible sense of whimsy about her which kept her childlike and adorable. Whoever got to spend his life with her would be very lucky.

He watched her interact with those around her, a cheery greeting to a stranger, every dog that went past getting treated to some attention, and her out-of-tune singing along with the Christmas tunes blaring out from nearby speakers. Evie was a ray of sunshine on this cold and dreary winter afternoon.

As she passed a young father struggling with a toddler in the midst of a temper tantrum, instead of walking on by as most had already done, casting a dirty look, she stopped and knelt down.

'Who's making all this racket?'

At the sound of her voice, the little girl paused her histrionics, though still refused to take her father's hand.

'She doesn't want to go without a tree but I think they're all too big for our flat,' the dad sighed.

'Oh, sweetie. It's not Daddy's fault. Maybe you'll find one somewhere else,' Evie soothed.

'I want one here,' the little diva insisted with a stamp of her foot.

'Maybe if you're a really good girl and take Daddy's hand we can find you a really special tree, just for you.' She gave the harassed father a wink, and both he and Jake watched on, intrigued, as Evie walked over to the man selling the trees.

The child too seemed curious. Enough to take her father's hand without a further fight and follow Evie.

Jake hid a smirk as he saw her charm the salesman into giving her what looked like the broken top or offcut of a full-size tree. With a little more persuasion, she managed to secure a small plastic pot and a handful of soil to plant it. It wasn't more than a couple of small branches sticking up out of the pot but when she handed it to the little girl it might as well have been a ten-foot Norwegian Spruce.

'Now, this is a very special tree. You have to look after it very carefully. Make sure you water it, and if you're a very good girl for your daddy, maybe he'll let you decorate it all by yourself.'

The child looked up hopefully at her father. 'I promise, Daddy.'

'Good girl. I'm sure we have some tinsel and lights you can put on it.' The dad took the tree from Evie and gently delivered it into his daughter's open hands.

'Thank you so much,' he said with genuine appreciation.

Jake felt a little twinge of something uncomfortable at watching the interaction. Perhaps if he hadn't been here this scene might have played out differently. Though he wasn't aware of the man's circumstances, if he was single, this would've been the perfect meet-cute. A ready-made family for Evie. Everything she wanted.

Jake's choice of clothes today didn't really matter. He was the city guy in a suit about to lose the girl to a hometown boy.

Okay, so he was being a tad melodramatic, Evie was just being her usual kind self, but it was obvious she was born to be a mother, and she was going to make someone a fantastic wife. It just couldn't be him. Even if it wasn't this guy with his daughter, there was going to be someone else who could give Evie everything she longed for. But marriage, babies, a family…just weren't for him. That meant sharing his life completely with other people, and he wasn't ready for that. If ever.

Marriage and children were the ultimate commitments of himself, and his heart. If it didn't work out, as had been his experience so far in life, he knew he wouldn't recover. It would be too great a loss for him to bear, and he'd been hurt too much in the past.

Evie had helped him open his heart a little bit to let

her in, and whilst he liked what they had now, by her own admission, it wasn't going to be enough for her long-term. Though he'd sworn he didn't want a serious relationship, the thought of not having her in his life was already causing him pain. Jake was beginning to wonder if he had finally found someone who made him want to make room in his life for her. Only time would tell if he was strong enough, and willing to do so. Unfortunately, the countdown was already on.

CHAPTER TEN

'THANK YOU SO much for doing this, Jake.'

'I forgot you didn't live on the ground floor when I volunteered,' he huffed, carrying the heavy end of the tree up the stairs to Evie's flat.

She might have been better thanking him when he could breathe again and was in better form after they'd discovered the lift was broken. Despite his assistance today, she could sense a distance between them that hadn't been there before. It wasn't just about last night either.

Earlier, at the Christmas tree lot, when she'd interacted with the father and daughter, she'd felt a little pang. The scene had reminded her of Christmases spent with her own father, just the two of them getting ready for the big day. It had made her realise that she did want that some day, with her own family. Something she was never going to have with Jake. He'd made it clear having children was not on his agenda. However, she was already having feelings for him, and if they had very different ideas of the future it seemed as though a relationship with him was doomed. By carrying on, pretending otherwise was just going to cause more heartbreak.

Jake had backed away when she'd even hinted at

something more, and today had been a reality check. Despite her growing feelings for him, she was beginning to think he couldn't be the man for her and she was only breaking her own heart by pretending otherwise.

'Can I make you a hot chocolate?' she offered once they had it in situ in her living room after a lot of huffing, puffing and swearing, thinking she should offer some kind of thanks for inconveniencing him even though she would prefer to put some space between them.

'I should probably get back to work.'

'Of course. Thanks again for your help.'

'Listen, Evie, about last night… I'm sorry about bailing on you.'

Hearing him raise the subject and knowing the conversation she needed to have made Evie's insides lurch.

'Don't worry about it. I know that sort of thing isn't your scene and I shouldn't have pushed you into it.'

'I've been thinking a lot about us today…'

Evie took a deep breath. He was giving her the perfect opportunity to get out now before she completely lost her heart to him.

'Me too. I know the plan was to keep seeing one another over Christmas, but I think it's pretty obvious we're very different people. We want different things, and I don't see the point in pretending otherwise.'

'Oh.'

He looked stunned. Probably because she'd beaten him to the punch.

'We did what we set out to do. We were there for each other when we needed it and we had fun. But I think we're just putting off the inevitable by continuing this. It's probably time we both got back to real life.'

The nausea was overwhelming now, because she didn't want it to end. She didn't want to lose Jake now, when she was just beginning to feel like herself again, but waiting for him to feel differently about her, and about what he wanted in life, seemed like a futile exercise. Though a broken heart definitely hadn't been on her Christmas list.

'If that's what you want.' It was a verbal shrug, as if it didn't mean anything to him. He wasn't putting up a fight, simply accepting the end. Likely because he'd come to the same conclusion, albeit for different reasons.

If it was really so easy for him to move on then he clearly didn't feel the same way about her as she did about him. Because the thought of never seeing him again was devastating. But she wasn't going to humiliate herself again by begging him to love her. She'd invested too long in a relationship with a man who didn't want her before, and she wasn't about to do it again.

'I'd rather leave things on good terms now than wait until our differences really start to make themselves known.'

'I guess...'

'What will you tell the family?' She was asking questions, faking her acceptance of the situation, but she was feeling kind of numb.

'Nothing, unless they ask. It won't come as a surprise even if I do say we've split up.'

Evie felt foolish to have imagined a rapport with his family, believing that anyone would care that she was no longer part of their lives. Clearly, she was the only one who'd thought there was a possibility that this could have been a long-term thing.

'Okay. Then I guess this is it. Thanks for walking into the studio that night.' Her voice cracked and she stopped herself from saying anything else.

'Thanks for everything, Evie.'

Jake moved as if to offer a hug, but she didn't want that. She knew if he touched her she'd break down and never want to let him go.

Instead, she ducked past him and opened the front door. 'I'll let you get back to work. Have a good Christmas, Jake.'

He hesitated in the doorway as if to say something more, then simply gave a lopsided smile and walked away.

She felt numb. As he disappeared out of sight down the stairs it felt like a death, the loss was so great. The death of her hopes and dreams, and the misplaced belief that she'd found 'the one'. If she couldn't find happiness with Jake, she knew she'd never find it with anyone.

'I can't believe it's Christmas Day tomorrow already.' Donna was perched on Jake's desk when he came back from making himself a coffee. He'd been in work at six a.m., as he had every day since he'd walked out of Evie's apartment. It was either that or lie staring at the ceiling for another couple of hours, wondering what had happened between them, and he was sure he knew every crack and fleck of paint on it by now.

'It's just another day as far as I'm concerned.' He'd probably be in work like every other day, but he didn't want to tell her that and have her tut and roll her eyes at him in despair. He was feeling low enough at the moment.

'I assumed you'd have special plans with Evie, like Mum and Gary do for their first Christmas together. I mean, *I* wouldn't want to spend Christmas Day in a hotel, but as long as they're happy. So are you not seeing Evie at all?' She lifted the pen from his desk, not making eye contact, and started doodling on his desk pad.

Jake took it off her and set it down again, hoping she hadn't seen him wince when she'd mentioned Evie. 'Nope.'

'Are you two not together any more?' It was a fishing exercise, but he was just surprised she hadn't quizzed him about his love life before now.

'Nope.'

He didn't want to get into it. There was no burning desire to hear her tell him how stupid he was to let her go out of his life, because he already knew it. He felt it every time he went home to an empty house and bed, and when he had no one to have a laugh with at the end of a difficult day.

Evie had taken him by surprise when she'd told him she didn't want to see him again, because he'd been on the verge of telling her the opposite. That he wanted to commit to something beyond Christmas. However, he hadn't argued with her reasoning. It had become clear that she was looking to settle down, and he wasn't the man who could offer her that stability. He'd opened his heart to her, but with such differing views of their future, they would never have survived. In the end he'd thought it best to go along with her decision rather than prolong the pain.

Except he didn't feel any better not having her in his life any more. He hadn't realised the misery he'd be in simply by walking away.

'That's a shame. She was nice.'

'Yes, she was.' He carried on typing, even though he couldn't see the words on the screen clearly.

'There's no chance—'

'No.' He cut her off before she even asked about a reconciliation. He'd clearly underestimated the impact she'd made on him and how much he'd miss her. However, how he felt about her didn't change the reasons they'd had to part. It would've been selfish of him to keep things going, knowing he couldn't fulfil those dreams she had for the future.

'You could come around to mine. We'll make dinner and put on some of those Christmas films you love.' She was teasing him, but nothing could raise his spirits, knowing he could've been spending the day with Evie if only he hadn't been so cowardly.

'We'll see.' He had no intention of listening to the pity and recriminations, but it would be enough of an answer to hopefully get rid of his sister in the meantime.

'I don't want you to spend the day on your own, wallowing.'

He was about to ask her how she knew he was wallowing, but instead found himself asking, 'How do you do it, Donna? How do you pick yourself up after a breakup and start all over again?'

This wasn't his first breakup, of course, but usually

he was the one to end things and he didn't dwell too much on the person he'd had to let down. Other than his ex, of course, but this was different. He'd opened up to Evie in a way he had never done with anyone else. Now it felt as though he'd lost a part of himself with her. As if those parts of himself which he'd shared with her were hers for ever, and instead of learning and evolving he'd fallen back into his old ways, completely shutting down emotionally rather than dealing with his feelings. Telling her what she meant to him.

He was opening himself up now to Donna for another lecture, and he half expected her to point out the obvious, that this felt different because Evie had been more than a passing fancy.

'I cry, I rant and rave, then I realise that I wasn't with the right person. Otherwise, they would've fought harder for me, for us. So I dust myself off and put myself out there, until some day the right man will find me.'

He knew his sister was a romantic, but he'd never had her down as an optimist. The exact opposite of his outlook. If he lived the way she did, he would've told Evie how he felt, asked her to give him a chance. Maybe even some day contemplating marriage and starting a family, and hoping they'd live happily ever after.

Now he was beginning to wonder what was wrong with that. There was nothing to lose for someone who'd already had their heart broken and didn't know how he'd ever live without the woman he'd come to love. He realised now that was how strong his feelings had been for Evie. That was the reason he'd panicked and run as soon as she'd given him an out. As if he could shut down those feelings and go back to life the way it had been before he'd walked into that pottery studio. These past days without her had proved that wasn't possible.

He didn't know if marriage and children were something he wanted right now, but he did want to be with Evie. Only time would tell if he'd ever be ready for that kind of commitment but, as Evie had reminded him, she'd never asked him for that. All she'd wanted was to be with him. She hadn't tried to label anything, or catastrophise the future, but simply tried to live in the moment with him.

Maybe it was about time to see where those feelings took him. And share them with Evie. If she still didn't want him at least he would know he'd tried. He might be pleasantly surprised, and anything had to be better than this torturous limbo he was in without Evie.

He got up from his desk. 'Donna, tell everyone to go home.'

'What? Really?'

'Yes. It's Christmas Eve. Everyone should be with their loved ones. Including me.' He just hoped it wasn't too late for this fake commitment-phobe to prove how he really felt.

'It looks as though it's just you and me for Christmas, Dave.'

Evie tossed the dog a piece of the turkey she'd brought with her to the studio. She'd spent the evening at home cooking it in the hope the smell at least would put her in a festive mood. To no avail. All she could think about still was Jake, and how they should've been spending tomorrow together. How they should've been spending every Christmas together, but self-preservation had caused her to push him away before she fell any further for him.

Instead of cosying up with Jake in a Christmas card scene, she was talking to her dog in her cold pottery studio on Christmas Eve. She'd had a last-minute booking for a private lesson. Any other time she would've turned it down, but she needed the money, as well as the distraction.

The knock on the door signalled her student's arrival.

'Come in,' she called, busying herself with setting up the wheel for the lesson.

She had her back to the door when her guest walked in.

'Just hang your coat up and put an apron on. You can make yourself a cup of tea if you want whilst I'm setting up.'

'Do you have any hot chocolate?'

The sound of Jake's voice froze her to the spot. Until she heard his footsteps crossing the floor and she turned before he could reach her.

'What are you doing here?'

'I'm here for my pottery lesson.'

It took her a moment to register what he was saying.

'You booked the private session?'

He at least looked shamefaced as he nodded, accepting that he'd lied about his name at least.

'I wanted to see you and I thought it was the best way to know for sure where you'd be, and that I could speak to you in private.'

Her initial shock and delight at seeing him again quickly changed into something more painful. By turning up here when she was doing her best to get over him he was making her go through that rejection and loss all over again when he left.

'Well, I've been paid to give a pottery lesson, but if that's not why you're here then I'm going home. It's Christmas Eve and I have better things to do than be the object of ridicule.'

She didn't, but he didn't have to know that. Up until recently her plans had been to spend the day with him, and she hadn't been able to face the fact she'd be alone instead. She hadn't even told her stepmother they'd split up, afraid she'd be forced to go there for Christmas dinner and be ridiculed over her single status in front of a smug Courtney and Bailey. So her current plans simply included sharing a turkey dinner with her dog. None of which Jake needed to know.

When she rolled down her sleeves and prepared to pack away her equipment again, he quickly donned an apron and took a seat at the wheel.

'Can we at least talk while we work?'

'That's up to you, but you might need to concentrate unless you want to end up with clay in your lap.' She slapped a ball of clay in the centre of the wheel, splattering him with wet residue.

'I wanted to see how you were doing.'

'Fine.' Evie pushed the accelerator pedal down, forcing him to focus on the clay and stop it from flying off the wheel. She didn't have to play nice when he was deliberately goading her simply by being here. There was absolutely no reason for him to do this other than to watch her suffer.

'Good. Good.'

'Remember, you have to raise the clay up, then flatten it.' Pretty much the way her heart felt, she thought to herself, wondering why he'd come to torture her.

Annoyingly, he followed her instructions perfectly. 'Like this?'

'Yes. Now, we need to open up that divot in the middle.' She could feel him looking at her and she did her best to ignore it, not wanting her soft heart to give in if she should lock eyes with him. He had no business being here, or having an effect on her heart.

'I'm sorry.'

The words made her and the clay wobble, so she had to pull things back and re-centre everything.

'Just concentrate on the clay,' she warned.

'I'm not here for the clay.'

It was difficult to maintain that pretence of indifference when her hands were on his and he was practically begging her to look at him.

'Well, that's what you've paid for.' She dipped a sponge and squeezed the water over the clay.

'I'm sorry, Evie. I should have fought harder for us.'

'Okay.' She wasn't going to argue with him on that score, but neither did it change anything.

Jake gave up all pretence that he was here for a lesson, turning around so she was now trapped between his legs. If her heart wasn't beating so fast she thought she'd pass out, she might have made a joke about that.

'I had come that day to ask if we could make a

proper go of things. But when you pointed out that we wanted different things and it would inevitably come between us, I took the easy way out.'

'And has being apart been easy for you, because it sucked for me.' She offered a half smile, afraid to believe that he had real feelings for her in case she got hurt again.

He shook his head. 'No. Apparently, feelings don't go away just because they're inconvenient.' The way he looked at her now, so open and vulnerable, Evie had to stop pretending she didn't care deeply for him too.

'So now what? What's changed? I want security, and a family some day. You don't. I can't see how we can reconcile those differences.'

'All I can tell you is that I've fallen for you, Evie. Maybe it took you ending things to make me admit that. Afraid if I didn't tell you now, I'd lose you for ever. You have to understand that I'm still traumatised by my childhood. I was forced to leave people I came to care about so often I learned to shut myself off emotionally, to stop it hurting so much. Somehow, you managed to break through that barrier.'

'I'm sneaky that way,' she joked, trying to make light of the situation because she was afraid to take it too seriously just yet.

'I know I want a future with you. I just need to know if you feel the same way. I've missed you, Evie.'

That simple statement was enough to break her. He was putting everything on the line for her. Fighting for them. Treating her as though she was the most important thing in his life, and no one had done that since her father passed away. That didn't mean she wasn't afraid of investing her heart, and her future, in Jake again.

'You know the damage Bailey did to me, and putting my trust in a relationship with you is a big deal for me.'

'I know. I was afraid of making a commitment to you because I knew that meant leaving myself vulnerable again too if things didn't work out between us.'

'And now?'

'I'm more afraid of not having you in my life. I don't know what the future holds, but I do know that I want to be with you, Evie.'

'How do I know that anything's going to change? You're not the only one afraid of getting hurt again.'

'I've taken some time off work. I want to spend Christmas and New Year together, and focus on us. I'll do whatever it takes to have you back in my life.'

Already won over, Evie walked further in between his legs. 'Anything?'

'I'm yours completely.'

She knew Jake wouldn't make such a gesture if he didn't mean what he said. He was willing to take a chance on them in the hope of nurturing something special, and she knew she wanted the same.

'I'm yours too. I was from the moment you agreed to be my fake date.' Now she was ready to embrace the real thing.

Jake kissed her and she knew without doubt she'd finally found someone willing to give her the love she'd always deserved.

'THAT'S THE TREE almost finished,' Evie said, taking a step back to admire her handiwork, though Jake had paid for it to be delivered this year from the Christmas tree farm.

'Almost?' Jake wandered in from the kitchen, where he'd been making dinner as he did most evenings after work. This was their time together, both learning that work ended once they came home. The home he'd invited her and Dave to share with him at the start of the year, showing how invested he was in their relationship.

She knew what a big step that was for him, and hoped the next stage of their life together wasn't going to ruin what they had.

'I need the angel to go on the top. Can you do it?' She handed Jake the precious angel her father had left to her, once belonging to her mother. A real family heirloom she hoped to hand down to the next generation some day.

Jake gave her a puzzled look but took it from her and gently placed it on the top. 'There. Is that okay?'

'Perfect. I'd have done it myself but I don't want to stretch up that far. It's early days but I don't want to take any chances.'

He frowned again at her ramblings. 'Any chances of what?'

'Doing anything that might hurt the baby.'

She'd spent days worrying and wondering how to break the news to him, and in the end she couldn't find any right way of doing it. There was nothing that was going to prepare him for an unexpected pregnancy, and she only hoped that their relationship was strong enough to survive it when he'd made it clear he hadn't intended starting a family.

She watched his face, waiting to interpret his expression, her breath caught in her throat. This past year together had been wonderful. He was so attentive and loving she didn't know why either of them had been so worried about committing to one another. Now she was worried that three in the relationship would prove too much for him to cope with.

'Baby?'

She bit her lip as she nodded.

'We're going to have a baby?'

'Yes. I know we hadn't planned on a family. At least not yet, but I don't see why this has to change anything. I think you'll make a great father.'

Jake was nothing like his own, and was always present. Evie was sure he would be the same for their child.

However, his reaction when it came was worse than she could ever have imagined. He simply turned and walked out of the room. Panic rose inside her, the fear that she'd be left homeless and having to raise this baby on her own very real. It wasn't as though she had her family to support her when she'd distanced herself more than ever since last Christmas. She hadn't needed their toxicity in her life when she'd had Jake's love and support. Now she was going to be completely on her own.

'Jake? Can't we talk this through?'

To her relief, he strode back into the room.

'I'm sorry this happened, Jake, but I'm sure we can survive this. We're strong.'

'I know, that's why I went to get this. I was going to wait until Christmas, but I don't want you to think I'd only ask you because you were pregnant. I was already planning this.' He produced a small velvet box and opened it to reveal a beautiful emerald-cut diamond ring.

Evie blinked at it, then Jake, not knowing what to say.

Then he got down on one knee. 'Evie Kerrigan, I love you. You're the family I never knew I needed, and now this baby is just the icing on the cake. Will you marry me?'

She had no reason to hesitate. 'Yes. Of course I'll marry you. I love you.'

Jake slid the ring onto her finger and she knew they had a happy future together to look forward to. Her fake date had turned out to be her Prince Charming after all.

* * * * *

MILLS & BOON®

Coming next month

BEAUTY AND THE BROODING CEO
Juliette Hyland

The candlelight caressed her features. This was another painting. All the walls in the closed-off wing were going to be Cora. His masterpieces. Memories of her.

'May I have this dance?' He offered a small bow, enjoying the grin spreading on her face.

'I feel like Beauty in the fairy tale.' She put her hand in his and he wrapped his other arm around her waist.

'Does that make me the Beast?' He spun them in a wide circle.

'You are not a beast.' Cora ran her hand down his cheek. Her fingers brushed his scar but she didn't recoil.

'In your arms I feel like that might actually be true.' Everett skimmed his hand up her back, pulling her a little closer.

'Everett.'

This time it was his turn to silence her rather than touch the uncomfortable subject. He bent his head, capturing her lips. She let out a little moan, pressing her hips against his as they moved in sync around the room.

When the song shifted to a faster beat, neither pulled away or adjusted the dance's speed. He simply held her. Reveled in the moment, the majesty.

Continue reading

BEAUTY AND THE BROODING CEO
Juliette Hyland

Available next month
millsandboon.co.uk

COMING SOON!

We really hope you enjoyed reading this book.
If you're looking for more romance
be sure to head to the shops when
new books are available on

Thursday 19th December

MILLS & BOON

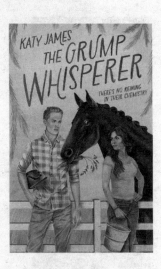
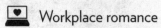
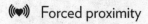

OUT NOW!

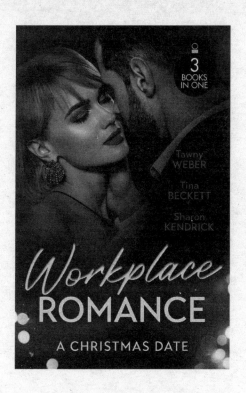

3
BOOKS
IN ONE

Tawny WEBER

Tina BECKETT

Sharon KENDRICK

Workplace
ROMANCE

A CHRISTMAS DATE

Available at
millsandboon.co.uk

MILLS & BOON

OUT NOW!

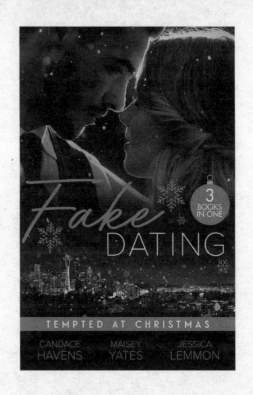

Available at
millsandboon.co.uk

MILLS & BOON